"Martin excels at writing characters who exist in the margins of life. Readers who enjoy flawed yet likable characters created by authors such as John Grisham and Nicholas Sparks will want to start reading Martin's fiction."

—*LIBRARY JOURNAL*, STARRED REVIEW, FOR *THE WATER KEEPER*

"*The Water Keeper* is a wonderfully satisfying book with a plot driven by both action and love, and characters who will stay in readers' heads long after the last page."

—*SOUTHERN LITERARY REVIEW*

"Charles Martin fans rejoice, because he's done it again. Martin's newest, *The Water Keeper*, is a multilayered story woven together with grace and redemption, and packed tight with tension and achingly real characters. This one will keep you turning pages to see what else—and who else—Murph will encounter as he travels down the coastline of Florida."

—LAUREN DENTON, *USA TODAY* BESTSELLING
AUTHOR OF *THE HIDEAWAY*

"In *The Water Keeper* Charles Martin crafts a compelling story with skill and sensitivity. Open the pages of this book and you'll enter the world of characters caught up in a real-life drama that grips the heart. As with all of Charles's books, you never finish it—you continue to live there in your own imagination. Current fans won't be disappointed; new readers will understand why Charles Martin is on the short list of contemporary authors I recommend above all others."

—ROBERT WHITLOW, BESTSELLING AUTHOR

"Martin explores themes of grace, mercy, and forgiveness in this sweeping love story . . . In this relatable tale of recovery from physical and emotional trauma, Martin beautifully captures the essence of Christian principles of sacrifice and forgiveness."

—*PUBLISHERS WEEKLY*, STARRED REVIEW, FOR *SEND DOWN THE RAIN*

"Martin's latest is another beautifully written winner . . . Amazingly heartfelt statements about love, loss, and the true meaning of friendship will resonate deeply with readers."

—*RT BOOK REVIEWS*, 4 STARS, FOR *SEND DOWN THE RAIN*

"Another stellar novel from Martin. His fabulous gift for characterization is evident on each page. Layers of the story are peeled back to show the spiritual truth underneath the gripping plot. Cooper is an intricate character with an amazing story to tell, and the supporting cast is just as important to provide additional depth and understanding. This novel should be on everyone's must-purchase list."

—*RT Book Reviews*, 4½ stars, TOP PICK! for *Long Way Gone*

"Martin crafts a playful, enticing tale of a modern prodigal son."

—*Publishers Weekly* for *Long Way Gone*

"Cooper and Daley's story will make you believe that even broken instruments have songs to offer when they're in the right hands. Charles Martin never fails to ask and answer the questions that linger deep within all of us. In this beautifully told story of a prodigal coming home, readers will find the broken and mended pieces of their own hearts."

—Lisa Wingate, national bestselling author of
Before We Were Yours on *Long Way Gone*

"Martin's story charges headlong into the sentimental territory and bestseller terrain of *The Notebook*, which doubtless will mean major studio screen treatment."

—*Kirkus*, starred review for *Unwritten*

"Charles Martin understands the power of story, and he uses it to alter the souls and lives of both his characters and his readers."

—Patti Callahan Henry, *New York Times* bestselling author

"Martin is the new king of the romantic novel . . . *A Life Intercepted* is a book that will swallow you up and keep you spellbound."

—Jackie K. Cooper, book critic, *The Huffington Post*

"Martin's strength is in his memorable characters . . ."

—*Publishers Weekly* for *Chasing Fireflies*

"Charles Martin is changing the face of inspirational fiction one book at a time. *Wrapped in Rain* is a sentimental tale that is not to be missed."

—Michael Morris, author of *Live Like You
Were Dying* and *A Place Called Wiregrass*

"Martin spins an engaging story about healing and the triumph of love . . . Filled with delightful local color."

—*Publishers Weekly* for *Wrapped in Rain*

THE

WATER

KEEPER

ALSO BY CHARLES MARTIN

THE MURPHY SHEPHERD NOVELS

The Water Keeper

The Letter Keeper (Coming June 2021!)

Send Down the Rain

Long Way Gone

Water from My Heart

A Life Intercepted

Unwritten

Thunder and Rain

The Mountain Between Us

Where the River Ends

Chasing Fireflies

Maggie

When Crickets Cry

Wrapped in Rain

The Dead Don't Dance

THE

WATER

KEEPER

CHARLES

MARTIN

THOMAS NELSON

Since 1798

Published in Nashville, Tennessee, by Thomas Nelson. Thomas Nelson is a registered trademark of HarperCollins Christian Publishing, Inc.

Published in association with The Christopher Ferebee Agency, www.christopherferebee.com

Interior design by Mallory Collins

Thomas Nelson titles may be purchased in bulk for educational, business, fundraising, or sales promotional use. For information, please email SpecialMarkets@ThomasNelson.com.

All Scripture quotations are taken from the New King James Version. © 1982 by Thomas Nelson, Inc. Used by permission. All rights reserved.

ISBN 978-0-7852-3094-6 (trade paper)
ISBN 978-0-7852-3091-5 (HC)
ISBN 978-0-7852-3092-2 (epub)
ISBN 978-0-7852-3093-9 (audio download)

Library of Congress Control Number: 2019042760

Printed in the United States of America
HB 09.07.2023

To Johnny Sarber
My brother

Three miles distant, the trail of smoke spiraled upward. Thick and black, it poured from the twin supercharged diesels housed in the engine room. Orange and red flames licked the smoke against a fading blue skyline, telling me the fire was hot and growing. When the heat hit the fuel tanks, it would blow the entire multimillion-dollar yacht into a zillion pieces, sending fragments to the ocean floor.

I turned the wheel of my twenty-four-foot center console hard to starboard and slammed the throttle forward. The wind had picked up and whitecaps topped the two- to three-foot chop. I adjusted the trim tabs down to bring the stern higher in the water, and the Boston Whaler began skidding toward the sinking vessel. I crossed the distance in just over three minutes. The 244-foot *Gone to Market* sat listing on her lee side, adrift. The hundred or so bullet holes across her stern explained her loss of rudder and engine. And possibly the fire.

They also told me that Fingers had made it to the boat.

Waves crashed over the bow and water was pouring into the main-level galley and guest rooms. The stern was already lifting in the water as the bow filled, pulling her nose dangerously toward the bottom of the Atlantic. Whether by explosion or water, she wouldn't be able to take much more. I ran the Whaler up her stern, beaching it on her swim platform. I rigged a bow line loosely to a grab rail and jumped onto the main-deck lounge, where I found three bodies with multiple bullet holes. I climbed the spiral staircase up one level to the bridge-deck lounge, finding two more bodies.

No sign of Fingers.

I kicked open the ship's-office door, tripped over another body, and ran into the bridge, where I was met by a wave of salt water pouring through the shattered front glass. Anyone in there had already been washed out to sea. I climbed to the top floor and onto the owner's-deck lounge. Victor's wife lay awkwardly across the floor. She'd been shot three times, telling me Fingers had gotten to her before she got to him. But the gun in her hand was empty. Which was bad. I pulled an ax off the wall and cut through the Honduran mahogany doors into Victor's stateroom. Victor, also shot three times, lay twisted with his neck forcibly broken. Suggesting he'd suffered pain on his way out. Which was good.

The vessel rocked forward, telling me she was reaching the tipping point. Telling me I only had moments to find Fingers and the girls and get off this thing before she dragged us down with her or blew us into the sky. I descended the stairs and turned aft into the engine room, but it was flooded. I waded fore through waist-deep water into the crew cabins, past Victor's prayer shrine, and toward the door of the anchor room where the water had turned red.

And there I found Fingers.

Actually, I heard him before I saw him. The gurgle of his breathing. When I turned the corner, he smiled but the laughter was gone. He held his Sig Sauer but couldn't raise his hand even though the pistol was empty. I cradled his head and started to drag him topside, but he pointed at the anchor-hold door. All he could muster was "There . . ."

Water poured through the crack beneath the door, proving the room had flooded. I pulled on the latch, but pressure from inside made opening the door impossible. I waded back into the engine room, swam to the far side—trying not to breathe the toxic and eye-burning smoke—lifted a wedge bar off the wall, and returned to the anchor hold. I slid the tip in against the lock mechanism and pulled, using my legs as leverage.

I heard laughter behind me. "That all you got?" Fingers choked, splattering me with blood. "Pull harder."

So I pulled with everything he once had. When the pressure from the inside and my leverage on the outside broke the lock, the door slammed open, pinning Fingers and me against the wall until the water level balanced out. As it did, I could hear girls screaming, but the sound was muted by the water. Fingers pointed at the scuba tank just inside the door. Next to it hung an assortment of weights and gear, including an underwater spotlight. I checked the regulator, fed my arms through the straps, clicked on the light, and swam down the stairs leading into the dark belly of the ship.

There I found seven scared girls in a tight group breathing the last of a trapped air bubble in the now-submerged nose of the bow. With a little prompting and a quick comment about the *Titanic*, we formed a daisy chain, and I led them through the dark water and up the stairs. When the girls saw daylight, they swam out and started climbing up the now-inclining keel toward the main-deck lounge and the Whaler.

Each of them was scared, shaking, and mostly naked. Marie was not among them. I swam back into the dark hole but Marie was not there.

I returned to Fingers, who was nodding off. I shook him. "Fingers! Fingers!" His eyes opened. "Marie? Where's Marie?"

He tried to speak.

I leaned in.

He shook his head. The admission painful. "Gone."

"What do you mean, gone?"

He uncurled his hand, and an empty pill bottle splashed into the water. A tear filled his eye. "Overboard." He paused, not wanting to say what happened next. "A weight tied to her ankle."

The picture haunted me. The finality crushed me.

I got Fingers' arm around my shoulder—which is when I felt the entry hole I had not seen. I ran my hand around his chest, only to find Fingers' right hand covering the exit hole. He shook his head. The bullet had entered to the side of his spine and exploded out of his chest.

I stuffed a portion of his shirt in the exit hole, tucked his Sig behind my vest, and dragged him through the growing smoke and up to the main-deck lounge. While I dragged him, he eyed his worn Sig and said with a smile, "I want that back." He coughed. "If that pistol could talk . . ."

The waves were tossing the Whaler around like a bobber. With all seven girls safely aboard, I lifted Fingers on my shoulder and timed my jump to the bow platform. We landed, rolled, and one of the girls threw off the line as I slammed the throttle forward. We had cleared a quarter of a mile when the explosion sounded. Fingers turned his head as a fireball engulfed the *Gone to Market* and a zillion pieces of super-luxury yacht rained down on the Atlantic just off the coast of Northeast Florida. Fingers rested in the bow, filling the front of the Whaler with a deep, frothy red and laughing with smug satisfaction. I cut the wheel toward shore, killed the engine, and beached the keel on a sandy paradise Fingers would never see.

He was having trouble breathing and couldn't move his legs. How he'd held on that long was a mystery. Patrick "Fingers" O'Donovan had been both hard as nails and tender as baby's breath from the day we'd met. Stoic. Wise. Afraid of nothing. Even now he was calm.

My lip trembled. Mind raced. I couldn't put the words together.

Fingers was having trouble focusing, so I started talking to try to bring him back. "Fingers, stay awake. Stay with me . . ." When that didn't work, I used the only word I knew would rouse him: "Father." Fingers had been a priest before he started working for the government. And if you pressed him, he would tell you he still was.

Fingers' eyes returned to me. He feigned a smile and spoke through gritted teeth. "Was wondering when you were gonna show up. 'Bout time you did something. Where the heck you been?" Everything about him was red.

It was never supposed to end this way.

Fingers reached for and then pointed to a worn, orange Pelican case tied to the console. He never traveled without it, which was why the box alone had logged several hundred thousand miles. Whenever I thought of Fingers, the image of that stupid orange box wasn't far behind. And while he and I seldom talked about our work with anyone, he was—if caught in the right mood—oddly vocal about two things: food and wine. Both of which he protected with a religious zeal. Hence, the crash-rated, watertight, drop-proof box. He fondly referred to it as his "lunch box." No one, not me, not anyone, ever got between Fingers and a meal or a glass of wine at sunset. Some people marked memorable moments in their lives with a cigar or cigarette. Fingers marked them with red wine. Years ago, he'd converted his basement into a cellar. Visitors were routinely treated with a tour and tasting. A total wine snob, he'd often hold his glass to the light, swirl it slightly, and comment, "The earth in a bottle."

One of the girls loosed the bungee cord and brought me the box. When I opened it, Fingers laid his hand on the wine and looked at me.

He was asking me a question I didn't want him to ask, and one I certainly did not want to answer. I shook my head. "You're the priest, not—"

"Stop. No time."

"But—"

His eyes bored two holes in my soul.

"I—"

He pushed out the words. "Bread first. Then wine."

I tore off a small piece of bread and mimicked the words I'd heard him say a hundred times, ". . . the body, broken for . . . ," then I laid the bread on Fingers' tongue.

He pushed it around his mouth and tried to swallow, which brought a spasm of coughing. When he settled, I pulled the cork, tilted the bottle, and rolled the wine up against his lips. "The blood, shed for . . ." He blinked. My voice cracked again. "Whenever you do this, you proclaim the . . ." I trailed off.

He spoke before letting the wine enter his mouth. The smile on his lips matched that in his eyes. I would miss that smile. Maybe most of all. It spoke to the deepest places in me. Always had. The wine filled the back of his mouth and drained out the sides.

Blood with blood.

Another spasm. More coughing. I clung to Fingers as the waves rocked his body. One breath. Then two. Mustering his strength, he pointed at the water.

I hesitated.

Fingers' eyes rolled back; he forced their return and they narrowed on me. Calling me by my name. Something he only did when he wanted my attention. "Bishop."

I pulled Fingers over the gunnel and into the warm water. His breathing was shallower. Less frequent. More gurgle. His eyes opened and closed. Sleep was heavy. He grabbed my shirt and pulled my face close to his. "You are . . . what you are, what you've always been . . ."

I walked out into the gin-clear water up to my waist while Fingers' body floated alongside. The girls huddled and said nothing, crying while a trail of red painted the water downcurrent. Fingers tapped me in the chest and used one hand to make the numbers. First he held up all five fingers, then quickly tucked three, leaving two. Meaning seven. Without pausing, he held up all five only to tuck two. Meaning eight. Then he paused briefly and continued, making a seven followed by a zero. His cryptic motions meant 78-70.

Having learned this rudimentary code from him years ago, I knew Fingers was quoting the Psalms, which he knew by heart. The numbers 78 and 70 were a reference to King David and how God "took him from the sheepfolds." In short, Fingers was speaking about us. About the beginning of my apprenticeship. Twenty-five years prior, when I was a sophomore at the Academy, Fingers had pulled me out of class and said the strangest thing: "Tell me what you know about sheep." We'd walked a million miles since. Over the years, Fingers had become a boss, mentor, friend, teacher, sage, comic, and sometime father figure.

Life had been different with him in it.

Over the course of his career, Fingers had been in multiple places where making noise could get him killed, which is why he learned to communicate with numbers corresponding to the Psalms—earning him the nickname "Fingers." The trick meant whoever he was talking with either had to know the Psalms as well as he did or have access to a Bible.

As Fingers' life drained out into the ocean, he pulled me toward him and forced out, "Tell me . . . what you know . . . about sheep."

We had started this way. We would end this way. I tried to smile. "They tend to wander."

He waited. All of these were lessons he'd taught me. Each a year or more in the learning.

"They get lost often."

"Why?"

"Because they can."

"Why?

"Because the grass is always greener . . ."

"And that's called?"

"Murphy's law."

"Good."

"They're easy prey. The lion is never far."

A nod.

"They seldom find their way home."

He prompted me. "So they need . . ."

"A shepherd."

"What kind?"

"The kind who will leave the warmth of the fire and the safety of the flock to risk the cold, the rain, and sleepless nights to . . ." I trailed off.

"To what?"

"Find the one."

"Why?"

I was crying now. "Because . . . the needs of the one . . ." The words left me.

He closed his eyes and laid his hand flat across my chest. Even now, he was taking me to school—showing me the reason he lay dying in my arms. He'd gone after the one and turned her into seven.

He pulled himself toward me. One last moment of strength. "Need to give you—" He reached inside his shirt and pulled out a blood-soaked letter. The handwriting was hers.

He placed it flat against my chest. "Forgive her."

I stood incredulous. "Forgive her?"

"She loved you."

Blood spilled from the corner of his mouth. The flow was deep red. He shook me. "To the end—"

I held the letter and forgot how to breathe.

He spoke through the gurgle. "We're all just broken children—"

7

I stared at the paper. The weight of hopelessness. Tears spilled out of my eyes.

He reached up with his one working hand and thumbed them away. He was crying too. We'd searched for so long. Gotten so close. To have failed at the end was . . .

He tried to smile and then to speak, but his words were failing. Instead, he wrapped his fingers around the chain hanging around my neck. The weight of his arm broke the chain, and it spilled over his fingers; the cross he'd brought me from Rome swayed with the movement. "She's home now. No regret. No pain. No sorrow."

A moment passed. He closed his eyes, floated, and whispered, "One more thing . . ."

My hands were warm and slippery from the water and the blood. I could no longer feel his pulse. I knew what he wanted, and I knew it, too, would hurt. Not able to let him go, I just pulled him to my chest and held him while the life drained out and the darkness seeped in.

He whispered in my ear, "Spread my ashes where we started . . . at the end of the world."

I held back a sob while my tears puddled. I stared six hundred miles south in my mind's eye. "I can't—"

He crossed his arms, the chain still dangling. He was smiling just slightly. I looked out across the water, but my heart had blurred my eyes and I couldn't see a thing. I nodded for the last time. He let go and his body lay limp in my arms. His words were gone. He'd spoken his last. Only his breath remained.

I leaned in, managed a broken, "I'll miss you." He blinked. It was all he had left. I rallied what little strength of my own remained. "You ready?"

His eyes rolled back, then he drew a last surge of energy from the depths and focused on me. While he may have been ready, I was not. The words of his life were draining off the page, black to white. From somewhere, he mustered a final word. With his eyes closed, he tapped me in the chest, murmuring, "Don't carry her. That one'll kill you—"

With one hand beneath his neck and one hand covering the hole in his chest, I spoke out across the water. Echoing what he'd taught me. "In the name of the Father . . . the Son . . . and the . . ." He blinked, cutting a tear loose, and I pushed him beneath the surface.

I held him there for only a second, but it was long enough for his body to go limp as the last of the air bubbles escaped the corner of his mouth and the water turned red.

Though bigger than me, his body felt light as I lifted him. As if his soul was already gone. When he surfaced, his eyes were open but he wasn't looking at me. At least not in this world. And the voice I'd heard ten thousand times, I could hear no more. I dragged him to shore and laid him on the sand, where the waves washed over his ankles. That's when I noticed his hands. His crossed arms lay flat across his chest, and yet his fingers were speaking loudly enough for heaven to hear: "2–2."

"It is finished."

I pulled him to me and cried like a baby.

The Coast Guard wrapped the girls in blankets and started IVs in three of them. Having known Fingers, the captain of the ship waded into the water to help me lift his body off the sand. One of their guys offered to let me ride alongside Fingers while they piloted my Whaler back to port, but I declined. Marie's body was out there somewhere.

I had failed.

I followed the current and beached the Whaler. The sea would do one of two things: bury her in the depths or lay her body on the shore. Hours later, as the sun dropped behind the edge of the water, with both salt and blood caked on my skin, I stood at the water's edge and unfolded the letter. The weight of it drove me to my knees, where the waves washed over my thighs.

The words blurred:

My Love,
    I know this letter will hit you hard . . .

I thumbed away the tears, walking the shore until daybreak. Reading the letter over and over. Each time hurt worse. Each time her voice grew more distant.

The tide washed her ashore as the sun broke the skyline. I pulled her limp, pale body against my chest and cried again. Angry. Loud. Broken. Her body in my arms. Skin transparent and cold. I could not make sense of my life. Either what it had become or what it would be. I was lost. I kissed her face. Her cold lips.

But I could not bring her back.

The rope around her ankle had been cut with a knife, telling me she'd changed her mind somewhere in the darkness below. Though gone, she was still speaking to me. Still clawing her way back. We lay there as the waves washed over us. I pressed my cheek to hers.

"You remember that night I found you out here? Everybody was look-ing for you but nobody thought to look that far out. But there you were. Floating six or seven miles out. You were so cold. Shaking. Then we ran out of gas a mile from shore, and I paddled us in. You were worried we wouldn't make it. But I had found you. I could have paddled the coast of Florida if it meant we could stay in that boat. Then we built a fire and you leaned in to me. I remember feeling the breeze on my face. The fire on my legs and the smell of you washing over me. All I wanted to do was sit and breathe. Stop the sun. Tell it to wait a few more hours. 'Please, can't you hold off just a while?' Then you placed your hand on mine and kissed my cheek. You whispered, 'Thank you,' and I felt your breath on my ear.

"I was nobody. A sixteen-year-old shadow walking the halls. A kid with a stupid little boat, but you made me somebody. That night was our secret, and seldom did a day pass that we didn't see each other. Somehow you always found a way to get to me. Then my senior year, you were the only one who thought I could break the record. Forty-eight seconds. I crossed the line and the watch showed 'forty-seven-point-something' and I collapsed. We did it. I remember the gun going off but I don't remember running. I just remember flying. Floating. A thousand people screaming and all I heard was your voice. It's all I've ever heard.

"I don't know how to climb off this beach. I don't know how to walk out of here. I don't know who I am without you. Fingers said to forgive you but I can't. There's nothing to forgive. Nothing at all. Not even the . . . I want

10

you to know I'm sorry I didn't find you earlier. I'm real sorry. I tried so hard. But evil is real and sometimes it's hard to hear. I wish you could have heard me. So before you go, before . . . I just want you to know that I've loved you from the moment I met you, and you never did anything—not one thing, ever—to make me love you less.

"My heart hurts. A lot. It's cracking down the middle, and it's going to hurt even more when I go to stand up and carry you out of here. But no matter where I go, I'm carrying you with me. I'll keep you inside me. And every time I bathe or swim or take a drink or walk through the waves or pilot a boat or just stand in the rain, I'll let the water keep you in me. Marie, as long as there's water, there's you in me."

As the sun rose above me, I called in the Coast Guard. The helicopter landed on the beach, and when the crew offered to take Marie from me, I declined. I carried her into the bird myself, crossed her arms, pressed her head against my chest, and for the first time since I found her, I uncurled her fingers and slid my hand inside hers.

They could hear me crying over the sound of the helicopter blades.

CHAPTER 1

A week passed. I ate little. Slept less. Most afternoons I found myself staring out across the water. Days ticked by. Both Marie and Fingers' last will and testament stipulated they be cremated. Which they were.

While Fingers had asked me to spread his ashes at the end of the world, Marie had chosen a spot a bit closer to home. In her final letter, Marie had asked me to spread her ashes in the shallow water just off the island where we played as kids. For a week, I clutched the urn in my hands and watched the tide roll in and wash out. High tide. Low tide. High. Low. But I could not convince my legs to carry me out into the water. So, despite Marie's final wish, I returned to my house and placed the urn on the kitchen table alongside Fingers' ashes, which I had placed in his signature orange lunch box. An odd pair and a strange sight. A purple urn and a bright-orange box. I stared at them. They stared back at me.

For another week, I orbited them like a moon. Daylight. Darkness. Daytime. Night.

Fingers had taught me all I knew. Found me when I was lost. Patched me back together when all the king's horses and all the king's men could not. I had been Ben Gunn; he had been Jim Hawkins. I had been Crusoe; he had been Friday. In my darkest moment, I had awakened on a shoreline, a castaway with sea foam and fiddler crabs tickling my nose. I could not rescue myself and did not speak the island language. Fingers lifted me from the sand, brushed me off, fed me, and taught me how to walk again. He rescued me when I was beyond rescue. His impact was immeasurable. The absence of his voice deafening.

Life without Marie was like waking up in a world where the sun had been removed from the sky. I kept her letter close. Read and reread it ten thousand times. Set it next to my face when I lay down to sleep so I could smell her hand, but it brought little comfort. I could not turn back time. Nor could I, no matter how hard I tried, wrap my head around the finality. It didn't seem possible. It wasn't. How was she gone? The picture of her alone, terror-filled, a rope around her ankle, leaving this world consumed by shame and regret, was tough to stomach. I had exhausted myself in the search. Spent all I had. Come so close, and yet failed so completely. When she needed me, I had not been there.

Maybe that hurt most of all. I'd spent my life rescuing the wounded, and yet I could not rescue the one I loved the most.

Fort George Island sits north of Jacksonville, Florida, protected from the Atlantic by Little Talbot Island. Someone with knowledge of the waterways can navigate the Fort George River from the Atlantic Ocean through the sandbars and shallow waters around Little Talbot into the gentler waters surrounding Fort George. And while protected, Fort George Island is anything but hidden. The reason for this is a confluence of geography. The Intracoastal Waterway—which in North Florida is known to the locals as Clapboard Creek—runs north from the St. Johns River and the Mayport basin to Amelia Island and the Nassau Sound. In between the two, the Fort George River connects the Clapboard with the Atlantic.

That means the Fort George River is easily accessible by either the ICW or the Atlantic, and thereby party central for the boat culture of North Florida—which includes the wealthy who winter or weekend on Amelia, St. Simons, and Sea Island. At high tide, the Fort George River looks like any other. Water everywhere. But inches below the surface lies a different reality. As the tide recedes, the sandbars around Fort George emerge like Atlantis and become a playground the size of twenty or thirty football fields. High-traffic weekends will see a hundred boats anchored or tethered in daisy chains—boats ranging from twelve-foot Gheenoes to sixteen-foot

Montauks to twenty-four-foot center consoles to thirty-two-foot triple engines to forty-foot go-fast boats and every variation in between. Even some sixty- or seventy-five-foot yachts will moor in the deeper water and then send their tenders into the playground.

Weekends are a kaleidoscope of color and an explosion of sound. Boat captains attract attention three ways: the color and design of their boat, the bodies filling the bikinis aboard, and the noise emitting from their speakers. Dotting the periphery are glass bottles in coolies, beach chairs resting in the water, kids on floats, dogs chasing bait fish, boys throwing cast nets, kids on jet skis, sandcastles in disrepair, straw hats of every size and shape, old men flying kites, barbeque grills, and generators. From sunup to sundown, the Fort George system of sandbars is a city that emerges and disappears with the tide.

My island is one of the many smaller ones surrounding Fort George. With the deepwater access of the ICW to the west and the shallower waters of the river to the south and east, I, too, am hemmed in by water. But unlike Fort George Island, my island is smaller and only accessible by boat. And while Fort George is dotted with homes and churches and clubs and tourists and an old plantation, I live alone.

Which is how I like it.

I sat at the kitchen table, sipped my coffee, and tried not to stare at the urns. To give my hands something to do, I cleaned Fingers' Sig. Then I cleaned it again. And again. I liked the worn feel of it in my hand. It reminded me of him and the umpteen times I'd seen him holster or unholster it. I tried to remember the sounds of his and Marie's voices or see their faces, but both were muffled and muddled; I couldn't make them out. With each day, the regrets mounted, and I kept hearing myself speak the many words I'd left unsaid.

Fingers' leaving was sudden, and while I always knew it might happen that way given his and my chosen line of work, I wasn't ready for it. He was here, big as life itself, filling my heart and mind—and then he was gone. I thought through the details of that last day a thousand times over. "We'll cover more ground if you take the coastline and I take the horizon," he'd said. I knew we never should have split up. I knew if and when he found Victor's yacht, he wouldn't wait. Older and maybe a step slower, he'd charge in. Bull in a china shop. Sig blazing. He was stubborn that way. He knew the moment he grabbed the swim ladder that entering the *Gone to Market* was a one-way trip.

It's why those he rescued trusted him. And why so many more loved him.

Stories were Fingers' mechanism for dealing with the memories. They rolled off his tongue one after another—the scent of one pointing to the next. Of course, getting him to sit still long enough was the key, but pour him a glass of earth and the gates would open. When they did, I'd sit, listen, laugh, and cry. We all did.

I stood at the orange box and mourned the silence. I knew I needed to get going, but I was stalling. The loss of one was crushing. The loss of both was . . . No matter how hard I tried or how long I sat there staring down the table, I could not make sense of the fact that everything I knew about them and had experienced with them was now held in two containers sitting three feet in front of me. I would walk out of the kitchen only to walk back in and be amazed that they had not moved. Purple and orange still staring back at me.

It was a dream I did not like and from which I could not wake up.

Sunday afternoon meant much of the crowd had thinned on the sandbars, yet one boat emerged from the ICW pushing a wake against the outgoing tide. A twenty-eight-foot, dual-engine tender for a larger yacht moored in the channel. Two guys and ten girls. Piercingly loud music. They ran the nose up on the beach, and the girls and one guy exited while the captain secured a Bahamian moor so the wind wouldn't spin him and beach him in the shallows, forcing him to wait about eight hours to nudge his boat loose. Evidently he knew what he was doing.

His guests roamed the sandbar and set up a volleyball net. The two guys were not remarkable. Tattooed. Muscled. Chains and earrings. Like every other wannabe. But the girls were. As were the sizes of their bikinis. With the beer and umbrella drinks flowing and sundown approaching, the sandbar soon became a topless dance competition.

I'd seen it all before.

With the noise of their party over my shoulder, I waded through the waist-deep water several hundred yards away, pulled the crab trap, lifted out the angry blue crab, placed it on a medium-size circle hook, and cast a Carolina rig out into the deeper channel. Twenty minutes later, my drag started singing. A keeper redfish, or red drum as they are technically known, bronzed from the tannins in the St. Johns and St. Mary's Rivers. Hooked well.

Redfish is good eating. Dinner served.

Fingers' watertight, bright-orange, beat-up Pelican case had probably circled the globe a half dozen times. One more trip wouldn't hurt. I figured he'd like that. Besides, if the boat took on water, the case could serve as a flotation device and save my life—something Fingers was good at. The trip south would take me several hundred miles through temperamental and sometimes unforgiving waters, so I was planning like the airlines do— "In the event of a loss of cabin pressure." Unlikely but possible. I secured Fingers' box on the bow because I knew he'd like the wind in his face.

I had intended to spend the afternoon readying the Whaler for my trip down the coast, but more often than not I found myself staring at that box. Thinking about the number of times I'd seen Fingers do what Fingers did—make everything better. Years ago, I'd named the Whaler *Gone Fiction* for reasons that mattered only to me. Fingers told me it was a stupid name. I told him to get his own boat because I wasn't changing the name. He knew why, so he didn't fight me on it.

I changed the oil. Swapped out the prop for something with a little more pitch, which would bring down the rpm's at higher speeds over long distances. Conserving fuel while bringing my top speed to fifty-five-plus if I trimmed it out.

I cleared the bills off my desk and then did the one thing I'd been dreading. I composed the email I did not want to write. Then another. How do you tell a person that someone they love has died? I'm not sure I can answer that. When finished, I sat staring at my screen. For an hour. A phone call would have been better—they deserved that—but I didn't have the bandwidth. I would not be able to control my emotions. So I clicked Send, turned off my computer and my phone, and was in the process of turning out all the lights when I heard a knock. It echoed off the massive doors, crossed the lawn through the rain, and bounced into the second-story open window of my loft inside the barn. Given that I am surrounded by water, visitors are rare. I waited, and there it was again, this time accompanied by a muted female voice.

A girl's voice.

I pulled on a shirt, climbed down, crossed the yard in the rain, and crept barefooted through the darkness, staring at her back. Even from behind, she was beautiful.

"Hello," I said.

She jumped a foot in the air, fell into a squatting position, and screamed. Following that with relieved yet uncertain laughter as I stepped around her and into the light.

She stood and pointed at me, but her aim was slightly off and most of her words ran together. "You shouldn't sneak up on people. Now I really have to pee. You open?"

I unlocked the latch and swung open the massive oaken doors. Our movement turned on the motion lights, which gave me a better look at her. She was a beautiful young woman. Fashion magazine face. Runway legs. Pilates figure. Bare feet, muddy at the edges. She was holding a rain jacket above her head to ward off the drizzle. She laughed uncomfortably. "You scared the sh—" Suddenly aware of her surroundings, she covered her mouth and said, "I mean . . . I wasn't expecting you. That's all. Sorry."

I recognized her from the sandbar.

CHAPTER 2

S he shook off the rain, tracking mud. She was dressed provocatively.
Daisy Dukes. Bikini top. Several piercings—nose, ears, and belly button. Black eyeliner. Maybe the eyelashes were not hers. She smelled of
smoke but not cigarettes. Possibly a cigar but I doubted it. Her fingers nervously turned the bikini strap behind her neck. She stepped inside and
twirled like a dancer. Something she did both to take in her surroundings
and because it was natural. Like she'd danced as a child. Her jet-black hair
was not her real color. A recent change. As was the tattoo at the small of her
back. The red edges looked slightly irritated.

Her rain jacket belonged to a man and was several sizes too large. I
pointed. "May I?"

She folded it over her arms. "I'm good." I wondered if her present dis-
trust of me was fueled by whoever gave her that rain jacket.

She was fifteen. Maybe sixteen, but I doubted it. The world before her.
Something ugly behind her. Her glassy eyes betrayed a stormy and medicated mixture of excitement and fear. Going up or coming down, there was
more in her blood than just blood.

Silence followed. I folded my hands behind my back. "Can I help
you?"

Her words grew more slurred. "You have a baaaa-throom?"

I pointed at the door, and she went in. Walking provocatively. After
a few minutes, her phone rang and I could hear her in there talking more

to someone than with. Her raised voice suggested the conversation did not go well. When she returned, she'd settled the jacket loosely around her shoulders.

"Thaaaank you."

Curious, she studied the small chapel. My voice broke the silence. "How old are you?"

She laughed but wouldn't look at me. "Twenty-one."

I paused long enough to force her to look at me. "Are you okay?"

More discomfort. Less eye contact. "Why do you ask?"

I waved my hand across the water where she'd spent the afternoon. "Sometimes getting off a boat can be more difficult than getting on."

"You know about boats?"

"Some."

She studied the intricate woodwork. Hand carved. The tops of the pews had been darkened over the years by hand oil and sweat. Her eyes landed on the ornate altar and steps. "It's beautiful."

"Slaves built it. About two hundred years ago."

The moon filtered through the glass and cast her shadow on the worn stones below her. She ran her hands along a pew. Letting her fingertips read the stories it told.

She glanced out the window, which did little to mute the sound of the Atlantic crashing on the beach some several hundred yards distant. "It's amazing the hurricanes haven't erased it."

"They've tried a couple times. We pieced her back together."

She continued, "Slaves, huh?"

I pointed at the wall. At all the names carved into the stone by hand. "Each one a mom . . . a dad . . . a child."

She walked to the wall and ran her fingers through the grooves of the names, then the grooves of the dates. Some deeper than others. A wrinkle formed between her eyebrows. She asked, "Slaves?"

"Free slaves."

Hundreds of names had been etched into the stone wall. She tiptoed to the right. A half smile spread across her face. She craned. Quizzical.

I continued, "Most date prior to the Civil War, when this place was one of many stops on the Underground Railroad."

She studied them and asked, "But some of these dates are from the last decade? Last year?"

Another nod.

"But slavery's over."

I shrugged. "People still own people."

She read the names. "All these people found freedom here?"

"I wouldn't say they found it here as much as they stopped by on their way to it."

Her fingertips read the wall again. Her voice was loud and didn't match the quiet of our conversation. "A record of freedom."

"Something like that."

"Why do these just have one date?"

"Once free, always free."

She walked to the wall, coming to another list. "Why do these have two dates?"

"They died before they tasted it."

Outside, a foghorn sounded. One long blast followed by a shorter second and third. It pulled her eyes off the wall. She walked to the door only to turn and stare at the wall of names. She turned to me. "Am I the only one here?"

"Just us."

"You mean you-and-me us, or . . ." She shot a glance upward. "You-me-and-Him us?"

"Just us."

She considered this and smiled, twirling again. More dancing, but her partner was only visible to her. "I like you, Father." She pointed at the ground beneath her. "You live on this island?"

"I'm not the priest. And yes, I live here."

"What do you do?"

"Groundskeeper. Make sure people who sneak up at night aren't here to spray-paint graffiti."

She grabbed my right hand and turned it over. Running her fingertips along the calluses and the dirt in the cracks. She smiled. "Where's the priest?"

Short question, long answer. And I wondered if this was the real reason she'd come to my door. "We're in between priests at the moment."

She looked bothered by this. "What kind of da— I mean . . . What kind of church is this?"

"The inactive kind."

She shook her head. "That's silly. Whoever heard of a church being in-active? I mean, doesn't that sorta go against the whole reason for a church?"

"I just work here."

"Alone?"

I nodded again.

"Don't you get lonely?"

"Not really."

She shook her head. "I'd lose my ever-loving mind. Go bat-shi—" She covered her mouth again with her hand. "Sorry . . . I mean, I'd go crazy."

I chuckled. "You're assuming I'm not."

She stepped closer, her face inches from mine. Her eyelids were heavy. Her breath reeked of alcohol. "I've seen crazy and you don't look the part." Her eyes walked up and down me. "I don't know. You loooook pretty goooood to me." She reached out with her finger and touched the scar above my eye. "That hurt?"

"Not anymore."

"How'd you get it?"

"Bar fight."

"What happened to the other guy?"

"Guys. Plural."

She put a hand on my shoulder and patted me, proving that whatever boundaries of personal space she'd once possessed had been erased by the cocktail in her blood. "I knew I liked you, Padre." She considered me again. Ran her fingers down my arm, tracing the vein on my bicep. Then she squeezed my muscle like someone would test the air in a bike tube. "You work out?"

"I keep busy."

She squeezed both arms, and then—invading every barrier of personal space I'd ever erected—she squeezed my pecs and patted my abs and butt. "I'll say." She thumbed behind her. Toward the water and what I could only assume was her boat. Lifting her rain jacket, she said, "He's always working out. Nothing but muscle."

I said nothing.

She continued, "What all you do here?"

"I mow the grass and keep the weeds down, and they give me a free place to stay."

She considered this. "I never been in a church like this."

She was looking at a far wall covered in weapons of archery from around the world. Handmade bows from more countries than I could count. Matching arrows. She walked an unsteady S to study the mementos. "These yours?"

"I used to travel a lot," I responded.

"You've been a lot of places. I never . . . uh . . . I never been anywhere . . ." She feigned a smile. "But I'm about to." She ran her fingers across the bows and arrows. "You Robin Hood?"

"No." I've always had a thing for archery—seeing how various countries created energy through a stick and string amazed me—so I collected them on my trips. Whenever I bumped into one, I'd bring it home.

She mimicked the motion with her arms. "You shoot these?"

"No."

"Why you keep them?"

"They're reminders."

"Of?"

"What I am."

"What are you?"

I didn't respond immediately. When I did, my voice was lower. "A sinner."

She looked confused. "Well, me too, but what's that got to do with . . ." She flipped her hand across the wall. "All this?"

"The term *sinner* grew out of an Old English archery term from the thirteenth century."

"What's it mean?"

"To miss the mark."

She laughed. "Well, hell, we're all—" She covered her mouth with her hand, then wiped her mouth on the back of her arm. "I mean . . . They sure got that right." She twirled again and then walked in between the pews, staring at my world. "So, you're a sinner, huh?"

I stared at her but said nothing.

"Can't imagine what that makes me." She walked around me in a circle, sizing me up. "You can't be that bad." She gestured toward the walls. "God keeps you here."

She eyed the old, worn confessional. "When they gonna get a new priest?"

"Don't know."

"So . . . what you're saying is that there won't be a priest here anytime tonight? Say in the next twenty minutes?"

A nod. "Yes."

"So he isn't coming?"

"Yes, that's what I'm saying. No priest tonight."

She let out a deep breath. "So I'm stuck with—" She waved a disapproving hand across the whole of me. "You."

Whatever was in her blood had made its way to her head. She was swimming. Ghostly pale. Sweat beaded on her face. She closed her eyes, swayed, began humming quietly, and raised her arms. An act of which I was not certain she was conscious. For nearly a minute, she stood in the chapel, arms raised, swaying, humming a song buried somewhere deep in her memory. I have this thing that happens in my rib cage when I'm around kids who are a long way from home—and getting farther. I've had it for years. While she stood there, I felt the knife enter between my ribs.

When she opened her eyes again, the sweat had trickled down her temple. She lowered her arms. "Whoa . . . This place is legit." She caught herself on a pew, only to look at me a long time. After a minute, her head tilted sideways like a puppy, and then a sour look shaded her face. Her hand touched her stomach and her eyes began blinking excessively.

"Uh-oh." Her cheeks filled with air and she convulsed slightly. The beginnings of a dry heave. Frantically looking for ground that was not sacred, she exited the pews and ran into the center aisle, swaying, only to pause midway. "I think I'm about to pu—" She tried to step toward the door, but the floor was uneven and her steps uncertain. With too many hurdles, she dropped to her knees, collected herself, and emptied her stomach. Then she did it again. The sounds of splattering and heaving echoed off the stone walls.

Wiping her mouth with her jacket, she sat back against a pew and closed her eyes. Pouring sweat. She spoke without opening her eyes. "I cannot believe I just—" She cut herself off and crawled down the center aisle. Stopping two pews away. She leaned against a pew and closed her eyes again. "If you've got a towel or a mop, I'll clean that—"

"I got it."

She opened one eye. "You're really gonna clean up my puke?"

"I've seen worse."

She leaned her head back, closed both eyes, and placed her palms flat on the floor. As if she were trying to stop the world from spinning. "If you weren't a padre, I'd kiss you on the mouth."

"I'm not the padre."

"What, you wouldn't kiss me?"

I said nothing but pointed at the trail of saliva dangling off her chin and pooling on the top of her breast. She wiped it on her other arm and said, "Okay, so maybe I wouldn't kiss me either, but—" She closed her eyes again. "I'm a goooood kisser." Opening her eyes, she studied me a minute. "You ever kissed a girl, Father?"

"Yes."

She looked around as if she was afraid somebody was listening to our conversation. "They allow that around here?"

I laughed. "Yes."

"What are you?"

"Just a guy."

"So you're married?"

"I was."

"Was?" More of a statement than a question.

"For a short while."

"So . . ." She smiled. "It's been a while since you been kissed?"

"Yep."

"Then you could probably use a good kissssssing."

I didn't disagree with her.

She puckered her lips and closed her eyes. Held that pose for several seconds. "You sure you don't want to kiss me? I'm pretty good at it."

"I believe you."

She unpuckered, then puckered again. Doing so made her look like a fish. If she wasn't so high, it would have been comical. "You're missing out."

"I can see that."

She opened both eyes, but the space between them narrowed. "How old are you?"

"Forty-nine. How old are you?"

She responded without thinking. "Sixteen." She leaned her head against the pew and closed her eyes again. "If you weren't, you know, stuck in here with God breathing down your back, I'd introduce you to my mom—although we're not on the best of terms right now, so you might neeeeed"—she raised a finger in the air to add emphasis—"to take a rain check on that." She opened her eyes. "You like to dance, Padre?"

It wasn't worth the effort to correct her. I shook my head. "Not much."

She attempted to point at me but her finger missed again. This time by a couple of feet. "You'd like my mom. She's one helluva—" She covered her mouth again and began crawling toward the door. "I need to get out of here." She held her hand close to her face and began counting out loud, touching her fingers with each count. "Thirty-two, thirty-three . . ." She stopped and looked at me. "You're old enough to be my dad. You should meet my mom."

"Technically, I'm old enough to be your grandfather."

She pursed her lips. "You're pretty good looking for a grandpa." She pushed off her knees, climbing up the pew one hand over another. Now standing, eyes closed and legs wobbly, she tugged on her bikini top, which came off rather easily. Chest bare and sunburned, she stood with her eyes closed, lips puckered, and waited for me to accept her invitation. A girl trying ever so hard to become a woman when being a girl was what she needed. A silver Jerusalem cross hung in the space between her breasts. Whenever she moved, it bounced off her skin and spun slightly, exposing the honeycomb engraving. She noticed me eyeing it.

"You like my cross?"

"I do."

"You take it off me and you can have it."

I pulled a robe off the hook on the back wall and hung it across her shoulders. Draped in white, she looked disappointed. "Not pretty enough for you?"

"You're plenty beautiful."

Twirling her bikini top, she was playing with me now. "Too dirty?"

"Nope."

Suddenly, her eyebrows lifted and her eyes grew large, followed by a sly smile. "Oh . . ." Another point. Another miss by several feet. "This is one of *those* churches. You're gay? I'm sorry . . ." She fumbled with her bikini top but got nowhere. "Here I am coming on to a—"

"Not gay."

"You sure?"

"Pretty sure."

The space between her eyes narrowed and she held her chin in her hand. "Too young?"

I relented. "Something like that."

Her nose caught scent of the puddle on the floor that separated us. Her lip curled. "You sure you don't want some help with that?"

"You sure you want to go back to that boat?"

She closed her eyes and puckered her lips, holding the position several seconds. "I'm a good kisser, Padre. You should get it now while the getting's good. You worried I'll tell?"

"Not really."

"I won't tell a soul. It'll be our secret."

"You good at keeping secrets?"

She smiled knowingly. "I'm fr-fri-fricking Fort Knox." She eyed the confessional again. "Can you call maybe a fill-in priest?" She pointed at the kneeler. "Anybody will do. I wanted to, uh—"

"No."

"Seriously?"

"Seriously."

"This is a weird fri-fricking church."

I laughed out loud.

The words she spoke circled her fuzzy and incoherent mind and settled somewhere near her understanding. When the reality of what she said sank in, she covered her mouth again. "Oh, I'm sorry. I need to shut my—"

"Will you let me give you my phone number?"

"What, you gonna have the priest call me?"

"No, I'm giving you my number. Not the other way around."

She waved me off. "Padre, I'm not that kind of girl. I don't ever give my number on the first date."

"Is that what this is?"

She looked disappointed. "Not really. You won't kiss me."

I held out my hand.

She slipped her phone from the back pocket of her Daisy Dukes and held it in front of her. One finger unbuttoned the top of her Daisy Dukes, exposing the matching bikini bottom. "I'll give you my phone if you kiss me."

"Close your eyes."

She did, then puckered and waited, swaying a little. Had I been thirty years younger I might have taken her up on it. Actually, I'm positive I would have. I gently took her phone, but it was locked so I pressed her thumb to the home button and unlocked it. She smiled, eyes still closed. "Padre, my lips are cramping." I typed in my number and saved it under the name

"ICE—Padre," then handed her back her phone. She opened her eyes and read the new contact.

She looked confused. "ICE?"

"In Case of—"

She smiled and held out her right hand like a stop sign. "Emergency."

Forcing her eyes to focus, she read my number out loud. Halfway through it, she said, "That doesn't look like any phone number I've ever seen."

"It's a satellite phone."

"Does that make me special?"

"It makes you one of a few select people on this planet who've ever had that number."

She winked at me. "Oh . . . that's a good one. You're smooth, Padre. I'll bet you get all the girls with that one."

She held the phone over her heart and nodded. I didn't know if she'd ever remember this conversation or even who "Padre" was, but maybe she had enough sober brain waves to recall it if she had an emergency. Then without notice, she raised her hands, twirled, then twirled again.

She strolled down the center aisle, shedding the priest's robe as she walked. It lay in a pile on the floor. Stopping at the door, she clung to the massive iron latch. My voice stopped her. "Can I ask you one thing?"

She twirled again, eyes closed. "You gonna kiss me?"

"What's your name?"

She stuck one finger in the air and waved it like a windshield wiper. "You gotta do better than that, Padre."

I took one step closer. "Let's say we get a new priest, and he asks about you—"

"Why would he do that?"

"So he can ask God to watch over you."

She put her finger to her lips. "Ooh, that's a good one too." For the first time, she covered her chest with her arms, but her covering was playful. Not ashamed. "You got game, Padre. You tell that to all the girls?"

"Just you."

She tied on her bikini top and eyed the walls that surrounded us. A girl again. Then without speaking, she walked to the wall of names, slid a lipstick tube from her back pocket, and wrote "Angel" at the bottom of the list.

"That your real name?" I asked.

She spoke without looking. "It's what my momma calls me." A pause. "Or used to."

The soft light shone on her face. Drowned the pain. I held up my phone and clicked a picture. She liked the fact that I'd finally noticed her. She smiled. "Something to remember me by?"

"Something."

She twirled her finger through the strap of her bikini. "Should've taken it a few minutes ago. More fun to look at."

"I got what I needed."

"Needed or wanted?"

This girl was smart. "I'll bet somebody's looking for you right now."

Something rested on her tongue but she smiled and swallowed it. "You ever write letters, Padre?"

"I write some."

Her eyes wandered across the pews and everything about her darkened. Even the playfulness of her voice. "I wrote a letter."

"Can I read it?"

She looked directly at me. "It's not addressed to you." She swallowed again. "I wrote it to my mom, but I'm pretty sure she didn't like it."

"Why?"

She didn't answer.

The foghorn sounded again. Last time she heard it; this time she considered it. Having done so, she turned and studied me as if she were taking a picture of her own. Then she glanced up at the confessional, took another, and hesitated. Finally, she spoke without looking at me. "You think God gives us credit for showing up even when the priest didn't?"

For the first time, I spoke through the cloud, directly to her. "If this life is based on credits and debits—" I shook my head. "Then we're all gone anyway."

In a rare moment of lucidity, she turned to me. "What do you think it's based on?"

The wall of names painted the backdrop behind me. "The walk . . . from broken to not."

She nodded, wrapped herself in the rain jacket, and silently stumbled out into the rain.

I stood at the water's edge, my face shrouded in shadow, and watched her walk out my dock and step aboard the waiting vessel. A yacht. Eighty feet or better. The muscled captain tipped his hat to me, cranked the engines, and used his thrusters to move ninety degrees away from the dock. He did so against the current and a contrary wind—again suggesting experience. Moving fore to aft, the girl swayed, bouncing between railing and cabin wall as she walked toward the rear deck and the other party-goers. Blue lights lit the aft deck, revealing a Jacuzzi. A bartender. DJ. No expense spared.

The girl was met by a man, older than her. Even in the darkness, his eyes were dark. He was fit. Muscled. Tight shirt. Veins in his neck. Gold hanging from it. She handed him the rain jacket, and he wrapped an arm around her waist. He handed her a shot glass of something, which she turned up and downed, and then he held something glowing to her lips. She inhaled, causing the tip to flare. Having rallied, she fell out of her clothes and into the hot water along with what I could only guess were a dozen or more equally plastered people. Then the lights of the yacht faded south down the Intracoastal. Another promised party on the sunrise.

Yachts that size were a statement. In my experience, the wealthy invested in homes, but they bought yachts to draw attention. To showcase their power. Something akin to artwork hung on the water. And whereas most boat owners wanted everyone to know who they were and how cunningly they'd imagined the name of their vessel, the name of this boat was covered, shrouded in darkness.

That meant people got on, but not everyone got off.

And that was bad.

CHAPTER 3

The slaves who once inhabited this island worked just across the river from the plantation that encompassed Fort George. At low tide, the slaves could walk from home to field without getting more than knee-deep; most of that walk was on a dry sandbar. For community, and possibly protection, the slaves arrayed their tabby homes in a circle, at the center of which sat the chapel.

The walls of the chapel were made from cobblestone ballast rescued from English trade ships. The ships would navigate the Atlantic, arriving in one of several nearby ports, and dump their ballast of cobblestones to make room for cargo. Over the decades of trade, islands of stone rose up from the sea floor. The slaves gathered the cut stones and built the chapel, which looked like something straight off the streets of London. Given that the walls were four stones thick, almost two feet, it was cool inside during the summer and, come September, a strong shelter against the Atlantic storms. On the other hand, the slaves' homes were made from tabby—a form of durable, pourable concrete made from available elements, including small shells.

I lay in bed listening to the rain on the tin roof above me. Soft at first. Then a downpour.

The dream is always the same, and unlike most dreams, I know I'm dreaming this one. I just can't wake up. Or maybe I don't want to. It's my wedding day. Sunshine. Breeze. She is resplendent. Glowing. She walks the aisle. Takes my hand. "I will." "I do." I lean in and try to kiss her. Millimeters from her touch, I can feel her breath on my face. But it's a dream where one millimeter equals a million miles. No kiss.

We are whisked to the limo where my best man dons a "James" hat and cracks jokes. "Yes'm, Miss Daisy." She and I sit in the back seat. Giddy. Over the moon. It's a dream, so I can say things like that. She looks with longing out the window, places a hand on my thigh. "Can't we just skip the reception? I don't want to wait."

We arrive at the reception. There is champagne. She pulls me aside, her bottom lip trembling. A tear in the corner of her eye. "You sure you want me?"

I lean in, try to kiss her. A millimeter stands in the way.

We process in. Or parade as the case may be. First the wedding party. Then us. Applause. Shouts. Whistles. A band plays. Lights flash. A disco ball spins. We wind our way around to the head table amid well wishes and handshakes and hugs. The room is a sea of flowers and tuxedos and diamonds and high heels and laughter. Another toast, another attempted kiss, but the distance is now two million miles. We stand, and she takes my hand to lead me to the dance floor. Our first dance. Mr. and Mrs.

All the world is right.

My best man stands. Wobbles. He'd started early. He toasts us. *Just so happy for you.* He has a gift. From him to us. He'd worked hard on it and wanted to wait until now to give it to us.

The room is silent as I open it. She watches. She has slid her hand inside my arm.

Even in my dream I know I'm about to wake up. I try to stop. To stay sleeping. But it's no good. I never make the dance. Not in the dream. Not in real life. Not once.

I wake sweating. Heart racing. Unable to catch my breath. It's always the same. I hate that dream.

On that morning, I splashed my face and was in the process of boiling water for my Chemex when the phone rang. I didn't need to look at caller ID. Obviously, she'd read my email. She was crying when I answered. She collected herself enough to say, "Hey . . . You okay?"

"I'm staring at the green side of the grass." She laughed, a release of emotion. I continued, "How are you making it? How's New York?"

Another sniffle. I heard paper shuffling. "Didn't know I could hurt like this. Even for someone as jaded as me." She blew her nose. "You really doing it?"

"Told him I would."

"And Marie?"

I leaned against the wall and my eye fell on the purple urn. Resting on the kitchen table. "Not yet. One at a time."

"Want some company? I'll fly down. Whatever you need, you know that."

"City girl like you? No A/C. No Wi-Fi. No Starbucks. You'd lose your ever-loving mind." She laughed. Let out the breath she'd been holding. I continued, "Think I'd better do this one on my own."

"How long will you be gone?"

I didn't have an answer. "Week. Month." I rubbed my eyes. "Don't really know."

"Last time you were down there a year." She faked a laugh. "Don't make me come down there and find you."

"You're good at that." The memory of the bar returned. "Might be tough to find me this time."

"I did it once."

I laughed. "True. But I think that was luck."

I heard her smile and light a cigarette, which meant she was remembering something she'd not told me. "I think love had more to do with it than luck."

I smiled. "Strong words for a woman who swore off any affection for the male race."

She laughed. "Murph?"

"Yes."

"The obituary . . ." A pause. "Beautiful. I've never . . . She would . . ." Her voice faded.

I waited.

"I want to . . ." She choked up. Silenced a sob and said, "Thank you for . . . Without you, I'd never have known either of them. Fingers was the father I never had. He taught me what a man should be. What it looked like to be loved by a man." A pause as the line fell silent. "Maybe that's why it's been so tough to find someone who measures up. He set the bar rather high."

"God broke the mold when He made him. One and only."

She held back a sob. "Marie . . . if I could be anyone, I'd be her."

I couldn't answer. The urn stared at me. Silently.

"You will come back, right?"

My teakettle whistled as the water boiled. "I'd better get going."

"Murphy . . . ?"

I knew what was coming. One last attempt. She had to try. "You sure? I mean, really. You don't have to . . ."

I stared at the boat and then south at all the miles staring back at me. There and back again. "I promised him." A long pause. "I owe him." I wiped my eyes.

"Still keeping your word."

"Trying."

"He taught all of us that."

"You're the best. I'll be seeing you. Take care."

The emotional tug she held on my heart convinced me of what I already knew—I needed to cut all the tethers. If I didn't, I'd never make it to Daytona. Much less the southern tip of Florida. I couldn't do what I had to do looking in my rearview. And once I got there, I had to return. Marie was here waiting. The view out the windshield would be painful both going and coming. Pain waiting on me there. Pain waiting on me here. I read Call Ended across the faceplate of my phone, walked to the water's edge, and skimmed it like a stone out across the shallow waves.

Daylight found me walking the perimeter of the island. I care for more than two hundred rose and citrus trees, so I fertilized each one and checked the automatic sprinklers, making sure they were functional. Over the years, I'd run miles of rubber tubing and PVC pipe to bring water to the roots.

Something else Fingers taught me. I didn't know how long I'd be gone, so I locked up my apartment in the barn but not the chapel. I never locked it. Fingers and I had rebuilt much of it, and I had hundreds of hours of sweat equity invested, but I didn't consider it mine. Who really owns a church? If someone needed shelter, they were welcome to it. I certainly wouldn't stop them. I left a note pinned to the door:

> If you are looking for the priest, he died. If he were here, he'd tell you that he's gone home and you can read the details in the obituary. If you need God, you'd better talk to Him yourself. He'd like that. And he'd wish that for you. It's why he lived the life he lived. The door is unlocked.
> —Murph

I wound down the path to the water, stepped onto my small dock, then onto my boat.

I stood a long time staring at the water. Marie and I fell in love here. In these waters. Knee-deep. We'd met as kids. Shared our secrets. Watched each other walk over from kids to man and woman. Then there was that night. The party. The riptide. How they were all looking in the wrong place and how I found her washed out to sea. Back onshore, tender and trembling and full of hope, she put her hand in mine and we waded in. Love washed over me. A riptide. I'd like to think it washed her too. We dove to the bottom—where the water is clear—then climbed up on the bank and let the moon and fire dry our skin. In the weeks that followed, we combed the beach looking for shells and each other. Just two hearts reaching for each other, standing against the world, wishing the tide would stay out forever.

But that's the thing about tides. They always return. Nothing holds them back. And when they do, they erase the memory of what was.

A week before our wedding, she had tugged on my arm. "I need to tell you something." Her eyes were glassy.

"Sure."

"Not here."

We climbed into my Gheenoe, a sixteen-foot skiff, and she brought me here. We beached the skiff just over there and walked these woods. Into the chapel. I had proposed in there. The place held a thousand tender memories. She pushed open the massive doors and led me up the center aisle toward the altar. Abandoned years ago, the chapel lay in disrepair and ruin. We stepped over and around pieces of the roof that had caved in decades ago. She held both of my hands and through tears said, "I just wanted you to know . . ."

I waited. She was hurting and I needed to let her talk.

"Just wanted you to hear from me that . . . I will and I do." She patted her chest. "With all of the broken pieces of me."

I brushed the hair out of her face. "What's wrong?"

"I can't give you what I promised you."

"What do you mean?"

"I mean . . ." She looked away. "Something was taken from me . . . when I was younger. Once it's gone . . ." She shook her head. "It never comes back."

"What're you—"

"My father." The tears broke loose and she reached for me. Clinging. "Please don't think I'm dirty. It was a long time ago."

Wasn't tough to put the pieces together.

She spoke in my ear. "Mom found out. Divorced him. I haven't seen him since he got out of prison."

I held her, and what started low and quiet became loud, angry, and painful. Something she'd been holding a long time. Maybe since it happened. I held her face in my hands and kissed her. Her lips tasted salty. "I loved you from before the moment I met you. Always have. Nothing changes that. Ever."

"You still want me?"

I wrapped my arms around her waist and smiled. "Yes."

"You're sure?"

"Positive."

"I wouldn't blame you if—"

I pressed my finger to her lips. "Stop. I love you. All of you. Just the way you are. I'm not making light of any of this, but love . . ."

Desperation wrecked her eyes. "Does what?"

I searched for the words. "Writes over the old memories. Makes beauty out of pain. Love writes what can be."

"You promise?"

"I do."

She pressed her body to mine. "Then write me."

How do you bury the two people you love most in this world? The trip south to spread Fingers' ashes would take several days, a couple weeks even. Then I had to turn around. Get back. The round trip would allow me time to get used to the idea of spreading Marie's ashes upon my return. Who was I kidding? Get used to? I think not. The only thing the time gave me was more time to wrestle with the idea.

Which was both good and terrible.

Earlier in my apartment, standing there staring at the purple urn and the orange box, I knew I couldn't deal with both at once. I had to take them one at a time. And while I didn't know who to bury first, I knew I couldn't just walk out into that water and spread Marie's ashes. My heart wasn't ready for that. Too sudden. Too final. So I'd moved Marie's urn to the center of the table, kissed the lid, and tucked Fingers' orange box under my arm.

Now the current lapped against the hull, tugging against the boat, tugging against me. Southward. My Whaler is a center-console bay boat. The steering wheel is connected to a console that rises out of the center of the boat. Which means you can walk around it while still inside the boat. The console holds the electronics and throttle and steering control, as well as space for storage and a tiny toilet. It was meant for kids or women who weren't comfortable going over the side of the boat or just needed some privacy. I'd never used it.

When Fingers met me, I was just a teenager, no more than thirteen. He'd discovered I had a thing with fish. Meaning I could catch them when others couldn't. He'd hire me to take him fishing. And there in that boat, I got to know this priest who wore a robe, and he got to know me, this kid with a lot going on in his head and little ability to get those words out of his mouth. Over time, he dug in and helped pull me out of me. He gave me the words.

Years passed. Sometime later he learned I had a bit of a green thumb and that I had an inherent hatred of weeds, so he offered me a permanent position at his parish. "I see what you're doing," I joked. "Two birds with one stone: somebody to mow the grass—and pole you through the grass flats."

He'd smiled. He loved to fly-fish a flood tide, where he could sight the fish.

I didn't see it then, but he was grooming me. Every interaction was purposeful. Calculated. Intentional. He was not only teaching me to see—he was teaching me what to look for. It was in those moments at early dawn, watching the sun rise as he cast off my bow, that he taught me about the one, and how the needs of the one outweigh those of the ninety-nine. It would be years before I understood what he meant.

I started to stow Fingers' lunch box in the head, where it would be safe and protected from the elements, but I thought better of it. He wouldn't like that. He'd want to be where he could see. Where he could feel the wind in his face. So I strapped him to a flat section on the bow and secured him with several ropes. A hurricane couldn't rip him off there. Once he was secure, I checked the time. Fingers' Submariner was worn, scratched, and lost a few seconds every day, but that didn't bother me. He'd bought it thirty years prior while serving on an aircraft carrier in the Mediterranean. Told me it was the best $600 he'd ever spent.

I asked him one time, "What're you doing with a Rolex?"

He had smiled and scratched his chin. "Telling the time."

I raised my jack plate, thereby lifting my engine as far up as it could go while still spinning the propeller in the water, cranked the engine, nudged the throttle into drive, and idled out of the backwater.

My boat is a twenty-four-foot Boston Whaler. Called a 240 Dauntless. It's a bay and backwater boat, though better suited to the bay. It'll float in fifteen inches of water, but in truth I need twenty-four to thirty inches to get up on plane. She handles well in a one- to three-foot chop where I can lower the trim tabs, push the nose down, and skid across the tops of the whitecaps. But where she earns her reputation as a Cadillac ride is when the wind dies down. I push the throttle to 6000 rpm, trim out the engine to bring the rpm's up to 6200 or 6250, and she glides across the water like she's riding a single skid. In rare moments, she'll reach fifty-five mph. True to the Whaler name, she's unsinkable, which is a comfort when the storms come. And her range is decent enough. If pressed and conditions allow, I can run an entire day on her ninety-gallon tank, making more than two hundred fifty miles. The T-top is powder-coated stainless steel and built like a tank. It makes a good handhold for purchase in rough waters, you can stand on it if you need a better view, and it'll keep even the hardest rain or intense sunshine off you—both of which are welcome after long days on the water.

I like my boat. It's not sexy, but it is a comfort when other things are not.

When I was a kid, I read Robert Louis Stevenson's *Treasure Island* a dozen times. Maybe more. I loved everything about it. And although it filled many a long night, I never learned to talk about boats or ships or anything having to do with seafaring vessels the way Robert did. He owned the language of ships and boats like he lived it. I, on the other hand, did not grow up a deckhand. I simply grew up with my hand on the tiller. Boats were boats. The left side was the left side, not the port side. Right side was right side; starboard always confused me. Fore, aft, forecastle—this was all Greek to me. Later in life, I'd find comfort in some of these terms but never like Stevenson. To me, he was the captain and I was just a pretender sailing in his wake.

CHAPTER 4

I idled out the creek toward the Intracoastal—or IC. Most just call it "the ditch." Above me, gnarled and arthritic live oak limbs formed a canopy shading my exit from land and my entrance to water. Spanish moss dangled overhead, swaying slightly. Waving. I lit the Jetboil, then sat sipping instant coffee with my feet propped on the wheel while I counted the dolphins rolling off my bow. Over the next hour, I covered only four or five miles. I had no interest in pushing the throttle forward. No real desire to get going.

Saying yes was one thing; doing yes was another entirely. Besides, that purple urn awaited my return.

I traveled south into the larger waters of the Mayport basin and the intersection of the St. Johns River with the IC. The Atlantic Ocean was two miles to my left. On a calm day I could exit the jetties, turn south, and arrive in Miami tomorrow. Tonight even. The end of the world the day after that. Two days and I'd be done with all this. But that's not what Fingers would have wanted. He liked the inside, and he always took the slow way home.

The radar on the Weather Channel on my electronics, along with the digital voice of Weather Radio, told me that a confluence of storms in the Atlantic was pushing a steady barrage of wind and water against the East Coast and would be for the better part of two or three weeks, maybe longer. Today, the average wind was thirteen knots out of the northeast. Tomorrow, it'd top twenty and then stay there a week, maxing at thirty where it would pause briefly, only to pick back up and hammer the coastline again. Those conditions would push all small-boat traffic inside the ditch. For protection. Much of the larger vessels would soon follow suit as seasickness spread. That meant everybody going north or south would be rubbing shoulders in the IC for the next several weeks.

To my right glowed the city skyline of Jacksonville. The detour was a long way out of the way, and it'd cost me a day's time, but Fingers would have wanted to see it. Taste the water one last time. Black Creek is some of the prettiest and purest water in Northeast Florida. He used to make me bring him here, and when we'd pass under the Black Creek Bridge, he'd walk to the bow, tie both bow lines behind his back, and then give me his best *Titanic* impression. Every time. Without fail. Then we'd idle upriver, tie up beneath some giant cypress tree, and he'd pop the cork on some new wine. The earth in a bottle.

I turned right. Or, as a boat captain might say, "hard to starboard." As a city, Jacksonville, or Cowford as it was once known, grew up on opposite banks of the same river as men brought their cows to ford at a narrowing of the river. As it grew in population, it spread out from its epicenter and became a city of bridges. While most rivers run south, the St. Johns River is an anomaly of geography and runs north—as do the Red River, the Nile, and a couple of big rivers in Russia. I ran upriver, passing beneath seven ginormous bridges of various colors and materials, including one aggravating railroad trestle, and eventually crossed the big water of the St. Johns where, at times, the breadth of the river spans nearly three miles.

Throughout her history, the state of Florida has been home to some great writers, including some Pulitzer and Nobel Prize winners. Judy Blume, Brad Meltzer, Stuart Woods, Elmore Leonard, James Patterson, Mary Kay Andrews, Carl Hiaasen, Jack Kerouac, and Stephen King. Then there are the giants: Madeleine L'Engle, Ernest Hemingway, Patrick Smith, Marjorie Kinnan Rawlings. Preceding all of them was the abolitionist Harriet Beecher Stowe, who put a human face on slavery with *Uncle Tom's Cabin*.

Maybe there's something in the water.

South of the Buckman Bridge, the water is wide. Three miles or more in some places. Off my port side, in a little hamlet called Mandarin, Harriet Beecher Stowe lived seventeen years on a thirty-acre orange grove where the locals treated her like royalty. Prior to the Civil War, tourists rode paddleboats up this very stretch of water to the Ocklawaha River, and finally into the Silver River, which led them to Silver Springs State Park—later to be made famous by photographer Bruce Mozert. The water was so clear they developed glass-bottom boats through which they could view the "mermaids." The park became known as Florida's Grand Canyon and was unparalleled in popularity until a man named Walt introduced a mouse named Mickey just outside of Orlando.

Fingers loved the history. Soaked it up. He read and reread their books, took me in this very boat to Silver Springs and pointed to the shoreline. "Mrs. Stowe lived right there." But one of his favorite spots was a little creek known to few.

South of Jacksonville, I throttled down at the mouth, passed under my eighth bridge, and entered Black Creek. Like the Suwannee River, St. Mary's, or Satilla, Black Creek is dark water—but that doesn't mean it's bad water. It's actually very good water. It derives its color from the tannic acid generated by decomposing organic matter such as leaves. In short, the water looks like strong iced tea. At the mouth, Black Creek drops from six or eight feet deep down to over forty. Back when fresh water supplies were transported in barrels, the captains of seagoing vessels favored Black Creek for its purity and because the tannic acid kept the water fresh longer. They would sail up the St. Johns and into Black Creek, hit depths of forty-plus feet, and then use ballast stones to sink their barrels to the bottom where the water was especially good.

Some even claimed it tasted sweet.

I ran up the creek as far as it would let us, letting Fingers taste the air and water from inside his orange box. When the creek narrowed, two bald eagles descended out of the trees above us and then lifted on the updraft. Maybe they'd come to say goodbye. I ate lunch beneath a rope swing where Fingers liked to swim, opened a bottle of his wine, poured two glasses, and drank them both—not wanting to let his go to waste. I swam, napped lazily, and then idled my way back to the mouth.

When the depth finder read forty-three feet, I anchored, grabbed an empty milk jug with the top screwed on tight, and took a Peter Pan off the bow. I followed the bow line down, pressurizing my ears twice and pulling the jug with me. When I reached somewhere between thirty and forty feet deep, I screwed off the top and let the jug fill completely, then screwed back on the lid and swam to the surface where I took one sip and then stowed the jug inside the head. I'd seen Fingers do the same thing a dozen times. Every time he'd sip, swallow, and swear the water tasted sweet.

I returned through Jacksonville at dusk, the sun setting over my shoulder. I'd started to think about a protected shoreline where I could anchor for the night. When I reached the Jacksonville landing, I noticed something swimming in the water. Something not a fish. I pulled up alongside to find a Labrador retriever making his way downriver. And when I say downriver, I don't mean he was favoring one shoreline or the other. He wasn't trying to make it to shore. He was trying to catch a boat long since gone. I cut the engine and came alongside, but he made no attempt to climb in. He just kept swimming.

"You all right, boy?"

The dog barely noticed me. I lifted him from the water and set him inside the boat, where he didn't even take the time to shake. Finding himself no longer swimming, he immediately ran to the bow and stood sentinel-like, looking and listening downriver. He had no collar and no markings. Just a beautiful, almost white Labrador. From the looks of him, he was pretty fit. Teeth and strength of a young dog. I guessed him to be somewhere between two and three. I looked for any sign of a boat or somebody screaming some dog's name, but we were alone.

I couldn't very well throw him back in, and I figured if someone was looking for him, they'd have a much better chance of spotting him up there versus submerged in the water. Plus, we were headed the direction he'd been swimming. If we weren't, he never would've gotten in the boat. His beautiful color and regal lines, mixed with his unwavering commitment to his lookout vigil—not to mention the bright-orange box tied beneath his legs—meant if someone was looking for a dog, we'd be tough to miss.

When I took him to shore and set him on the Riverwalk, he simply ran along the shoreline downriver until something prohibited him from running any farther—at which point he launched himself into the river and started swimming again. After doing this three times, I pulled him up in the boat and told him to sit. Surprisingly, he did.

"Look, I can't very well leave you in the water. You'll drown."

No response.

I pointed to the bank. "You won't stay onshore, and I can't follow along behind you while you swim to the ocean and die."

Still no response.

"Do you have any suggestions?"

He looked to the bow, then back to me, but didn't move. Then he lifted his ears and tilted his head sideways.

I pointed to the bow. "Okay, but there are a couple of rules." He returned to the bow, pointing his butt in my direction. "No chewing on any-thing"—I pointed again—"especially that box beneath you, and absolutely no peeing in this boat. If you gotta go either one or two, you take it over the side."

If I was getting through to him, he made no admission.

"Did you hear any of what I just said?"

He stared downriver and wagged his tail.

Over the next hour, whenever we passed a sailboat or motorboat, I'd hail the captain and point to the dog. "This your dog?" I asked a dozen or more times. No takers.

The reality of the change in my condition was starting to settle on me. "I can't very well keep calling you Dog, so you've got to help me with a name. What do you want me to call you until we find who you're looking for? Or they find you?"

Again, no response.

"You're not much help."

He sat in the bow, staring straight forward, eyes downriver.

"How do you feel about Swimmer?" I pointed at the water. "You seem pretty good at it." I said the name a few times to myself and figured it sounded sorta stupid. "Okay, so maybe not Swimmer. What about Whitey?" That didn't sound too great either. His feet were pretty big, so I said, "How about Paws?"

He looked over his shoulder, then back at the water.

"Not so much, huh?" I scratched my head. "How about Ditch? It is where I found you."

His ears moved, letting me know he heard me, but he never turned.

"Okay, so maybe that's too close to another word, and you're not one of those, so . . ." The thought of my island and the remains of the slaves' tabby homes occurred to me. Oddly, the tannic acid in the water had made his white coat look almost tabby in color when I pulled him out. "What about Tabby? You do look like it—sort of. In a small way."

He looked over his shoulder and wagged his tail.

"Tabby it is."

I idled through downtown Jacksonville as the sun disappeared behind my stern and the moon rose off my bow. When the river dumped me into the IC, I turned south and was about to put the boat on plane when I gave him a final warning. "Last chance. You want off?"

He sat and glanced over his shoulder, acknowledging he'd heard me. Fingers' orange box was wedged beneath his feet. Fingers would like that.

"Okay. Suit yourself. But this is a working boat, and you'll have to carry your weight."

He lay down. Facing forward. Tail wagging.

We settled into an easy rhythm of checking off miles, one after another, while my silent friend straddled the orange box and let his ears flap in the wind. Every few minutes he'd leave his post, come to me, sniff my leg, look up, sniff the head and the door leading into it, then return to the bow. After the third time, I had a feeling he was trying to tell me something, so I pulled over at a beach on the west side of the IC. He hopped off, did his business, sniffed eight or ten crab holes, dug down into one of them, and then hopped back up on the boat.

This was a smart dog.

But we had one problem. His feet. "Look, dude. You can't go digging in the mud and then just hop up here acting all brodie." I pointed at the water. "Wash your feet first."

He pushed his ears forward and tilted his head. The expression on his face said, "You're crazy."

I pointed again. "I'm not kidding."

He jumped off the bow, dog-paddled in a circle around us, then climbed up on the swim platform in the rear. He shook and waited for my invitation.

"That's better."

We ran the ditch south through Jacksonville Beach. Ponte Vedra. Marsh Landing. And the eastern edge of the Dee Dot Ranch—owned by the same people who started Winn-Dixie. The Dee Dot is a ginormous private ranch where buffalo used to roam until mosquitoes and snakes drove them insane. I passed beneath the Palm Valley Bridge and on through Guana River State Park.

Midnight found me in the St. Augustine inlet. Not the best place to be at night, especially with a twenty-knot wind. Like all the pirates before me, I turned due west—away from the frothy Atlantic—and pointed my bow at the old fort of St. Augustine. The Castillo de San Marcos, which was the Spanish claim to the new world built somewhere around 1565. Jamestown claims to be the first colony in America, but by the time Englishmen set foot in Jamestown, the Spanish—aided by Europeans and Africans—had given birth to grandchildren in St. Augustine. If America has a birthplace, it's here in these improbable waters and mosquito-filled shores.

We passed beneath the Bridge of Lions and moored at the north end of the municipal marina. I was too tired to go in search of a hotel, so I spread out across the bench seat in the stern and slept five or six hours until a massive, slobbery tongue started licking my face just after sunup.

CHAPTER 5

I pushed him off me. "Dude . . . I know you're feeling like your world's been turned upside down, but we gotta set some boundaries here." I stuck up one finger. "First, you can't lick my face while I'm sleeping. That's gross. My mouth was open and I've seen what you lick and . . . and I don't want to even think about what's squirming around inside my mouth right now." I stuck up a second finger. "And two, we gotta get you some toothpaste." I wiped my face on my shirtsleeve. "You could gag a maggot."

He sat wagging his tail. The look on his face said one word: "Breakfast?"

I rigged a makeshift leash from an unused bow line, and Tabby and I headed for town. I needed some coffee. Walking out of the marina, I recognized a large yacht tied up on the far side, somewhat hidden from view. This time her name wasn't covered. The *Sea Tenderly* sat quietly pulling against her lines without a soul on deck. Either they were sleeping it off or they'd vacated in search of the next party.

I found coffee and bought Tabby a bacon, egg, and cheese sandwich, which he devoured in two bites before looking up at me, wanting more, while the egg yolk drained off his jowl. He ate four more before I put my foot down and found a grocery store where I bought him a large bag of food, a five-gallon bucket with a sealable top, a bowl, and a collar.

He didn't like the collar, but I sat in front of him and tried to explain. "I don't like this any more than you, but you gotta wear it."

He whined.

"I know, but . . . you just got to. It's the law." He sat up, regal like, and turned his head side to side, refusing to let me put it on him.

"I'm the boat captain, right?" He wagged his tail. "Boat rules. All dogs must have a collar, and that includes you." He whined again.

"Come on. I'll keep it loose." He walked around me in a circle, licked my face, and finally lowered his head. Somebody had spent some time both training and loving on this dog. I felt sorry for whoever was looking for him.

I tried to think like someone who'd lost a dog. I checked with newspapers and social media from Jacksonville south to Daytona and north to St. Simons, but nothing came up. Then I walked down to animal control. They thought he was beautiful, but they told me that if I left him there, his stay would be three days and then he'd take a really long nap.

I told them he wasn't sleepy.

Not knowing his history, I had no idea what to do about his shots, so I asked them to bring him current without killing his liver and kidneys. They did, which he wasn't crazy about. Especially the stool sample. He was looking a little puny when they brought him back to me.

To make it up to him, I took him to get one of my favorite things. I can't leave St. Augustine without it. Gelato on St. George Street from Café del Hidalgo. I ordered an extra-large, and he and I sat on the sidewalk amid the myriad of street performers and shared a cone. When finished, I brushed his teeth, which he tolerated.

This twenty-minute experience mixed with his nearly white coat and willingness to lick every human's face on the planet—especially those covered in ice cream or gelato—taught me something. Tabby attracted attention like a puppy at a park. Everybody wanted to pet him, and he was only too happy to oblige. We set up camp at the crosswalk of two busy sidewalks—the walking intersection of St. George Street with Hypolita, catty-corner between Café del Hidalgo and Columbia Restaurant. If I was to advertise something in St. Augustine, that street corner was better than FOX or CNN. Over the next several hours, it seemed like every child in St. Augustine had their picture taken with Tabby, and I turned down several offers to sell him. With every picture taken, I asked folks to post it on their social media under the hashtag #findmyowner and #whitelabrador. All to no avail.

The crowds thinned after dinner, so Tabby and I prepared for our trek back to the marina, both of us tired and hungry. I was in the process of standing up when I heard a voice behind me. While I'd heard voices behind me for the better part of eight hours, this one sounded different. It was distressed. And in pain. I closed my eyes and focused on the sound, trying to hear what the tone gave away. She was saying a lot but not with words.

Her appearance matched the frantic and defeated sound of her voice. Maybe early forties, head down, brownish hair, gray at the roots, quick steps, slight limp, a mission before her. She wore one flip-flop—which had blown out—and the other foot was bare. Both were muddy. Her legs, while beautiful, were scratched along the calves as if she'd run through briars or wiregrass. She was wearing what remained of a uniform. Something a server would wear at an all-night diner. Black skirt, provocative in an institutional sort of way. White oxford, no longer white. And an apron of which she did not seem cognizant. Like either she'd worn it long enough to forget it was there or she just didn't care what it said about her. A pad of guest checks had been stuck into the right front pocket. Pencils and straws rose up out of the other.

Both her hands and voice were trembling as she held the phone. "But, baby . . . you can't." She was unconsciously walking in circles around Tabby and me now. "They just want one thing and they'll promise you anything to get it." Another circle. A deep breath while she tried to get a word in edgewise. "I know I did, but . . ."

She passed me a third time, straightened, and began walking toward the marina. Her voice grew louder. More exasperated. "Wait. Don't—Baby?" Then I heard her say one word. One word I couldn't deny or overlook. One simple, five-letter word. She was crying as she spoke it. "Angel?"

I shook my head and cussed myself.

Tabby watched her go. Then looked at me. I scratched his head. "Come on, boy."

A block behind her, we returned to the marina where the woman began jogging along the docks, knocking on all the doors of every boat that seemed inhabited. Her voice echoed off the water. "I just need . . ." "Next marina . . ." "Daytona . . ." "No, I don't have any—"

Frustrated at another door slammed in her face, she spotted the marina boats. The first-come-first-serve, fourteen- to sixteen-foot runabouts used to ferry people and goods to and from larger boats. She hopped into one tied in the shadows, studied the outboard, flipped a switch, pulled the cord, and the forty-horsepower Yamaha outboard cranked on the first attempt. Something they are known for. She twisted the throttle on the hand tiller, revved the engine, cussed, found the gearshift, and slammed it into reverse, grinding the gears. The boat jerked in the water, tugging against its mooring line, sending waves and froth against the dock.

Realizing her mistake, the woman relaxed her death grip on the tiller, idled the engine, untied the line, and without bothering to check the gas level, backed up, banging into two yachts, one piling, and the bulkhead. Finally, she managed a circle like a one-legged duck and ran smack into the hull of a sixty-foot sport fisherman, which sent her rolling head over backside to the bow. Recovering, she returned to the stern, steadied the tiller, and began an erratic and serpentine path out of the marina. Free of the no-wake zone, she twisted the throttle and put the small boat up on plane, where she immediately stuck it in the soft mud. Cussing again, she stepped out of the boat, pushed it off the mudflat—finally losing the other flip-flop—found reverse, and backed out into the deeper channel. Once free, she again floored the throttle and motored southward down the ditch.

Her pinball path proved she'd never steered an outboard, but she was in the process of training her mind—push the opposite way you want to go. I admired her gumption but wondered how long it'd be before the marina sent the authorities to drag her back. Or she sank that boat.

Tabby and I loaded into *Gone Fiction* and slipped out of the marina. By then, the woman was gone. As was her wake. This time of night, the larger yachts had moved inside to escape the winds off the coast and were traveling north and south in the ditch—some as fast as twenty-five or thirty knots, thinking themselves safe from smaller vessels. Few people travel the ditch at night. Those yachts would be splitting the channel down the middle with their wakes—some as high as five or six feet tall, rolling and breaking toward the shoreline.

I thought about the woman. She and that boat didn't stand a chance.

Tabby and I left St. Augustine with thoughts of making Daytona by midnight. The problem was that it was dark, and while my electronics are accurate, hurricanes and storms have a way of moving boundaries and causing changes in depths. Nighttime navigation can be tricky, and while I knew these waters, I didn't trust my electronics. Never have. I only use them to confirm what the markers are telling me. That's not to say they're not accurate. They are. Generally. I've just learned to trust my eyes more than the screen.

CHAPTER 6

The moon was once again high and clear, casting our shadow on the water. This stretch of the IC was primarily residential, which made it poorly lit compared to a city like St. Augustine or Daytona or Jacksonville. Also, while the Florida Keys get much of the attention when it comes to the waters of Florida—and deservedly so, because they are lovely—some of the most beautiful water in North Florida can be found on the Matanzas River between St. Augustine and the Tomoka Marsh Aquatic Preserve. Or the waters leading into Ormond and Daytona Beaches. Right in the middle sits Marineland—the world's first oceanarium. Made famous by Hollywood moviemakers for eighty years with such 1950s classics as *Creature from the Black Lagoon* and *Revenge of the Creature*.

Half an hour outside St. Augustine, I throttled down through Crescent Beach, passed just west of Fort Matanzas, and then cruised along the stretch where A1A literally forms the border of the IC. I ran with my bow and stern running lights on, along with lights atop my T-top, but I turned off the light from my electronics as it interfered with my ability to find the center of the channel and the next buoy. With Marineland on my port side separating me from the Atlantic Ocean, I made the bend heading south-southwest when I spotted residue of a small craft's wake. It wasn't tough to spot. Foamy white powder on a sea of black glass.

The woman. Had to be.

And she wasn't alone on the water. Something else up ahead, traveling from south to north. Something big.

The problem with the Intracoastal here is that it narrows to less than a hundred yards. The further problem is that there is shoaling at either edge, meaning the actual channel is maybe forty yards wide and seven feet deep. Narrow and shallow, yes, but this is not normally a problem on sunny afternoons. When it becomes a problem is now—when it's dark and two vessels traveling opposite directions are fast approaching one another at the narrowest point.

I saw the white water from the cutwater of the northbound vessel and quickly judged her length at greater than a hundred feet. The woman in the dinghy had the sense to move to the right but only slightly, proving she was unaware of the havoc about to be unleashed on her small vessel. She could avoid the bow of the bigger boat but not the wake.

I nudged the throttle forward and kept my eyes on the coming vessel.

What happened next would have been amazing had it not been hor- rific. With the throttle high and traveling something between twenty and twenty-four knots, the naïve woman passed the perpendicular line of the bow only to meet the wake of the oncoming vessel, which was traveling closer to thirty knots. And unlike the cutwater, the wake was dark—same color as the water. Which was the same color as the night.

The speed of her boat meeting the speed of the wake ejected her at bet- ter than fifty knots. Shot out of a cannon, she spiraled some fifty feet in the air. Her small boat road up the first wake, only to leave the water entirely. The propeller spun dry just briefly, maxing its rpm's. Then the nose of the small boat slammed into the second wake. The collision broke the dinghy in half, both pieces disappearing into a sea of foam while the woman's flail- ing, screaming body flew through the dark night air.

Crossing the bow of the oncoming yacht, I pulled back on the throttle, turned slightly westward toward the shore, and rolled over the six-foot wake. First one, then a second, then a third. When clear, I slammed the throttle forward and ran three seconds to where I thought she'd landed. My depth gauge read five feet, then four. Then two. Given the height of her cannon shot, the impact would probably knock her unconscious. At the very least, it'd knock the wind out of her and might break a few ribs. The trick for me was to ride far enough to hear or see her hopefully on or near the surface of the water while not so far as to chew her up under my spinning prop. I pushed it as far as I could, watching Tabby's ears for any signs of life, and pulled back on the throttle when he sat up and looked to our right. I cut the engine when he stood and began barking, and then I shined a spotlight across the surface of the water.

Seeing nothing, I cut the wheel to the right and killed the engine, allowing my momentum to turn me ninety degrees while I scanned the surface of the water. When Tabby ran to the back of the boat and began barking his head off, I focused on the water at the stern. Seeing lifeless floating arms and what looked like hair, I stripped off my shirt and dove in, pulling hard in the water as the outgoing current tugged me from her and her from me.

Digging deeper against the water, I crossed the distance and was met by kicking feet, flailing hands, and a choking woman. She was sinking beneath the surface when I reached down, sank a hand beneath her armpit, and lifted her up and out. When her mouth cleared the waterline, she sucked in a giant breath of air, only to choke and cough and fight for more— pulling me down with her. Fighting me, she was making it impossible to get her to the boat, so I shoved her in front of me, snaked an arm around her waist, rested her head against my shoulder and chest, and began side-kicking toward the boat and Tabby. She was frantic, and if I didn't get her to the boat soon, she'd drown us both.

When Tabby saw us, he dove in, circled us, and led us back to the boat. When we got there, I held her up against the swim ladder, which she clung to. Coughing, choking, and shaking, she was about to lose it. I helped her climb up and sat her on the bench seat, where she cried, rocked back and forth, and hugged herself. Tabby climbed up the swim platform but couldn't find purchase with his back legs, so I lifted him by the neck and back and set him in the boat. He promptly shook and then sniff-checked the woman.

She was doubled over, crying from her belly, knees in her chest, and bleeding a lot. Tabby stood next to her, licking her face and ears. I grabbed a towel out of one of the fore storage compartments and wrapped it around her shoulders. Finally, I turned on the console and T-top lights. Even in the blue LEDs, covered in mud and blood, she was beautiful. Her hair was matted across her face and her fingers were cut. Several were bleeding, which meant the impact had sent her to the shoaling. Her face, too, was cut above one eye, with the wound trailing down her cheek. Shoulder scrapes too. Evidently her back had taken the brunt of the impact, since that's where the cuts were deepest. She quickly bled through the towel, spotting it red.

I figured she'd talk when able and the best thing I could do was get her some help, so I cranked the engine and turned north back up the ditch, and only when I got the boat up on plane did I turn to look at the woman. She was staring up at me while Tabby licked the blood off her face.

I pulled into the municipal marina, threw a bow line around a cleat, cut the wheel, and allowed the current to turn the Whaler and bring her alongside the slip while I secured the stern. Hopping onto the dock, I was met by a young attendant. When the lights of the small marina lit the bench seat, he noticed the woman. "Dang. She need help?"

I helped her stand only to realize her skirt was gone. The woman was wearing underwear but not much of it. I grabbed a second towel and wrapped it around her waist, and he helped her up out of the boat. She was in shock; speech wasn't happening. I looked at the attendant. "You got a doc in the box? Anything close or open this time of night?"

He shook his head. "Closest medical is Baptist South. Forty-five minutes that way."

"You got a car?"

He frowned. "Do I look like I have a car?"

My options were limited. An Uber driver would never let me in the car, and while paramedics would certainly help with the woman's physical condition, they couldn't help her where she needed it. I, on the other hand, maybe could.

First I needed to get her cleaned up before infection set into these cuts. "Where's the nearest motel?"

He pointed at the lights up the dock and across the street. The doors of the motel were all outward-facing with a view of the marina. I handed him a hundred-dollar bill. "You get me a room, bring me a key, you can have the rest."

His eyes widened and he disappeared up the dock. I turned to her. Her hair was still matted against her face. She had begun that convulsive crying in which she had no control of her breathing either in or out. The towel across her shoulder was one large spot of red. "Can you walk?"

She put her left leg in front of her right, only to buckle. I caught her, stood her upright, and she fell into me. I picked her up, threw her legs across my arms, and carried her up the gangway and across the street. The attendant came out of the office, pointed to his left. I followed. At the last room before the stairwell, he unlocked the door, stepped out of the way, and placed the key in my right hand.

"One more thing?" I asked.

He waited.

"Check on my boat. Make sure she's secure and will be there tomorrow when I show up."

He left without a word.

I carried her into the room and the door shut behind me. Tabby stood attentively. The look on his face said, "What now?"

I set her on the bed, where she curled into a fetal ball. Shaking. I peeled one corner of the towel off her shoulder, but it had begun to clot and stick, so the farther I peeled, the more it reopened everything. If I kept this up, it would hurt her. I stepped into the bathroom, turned the shower on warm, and knelt next to the bed. "Listen, I can call an ambulance . . ."

Staring through the wall toward the IC, she shook her head.

"I need to get a look at how badly you're cut, but if I keep picking at these towels, it's only going to make things worse. I need to get you to warm water."

She slid her feet onto the floor and I helped her stand. I couldn't figure out if she trusted me because she had no one else or because she was so delirious she didn't know better. Regardless, she leaned on me as I dragged her into the bathroom. While steam wafted above us, she stepped into the warm shower and just stood while the tub filled with red and mud and pieces of oyster shell.

When she was ready, I slowly pulled the towel from her shoulders, exposing fifty cuts and a myriad of tiny oyster pieces stuck in her skin. Evidently, her landing had skidded her across an oyster shoal. She turned to expose a shredded shirt and sliced back. I helped her out of her shirt and stood back while she leaned against the wall and allowed the warm water to wash down her back. Tabby stood next to the tub, tail wagging. I grabbed the bloody towels and set them aside, allowing the tub to drain. For three or four minutes, she just stood. Finally, she sank to her bottom and sat on the floor of the tub, head on her knees, while the water and steam brought her back to life.

I needed to pick the oyster pieces out of her back, so I pushed the control knob and converted the water from the shower to the tub spout. I sat on the edge of the tub. "Are you tough?"

She nodded without looking at me. I pushed in the stopper and began picking out the mud and oyster shells as she leaned against her knees. As the water in the tub turned a deeper red, I cleaned her back. Halfway through the process, she braced herself on the edge of the tub where Tabby took the opportunity to lick her hand clean. She hung her hand around his neck and allowed me to finish the process—which took the better part of an hour. When I'd finished her back, I said, "Can you stand?"

She did, and I continued washing the sides and backs of her legs. When I got her as clean as I could get her, I said, "I'm going to grab some clothes from the boat. You okay if I leave?"

She nodded without looking at me.

I grabbed a bag of clothes from the port side storage where I found the attendant watching my boat like an eagle. "Anyplace around here open this time of night? Food or something?"

He thought. Then shook his head. "Lots of bars."

"Anything else?"

"Grocery store. 'Bout a half mile that way."

"Thanks."

I walked to the store where the sign on the door read, "No shirt, no shoes, no problem." I walked in and found them closing up for the night, so I made a trip through the deli. I bought a fried chicken. Some cold chicken salad. A few apples. A mug of soup. Some mac 'n' cheese. Some saltine crackers and some applesauce. I topped it off with a bottle of wine and some Gatorade and herbal tea. I exited through the pharmacy, picking up antibiotic ointment, Band-Aids, gauze, pain pills to help with the swelling, and hydrogen peroxide. If she didn't hate me already, she would when I finished putting all that on her back.

I knocked, let myself in, and found her in the bed, lying on her side. Her back was bare. Arms crossed in front of her chest. Head on a pillow. The sheet covered her legs and most of her chest. She was still staring south through the wall—the direction she'd been heading when all this happened. I pulled a chair up next to the bed and showed her the ointment and peroxide. She nodded. I soaked a gauze roll and began patting her cuts clean. Doing so took some time. I continued until there were no more bubbles. Then I smeared antibiotic ointment onto all the cuts, which by my count were somewhere close to a hundred. They wrapped over her shoulder and onto the top of her collarbone and chest. It was impossible to cover each with a bandage without turning her into a mummy, so I didn't. When I finished, she slid the sheet off and I doctored the slices on her legs.

She'd live, but the next few days wouldn't be fun. As I worked, she never winced, suggesting either she'd known much pain or something in her hurt more than my doctoring.

I took out the food and set it on a chair before her. She reached for nothing. I opened the soup and offered a spoonful. She sat up, gently grabbed the mug, and sipped. Not taking her eyes off me. I opened the saltines and set them next to her on the bed.

I tried to make conversation. "You auditioning for the circus?"

She nodded and managed a whisper. "Evidently."

"What were you doing out there on open water in a boat the size of a bathtub?"

She shook her head.

"The guys at the marina are gonna be hacked when they find out their boat is at the bottom of the ditch."

She said nothing.

When she finished the soup, I offered her a mug of microwaved herbal tea. She accepted it, hovered over it. Sipping gently. The moon shone in through our window. Her convulsive cries had been replaced by shallow, controlled breaths.

"You picked a nice night for a swim." Trying to bring a smile.

She leaned her head back and laughed. At herself. "I can't swim."

That explained a good bit. "Really?"

She was staring into her mug when she spoke. "Never learned."

"You mean to tell me you stole a boat, navigated thirty minutes south of here having never had your hand on the tiller, and you can't swim?"

She placed a hand on her ribs, winced, and nodded.

"Seriously?"

A shrug.

"What were you planning to do had you gone overboard?"

Again only her eyes moved. "No plan for that."

"What were you going to do had I not showed up?"

Another shrug. "No plan for that either."

Gathering her strength, she sat up and pushed the sheet off her. Naked. She spoke in broken resignation. "I can't fight my way out of this room. If you're going to do something to me . . ." She lay back. "Just get it over with."

Sometimes people's pain is deeper than we can first see. I was sorry I hadn't seen it sooner.

I set my backpack on the bed, unzipping it. "There are some clothes in here. Not much, but it's what I've got. Maybe tomorrow we can get you something more feminine. Tonight you might sleep without a shirt. Give your skin time to scab over. Otherwise everything's just going to stick to you and you'll have to go through the whole warm-shower peel-off in the morning." I set the pain pills on the bed next to her. "Tomorrow you're going to feel like you've been hit by a truck. Two of these will help with the pain and swelling." I laid the room key on the nightstand next to her and walked to the door.

Standing at the exit, I said, "Get some sleep. I'll wake you in the morning."

Tabby stood looking at me, anticipation and saliva dripping from his mouth. I made a stop sign with my hand and he sat. Then I pointed to the bed, so he hopped up on it and lay with his head alongside her leg. Another stop sign. "Stay." He wagged his tail.

As I was pulling the door shut, I heard her say, "How do I know you're coming back?"

"Well, if I don't, you can keep my dog."

She wrapped an arm around his chest and almost smiled for the first time.

I pulled the door shut and looked down at the marina and Fingers' ridiculous orange lunch box staring back up at me. He'd like her. "I know. I know," I told the box. "Don't say it."

CHAPTER 7

Sunlight pierced the crack in my eyelids. I sat up to find my friend gone. Bench seat clear. Fingers' Rolex told me I'd been asleep a few hours, so I climbed out of the boat, walked up the dock, and met the attendant bringing me a cup of coffee. He handed it to me. "Didn't know how you took it."

I nodded and handed him twenty bucks.

He smiled. "Mister, if you need a keeper, I'm available for hire."

I sipped and stared up at the motel. "You'd be a good one too."

I knocked on her door and heard a rustling. When she answered, she was wearing my shorts and long-sleeve fishing shirt. Both of which swamped her. Tabby appeared, licked the outside of my fingers, and stood smacking me with his tail. Beneath the long sleeve was a short sleeve, which I guessed she was using to soak up the blood and protect the outer layer. She'd pulled her hair back, revealing cuts and scrapes and an otherwise beautiful face with roots still gray. I wouldn't say she was rested, but she looked like she'd slept. Barefoot, she swung the door wide and stepped aside. The room had been cleaned, bed made, groceries bagged. Both the bottle of wine and the pain pills sat on the table. Neither the cork nor the seal had been broken. A steaming mug sat with the tea bag dangling.

Her face looked slightly puffy above her eye. She sat on a chair, hands between her knees. "I don't have any money. For—" She waved her hand across the small world in front of her.

I stood opposite her. "You hungry?"

She said nothing and nodded.

I laid a pair of flip-flops at her feet. "Wasn't sure of your size, but . . ."

She spoke without accusation. Only honesty. "You have a way of avoiding some of the things I say to you."

I gestured to the flip-flops.

"You're doing it right now."

"I know, but I'm worried about your feet."

She slid her feet in and her toes curled and uncurled. Her feet were muscled, arches high, toes calloused, and calves defined in taut muscle. She stood and shoved her hands in the pockets of my baggy shorts.

"I talk better with food in my stomach," I told her.

She smiled.

We walked two blocks to a diner and took a seat in a booth against the window. "You drink coffee?"

She rubbed her eyes and attempted a smile. "People who don't . . . aren't people."

The waitress brought coffee, and we ordered breakfast. As the silence settled around us, I broke the ice. I extended my hand across the table. "Murphy. But most folks call me Murph."

She met my hand with hers. "Elizabeth. But everybody calls me . . . Summer."

"How'd you get from Elizabeth to Summer?"

"Made my Broadway debut as Anna in *The King and I*. The *Times* headline the next day read, 'Meet the Star of This Summer's Hit: Summer.' The misprint was a comical hit among the cast members. Been Summer ever since."

"You danced on Broadway?"

She nodded but there was no arrogance in it. Only a silent admission of something lost. "Sang too."

"How long ago?"

She shook her head and studied the ceiling. "Twenty-plus years."

"Just the one show?"

"No." Her eyes studied the ceiling. It was the first time I'd seen them in daylight. Emerald green.

She saw no need to promote herself, so I asked, "How many?"

"A dozen or so."

"You performed on Broadway more than a dozen times?"

"Well, no. I played a role in more than a dozen shows, which performed a couple hundred times."

"What happened?"

She stared out the window, then back at me. She folded her arms, bracing herself against a cold breeze I didn't feel. "Bad decisions."

"How is it that you never learned to swim?"

She shrugged and shook her head. "City girl trying to dance. Never made time."

"What were you doing out there?"

"Looking for someone."

"Looking for or chasing?"

Raised eyebrows told me I'd hit some corner of the truth. "Both."

"Someone who doesn't want to be found?"

Her eyes found mine.

I scratched my chin. "Is she sixteen, looks twenty-one, has legs like yours, a new tattoo at the base of her back, likes to twirl when she enters a room, and is now hanging out with some bad people she thinks are okay people?" I held up the picture I'd snapped with my phone. "Answers to the name Angel?"

She reached out and touched the screen with her fingertip. She held it there a long time. The waitress delivered our food, and I told her the story while she shoved eggs around her plate. The truth did not comfort her, as evidenced by the tears. Finally, she wiped her face and nodded.

I thumbed behind me. "I was on the dock when you perfected that seventeen-point turn in an attempt to exit the marina."

She nodded again. A little less uncomfortable.

"I had a feeling if you stayed in that dinghy long enough, you'd end up wet. So I went looking."

She looked up at me. "You always go looking for stupid folks you don't know?"

Funny how one simple question can sum up so much. I pushed my eggs around my plate and smiled. "Sometimes."

We sat in silence while the waitress refilled our mugs. The waitress asked Summer, "Baby, could I get you something? We make a pretty good apple pie. Oreo milkshake?"

She shook her head. "No. Thank you."

The waitress looked at me with suspicion and then turned sideways and whispered again to Summer while scratching her right eye. "Baby, you want me to call the police for you?"

She reached out and touched the waitress's hand. "No, but thank you."

Summer spoke as the waitress returned behind the counter. "I don't think she likes you."

"No, but I love the way she says 'Baby.'"

She laughed.

I sipped. "Tell me about Angel."

Summer told me about her daughter and their rocky relationship. As Angel grew and blossomed into a staggering beauty with an innate and easy dramatic ability—landing her the lead role in every musical since she was seven—Summer, based on her own mistakes, became more protective. In the last year or so, Summer had been unable to corral Angel at home. Eventually, Angel made her own poor choices. Culminating in the decision to hop on a yacht with a mysterious muscled man and a bunch of equally disoriented kids and spend a promised month in the islands bending reality with mind-altering drink and drugs.

"You got any family? Anybody you can call to help you out?"

"No. It's just us."

"Husband?"

Her eyes found mine, then looked away. Another single shake.

"Any idea where they're headed?"

She shrugged. "South. Miami. The Keys. Bahamas. Wherever the wind blows, the water's clear, and rum flows."

"You got a plan?"

She laughed. "Yeah." Wiped her face with her right hand. "But it's at the bottom of the Intracoastal right now." More silence. When I paid the check, she looked away.

She didn't like leeching off me. "On the dock, you were wearing a uniform. Like a server . . . ?"

"Angel has . . . had . . . a partial scholarship to this really good school. But seventy-five percent still leaves twenty-five percent. I was working three jobs. One was an all-night diner where I work six nights a week."

"And the other two?"

She didn't look at me. "I stock shelves at an auto parts store on Sundays when they're closed."

"And?"

"I own an appointment-only dance studio."

"Why appointment only?"

Her voice softened. As if the admission were painful. "I don't have enough clients to keep normal hours."

"What do you teach?"

"Mostly, I teach two people how to stand in the same space and not kill each other."

I laughed.

She continued, "Other than that, I teach women how to follow men who don't know how to lead."

"Sounds tough."

"Following is not as easy as it looks."

"How so?"

"Ginger Rogers did everything Fred Astaire did, backward and in high heels."

"Good point."

"Most guys think they're Patrick Swayze until you show them what to do. Then they melt into egg yolk."

"Sounds messy."

"Most of my appointments are wedding parties. A bride and groom."

I had a feeling she was growing slightly more comfortable with me, so I let her talk.

"I can tell you from the first five minutes of the first lesson whether they will make it or not."

"How do you know?"

"Not sure really. It's an intuitive thing. How he treats her. How she responds to him. How they communicate. How his hands touch her says a lot about how his heart holds her."

"You have a favorite type of student?"

"Older folks. Been married a long time. Their dancing is an expression of how they've lived."

"I don't know much about it."

"What, dancing or being old?"

I laughed. "Both, but . . ."

She was warming up to me. "No offense, but I already figured that."

You hang around people long enough and you learn their tells. Pain has a way of exiting the body, and most will let you know when it's on its way out. Seldom do they know what their "tell" is telling you. Most often it's silent. Sometimes it can be loud. However it comes out, it leaves a trail. Jittery fingers. Itchy skin. Headaches. Always tired. Always hungry. There are hundreds, I guess.

"How long you been clean?"

She bit her lip, tilted her head to one side, and looked at the floor. "Which time?"

"This time."

"Ever since things started going sideways with Angel. Two months. Give or take."

"What's your poison?"

"This time or other times?"

"This time."

"Opioids."

"That explains why you didn't touch the wine or pain pills."

"I've dated them too." She shook the memory. "I start swallowing stuff to numb my pain, and the next thing I know I'm chugging it like sweet tea or eating them like Skittles." She had a beautiful way of poking fun at herself. A disarming honesty. "I had spread myself really thin—"

She was returning to her story. As if compelled to tell it. I interrupted her. "You don't have to—"

"Feels good to hear myself say it."

I waited.

"Between rent and my lease and Angel's tuition and some debt, I was in over my head. Then I messed up some ligaments in my ankle when I got tangled up with a shopping cart in the grocery store parking lot. And then, because I needed the money, I made it worse trying to teach this idiot how to dance with a gimp ankle. Then one of my clients—"

I knew where this was going.

"—helped me out. Brought me whatever I needed. Said I could pay him later."

"But black-market pills aren't cheap."

She shook her head, and her eyes darted to the floor again.

I continued, "And he was all too happy to keep supplying you."

"My own private pharmacy."

I'd heard this before.

"But," she said with a shrug, "a few months passed. My ankle got better, and slowly, and not without difficulty, I weaned myself off the Skittles."

This I had not heard before. "How?"

She laughed. "You wouldn't believe me if I told you." Maybe sensing my skepticism.

"Try me."

"I read."

"You're right, that is a new one."

"Told you."

"What'd you read?"

"At first, thrillers. Love stories. Anything from the bargain bin that would take me"—she waved her hand across the world before us—"out of here."

"You unhinged your body from an opium addiction with a book?"

She smiled. "Not just any book. A series of thirteen books by one author. I've read them twenty or thirty times each."

"You've read one book twenty or thirty times?"

"Actually, I've read thirteen books twenty-seven times."

My face betrayed my questions. "Explain that to me."

"Drugs medicated my pain. Books medicated my reality. The second lasted longer with less downside and helped lessen the craving for the first. So I replaced one drug with another."

"Sounds like a good book."

That piqued her curiosity. "You like to read?"

I laughed. "No. Not really."

CHAPTER 8

I had opened Pandora's box. Summer took a breath and talked nonstop while our food grew cold. "Well, David Bishop is the man. He's written this impossible love story where his character, Bishop—a priest who's taken a vow of celibacy and poverty—uses the confessional and the secrets people reveal to open the story and introduce the problem, or to explain who the bad guys are and who he needs to rescue. Problem is, he's such a good priest and he's so good at his job that the government comes to him and asks him to work for them, which he reluctantly does. So he lives all these fantastic adventures around the globe working for both the church and this secret government agency.

"And on top of that, and this is the cherry on the whipped cream, in order to complete his cover, the government makes him travel with this beautiful woman, but—wait for it—she's a nun, and she was once beautiful but now she has this long scar across her face and a secret she won't tell him 'cause she's afraid if she does he won't have anything to do with her. She secretly loves him, see, and he secretly loves her, but neither one will tell the other. It's impossible all the way around."

Her face flushed. "In every story, they come so close. I finish each book and I'm like, 'Bishop, you're killing me. Just kiss the girl. God won't mind!'

"And here's the crazy part: the character writes the novels. That's right. Bishop writes his own stories. Everything is first person. Like a real auto-biography. But it's not. David Bishop is the author's name on the cover and he's the character's name inside, but nobody knows the identity of the real writer. Even the description on the jacket is fiction. Meaning the mystery guy, or girl, or whatever, has sold tens of millions of books all around the world and nobody but his editor has ever talked to him. The press offered to pay him a lot of money, but he's not talking. The news networks have offered the writer a lot of money to appear on TV, but he or she won't."

She raised a finger. "Which is why I agree with the prison theory."

"Prison theory?"

"Either the writer is in an actual prison and can't get out, or he's in a physical prison—I think the author is a guy—like a disease or something. Or he was in a horrible wreck or fire or something that changed his appearance, and so he's badly deformed like the hunchback. He knows if he shows his face, it'll kill the mystery. And kill book sales. Forever."

This entire chain of thought was incredible. As was her fascination with it. To think she'd spent so much time thinking about something and someone who only exists in the imagination. "How do you know all this?"

She continued, "There are internet forums devoted to research and theories and conversations and possible sightings and . . . Listen to this: the writer—which, mind you, no one has ever seen or has any idea if it's a man, woman, child, Neanderthal, eighty-year-old grandma, six-hundred-pound pervert, or serial killer serving forty life sentences—has his or her own social media pages and sites that readers and fans have created. Dozens of them claiming to be the real author. Some of them have hundreds of thousands of followers. Which means the fictional writer who writes fiction has given rise to even more fiction! It's bigger than the search for Sasquatch or Elvis." She trailed off.

"Anyway, whoever it is can write because the stories are exciting, fast-paced, take-your-breath-away thrillers-slash-love stories, and everybody—me included—is reading just to know when is he ever going to just get it over with and kiss the girl? I mean, enough already!" She slapped her thigh and raised a finger. "A woman's body will only make babies for so long." She pointed her fork at me. "There's a major rumor floating around the web right now that something big is going to happen in his next book."

I had her rolling. Might as well keep it up. I was enjoying seeing her so animated. "Like?"

"Most everyone agrees it's one of two things: either she leaves God and they marry, only to reveal her secret, which everyone thinks is that given her promiscuous past, she can't get pregnant, leaving them childless, or . . . he asks her to marry him, but someone out of his past catches up with him and kidnaps him, and while they torture him for information, she's stranded at the altar thinking he doesn't love her, so she goes back to the convent and takes a vow of silence. When he escapes, he can't find her 'cause she's not talking. Either way it could kill the series—which is both genius and crazy at the same time."

"You've really thought this through."

"These people are like family."

"Of course . . ." I was playing with her now. "There is a third possibility."

Her expression changed. "What?"

"He could just kill 'em off."

She shook her head. "Never happen."

I laughed. "How are you so certain?"

She was still shaking her head. Unwilling to entertain the possibility. "Marriage for sure, followed by a rollicking honeymoon where they don't see the light of day for three weeks. Nine months later she gives birth to the next Jason Bourne. Fast-forward and the spinoff series continues indefinitely. Although . . ." She raised her fork. "Their son does his time in the military so he can learn how to kill people with a rubber ducky, and then the church comes to his dad and tells him they need the son, so he—the son, whose name is something cool like Dagger or Spear or Bolt—fast-tracks through the priesthood only to be brought to Rome where he is special assistant to"—she snapped her fingers—"Bam! The pope. But in reality he's the pope's bodyguard. And you can run that story forever. Somebody's always trying to kill the pope, and then there's all that money . . ."

I was laughing. "You're really into this."

She nodded but continued, "The publisher is making money hand over fist. It's a cash cow. These things are in more than eighty countries and just as many languages. You think they're going to kill off that guy?" She raised a finger. "Listen to this: his—"

I interrupted her. "You're still assuming it's a him?"

"Yes, but it's pretty well accepted that no woman could ever write about his longing for her the way he does. Not to mention that the linguistics departments at five different universities have done some sort of analysis on the words of all the books—the way phrases are put together and word choice and combinations of words—and when they run all that through the computer, every time it's solidly in the eighty-five-plus percent chance it's a man. So for the sake of argument—"

I was amazed. "How do you know all this?"

"The man got me off drugs! Needless to say, I'm a fan."

I was laughing. "Evidently."

She continued, "His is the first book in publishing history where advertisers are offering him money—like six-figure money—to mention their products in his books. Automobiles, watches, computers, phones, sunglasses, motorcycles . . ." She paused again. "A winery in Napa even paid a junk-load of money to become the only type of wine he serves at communion. And they paid a bonus if he serves it to her—"

"That's ridiculous. May even be blasphemy."

She nodded. "There are some angry readers who agree with you. Anyway, whoever this writer is, he's no dummy. It's not like you're watching one big commercial. He's sly the way he does it. Like, he does it, you read past it, and then it hits you. 'He just mentioned another product.'"

"I'll bet Hollywood loves this guy."

"That's just it. He said no to Hollywood, which just makes everyone want it all the more. Two studios have sued the publisher for rights but lost in court. David Bishop is a genius—he has made a buttload of money and he's gonna make a buttload more in this next book 'cause he's giving people a little of what they want but not everything." She shook her head. "Kill the series? Not a chance."

"Of course, you're assuming that, whoever this person is, they're motivated by money."

"That's another thing. Several of the news networks investigated where the royalty payments go. Wanna guess?"

"Some fat, bald guy draped in cheesy gold chains and bad sunglasses living on the beach in Monaco, sipping an umbrella drink, collecting the interest, laughing at people like you?"

She smiled. "Close, but no. They tracked the royalties to an offshore holding account, but"—she held up a finger—"one of the reporters had a cousin or something who worked at Google, and he figured out that the offshore stuff was just a shell, and that most of the transfers, after they went through a few more shells, ended up . . . Are you ready for this? At a nonprofit."

She nodded knowingly. "That's right." She whispered for emphasis. "He's giving it all away." She raised an eyebrow. "Which only helps sell more books." She finished her food and spoke with her mouth half full. "I'm not sure what motivates him, but this whole idea—the writer who is both writer and character, and the nun with a scar and a secret, and their impossible love, the way their adventures bring them together but not 'together,' but oh so close, and how the royalties go to some nonprofit that nobody can find—the whole thing is what people like me dream of."

"Which is?"

She shrugged, speaking matter-of-factly. "The fairy tale. There are a lot of women out there who think we're just forever stuck on the island of misfit toys, and yet here's a writer who causes us to think that maybe someone might love us despite the scars and the baggage. Someone who knows what I'm thinking enough to finish my sentences. And what's more, would know how to fix my coffee if we were stranded on an island. Someone who"—she waved her hand through the air in front of her—"protects me from the world that wants to hurt me."

I laughed. "Sounds like a soap opera. Or maybe worse, pulp fiction."

She paused. Her voice changed. "I think he, whoever he is, is wounded. Something deep. Some days I think he writes to remember. And some days I think he writes to forget. Whatever the case, I read to believe."

"In?"

"A love I can only dream about."

"Sounds like you know him."

"I do. We all do. That's the mystery and the majesty. He's that good."

I laughed. "Somebody should find this guy."

"In his last book, the two of them are in Budapest. On this secret mission. And they're in this hotel in"—she made quotation marks in the air with her fingers—"'separate but joining' rooms, mind you, and he's in the shower trying to rinse off the blood from a gunshot wound, and she's leaning with her ear pressed to the wall listening to him shower, and she feels guilty but she can't pull herself away. They're separated by a single wall, eight inches at most, but it might as well be a million miles."

My voice turned sarcastic. "Yeah, I can see it in my mind's eye. Just tantalizing."

She waved me off. "Anyway, he's in there like a chiseled Adonis in a fountain, and he reads the label on the shampoo in the shower 'cause it smells good and drowns out the smell of his own blood. And you know what happened?"

"No, but I have a feeling you're going to tell me."

"The body wash in the book was real in real life. The week after the book released, that body wash was number one on Amazon." She raised both eyebrows. "I bought a case."

"Unbelievable."

She waved her fork in circles in the air. "I know how it sounds. What blows my mind is the fact that whoever that writer is, he or she has written something that is so good it took my mind off the drugs. Think about it. Better than drugs? And I'm not the only one. Therapists in rehab give these books to their patients. 'Read this. Let's talk.' Right now there are book club support groups across the country filled with junkies and addicts who are getting clean—all 'cause somebody wrote some words. If I could, I'd hug whoever it is. Kiss them on the mouth. I don't care. Man, woman, child, zombie . . . they did something that nothing else could."

"We're talking about a book, right?"

"If I hadn't read them, I wouldn't believe it either, but those stories, the characters, the way they talk with one another, the way he thinks about her, describes her, the things he notices about her that she doesn't even know—like a scar on her ankle where she cut herself shaving, or the sweat on the little hairs on her top lip, or how she moves when she's walking. All of it just shows how much he values her. Defers to her. In the last book, I nearly died. Cliffhanger at the end. She's leaning against the shower wall, listening to him, then without reason, she leaves a note on the table and disappears. Next morning, she's gone. He starts looking. Finds the letter: 'Dear Love, there is something I need to tell you . . .'

"This thing she can't tell him is killing her, so she basically leaves a suicide note. He turns himself inside out trying to find her before she goes through with it. Book ends right there. So we're all thinking this next book will be about how he and his mentor find her. Because everybody knows he's not about to kill her off."

"What makes you say that?"

"Which part?"

"The part where he kills the girl."

"Don't even talk like that." She pushed her food around her plate with her fork and stared out the window. As she did, I saw where she'd soaked through the bandaging on the top and side of her shoulder. Throughout breakfast, she had yet to wince or even draw attention to what had to be painful, suggesting she had a high pain threshold. More importantly, she wasn't working me. She wasn't using the injuries to get something from me. If anything, it was the furthest thing from her mind. She'd rather talk about some silly book than herself, which told me a lot about her heart.

"Those two gave me hope when I didn't have any."

"Hope in what?"

She stared at her plate and shook her head.

I paused. Her eyes found mine, and I spoke softly. "Hope in what?"

She looked away. "Hope that I'm not condemned to live and die alone and unloved on this island. That no matter what I do, how screwed up I become, maybe someday, somebody will . . ." She faded off.

"Will what?"

She looked down and spoke barely loud enough for me to hear. "Ask me to dance."

As we walked out I thought to myself that sometimes people need more than water to learn how to swim.

CHAPTER 9

Walking back to the marina, we passed a roadside cellular store. "Will you let me buy you a new phone?"

"Only if you let me pay you back."

"Whatever. It's just that if she tries to call and—"

"That'd be great."

I bought her the phone. Once connected, she restored from the cloud and checked her voicemail and messages, but none appeared. Then she dialed Angel. No answer.

We walked back to the marina where my eager friend had just finished scrubbing down my Whaler. He stood with brush in hand, suds up to his elbows. *Gone Fiction* was spotless. I handed him another hundred-dollar bill. Doing so did not escape Summer's attention.

He smiled. "Mister, you let me know if you ever do any hiring!"

I shook his hand, stepped into the boat, and cranked and warmed the engine. I looked up at her. She stood staring south down the ditch, then waved her hand across me. "If you give me your address, I can send you some money when I—"

"Forget it."

I busied myself with my electronics, but in truth I was stalling. Trying to look busy when in fact I was just giving her space. She turned the phone in her hands, finally asking me the question that had been on the tip of her tongue since I'd knocked on her door that morning. "Where are you headed?"

The truth hurt too much. I dodged it and patted the steering wheel. "Wherever *Gone Fiction* takes me."

She put two and two together. "Where's *Gone Fiction* headed?"

"Couple hundred miles that way. Where the world falls off into the ocean."

"Sounds perfect." She shoved her hands deeper in her pockets. "Want some company?"

"Water can be dangerous when you can't swim."

"And life can be sucky when you don't know how to dance."

I liked her. She was tough in a tender sort of way. And I had a feeling she was a good momma who'd been dealt a bad hand. The cold breeze I couldn't feel blew across her again, causing her to wrap her arms around herself. Her face was pale and she needed about three weeks of sleep. She pointed to Angel somewhere south of us. Tears appeared quickly. "She's all I have."

I spoke the obvious. "You realize that finding her is needle-in-a-haystack kind of stuff."

She nodded and thumbed away a tear.

"Okay, but I have two rules."

She waited.

"Two months clean, give or take, means you're tougher than most. Means you did the hard part on your own. You just gutted through it. Books or no books, that stuff pulls on you. From the inside out. It's like it wraps around your DNA. It can last months. So before you step foot on this boat and we go looking for your daughter who doesn't want to be found, you have to promise me one thing."

She waited as tears streaked her face.

I continued, "Please don't lie to me. Just tell me where you are. Don't hide you from me. I can't help you if I don't know the truth."

She nodded.

I stepped forward and looked up at her. "Words matter."

This time she spoke them. "I promise."

"Second . . ." I waved my hand across the bow where Tabby had resumed his vigil over Fingers' lunch box. "That's his spot. Move him from there at your own peril."

She was about to step aboard when she thought better of it and stepped back. She patted her chest and swallowed. "There's more I haven't told you."

I knew this, but first walk, then run. Fingers' face appeared front and center in my mind's eye. How I loved that man. I spoke both to her and to the orange box. "I was once in a bad way. On the . . . cusp of some bad stuff. Had a friend find me and tell me that none of us are who we want others to think we are. That despite the mask we are all so good at wearing, we somehow manage to wake up every day hoping there's still a chance. That maybe, somehow, we can balance the debt ledger we carry in our hearts. That maybe God is offering a special that week and one good equals two bad. But then there are the lies that the memories whisper."

Her tears were flowing freely now. She asked, "What do they say?"

"They say we are alone. That bad choices and mistakes have drained the value out of us. And that we are not worth the cost of getting to us."

"Are we?"

"I have yet to find anyone who is not."

"Even when we—"

"Even when."

"Where is your friend now?"

I stared at the orange box. "Gone."

"I'm sorry."

I nodded. "Me too."

Indecisive, she kept still. This time I spoke without looking at her. "I'll help you find her, but you need to be prepared for what and who you find."

She nodded.

I pointed to the boat.

She took one step, then—conscious or not—twirled. Like mother, like daughter. It was one of the most beautiful things I'd ever witnessed, and it took me back twenty-five years to a beach, a breeze, and the smell of a girl.

When she stepped aboard, she was immediately tongue-assaulted by Tabby, who spun in circles with happiness. I throttled into reverse, backing into the current where my friend the attendant threw me the bow line and saluted.

Idling south, I turned to find Summer standing next to me. A question on her lips. "Yes, ma'am?" I asked.

She held out her new phone and pointed at mine. "Could I have that picture?"

Summer sat on the back bench, pulled her knees into her chest, and pressed her phone to her bosom with both hands. When I pushed *Gone Fiction* up on plane, she laid her head back where the breeze tugged at her brunette hair and Tabby licked her face.

Ten minutes later, she was sleeping across the bench, arm wrapped around Tabby who lay next to her.

The phone rested beneath her cheek. The faceplate was wet.

I dialed a number I knew by heart. He answered after the fourth ring. I could hear female voices in the background. Happy female voices. He must have exited the room or turned a corner because they faded and his voice grew loud. "Murph?"

"I just sent you a picture with name, details, and identifying marks. I need to know everything. Plus what you've got on traffic and trade routes. Players, names, vessels, destinations."

I could hear him smile. "I thought you said—"

"I know."

He has this thing he does with his fingers when he's thinking. He pushes his beard away from the edges of his mouth—separating middle finger from thumb. "You got room on those shoulders for one more name?"

I stared out across the water, trimmed the engine, and pulled back slightly on the throttle. In truth, I didn't know the answer. "Do you?"

A long pause followed. "You okay?"

"Yeah, just bumped into someone on my run south. And time may be short."

"Shorter than usual?"

Another question to which I had no answer. "Not sure."

"I'll call when I know something."

I hung up, sat back, and stared out through the windshield while steering with my feet on the wheel. Fingers' lunch box sat oddly tied to the bow. When my vision grew blurry, I lifted my Costa Del Mars off the console and hung them on my face.

While Summer slept, we passed through Flagler Beach and into the Tomoka basin. Tabby lay on his stomach, tail wagging, ears flapping, eyes forward, tongue hanging out of his mouth. The sight of Ormond Beach told me Daytona wasn't far behind. Which was good. I was hungry and I had a feeling Tabby was too.

Like Jacksonville, Daytona is a city of bridges. As I entered the city's waterways, five towered overhead. I slowed, and we made our way into the narrow cut that leads into the Halifax Harbor Marina. I didn't need gas but did need information. The attendant, Bruce, told me where I could find a dog-friendly place to eat. I thought about waking Summer but then thought better of it and asked Bruce to let her know we'd be back shortly.

Tabby and I bought lunch. I led him to a patch of grass, and then we returned to *Gone Fiction*, where Summer had yet to stir. Bruce spoke as if his work was lonely. "Yeah, all the big boats come through here. Snowbirds heading south again." He rubbed his hands together and pointed to the IC. "Everything and everybody passes right here." He smiled. "The world on my own private conveyor belt of water."

"Seen any party boats? Loaded up with kids?"

He considered this. "From time to time. Nothing lately." He paused. "Although—" He pointed to a yacht on the far side of the harbor. I'd not noticed it when we arrived because it was hidden behind a hundred other boats. "That one came in night 'fore last. I was off. Don't know who was on it, but it just appeared. Nice boat too."

I could see enough to know what I needed to know.

"Any other boats missing since that one appeared?"

He scratched his chin. "Yeah, we had this crazy black, sleek, modern-looking thing parked over there for three weeks. Maybe longer. A hundred and twenty feet. Dang nice boat too."

"You know her name?"

This time he scratched his beard. "Something catchy. Like *Catch the Wind* or *Catching Fire* or . . ." He faded off.

He threw me the bow line. I reversed away from the tanks and said, "Thanks."

Summer stirred as I circled the marina, coming to stand next to me when she saw the *Sea Tenderly*.

CHAPTER 10

I tied up alongside and climbed aboard. She was empty, but I already knew that. The interior was a mess. Trashed. It smelled of burnt rope, incense, alcohol, vomit, and urine. The hot tub was an odd St. Patty's Day green color. The sound system was still blinking and the DJ's turntable was still spinning.

Summer studied the aft common area and kitchen. The stub end of marijuana joints filled the counter. Must have been thirty or forty. Wrapping papers. Beer and liquor bottles. Expensive tequila and vodka rested half full and half empty in what remained of the bar. Someone was courting and catering to these kids and sparing no expense.

All manner of clothing on the floor where it had been taken off.

Summer shook her head, disbelief painted across her face. We walked through the four staterooms, which were in no better condition. It'd take a cleaning crew a week to get this thing presentable, and I'm not sure they'd ever get the smell out.

Summer folded her arms. "They left in a hurry."

"They do this."

"Do what?"

"Change boats. Often at night."

"Why?"

"It keeps the kids interested. And throws off anyone looking for them."

"You've seen this sort of thing before?"

I nodded.

"How can anyone afford this?"

I tried to answer while not answering. "They are . . . financed."

"What do you mean?"

I turned to Summer. "Usually Russians. But also the Chinese and Koreans. Middle East."

Her eyes narrowed. "Who are you?"

"Just a guy who's spent a little time on the water."

She shook her head. "Not like any guy I've ever known." She waved her hands across the boat. "What are they buying?"

"Flesh."

The truth of this landed on Summer.

I continued, "They have teams of men who travel the coast, find attractive girls, and offer them a good time. Then they offer them drugs. Get them hooked. Move the party south. Then one day the girls wake up in Cuba or Brazil or . . . Siberia."

"Why do the girls fall for that?"

"The guys are well trained. They're gentlemen. And—" I stared at Summer. "They often target the mothers to get to the daughters. Do them a favor . . ."

Summer sat on the sofa and hung her head in her hands.

I rifled through the drawers and cabinets. "Don't. These guys are pros. They saw you coming a mile away."

"But—"

"Let's go."

"Shouldn't we call somebody? This is bigger than—"

"Not if you want to find her."

"What do you mean?"

"You alert any authority, and that boat will skip to Bimini in the next thirty minutes on the way to South America. You'll never see Angel again."

"But how—"

"They're smart and they don't joke around but they're also businessmen, and more girls equals more money. So they'll work the coastline until they feel real pressure."

"What will they do when they . . . ?" Summer trailed off.

"They'll post pictures on the dark web and sell them to the highest bidder—which I imagine they've done already. For the really special girls, they set up an auction."

Summer didn't speak.

"I don't know what you thought you were getting into or what you thought you'd find, but Angel is in a bad way. And these men, no matter how gentlemanly they seem, are anything but gentlemen. She's addicted to some ugly stuff, and even if and when you do find her, she's going to need to dry out for several months."

Summer sat shaking her head. "I should call someone. Someone who can do something."

I put my hand on her shoulder. It was the first time I'd touched her in tenderness and not in an effort to pick oyster shells from her body. "Do what you think is best." The moisture told me she'd soaked through her shirt. "But you'd better let me doctor that."

She turned sideways. "Have you done this before?"

"Done?"

She waved her hand across the boat, the water, and what lay before us. "This."

"Yes."

"How many times?"

I shook my head. "I don't know."

"But you've searched for . . . people?"

"Yes."

"And you've found them?"

"Yes."

"How many?"

"Officially?"

"Yes."

"Several."

"How many? Exactly?"

"One hundred thirteen."

"And how many have you not found?"

"Ninety-nine."

Confusion spread across her face. "Do you work for the government or something?"

"Or something."

"And the ones you found, were they in as bad a way as Angel?"

"Some."

Summer began sobbing and rambling about how this was her fault. I put an arm around her. She leaned into me. White as a sheet, soaking me with tears.

I'd been soaked before.

I tried to comfort her, but I had little to offer. "Boats like these have an incentive to make it as far down the coast as they can. They want more girls, but they want a specific type of girl. More time in the ditch allows them more time to do their homework and pick up people with no history. Loners who escape to the Keys—"

She interrupted me. "Impressionable girls fighting with their over-protective, helicopter moms."

I waited until she turned toward me. "Never beat yourself up for loving your daughter."

The enormity of what faced her began settling in her chest. I continued, "They're looking for people who won't be missed. Best thing you can do is keep calling Angel and leaving loving and apologetic voicemails. Chances are about a hundred and ten percent that they're monitoring her phone when she's passed out. Listening to you talk to her. So you need to tell her you miss her, but you need to sound like you're giving her freedom to figure it out. They need to think you're a long way from this water. That you're not chasing her. Otherwise . . ."

"Otherwise what?"

"They'll shoot her veins full of antifreeze and drop her body in the ocean. To them, she's just property."

She crossed her arms and held herself.

"These people are pros at psychological warfare. They will tell her repeatedly that she is free to leave anytime, but they will give her every possible reason and incentive not to. To stay on that boat. And that includes money and prizes. They'll make her feel safe and secure and wanted and appreciated. They will send her on day trips, maybe a jet ski ride under the guise of freedom. Possibly an overnight. A one-off. And they will buy her nice things. Stuff that glitters. Actually, the gifts aren't new. They're just recycled from the last girl. Most of these girls have or had absent fathers or they were abused by a man they once trusted, so they have this man-size hole that these sick bastards like to fill with counterfeit. They'll cause her to trust them like she's never trusted another human being." I paused. "They are masters at deception—at assessing and extracting value. Right now they own her. She's not free to leave. She can't. They'll never allow that. They have too much invested. Too much at risk."

Summer shook her head. "I can't call her."

"Why?"

"A few days ago, she canceled her number. When I dial it now, it just says, 'This number no longer in use.'"

"How were you talking to her on the dock in St. Augustine?"

"She called me from somebody else's phone."

"And that record of a received call is now at the bottom of the IC."

She nodded but said nothing. That caused me to wonder if I had put my sat-phone number into Angel's old phone or a new one her mom didn't know about. I let it go. Telling Summer about that might just produce false hope.

She spoke through the tremble. "How do I get her back?"

I tried to deflect. "We have to find her first."

She stepped in front of me. Blocking my exit. "And after we've done that?"

I weighed what to say. And what to keep. "Just help me find her."

CHAPTER 11

Tabby wagged happily when we stepped back onto *Gone Fiction*. I was about to work my way out of the marina when the sight of Summer caught my attention. She looked too much like me. We needed to find her some proper clothes.

By any standard, the Halifax Harbor Marina is huge. Used to catering to a lot of people with varying tastes from all over. Just like the stores that surround it. A clothing store shouldn't be too tough to find. Feeling a walk would do us good to stretch our legs, I tied up in a day slip and the three of us began walking the boardwalk north along South Beach Street. An ice-cream store, a hamburger joint, an electronics store, a hair and nail boutique, and finally a women's clothing store.

Summer hurriedly selected clothes with a singular criterion: price. Then she laid them on the counter without trying them on. The sales attendant was a girl in high school. When she saw what Summer had collected, she lifted an eyebrow. I stepped around the side and held up her selections. "Can you help her find something . . . that is not this?"

The girl laughed. "Gladly."

Summer was not in the mood for shopping, which I understood. But she couldn't leave looking like that. The girl took her to a dressing room and handed her several pieces of clothing, which I assume she tried on. Fifteen minutes later, she returned to the cash register. Now the clothes were beautiful, but shame shadowed her face.

"What's wrong?"

She held up the price tags.

I paid the girl and tipped her for her help, and we walked outside. That's where I realized just how beautiful Summer really was. She was stunning. I'd never seen emerald-green eyes like hers. Not even in the movies. And she had presence. Something I could only guess she learned on Broadway.

She held the two bags of clothes and studied the sidewalk. Unmoving. Finally, she looked at me. "I can't—"

I knew what was going on here, but there was little I could do about it. "You hungry?" I stepped out into the street and walked toward a dog park. Closing the gate behind us, I let Tabby off his leash and he began sniffing and peeing on a hundred bushes and poles. And one fire hydrant.

Summer and I sat on a bench in the shade, but despite my attempts at small talk, she wouldn't look at me. Finally, she spoke. "You're doing that thing again where you don't talk about what I'm trying to talk about."

"What are you trying to talk about?"

"I can't—"

I turned, faced her, and pushed my Costas up on my head.

"I'm trying to thank you."

"You're welcome."

"No, that's not . . ." She shook her head. "I'm not . . ."

To our right, the Daytona Beach Fire Department opened one of its huge bay doors, and a large red truck tore out of the parking lot, lights flashing and horn blaring. She looked up at me and studied my face a long minute. There was more but she swallowed it back, letting her eyes return to the bubble gum–dotted sidewalk. Pigeons circled in a Tabby-safe distance around us.

"I'm trying to tell you something that will change your opinion of me," she said.

"Why do you feel the need?"

She held up the bags. "Because I'm not deserving of—"

"Sometimes we need to let others do for us what we can't do for us."

"How do you make money?"

I laughed. "I have a job."

"Yeah, but I had a job once, too, and I never walked around with a wad of hundreds like that."

"I'm unmarried. I live alone. Rent free as long as I keep up the place. I eat little. Don't spend much. Don't have a gambling addiction. And I don't like credit cards, so the hundreds are sort of a necessity."

This gave her pause but didn't really convince her. She shook her head. "Look, I'm not really a good judge of men. I've made . . . mistakes."

"Welcome to earth."

"I need to know if I'm making a mistake with you."

"Not as far as I can tell."

"I'm being serious."

"Summer—"

Like Angel in the church, Summer was adept at invading my personal space. She stiffened. "Are you telling me the truth?"

"Everything I've told you is true."

Another step closer. "And what about the stuff you're not telling me?"

"It's true too."

"But—"

"Summer, I don't want anything from you. You are free to get off my boat anytime. I'll take you to whatever authority you like. I'll tell them everything I know, give them the picture on my phone, cooperate in whatever way you want. But you need to know that their chances are only marginally good at finding . . . a body. I'm trying to find a breathing person. Big difference."

She closed her eyes. She backed up and tried again. "That came out all wrong. It's not what I was getting at. I'm sorry. I just wanted you to know . . ." She tapped her chest. "I just wanted you to know."

"Summer, hang in there. You have some long miles ahead of you. And some of them might be difficult. Okay?"

She nodded and slung one bag over her shoulder, which must have still felt raw because she winced. I took the bags in one hand, Tabby in the other, and we strolled the sidewalk in search of food. Standing between us and a corner pizza parlor sat a bookstore. She tugged on my shirtsleeve. "You mind one more stop?"

She entered the bookstore and walked up to the counter. "Do you have book thirteen in the David Bishop series?"

The attendant walked to a shelf, pulled down the hardcover, and handed it to Summer—who clutched it to her bosom and then did that little unconscious twirl thing she did when she was happy. Her feet were moving like some sort of jitterbug dance move. "I've been looking for this, and my library hasn't had it in months."

The attendant spoke excitedly. "We're scheduled to get a galley copy of book fourteen in about three months. Online preorders have put it at number three on the *Times* list, and it's been at number one on our Indie list for seven weeks already. Two women got arrested in New York last week snooping around the editor's desk trying to find a copy." She shook her head. "I cannot wait!"

I paid the lady as the two book lovers yakked about the coming novel. As we walked out, you'd have thought I'd given Summer a golden ticket wrapped in a Wonka bar.

We stopped next door at a roadside pizza parlor that smelled like Italy. Our table gave us a view of the water and the Jackie Robinson Ballpark, home of the Daytona Tortugas. An easterly breeze pushed against our faces as we ordered a pizza, a couple of Caesar salads, and a bowl of spaghetti and meatballs with extra meatballs.

While we waited, Summer talked about the book she had yet to set down. "You seriously have not read this?"

"I don't read much."

"Where have you been living? Under a rock?"

"Actually, I live on an island."

"Okay. Same thing." She held up the book. "Best one yet. Can't wait for fourteen."

I let her talk. The more she did, the more the defeat disappeared.

She clutched it to her chest again. "In this story, Bishop is working his way up this line of Mafia henchmen and trying to get to the Godfather 'cause he kidnapped this girl, and Bishop is getting close to finding the girl. Yet despite the fact that they're all total sickos, all the bad guys are devout churchgoers. And get this, the Godfather makes them all go to confession! Where, unbeknownst to the Godfather, they all spill their secrets. So what does Bishop do? He uses the confessional—again. Problem is, the Godfather is no dummy and he suspects him."

"Where's the woman with the scar?"

"She's living in the convent next to the church. They're walking around each other like they've never met. And she thinks he's just blowing her off, so she's getting ticked. But he knows he's being watched twenty-four-seven and if he even acknowledges her, the mafia guys will kidnap her. So to keep her out of danger and get her transferred or kicked out or something, Bishop invents this cockamamie story about how she's been stealing from the church." She waved it in front of my face. "I can't believe you haven't read this. This one takes place along the East Coast mostly. Although a few of the stories have taken place in Europe, one in Mexico, one in South America, and one in Africa." She shook her head. "You don't know what you're missing. You should get out more."

"I have a tough enough time with reality to confuse it with make-believe."

Another squeeze of the book. "You should let down your hair and live a little."

I laughed. "I agree." I pointed at the book. "Okay, let's say you bumped into this guy and had ten seconds, what would you say?"

She opened the book and brushed her palm over the pages. "There are a bunch of girls like me. Middle-aged dreamers. With baggage and stretch marks and grown kids and bills and bunions and . . . with no chance of ever being rescued by a prince who storms the castle. And yet here's this guy who nobody knows, who makes us think that no matter how ugly we may be to the world, he might still show up. That's a gift and it's . . ." She shook her head. "Priceless."

Our food arrived, and we ate while Tabby lay at my feet, tethered to the stool by his leash, which he didn't like. Also, his attention seemed elsewhere. His bowl of spaghetti sat mostly uneaten, which was strange.

I knelt. "You okay, boy?"

Ears forward, he was sniffing the wind. When I lifted the bowl to his mouth, he stood up, stretched his leash taut, and began pulling the stool across the porch of the restaurant, pinballing off other patrons' chairs. I lifted the stool and attempted to grab the leash at the same time, but he has eyes in the back of his head and I was too slow. Free from his anchor, Tabby shot across the street at somewhere north of thirty miles an hour, dragging his leash behind him. He crossed Orange Avenue, turned due east, and began bounding over the East Orange Avenue Bridge, which spans the Halifax River. Avoiding swerving cars with honking horns, Tabby was running down the center double line. A dog on a mission.

The last time I saw him, he was running full out, ears flapping behind him, turning north between the ballpark and the courthouse. I dropped money on the table, and we began sprinting after him.

CHAPTER 12

I dodged the traffic, crossed the distance, turned left, and entered a tennis center where mixed couples were playing on six courts. "Anybody seen a dog?"

Guy closest pointed to a dog-size opening in the gate leading to the bleachers. I scaled the fence and ran around the side of the bleachers. The stands were empty save us, so it wasn't tough to spot him. Tabby's tail was wagging rapidly on the first row behind home plate. Down where all the guys with radar guns would sit.

The closer I got, the clearer it became that he wasn't alone. Tabby was straddling a dark-skinned man. More Brazilian or Cuban than African. His hair was totally white and combed back over his head. His eyebrows, mustache, and beard were likewise white. He lay on his back on the concrete between the first row of seats and the backdrop behind home plate. His head was propped on a bedroll of some sort, and his legs were crossed while Tabby straddled him and licked his face.

I walked below him into his field of vision and sat three seats beyond his feet.

The man's eyes were closed, hands folded across his chest. "Hello, sir?" No response. "Sir?" I shook his foot. Still nothing. I felt his wrist. His pulse was thin, so I shook him harder. He stirred but didn't wake. At the least, I'd say he was disoriented. Tabby sat alongside him, staring at me. I knew this guy needed medical help, but given the way he'd lay down here, I wasn't sure he wanted it.

The flag of the firehouse flapped behind the bleachers. I told Tabby to stay, which he planned on doing anyway, and ran back the way I'd come. Crossing the street, I passed Summer and asked her to sit with Tabby. I found a fireman waxing No. 29 out next to the street. After a quick explanation, he and two other men followed me carrying large bags over their shoulders and talking on their shoulder-mounted radios.

We found the old man as I'd left him. By now, Tabby was lying with his head on the man's chest. The firemen immediately ran an IV of fluids while one of them went back to the firehouse and returned with a gurney. We lifted the large man onto the wheeled stretcher, and they began rolling him toward the firehouse with Tabby jogging alongside.

Once there, the firemen were making plans to move him via ambulance to Halifax Medical when Tabby jumped up on his bed, straddled him once again, and continued licking his face. Within a few seconds, the old man came to, which I think had more to do with Tabby than the IV, but both helped. Surprisingly, the old man began rubbing Tabby's ears and talking to him. Tabby rolled onto his side, exposing his underbelly, and the old man rubbed his tummy until Tabby's rear left leg started jerking in a spastic movement.

"Sir, are you in pain?" The firemen had a lot of questions. "Do you know your name?" "Tell me what's going on."

The old man sat up. Slowly. I noticed he wore a hospital ID bracelet on his left wrist and a bandage on his left elbow—the kind you wear after you've given blood or been given an IV.

The old man answered their questions and sat patting Tabby.

The firemen scratched their heads for a few moments, then one returned to me. "Pal, he's not in any pain. According to him, we interrupted his nap. So we're going to let these fluids finish dripping into him with his permission, because he is a bit dehydrated, and then we're going to release him into your custody."

"My custody?"

"Yeah, he's your friend."

"I don't know him. I just found him."

"You don't know him?"

"My experience with this man is only about fifteen seconds longer than yours."

"Oh. Well, okay then."

As the fireman moved away, the old man nodded at me and spoke. "Afternoon, sir."

I extended my hand, which he shook. His hands were bear paws. Huge. The feel of them told me they were once muscled and calloused. While still muscular, they were more tender, sinewy, and the skin was thin. Tabby sat with his hindquarters perched on the old man's legs. He was almost sitting in his lap.

"Sir, this may sound like a dumb question, but do you know this dog?"

The old man looked at Tabby, who began licking his face. "I do." He laughed.

The impossibility of this struck me. "Really?"

"Raised him from a pup."

I scratched my head. "Did you lose him somewhere north of here?"

The old man nodded. "I was working on a boat, serving drinks, up Jacksonville way. I started to feel sick and checked myself into the hospital there. By the time I got out a week later, the boat had left me, but Gunner here was still waiting on me. I knew he didn't need to be tied down to a dying old, so I left a note on his bowl to whoever found him, snuck out the other end, and thumbed a ride on a tugboat."

"Did you say his name was Gunner?"

Tabby looked directly at me.

"Well, that's what I've always called him."

"Gunner?"

Tabby stood, walked to me, and rested his muzzle on my leg. I looked at him while the letters settled. "Gunner." Tabby wagged his tail.

I held his face in my hands. "So, your name is Gunner." Gunner wagged his tail and licked my face.

The old man pulled himself into a sitting position, evidently strengthened by the fluids, and crossed his legs. "How'd you two meet?"

"He was swimming down the middle of the St. Johns River. Chasing somebody. You, I guess."

He shook his head. "There were some good people at that hospital. I thought for sure somebody would take him home. I wrote it all in the note."

"I don't think Gunner liked your note."

"Evidently." The old man coughed, exposing lungs full of fluid and the reason for the ID bracelet. He hacked a minute, caught his breath, and sat quietly. Either feeling no need to talk or not wanting to expend the energy to do so.

I wasn't quite sure what to do, so I said, "Well . . . you've left him once and he's just navigated about ninety miles of water to find you. You want him back?"

"Never really wanted to be rid of him. Smartest animal I've ever known, but—" He shook his head once. "Not fair to him." The old man looked up at me. "You need a dog?"

I shook my head. "No, but I'm not leaving him here."

Summer stood off to my side, her shoulder touching mine. The old man returned his attention to me. "Say—" He coughed again, bringing another spasm. This time he took longer to catch his breath. "You say you got here in a boat?"

I nodded.

"Where you headed?"

I pointed south. "Couple hundred miles that way."

The old man stood. "Any chance you got room for one more?"

I glanced at his bracelet and his bandage, along with the now-empty bag of fluids hanging just above his chiseled face. When I spoke, I did so slowly. "They didn't really check you out of that hospital in Jacksonville, did they?"

He shook his head slowly side to side, saving his words for when he needed them.

"You trying to speed things along?"

He laughed. He had the look of a man who was used to sitting still for long periods of time. "Some things don't need my help. I'm just trying to get home. Maybe see somebody before I go."

I pointed at the field across the street. "What were you doing over there?"

His laugh was contagious. "Napping 'til you two woke me."

"You've got to do better than that."

He stared across the street, into the ballpark, and back into some memory I couldn't see. "Played minor league ball for the Yankees 'bout sixty years ago."

"What position?"

"Second. And—" He made a slight swinging motion with his hands and broke into a knowing smile. "I could hit from either side."

"What you been doing between then and now?"

"Wearing stripes of a different color."

I thought so. Noticing Summer, he tipped a hat he was not wearing and extended his hand. "Ma'am."

Summer shook his hand.

"Barclay T. Pettybone."

He turned to me. "But most folks calls me Clay."

"Murphy Shepherd. Most folks call me Murph." I pointed at him. "Is that really your name?"

"For the last sixty it's been I11034969, but now it's back to being letters. And when you put them in their rightful order, that's what they say."

I sat down. "You've really been in prison for sixty years?"

"Fifty-nine years, eleven months, twenty-nine days, and fourteen hours. But who's counting?" He smiled.

"How'd you get out?"

He made two fists, exposing his bear-like paws. "Broke out." He laughed again, and I could already tell he did that a lot. He gestured with both hands. "Health reasons." He weighed his head side to side. "I'm a lifer, but they figured I wasn't a harm anymore and they needed my bunk, so they flung wide the doors and set me on the street."

He pointed at Gunner. "We rode the bus to the coast in Brunswick because I needed to see the ocean. Thought maybe I could thumb a ride south. Find my way home. I got a job serving drinks on a private party boat moving south. Job paid in cash, came with a free bed, they didn't mind dogs and didn't ask for references. So I poured drinks, washed dishes, tried not to breathe the air, and fed Gunner scraps off the table. We stayed with them 'til Jacksonville."

"You say you got a home somewhere?"

He nodded. "Key West."

"When was the last time you saw it?"

He nodded and stared beyond me again. When he spoke, his voice had lowered. "Some time ago."

"You do realize there have been a few hurricanes in that time."

He laughed. "Tell me about it."

"You think it's still there after sixty years?"

"No, but it makes for a happy fiction."

Gunner sat quietly at his side.

Summer put her hand on my shoulder and whispered, "We can't leave him."

I turned to her. "Do you own cats?"

She nodded, smiling.

"How many?"

She held up both hands, extending six fingers.

"Strays from the neighborhood?"

She smiled.

"Mr. Pettybone," I asked, "what's wrong with you?"

"Clay, please."

"Clay—"

"Which part?"

"The part that's sick."

"Cancer mixed with pneumonia."

"How long do you have?"

He looked at a watch that wasn't on his wrist. "Five minutes. Five days. Five weeks. Nobody knows, but according to the guys in white coats, it's not long. I'm seventy-eight with a lot of mileage on my chassis. Prison ain't easy."

"What'd you do?"

"You mean what's my crime?"

"Yes, sir."

"I was a cocky ballplayer. Big. Strong. And—" He paused, shaking his head. "Young and dumb too. Found another man had my wife closed up in a closet. She was screaming. He was trying to do something she didn't want him doing. I stopped him." He spoke slowly, enunciating as best as he was able. "New York was not a good place for a black man sixty years ago. Especially when the boy I killed was white." He spat. "Folks tell me I'm lucky to be alive." He paused and stared at the sky. Then across the street to the field. "Maybe."

Summer whispered, "Murph, we can't leave him."

It was the first time I'd heard her say my name in casual conversation. He stared down at Gunner. "Mr. Murphy, you can leave me. I don't have long now. But I'd be obliged if you'd take my dog. He needs good people, and I reckon if he hung with you this long, then you're good people. He'd know the difference."

"It's just Murph. When was the last time you ate something?"

"I'm not hungry."

"When?"

"Ate a stack of pancakes maybe two hours ago. It's why I was sleeping so deep. All those carbs. Knocked me out." He smiled, exposing beautiful white teeth. "But I don't eat much."

"Got any family?"

"None that I know of. If I did, I doubt they'd claim me."

"Can you manage a boat ride?"

"How many feet is your boat?"

"Twenty-four."

He nodded and smiled. "Mr. Murphy, I can manage."

"It's just Murph."

He sucked through his teeth. "It may be to you, but when you've been locked up and beat down for six decades, everybody becomes 'Mister' whether they like it or not. My mouth doesn't know how to say anything different. The word is just there. And if your name is in my mouth, then 'Mister' is coming before it."

I liked this man. His honesty was disarming. "Mr. Pettybone, you call me whatever you like."

CHAPTER 13

With no real cause to send him to the hospital other than the inevitable end no hospital could stop, the firemen sent us on our way. We returned to the marina bearing clothes, a book, a tail-wagging dog, and one dying old man. Fingers' box stared up at me like a strobe light. He would have loved this. And he would have been laughing. While Clay was a big-boned man, he was also skinny. His clothes were baggy, and I wondered if he wasn't more fragile than he let on. I turned to Summer and Clay. "Make yourselves comfortable. I'll be right back."

They talked while I returned to the marina store and bought a waterproof beanbag made for boats and a large straw hat with a drawstring. I returned to the boat and wedged the beanbag in between the console seat and the front casting platform. "Clay, you might be most comfortable here." He climbed down into the boat, sat in the middle of the beanbag, and accepted the hat from my hands. "I thought that might help with the sun."

"I'll be just fine."

Summer was smiling at me as I cranked the engine. Letting it idle, I had a thought. Pulling out my phone, I sat in front of Clay and held up the picture of Angel. "You ever seen this girl?"

Summer began walking toward us. Listening intently. Clay held the phone, studied her face, and nodded knowingly. He pointed toward the Intracoastal. "She's on the boat. Name's Angel."

Summer sat, and Clay noticed the resemblance. He studied her a minute. When he spoke, there was pain in his voice. "She yours?"

Summer nodded.

He sucked through his teeth again, afraid to say more. "I see."

She put a gentle hand on his arm. "What are you not telling me?"

"They like her . . . a lot."

"What's that mean?"

"It means—" He chose his words carefully. "They do a lot for her and she likes it on that boat." He shook his head. "They're not giving her any reason to leave."

I asked him to tell me everything he could about the captains, their patterns, the phone calls they made, who else was on the boat, if they'd made plans to stop at any other ports, and if he knew what boat they were on now.

Barclay took his time and explained, in detail, everything he knew. People. Boats. Names. Places. Even what drinks people preferred. Drugs too. The two captains were of great importance to me, but he didn't know much about them. They were European, or maybe Russian, and he described identifying tattoos. They kept him busy or buried in the ship and didn't interact much. He said they weren't unkind, but not sociable either. There was a total of seven girls on the ship when he stepped off in Jacksonville, but Clay figured they'd picked up more now. More girls was all the two men talked about.

"What can you tell me about Angel?"

He looked at Summer, then back at me, and shook his head. "She's in a bad way."

"You talk to her much?"

"She talked to me mostly. Always asking me to dance with her. That girl likes to dance."

Summer both smiled and cried.

"If I was sixty years younger, I'd fight for that girl . . . but that's what got me into all this trouble, so . . ."

"Any idea what type of boat they're on now?"

He pointed at the *Sea Tenderly* across the marina. "Last I saw them, they were on that. Don't know what kind they're on now."

"If you went aboard, is there anything you could look at that would tell us what they're on now? Or maybe where they're going?"

He thought for a moment. "No, but I can tell you the name."

"You can?"

"*Fire and Rain.*"

"You sure?"

"Like the James Taylor song."

I climbed back out of the boat and returned to the harbormaster. I walked in and asked the kid behind the counter, "You guys had a boat here, *Fire and Rain*. Any idea when it left or where to?"

The kid sat up and exercised his single ounce of authority. "You got dealings with the vessel or its captain?"

The kid might have been twenty-two, and I doubted he shaved twice a week. I leaned on the counter. "Look, Scooter, I'm sure you're good at your job, but I'm not in the mood. I need to know what you know and I need it right now."

He was in the process of explaining how he couldn't give out that information when the real harbormaster walked out of his office. "Can I help you?"

When I repeated myself, he shook his head. "Sir, I can't give you that information any more than I would relay that information to anyone about you."

"You got CC video of the marina?"

He nodded. "Of course. But—"

"Can I see it?"

The harbormaster was in his sixties. This was not his first rodeo. His forearm tattoos told me he'd served in the navy. Emboldened by the presence of his boss, the kid stiffened and raised his voice. "Captain, you're not hearing me—"

I stepped closer and forced him to focus on my eyes. "They've kidnapped a sixteen-year-old girl and they're planning to sell her to the highest bidder when they hit South Florida or maybe Cuba. Then they're going to use her body for whatever they like and dump her in the ocean or a snowbank in Siberia. The clock is ticking." Scooter's eyes grew wide as Oreo cookies. I pointed at his computer. "The video would be a great help."

Scooter stuttered and finally spoke. "You mean it's a—"

I finished the sentence while looking at the harbormaster. "A flesh ship."

The harbormaster pointed at the computer and said, "Tim, bring up last night about midnight when *Fire and Rain* eased out of here under thick cloud cover."

Scooter, aka Tim, clicked a few buttons and brought up a remarkably detailed video of a large, sleek, black yacht darkened with mirror-tinted windows that stretched about a hundred feet as she slid out of the marina, causing barely a ripple on the water. I saw no one aboard. No faces. No lights. No nothing. The only helpful information occurred when she turned south and I got a good look at her tender—a matching black, thirty-six-foot, quad-engine Contender with blue LED lights and trim. The tender's name was *Gone Girl*.

I shook the harbormaster's hand. "Thank you."

He nodded. "If we can be of any help . . ."

I walked slowly back to *Gone Fiction*. I needed a few minutes to myself. The situation with Angel was getting worse, and now I was ferrying a dying old man to his grave.

When I dialed the number, he answered after one ring. "You in the Keys yet?"

I stared at Daytona Beach. "Not by a long shot."

He told me what he had on slave ships moving up and down the ditch. Which wasn't much, which told me these guys were pros. Not their first rodeo either. I told him what Clay had said about the two captains, their identifying tattoos, and about *Fire and Rain* and *Gone Girl*. He muttered as he talked because he was holding the pen cap in his mouth. When he finished writing, he said, "How you doing?"

"You wouldn't believe me if I told you."

"Try me."

"It's too much. Plus, I need you to look up Barclay T. Pettybone. Seventy-eight years old. Did sixty for murder somewhere in the South. Released in the last month or so. Admitted himself to Baptist Hospital in Jacksonville about a week ago. Then checked himself out. Prognosis bad."

"Where'd you meet him?"

"He's on the boat."

"Thought you worked alone."

He knew better. The comment was rhetorical.

"Clock's ticking. Wake somebody if you have to. I'll check in with you in a day or so. I need to get to West Palm by tomorrow at the latest. I think the clock is ticking faster than I can hear."

"Keep it between the markers."

"I intend to."

Back on *Gone Fiction*, I cranked the engine and we idled out of the marina. Clay sat in his beanbag and stretched out his legs and tipped his straw hat down over his eyes. In the miles ahead, I would learn that he hummed or whistled constantly, had a beautiful singing voice, and must have been a giant of a man at one time.

Summer stood next to me. She was clutching her book and staring down over the console at Clay. Gunner had dug himself a hole in the bag next to the old man. She put her hand on my arm. "Thank you."

I was lost in the chart in front of me, trying to calculate time on the water and how much I could push it and where we might take on food and fuel. She tugged on my arm. "You been on the water a long time?"

The downtown area of Daytona is one long no-wake zone, which meant we had a while before I could put her up on plane. "All my life."

"You love it, don't you?"

I stared into the water. Through it. Back to my beginning. "I do."

"Why?"

I waved my hand across the sea of rippled glass in front of us. "Thousands of knife-edged keels and spinning razor blades have cut this water right here. Sliced it into ten billion drops that somehow come back together again. No scar. Nothing can separate it. You could drop a bomb right here and within a few minutes, it'd look like nothing ever happened. Water heals itself. Every time. I like that. And if I'm being honest, maybe I need that."

She slipped her hand farther inside my arm. Now she wasn't tugging on my sleeve so much as winding her arm inside mine like a vine. She said nothing as the prop cut the water for the umpteen-millionth time. But despite the damage and the terror we inflicted on that spot of liquid earth, when I looked behind us, the water had come back together. It had healed. Farther on, there was no sign we'd ever been there.

She saw me staring behind us. "Can I ask you something?"

She was pressing closer against the walls I'd erected around myself. The walls I lived behind. The ones that protected me from people who tried to find my heart. I turned and pulled my Costas down over my eyes. "Yes."

She lifted them up again, setting them at an odd angle on top of my head. "Is Murphy Shepherd your real name?"

The no-wake zone ended. To the west, a deserted plantation house sat back off the water. Four chimneys, missing sections of roof, boarded-up windows, spray-painted graffiti, pigeons flying in and out—a shadow of her former beauty. The remains of a dock, outlined only by the barnacled posts that pierced the water, led from the marsh to the boathouse, a single sheet of rusted tin rubbing against its single remaining post. The hull of a fishing boat bobbed in the water feet away. In the water farther south, two dozen half-submerged sailboats lay at twisted angles. Beached. Run aground. Abandoned. No difference between the sea outside and the sea in. Single masts rose like sentinels at forty-five-degree angles, driven like stakes in the oyster shells. A rusted-out shrimper, rotten nets hung like Spanish moss, sat high in the marsh where the last storm surge had buried her and where she will remain. Forever.

We rode silently through the cemetery. So many muted memories, laughter that would never be heard again. What happens to old boats and those who rode them?

I pushed the throttle forward, bringing *Gone Fiction* up on plane and easing off when she reached four thousand rpm's—or thirty-two miles per hour. While Clay napped up front, caressed by the wind, Summer and I stayed in the bubble behind the windscreen. The eye of the hurricane. That safe place where you can hide from the noise and the wind and the stuff that tears at you. As I turned, a tear rolled down my face. I shook my head a single time. "No."

CHAPTER 14

We left Daytona in our wake and wound into and through the S-turn at New Smyrna Beach, eventually turning due west around Chicken Island and then due south through the northern tip of Turner Flats and Mosquito Lagoon. It's here in these frothy waters that mangrove trees grow en masse. Mangroves grow farther north, on up through Palm Coast and into St. Augustine, but it's down here where the water stays a bit warmer that they really thrive and spread out into islands. It's this island-spreading tendency that gives the Ten Thousand Islands their name on the southwest coast of Florida.

While Mosquito Lagoon may be great fishing, local knowledge of the waterways is a must. Fraught with hull-shredding debris just inches below the water, it's a no-man's-land outside the channel. The waters both east and west of the channel are littered with boats that strayed too far from the safety of the ditch. With nighttime an hour away, and with a thirty-knot northeast wind pounding the coastline east of us just beyond the mangroves, I needed to make a decision. We would not make West Palm tonight no matter how far I pushed the throttle, and the relatively wide-open water of the lagoon meant we'd be riding in two- to four-foot chops. Doable but not enjoyable. Especially for an old man.

And once we passed through the Haulover Canal and popped out into the open and wide water of the north end of the Indian River, which borders the eastern side of the Cape Canaveral security area, we'd be exposed for the better part of an hour—maybe three, depending on conditions—which would be miserable but necessary if we hoped to make West Palm tomor-row. And we needed to. The clock in my mind was ticking.

With the afternoon sun beginning to fall and only a few hours of day-light left, I knew Clay needed to stop. Despite the beanbag, he needed a break. We stopped on the side of the IC at the Sand Hill Grocery and Bait, and Summer and I loaded up with enough food for both an afternoon snack and dinner if things got bad. Twenty minutes farther south, I turned hard to starboard and entered the no-wake zone of the Haulover Canal.

The canal is an arrow-straight, three-quarter-mile, man-made cut through the finger of land that connects the Canaveral land mass to the mainland of Florida. Inside the protection of the canal, tall juniper trees form a windbreak, calming the water to a sheet of glass. The break from the constant pounding was a welcome relief.

I beached the boat on a sandy stretch on the northwest side of the canal. We helped Clay out of the boat while Gunner surveyed the landscape, marked his territory, and chased a rabbit. I gathered driftwood and built a fire. Then I asked Clay, "Thirty minutes okay with you?"

He knew what I was asking him. He nodded and gave me a thumbs-up.

I stretched a tarp to protect him from the sun and then hung a ham-mock beneath it. Clay tested the strength of the ropes, then lay sideways using the hammock as a chair. His smile spread across his face in much the same way as the hammock between both trees. Summer brought him a hastily made ham sandwich along with a bag of Doritos—each of which he savored.

I liked to watch Clay. His movements were purposeful. Singular. And he lived in the moment. Never outside of it. He ate each Dorito as if it were the last Dorito on earth. Thankfully, his cough had abated. For now.

I didn't like stopping but we all three needed a bathroom break, and that boat isn't the easiest place for a woman. It can be done, but there's noth-ing graceful about it. Clay swayed back and forth, singing in his hammock, while Summer fed Gunner half her sandwich. I cranked the Jetboil and started water for coffee, giving my fingers something to do while my mind turned.

Beach before us, a gentle breeze washing over us, and the sound of Clay humming. I wondered if this was the calm before the storm. I questioned if Summer would be able to weather what was coming.

As the water boiled, I noticed I had Clay's undivided attention. He was watching my every move. I spooned some instant coffee into an insulated stainless mug and took it to him. He tried to stand to accept it, but I wouldn't let him. He sipped and said, "Mr. Murphy?"

I smiled. "Yes."

"My bones thank you."

Moving from North Florida to South, the water slowly changes from dark to clear. From tannic tea to gin. We were not yet halfway through the Haulover Canal, still in the dark area, but I could see signs of clearing. With a beach next to us, I said, "Summer?"

She looked up at me.

"How 'bout you let me teach you how to swim?"

She stood and eyed the water with skepticism. Then shook her head.

"You do realize it's rather a good idea to learn how to swim?"

She nodded but stepped no closer.

I waded down in the water, thigh deep. The water was warm and felt good. She approached but kept her distance.

I waved my hand over the water. "Did you have a bad experience somewhere?"

"You mean other than two nights ago?"

"Yes."

"Not that I know of."

"So you're just old and set in your ways."

She shoved her hands in her back pockets and weighed her head side to side. "Pretty much."

"Okay, what if your daughter was passed out and they threw her off some boat and she was floating in the water and you had about ten seconds? Would you wish then that you could swim?"

She walked into the water up to her waist and stood with arms crossed, staring at the water around her. "Yes."

I waded out deeper. When the water got to my neck, with my feet still on sandy bottom, I reached out my hand and said nothing. She inched closer. The water now up to the middle of her stomach. I swam across the canal. It was a short distance. Maybe forty feet. I knew from my depth finder that it ranged from ten to twelve feet to the bottom, so to get to me she'd have to leave her feet and pull with her hands. Which was what I wanted. A simple dog paddle.

I held out my hand. She shook her head.

"Summer?"

She stepped farther in. Water to her collarbone.

"Make a cup with your hand and push against the water. You don't have to go anywhere. Just stand right there. I want you to feel that you can push against the water."

She did but said nothing to me.

"Now I want you to push down, hard enough to lift your feet off the sand."

She make a rather pitiful attempt, barely coming up an inch.

"You can do better."

She tried again. This time she bobbed up and down, always quickly returning to the safety of the bottom. Summer's problem was that despite her fearless courage in looking for her daughter, she was afraid of the water. Something had happened. I just didn't know what it was. Maybe she didn't either. Regardless, she was scared, and I didn't have time for her to be scared.

I swam back across the canal, turned her so she was facing away from me, put my hands on her hips, and said, "Do you trust me?"

She placed her hands over the top of mine and shook her head. "Absolutely not."

"Are you willing to be willing?"

She paused and eventually said, "Yes."

"I'm going to lift you slightly, move you to water that's deeper, and hold you while you kick and pull. Deal?"

She hesitated and then nodded quickly.

Hands on her hips, I lifted her and moved her just a few feet into deeper water. With a death grip on my hands, she stood arrow straight in the water. I thought we'd start with something easy, so I said, "Kick with your feet like you just did with your hands."

She tried with little success.

"You mean to tell me with as much muscle as you have in this body and those dancing legs of yours that you can't kick harder than that?"

Summer was trembling but the thought registered. Still holding my hands, she kicked harder and actually lifted herself up in the water. Had I not been holding her, she might have treaded water. By this time, we had Clay's attention too. He'd inched himself up in his hammock and could see from where he sat.

Gunner, never one to waste an opportunity to get wet, launched himself in the water and paddled himself around us in circles. All the while, he'd lick Summer's face and then mine and then hers again. Aside from the licking, he was actually helpful.

I nodded at Gunner. "You see what he's doing?"

She quit kicking and returned to an arrow with a death grip on my hands. "Sort of."

"I want you to do that. So start kicking." She did. "Now let go of my hands and start pulling. Just like Gunner."

One hand slowly let go, then quickly latched back on. She shook her head.

I pulled her to my chest where she quit kicking and wrapped her legs around my waist like a vise. "Trust me."

She stared at me a long minute.

I know the fear of drowning is a primal thing. We're all born with it, and it's tough if not impossible to reason ourselves out of it. Takes serious strength of will to do so. I said it again: "Trust me."

She loosened her grip, and I turned her facing away from me. She began kicking again while still holding my hands. Then slowly, one by one, she let go and began treading water. To comfort her, I pressed my hands against her hips. To let her know I was still there. But she was so strong that I had a difficult time holding her down. So as she found a rhythm and began holding herself at the surface of the water, I slowly eased off. After a minute, I was only making contact with her skin so her mind registered my fingers, but I was offering her no help whatsoever.

Having stayed afloat for the better part of a minute, she let her fear begin to take over and her hands returned to mine. But her legs kept kicking. I could work with that. Summer's problem wasn't that she couldn't swim. She could. Her problem was fear, but I knew she'd figure that out soon enough.

I pulled her to the shore where her feet found purchase on the sand, and she walked up the beach to the sound of Clay clapping. She looked like a soaked kitten, smiling and proud of herself. The next lesson wouldn't be as fun, but she didn't need to know that.

Yet.

We loaded up, pulled off the beach, and started the journey to Stuart. The no-wake zone continued another half mile, so Summer sat next to me while Clay resumed his perch on the beanbag. Summer caught me looking at my hands. She was smiling, apparently having enjoyed her lesson. Feeling like she'd accomplished something. She thumbed over her shoulder. "That reminded me of dancing. Back when I could really dance. On the . . . on the stage . . . my partner—depending on the show—would hold my hips the way you did and then throw me into the air." She paused. "Sometimes, when all the world was right"—she smiled—"which wasn't often, I'd catch a slow-motion glimpse of the audience somewhere in my spin. I can still see those pictures. Dim now, but I can still see them."

I was extending my fingers and then making a fist, stretching my hand. She asked, "You okay?"

I've used my hands for lots of things, but a tender touch on a woman's hips was not one of them. "Yeah, I'm good."

Truth was, it was the first time I'd touched a woman with tenderness in a long time. She put a hand on my shoulder. "You're a good teacher."

CHAPTER 15

I needed to get to Stuart, and having made the turn across the canal, we now had a bit of a tailwind. I pushed the trim tabs down, forced the boat up on top of the chop, and moved across the water at thirty-five mph or better. One of the beautiful aspects of my boat is that it's a little heavy for its size, which produces a Cadillac-smooth ride in choppy water. That has its downside in skinny water, but I'd face that when the time came. *Gone Fiction* was made for water like this, and so we churned across the top of it, eating up the miles.

We entered the waters of the Indian River and the no-man's-land of mudflats north of Cape Canaveral. Mars on earth. For several miles the channel is marked by twisted poles stuck at odd angles into the soft earth. The remains of an enormous tree and its massive root ball lay resting in the water a hundred yards south of us where the water depth shrank to two feet across a two-mile-wide mudflat. The wind picked up and Summer felt it. As did the sideways chop, which pushed ocean spray over the side of the boat. It's difficult to talk near forty mph, so I motioned for Summer to stand on my other side—back in the safety of the eye of the hurricane. Moving from my left to my right, she twirled. Unconsciously.

Clay, meanwhile, sat without a care in the world. One hand on Gunner, the other flat across his chest. Occasionally he would cough, but somehow he held the spasms at bay. As the sun fell off to our right, my attention turned to Angel and the satellite phone. Normally I kept it stowed until I needed it. I used it more for making calls than receiving them. But coverage in the Keys, which is where I figured her boat was headed, was spotty, and if she had coverage and tried to call, I wanted her to connect. I made a note to dig it out when we stopped.

We crossed Mars, turned south, and passed through the bascule span of the Florida East Coast Railway Bridge. The bridge sits low to the water and remains in the open position, flashing green lights notifying boats that entrance is permitted. When a train approaches, green changes to flashing red, a siren blasts four times, pauses, blasts four more times, and after an eight-minute delay, the bridge lowers and locks.

I saw the bridge some two miles distant and watched as the green light flashed to red. I also saw the train on my right. It was a long one, and I could not see its end. That train could delay us thirty minutes or more while we floated like a bobber in a thirty-knot crosswind and the engineer picked his teeth. That did not sound like my idea of fun.

Knowing I had about eight minutes, I pushed the throttle forward, bringing the engine to six thousand rpm's, and moved across the top of the water at more than fifty mph. Approaching the bridge, Clay raised both hands and sang loudly. I had no idea what he was singing, but I knew the tone and it sounded like freedom.

As we approached the bridge, the horn blasted again. The bridge tender must have seen my intention to sneak through, because he sat on that horn. If we didn't make it, *Gone Fiction's* T-top would contact the bridge span and rip it off at about shoulder level. I thought we could make it. The bridge tender thought differently. Summer squeezed my arm. Tightly. As I closed the distance, I pushed the throttle to full and aimed for the center of the span. I had trimmed the engine so that only the propeller and lower unit were in the water.

We passed through the span as the bridge started to descend, clearing it by well over twenty feet. On the other side, with the bridge tender still communicating his distaste for my theatrics on the radio, Summer released her white-knuckle grip on my arm. Her face was flushed with excitement and she was breathing heavily. Up front, Clay sat lounging with his legs crossed and both arms raised. Fingers' lunch box sat unmoving.

Knowing I could refuel in Stuart, I threw fuel conservation to the wind and maintained forty-plus mph. To our left, the Kennedy Space Center morphed into Merritt Island. With the city of Cocoa appearing on our starboard side, I pointed to our port side and brought Summer's attention to a small, almost imperceptible barge canal. She leaned closer and I said, "That cuts across the island and into Port Canaveral, where they dock the Trident submarines."

From Cocoa, Merritt Island encroaches on what was once the wide water of the Indian River and narrows the channel, offering protection from the wind. With the water smoothing out, I eased the throttle forward once again and leveled out at forty-five mph. We were skimming across the water.

We passed Cocoa Beach, Patrick Air Force Base, Satellite Beach, and into the waters around Melbourne and Palm Bay when I finally throttled down to thirty. Clay had started coughing, and I wondered if my speed had been the cause or his singing.

Either way, slowing down seemed to abate it.

Making good time, we put Palm Bay, Malabar, Sebastian, and Winter Beach in our wake. At Vero Beach, the IC narrowed and congestion picked up. We encountered several boats moving north and fishermen returning from a day in the mangroves.

Racing daylight, I navigated the wakes of oncoming vessels as best I could, but they pushed Clay around more than I would have liked. Were it not for the beanbag, he wouldn't have made it. Vero Shores gave way to the no-wake zones of St. Lucie and Fort Pierce. Passing beneath the A1A fixed bridge and cut free from the no-wake tether on the southern end of St. Lucie, I glanced over my shoulder and realized I was losing in my race against what remained of the sun. I pushed the throttle well forward and didn't slow again until we passed back under A1A at Sewall's Point, which in my mind marked the beginning of Stuart.

With darkness falling and boats dotting the waterline with their red and green running lights visible, I knocked the engine out of gear and glided along the surface of the water. Summer seemed excited. Both by the day behind us and by the possibility before us. We'd made good time and covered a lot of ground. *Gone Fiction* moved with the current in the now clear and open waters of Stuart. Hutchinson Island sat off to our left. As did the inlet that led out into the Atlantic. In between us lay an underwater sandbar that stretched for the better part of a half mile and appeared at low tide—a favorite party destination for boaters and jet skiers. Sandbars like that were much of the reason folks around here owned boats.

With the boat floating along with the current, I led Summer to the back of the boat, where she stood unsuspecting and expectant. Without comment, I pushed her into the water. This even surprised Clay, who stood, grabbing the T-top for support. Gunner ran to the back of the boat and barked while Summer thrashed in the water. When her head bobbed to the surface of the water, her hands scraping the air like an eggbeater, I said, "Swim, Summer."

She was screaming, thrashing, and choking. Out of her mind. The current was pulling me farther from her, so I turned the wheel and beached the bow on the sandbar she couldn't see and dove in. Summer was sinking.

I lifted her hips, forced her head out of the water, and said, "Summer..."

For one clear instant, her frantic and fearful eyes found mine. "Just swim."

Then I let go.

I don't know if it was Broadway and dancing, or the fact that I'd let go and she was so angry she just wanted to punch me in the face, or if it was unbridled fear. Whatever the cause, Summer began kicking and pulling—treading water. And when she did, her face and head broke the surface like a bobber. Where she stayed. First one breath, then two, then several. Realizing that she wasn't sinking and not going to drown, she began involuntarily rotating in a counterclockwise circle. When she reached six o'clock, she saw me, and the excitement of actually swimming faded away from her face. Making way for anger.

She spoke hastily. "I don't like you."

"I know."

She continued to tread water.

I moved two steps away from her. "Swim closer."

She shook her head. "I don't like you."

I took two more steps away, increasing the distance and her sense of insecurity. "Closer."

Reluctantly, she dog-paddled her way closer. Not close enough to touch me but almost. When she finally spoke, there was no humor in her voice. "You're an evil man."

"Put your feet down."

She looked confused. "What?"

"Put your feet down."

She stopped kicking with one foot and reached. When she did, she quickly touched bottom. Putting both feet on the sand, she quit paddling with her arms and stood still, the waterline at her collarbone. She stood, hair matted across her face, staring at me. A vein had popped up beneath one eye. I reached out and tried to push her hair back, but she slapped my hand and did it herself.

"You okay?"

She shook her head. "No."

I waited.

"You made me pee myself."

I laughed. "Well, no one but you and the sharks will ever know."

"Sharks!?" She launched herself off the sand and immediately started treading water again, but this time her movements were twice as fast. "Where?"

"All around."

"You being serious?"

I was laughing. "Yep."

She started inching toward the boat. "Get me out of this water."

"Summer."

She turned and looked at me. And when she did, she was almost smiling.

I stepped closer. "You were swimming." She put her foot down, then the other. This time she let me push her hair behind her ear. "All by yourself."

She smiled but reached out with her foot and those muscled toes and pulled a patch of hair from my leg. She raised both eyebrows. "You ever do that again and I'll—"

I smiled. "What?"

"You scared me."

"I know. I'm sorry."

"No, you're not. If you were sorry, you wouldn't have done it."

The water was warm and it felt good. I looked at the water below me. Summer thought I'd seen something. "What? A shark?"

"No, I just felt a warm spot—"

"Not funny." Without saying a word, Summer left the safety of the sand and dog-paddled into deeper water a few feet away. Keeping her head above water, she looked up at Clay, who stood staring down at the both of us. He said, "Miss Summer, you're swimming."

She seemed proud of herself. "Yes, sir, Mr. Pettybone, I am."

I climbed onto the sandbar as darkness fell in earnest. Summer paddled over, and when her feet sank knee-deep in the soft sand, I offered her my hand. She reluctantly accepted it. Climbing out and standing on the hard-pack, she stared out across the water while the wind dried her face. In the distance, we could hear the crash of Atlantic waves along the shoreline. She whispered, "It's just water."

I nodded. And when she turned back to face me, I whispered, "Forgive me?"

She studied my face. "Do I have a choice?"

"Yes."

"Can I get back to you on that?"

I admired her strength. If ever a momma had a fighting chance at finding a daughter, this one might. You had to be tough to make it through something like this. And in my experience, she had tough coming.

Clay met Summer on the boat with a towel while we idled up Willoughby Creek toward the waterside efficiency hotel connected to Pirate's Cove Resort and Marina. We tied up along the bulkhead, and I left them to tend the boat while I walked up to the office and rented three rooms. Returning, I gave them each a key and pointed. "How 'bout we meet back here in ten? Fried shrimp on me."

CHAPTER 16

Farther upriver, the lights of two bars shone festively on the water. Summer disappeared while Clay walked to his room just feet away. He was moving slower, walking from chair back to column to doorframe—anything he could grasp to steady himself. When he reached his door, he unlocked it and walked in. Before he shut it, he looked back at the boat but not at me.

Fifteen minutes later, we moored alongside two waterfront restaurants. I gave them a choice between live music at the Twisted Tuna or something quiet at Shrimper's Grill and Raw Bar. Summer and Clay picked live music. We sat outside, along the water. Moon high and shining down. I'd made Gunner stay in the boat, which he did, but his whining told me he didn't like it. His vocal protest attracted a few kids who were feeding the fish along the dock. A minute later, three kids were scratching his belly.

Smart dog.

We ate shrimp and talked little. I figured Summer was trying to decide if she was mad at me and Clay was conserving his energy, trying to keep the spasms at bay. While his eyes focused on his food, which he chewed slowly, every few minutes he'd glance at the boat.

When she'd finished eating, Summer wiped her mouth, pushed back from the table, and offered her hand to Clay. "Mr. Pettybone, would you be so kind as to dance with me?"

Clay set down his iced tea, wiped his mouth, and pushed back his chair. "Well, yes, ma'am."

Clay stood possibly six feet three inches and Summer was about five foot nine, so he reached down and she reached up. They walked to the makeshift dance floor. He held out his arms, she placed hers alongside his, and they danced. He was a good dancer. Summer laughed as the two slowly shuffled beneath the sound of his humming. Every few steps he'd raise an arm and send her into a spin. It was one of the more beautiful things I'd seen in a long time. An older, dying lifer full of regret and sorrow and a broken-hearted, middle-aged woman full of sorrow and regret. The two together made a happy sound out across the deck. The laughter was the proof.

When he grew tired, Clay stopped and bowed. All of the tables around us clapped for Summer, who was an accomplished dancer. Any idiot could see that. She returned him to his seat, where he sat smiling like he'd just won the lottery. Then she turned her attention to me.

Which I was afraid of.

She walked around the table and leaned in close to my face. She was happy, her cheeks flushed. "And you, kind sir?"

"I don't dance."

She held out her hand. "And I don't swim. Get your butt out of that chair."

She had a point. I stood, and she led me to the dance floor. "I've only really danced once in my life, and that was—"

"Well, before about an hour ago, I'd never been swimming. So you're in good company."

With most every table watching her instruct me, she lifted my arms into the position she wanted. I felt like the straw man in *The Wizard of Oz*. "You ever see *Dirty Dancing*?"

"No."

She mouthed the words without vocalizing them. *You've never seen* Dirty Dancing*?* Sweat beaded on her temple.

"Nope."

She continued to make fine adjustments to my arms, shoulders, and stance, and spoke without looking at me. "What is wrong with the educational institutions of America?"

"Are we finished yet?"

She sized me up. "You're no Patrick Swayze, but you'll do." She hung her right hand into my left and placed my right hand around her waist, with her left hand on my right shoulder. Then she began telling me where to put my feet. "Step here." "Step there." "Good, now raise your left hand straight up." "Step backward." "Now bring your left hand across your face, like you're looking at your watch."

While I followed instructions and she led me in the art of leading her, she said, "Nice watch."

"Friend gave it to me."

"Nice friend."

I focused on everything she was telling me while she moved as easily as someone breathing in their sleep. While she moved around me, making me look like I knew what I was doing, she said, "Did you just say you have only danced *once* in your life?"

"This makes twice."

"What on earth is wrong with you?"

"We're gonna need a bigger dance floor to answer that question."

"What's the short version?"

"I've only been married once."

"Certainly you danced with your wife somewhere?"

"Nope."

"Why not?"

"She left."

"What, a year? Two?"

"No. More like an hour."

She stopped spinning and returned to face me. This time she moved closer. "You were married for an hour?"

"Almost."

She looked embarrassed. "Something terrible happened, didn't it?"

"Yes."

"I'm sorry."

"It was a long time ago. And to be honest, I think this dance was much better. At least one of us knew what we were doing."

The music stopped and people actually stood at their tables clapping for Summer, who pointed to me, clapped, and then bowed. She was sweating, breathing slightly heavily. I wondered how someone so beautiful, so talented, so . . . wasn't married.

Clay seemed distracted as we idled back to the hotel. After I tied up at the dock, I helped lift him out and said, "Mr. Pettybone, you okay?"

He coughed and wiped his mouth with a cloth handkerchief. "Yes, sir. Would you mind . . . ?" He eyed his door, so I locked my arm in his and walked him to his room. As he inserted the key, he said, "Mr. Murphy, I don't want to tell you your business, but you've got somebody else on that boat."

I glanced back at *Gone Fiction*. Summer stood on the dock, tying up the stern line. "What do you mean?"

He threw his head to the side and rear, suggesting something from his past. "In my life, I learned to listen. I'm still pretty good at it. There's somebody else on that boat."

I glanced at Fingers' orange box tied to the bow. Not sure what to reveal, I shook my head. "Still not following you."

He pointed to the small door that led into the even smaller head housed in the center console.

CHAPTER 17

It dawned on me that I had not opened the latch door to the head since I'd finished packing the boat at my island the night before I left. I had thought about it when I almost stowed Fingers' box in there, but I'd never done it. That meant it had sat untouched since I'd left the island.

Summer noticed the wrinkle between my eyes. "You okay?"

I didn't want to leave the orange box out overnight, plus it gave me the excuse I needed. So I untied it and said, "Yeah . . ." I pointed to the head and placed one single finger to my lips. I spoke to her while looking at the door. "I just need to lock this up for the night." I didn't know what or who might be in the head, so if need be I planned to use Fingers' lunch box as a weapon.

I pulled on the latch leading into the head and gently swung the door open until it clicked into its magnetic hold. When I did, I found two wide eyes staring at me from the darkness. They darted from me to Summer and back to me. Slowly a shape took place. She was small. Sitting inside the console, surrounded by towels and a cushion. I scratched my head and started thinking back through all the rough water we'd crossed. The idea that someone had been in there for any length of time at all was mind-boggling. A pinball would have had an easier go.

Seeing another face to lick, Gunner moved in for closer inspection. Finding willing hands, he began licking her face, which brought a giggle. A beautiful laugh. Which explained all the time Gunner had spent sniffing the crack around the door. With Gunner's tail wagging at full speed, I

126

pulled him out and stuck my head inside the console. Then my hand. A much smaller hand took mine, and she climbed out of the head.

A girl. Maybe not quite a teenager. Jeans. Backpack. Running shoes. Short, Audrey Hepburn–length hair. She stood studying me and said nothing.

Summer looked at me, the girl, then me again. She stepper closer. "Honey, are you okay?"

The girl shrugged.

"You lost?"

The girl shook her head but didn't take her eyes off me. It was as if she was looking at something she'd heard about but never seen. Like something hanging on a wall in a museum.

Summer kept trying. "You're not lost?"

Another shake. Matter-of-fact. She looked around. "No."

"Well, baby doll—" Summer tried a laugh to break the ice. "What are you doing?"

The girl looked at me. "I'm wondering if you can tell me who I am."

I pointed to myself. "Why me?"

She held up a yellowed piece of paper.

"May I?"

She passed it through the air that hung between us. It was an older, detailed navigational chart showing the island I call home. The grounds around the chapel had been circled in red pencil. There was no name. No writing. "What's this?"

Her voice had an edge. "The girls at school were talking about their homes, parents, what they were doing for fall break, where they were going, and all that. I knew nothing. I've never known anything about me. All I knew was that I was going to spend one more sucky holiday alone. With the same old sucky questions. I got tired of them always talking behind my back. So I broke into the room where they keep the files and dug around. Most of the files were an inch thick. Each a pedigree of royalty. So-and-so is related to so-and-so, who did such and such. More money than God. My file had two pieces of paper."

"The second?"

She handed me a smaller sheet the size of an index card. It was a picture.

Of me.

She pointed. "That's you, right?"

I looked to be about fifteen years younger. I did not know when it was taken or who had taken it. It showed me standing in the water on the south side of my island, shirt off, a cast net in my arms. Doing what I love. The look on my face was one of peace. Contentment. Whoever had taken it knew enough about me to know when to snap the shutter. They must have been standing in the trees along the bank and snapped it when I turned to throw the net. Taped to the underside of the picture was a newspaper headline from the *New York Times* dated sixteen years ago. The headline read, "Kidnapped Senator's Daughter Rescued and Returned Unharmed by Mystery Man. Shot 3 Times He Paddled Seven Miles Navigating by the Stars."

The article was not attached to the headline. Which was all right with me. I knew what it said. I held the pieces in my hand. "Anything else?"

She pulled a shoestring-size piece of leather from around her neck. It held a large brass-looking key.

She offered the key. "Ever seen this?"

I studied it, flipping it over and back in my hand. "Not to my knowledge." One side of the key read "27"; the other side had the address of a bank in Miami.

I had grown somewhat annoyed. "That's all you got?"

Her eyes never flickered when she spoke. "It's what I've got."

Summer continued, "Baby, where's your school?"

She turned to Summer. "I'm not your baby."

Summer put her hands on her hips. "Can you tell me your name?"

"Ellie, but it's not my real name."

"Why do you say that?"

"Seven foster homes. Four boarding schools."

Summer stepped closer. "What's your real name?"

Ellie spoke without emotion. "You mean like on my birth certificate?"

Summer nodded.

"Jane Doe."

Summer's voice softened. "Is somebody looking for you?"

Expressionless, Ellie shrugged. "No idea."

Summer leaned in closer. "Where's your mom now?"

Ellie spoke with governed sarcasm. "If I knew that, do you think I'd have stuffed myself in that box?"

Summer asked again, "Where's your school?"

"New York."

Ellie stared at me. "Look, I don't like being here any more than you, but can we just skip all this? Did you have some kid you didn't want? Maybe dropped her on the curb somewhere? If so, just tell me. It's no big deal—"

I interrupted her. "My wife died before we were able to have kids."

Summer asked, "How'd you get from New York to Florida?"

"Train."

"And the island?"

"Uber."

"How'd you pay for it?"

Ellie frowned. "The girls at my school are rich. Daddy's money and everything. They never miss it."

Summer stepped closer. "Honey, how old are you?"

"I'm not your honey either."

"Okay."

"What's it to you?"

"You just look so young."

"Just how old should I be? I can actually hold my own sippy cup and change my own diaper."

Summer passed her off to me with a look. The lights shone on the girl's features. Eyes. Chin. Cheekbones. She was beautiful, tough, and her body language suggested she was not afraid of a scrap.

I took a go. "How long have you been looking for me?"

"Couple of weeks."

Summer spoke up. "You've been on your own for three weeks?"

She shrugged. "I've been on my own since I was born."

Summer kept at it. "Do I need to call someone and let them know you're okay?"

She raised an eyebrow. "Who would you call?"

This girl really was on her own. I could hear her stomach growling. "You hungry?"

Another shrug. "Not really."

Summer took the baton. "Would you like to shower?"

"No, I don't want a shower and I don't want any food. I don't want anything from you two." She looked at me. "I just want to know if you have any idea who I am or where I might have come from. If not—" She tapped the key on her chest. "I'm headed to Miami."

I didn't have time for this girl. But that picture kept staring up at me. I tried to speak calmly. "The bank won't let you access that."

"Watch me."

I stepped closer. It was the first time I intentionally intruded on her personal space. "You have an ID showing that you're eighteen?"

She nodded.

I held out my hand.

"Why?"

"I'd like to see it."

She flashed it but didn't let me hold it. "See."

She was right. She had learned how to work the system.

I glanced at Clay, who shrugged and coughed once.

The ID wasn't hers. A close likeness, yes, but it'd never pass in the bank.

I was tired. Thoughts were firing and I had no answers. I also felt like Angel was slipping further from my grasp the more I stood here and talked. But there was that picture. "Listen, I don't know who you are. I'm sorry. I don't. But we'll be in Miami tomorrow, and if you'll just hang out one more night, we'll go to the bank."

She stiffened. Raised a finger. "On one condition."

I didn't think she was in a position to make demands, but I went along with it. "Okay."

"I keep whatever's in that box."

I nodded. "Deal."

"Even if it's a million dollars."

"Even if."

Her head tilted sideways. "Really? You're not going to fight me for it?"

I shook my head. "No."

"Why not?"

"Honestly?"

"Yes."

"Because I don't want what's yours and right now I'm too tired to fight you or anyone else for anything."

She folded her arms. "Can I ask you something?"

I wiped my face with my palm. "Sure."

She held up the picture. "This you?"

"Yes—although I have no idea who took it or when."

Next, she waved the news headline. "And this?"

I nodded.

She did not seem convinced. "Prove it."

"No."

She gestured with both hands. "Why not?"

It was late, and I still had some thinking to do. I spoke to everyone. "We'll leave early." Turning to Summer, I said, "Can she stay with you?"

Summer put her hand on Ellie's shoulder. "Sure."

"I'll find some takeout and bring it back." I spoke to Ellie. "Chinese or something?"

"You didn't answer me." A pause. "Why not?"

"I quit proving myself to people a long time ago. You can stay or go. Up to you. But—" I could hear her stomach growling. "I'm offering dinner."

She considered my offer, hesitated, and spoke softly. "All right."

Clay walked to his room. Slowly. His cough had worsened and it was producing more. Gunner walked alongside him. The two disappeared into Clay's room.

The world just got a lot more complicated.

Summer kicked into momma-gear and slipped her hand into Ellie's. "Let's get you cleaned up and then something hot to eat. Deal?"

The two disappeared into Summer's room. I set Fingers' box inside the head and saw how Ellie had been living the last few days cooped up inside that small area. She'd made a pallet of towels to cushion her ride. Before I locked up the boat, I pulled out my sat phone.

When I turned it on, the screen immediately read, "You have 0 new voicemails."

As I turned the phone in my hand, my cell phone rang. Caller ID put the area code as Colorado. I answered after the second ring.

He asked, "Late for you, isn't it?"

"A little."

"What's going on?"

I stared at the lights of Summer's room. "Well—" My eyes wandered to the hotel, then to the water slowly flowing south. "I'm traveling with a woman who's looking for her daughter who doesn't want to be found. The mom is on the verge of cracking. Fragile. Frayed threads holding it together. Fighting images in both the windshield and the rearview. Next to her sits a dying man who's trying to get south for the first time in over sixty years. His eyes are tired and tell of a life lived hard, and there is sorrow behind them. I'm not sure where we're headed, but I think he loved someone many years ago. He's returning to that memory. Next to him is possibly the smartest dog I've ever seen anywhere. And next to him is a teenage girl who's been hiding in the head since I left the island. She's friends with no one but trying to dig up her past, which brought her to me—for reasons I can't quite figure. Discovered her an hour ago. And tied to the bow is a box holding the ashes of my best friend. Before me is a lot of water and possibly a lot of pain. Behind me is an email. And back on the kitchen table is a purple urn. That's pretty much it for starters."

"Who's the girl?"

"Thanks for the sympathy."

"Oh, I'm sorry. Were you looking for some of that?"

I told him Ellie's story.

He was silent for several moments. When he spoke I knew he was serious. He said, "I could be there—"

"If we find Angel, you'll be needed where you are." He knew I was right. I was tired. My filter weak. "Did you have a reason for calling me?"

"Two things. First, Barclay T. Pettybone did in fact do sixty for murder. In Alabama. Which probably wasn't easy for a man of his color. He is also dying of cancer, but . . ." He cleared his throat. "He doesn't have to."

"What do you mean?"

"Surgery and treatment will help him. Extend his life. But it's expensive. Somewhat experimental. And he would need to travel. Quickly."

"How long does he have?"

"That depends on the infection in his lungs and . . . whether or not he wants to keep living."

I stared at Clay's door. "He's pretty weak. I have a feeling he's not going anywhere until he finds what he's looking for in the Keys."

"He may not make it that far. Can you lean on him?"

"I can lead a horse to water, but I can't make him drink. I think you were the one who taught me that."

I could see him nodding in my mind's eye. "I might have said something like that over the years . . . a time or two."

"You said 'two things.'"

He cleared his throat. His tone changed. "There's a body in the morgue at Jupiter Medical. Fits the description of your girl. Runway-model looks. Recent tattoo that reads 'Angel.' Toxicology suggests opioid overdose. Body showed up last night. Nobody's been to see her and nobody's claimed her."

I rubbed my face and cussed beneath my breath.

He continued, "And because you're not family, they're not going to let you in to see her unless you use that ID you keep hidden behind your driver's license."

Seconds passed. "Do me a favor?"

"Anything."

"Have them ready to look at Clay when we get there."

"Done." His voice softened. "You got any sleep in your future?"

I stared at my boat, then the lights of the street and a twenty-four-hour Chinese takeout. "Doubtful."

I was about to hang up when he said, "Murph?"

The tone of his voice changed again. The first time I'd heard that tone, I was facedown in the sand and had been drunk for the better part of a year. "Yeah?"

"You all right?"

"Why do you ask?"

"The hair's standing up on the back of my neck."

I rubbed my face. "Mine too."

CHAPTER 18

Clay's feet shuffled as he walked to the boat. Between his door and *Gone Fiction*, he stopped twice to cough. Both times left him doubled over. The wind had picked up so I offered him my windbreaker and brought him a cup of coffee and a blanket. All of which he accepted. He'd aged overnight. He collapsed into his beanbag, Summer joined me in the eye of the hurricane, and Ellie moved aft. Sitting on the back bench, pulling her knees into her chest, and not taking her eyes off me. Gunner floated around the boat, licking each of us good morning.

We pulled out of the marina and the sky shone crimson red as the sun broke the skyline. I whispered to myself, "Red sky at night . . ."

Summer leaned inside the eye of the hurricane. "What's that?"

"Sailor lore. 'Red sky at night, sailor's delight. Red sky at morning, sailor's warning.'"

"What's it mean?"

"It's a warning about the day's weather."

"Where's it come from?"

"Its roots go back about two thousand years when it was a warning about the days ahead. Has something to do with the life of a shepherd. Over the years it's been shortened but it goes something like, 'Red sky at night, shepherd's delight. Red sky at morning, shepherd's warning.'"

"Who said it?"

"Jesus."

She slipped her hand inside my arm. "The farther we get down this river, the more interesting you become."

And the farther we traveled down this river, the tighter her grip became on my arm, which spoke volumes about the condition of her heart and the fear she was fighting.

I looked at her hand, interwoven with mine. "Has anyone ever told you that you're a touchy-feely kind of person?"

"As a dancer, your hands tell your feet where they're going. Good dancers learn to close their eyes and follow the lead. It's like braille."

"Does following get old?"

"Two can't lead, and no matter what these young kids think today, one can't dance alone. By definition, the leader is only leading when someone is following. If no follower, then no leader. And if you're leading, then you're judged by how well another follows. They need each other."

"Is the same true for the heart?"

She tugged slightly on her hand, attempting to withdraw it, but then thought better of it, sinking it farther. "Sometimes my hands tell my heart how to feel, and . . ." She turned toward the back bench where Ellie sat staring at the shoreline. "In my experience, that's another dance that very few men know how to lead."

Summer and Ellie sat on the back bench as we motored out of Stuart. Getting to Jupiter would take a while as one no-wake zone led into another. Up front, Clay coughed. One spasm leading into another. To say he was worsening would be an understatement. One episode lasted twenty minutes and left him sweating, pale, and struggling to catch his breath.

The Indian River took us south out of Stuart to the beginning of Florida's ultrawealthy who live along Jupiter Island. Little more than a spit of land, Jupiter Island is an elevated sandbank that separates and buffers the Atlantic from the IC. Those who live there look out their front doors onto the Atlantic and out their back doors onto the IC. It's home to actors, TV moguls, entertainers, and professional athletes.

We idled south under the shadow of the huge banyan trees that sprouted along the waterline—each carrying countless HD security cameras. The water brought us into Jupiter proper where I rented a slip at the Jupiter Yacht Club. With Ellie's help, we Ubered to the Jupiter Medical Center.

When I told him where we were going, Clay didn't give me much argument. His breathing was shallow and his face ashen. Without medical intervention, he didn't have long. The Uber driver wasn't crazy about Gunner getting in his car, but Ellie saved the day. "He's a service dog." The driver relented.

We walked in the doors of Jupiter Medical as Clay doubled over, coughing. I spoke to the receptionist. "Ma'am, this is Mr. Barclay T. Pettybone." A question in my voice.

She typed some letters into her keyboard and stared down her nose at a monitor. A few seconds later, she spoke into a radio and then stood and rolled a wheelchair from a corner. Clay didn't need an invitation. She pointed at Gunner. "Service dog?"

I spoke before anyone could mess it up. "Yes, ma'am."

She pursed her lips. "Thought so."

Catching his breath, Clay waved his hand across the hospital. "You do this?"

"Not directly."

"Who did?" he asked between coughs.

I held up my phone.

He nodded. "I like them." He placed his hand on mine. "Promise me something?"

"Okay."

"You won't leave me." He made sure I was focused on him. "Alive or dead."

When I hesitated, he squeezed my hand. Not harsh. Just firm. "Mr. Murphy?" His grip softened. "Please, sir."

"One condition."

He raised both eyebrows while trying not to cough.

"You quit calling me Mister."

The nurse began pushing his chair down the hall where Gunner followed at his hip. Clay put his hand on the wheel, stopping her, then pulled backward, turning to face me. "Taking a man out of prison is one thing." He coughed. "Taking prison out of the man . . . is another thing entirely."

I turned to Summer and took her by the hand. Ellie stood listening. "I need to tell you something."

Summer waited expectantly. Eyes wide. Hopeful. Hand warm and trembling.

There was no easy way to say this. So I just said it. "There's a body in the morgue here."

The words rattled around her mind. When they settled, her bottom lip started to quiver and her spine straightened.

I spoke slowly. "She fits the description of Angel. I need to—"

She grabbed my arm. "Not without me."

I whispered, "This is never fun."

"If she's mine . . ." She trailed off.

If the body was Angel, then Summer would need the closure. But it'd be hell. "This . . . can change you forever."

She shook her head once, bit her lip, and collapsed onto a bench behind her.

Gathering herself, she took several breaths, wiped her face, and then stood and nodded. I held her hand as we walked through two buildings and rode the elevator down to the basement. Ellie followed silently behind. Her defiant posture had weakened slightly, and her face showed she understood what was really going on here and what might be about to happen.

The temperature in the basement was icebox cold. Summer wrapped her arms around herself. I spoke to the guy sitting at the desk.

He interrupted abruptly. "You family?"

I didn't want to give away too much. "I won't know until I see her."

"Cops call you?"

I shook my head.

"Then you can't—"

I didn't have time to argue. I pulled out my wallet, flipped it open, and laid my credentials on the countertop.

He nodded, raised both eyebrows, and wrapped a bracelet around my wrist. I pointed to Summer. "She's with me."

The guy wrapped a bracelet around Summer's wrist. I turned to Ellie and pointed to the waiting area. "You mind?"

She sat without protest.

The attendant pushed open the door and led us down a hall to a room where the temperature was colder still and the smell reminded me of dissection lab in high school. He opened the door, and we walked in to find six bodies covered in blue sheets on tables. Summer sucked in a deep breath and covered her heart with one hand. The bumps beneath the sheets suggested three men and three women. He pointed to the far left.

Summer walked to the table slowly. Unsteady. Her hands shaking. Torment rippled across her face. As we stood over the body, Summer began making a low, almost inaudible moan. The man placed his hand on the sheet and slowly pulled it back, revealing the face.

Summer crumpled, tried to suck in a breath of air but sat, unable to finish it. For over a minute, no air and no sound emitted from her lungs. As veins bulged on both temples and tears and snot poured from her eyes and nose, Summer let out some fraction of the pain buried in her womb. The cry lasted a long time. It echoed off the walls, the stainless steel tables, the tile floor, and the ceramic sinks.

I looked at the man and shook my head.

The body on the table was not Angel.

He returned the sheet over the woman's face. I lifted Summer off the floor and carried her to the elevator, where we rode to the surface.

The human body does not like pain. Either physical or emotional. In order to protect ourselves, our bodies do stuff that sometimes we can't control. Especially when that pain is intense. Somewhere en route to the elevator, Summer's body had had enough. She passed out, falling limp in my arms and becoming deadweight.

Ellie followed as I carried Summer to a bench beside a fountain. Ellie asked one of the nurses for a bag of ice, which we placed on the back of Summer's neck. Minutes later, her eyes opened.

She sat for a long moment, shaking her head. Finally, she lay back down and curled into a ball. She spoke to whoever would listen. "I'm sorry. I'm sorry for everything I've ever done wrong in my life. I'm sorry for every—"

Words wouldn't help this. I wrapped an arm around her and held her while she tried to make sense of the nonsensical. Finally, the emotion overwhelmed the words and she just wept.

CHAPTER 19

Ellie sat and I held Summer while she emptied herself. It wasn't pretty. An hour passed. Toward lunch, my phone rang. Colorado again. Soon as I answered, he launched in. "*Fire and Rain* is docked in West Palm. Taking on crew and fueling as we speak."

"Where?"

"Just sent you the location."

The world was spinning pretty fast. I needed to focus. To think beyond today. "You got any room out there?"

"What?" He chuckled. "You mean like available rooms?"

He knew what I was asking. "If I find Angel—"

"What about her mom?"

I studied Summer. "Yeah, probably her too."

He continued, "You know I do."

"Can you send the—"

He interrupted me. "Already there. West Palm Executive. Parked in hangar number two."

I studied the world around me. "Thanks. I'm not sure how long any of this will take."

"We never do."

I hung up and spoke to Summer. "I think we found the boat."

She stood, wobbled, and caught her balance. "I'm going with you."

"I think—"

141

She cut me off and something chiseled her face. As if it were cut from stone. She spoke through gritted teeth. "I'm going with you." I tried to object, but she was having none of it. "Murph, or whatever your name is—" She gripped my bicep like a vise. "I'm with you." While I heard her voice, my mind was focused on her hand squeezing my arm and the absence of fingernails.

She'd bitten them to the quick.

I turned to Ellie. "What about you?"

She pointed over her shoulder. "I'll stay here."

"You got any money for food?"

"Maybe."

I handed her several twenty-dollar bills. "If you think of it, you might take Clay something as well. He looks like he could eat."

Ellie pocketed the money, suggesting she had agreed to stay with Clay and Gunner. As Summer and I walked out of the hospital, footsteps sounded behind us. I turned to find Ellie staring up at me. A question in her eyes. It was the first sign of weakness I'd detected.

In my line of work, I'd encountered my fair share of the abandoned. The forgotten. I'd done my time on the island of misfit toys. And in my time on that beach, I'd learned something. Rejection is the deepest wound of the human soul. Bar none. And only one thing can heal it.

When Ellie opened her mouth, she exposed that wound. Her voice was weak. Unsure. "You coming back?"

I stepped toward her. "Yes."

She half turned but then turned back. "You lying?"

"No."

"Prove it."

I took off Fingers' Rolex and held it up. "You know what this is?"

She eyed it and nodded.

I clasped it about her wrist. "I want it back."

I turned to go but then thought better of it. I held up a single finger and motioned for her to do the same.

She protested. "What?"

"I'm wanting you to touch my fingertip with the tip of yours."

"I'm not a real touchy-feely kind of person."

I knew this. I waited. Both my silence and my waiting were purposeful.

Finally, she held up her finger and touched the tip of mine. With my index finger extended, I uncurled the other four fingers, leaving my palm facing outward toward her and all five fingers extended. At my prodding, she mirrored my hand, allowing our five fingertips to touch. Finally, I pressed my palm and fingers flat against hers, then slowly curled our fingers together. Locking hands.

She looked at our two hands the way people inspect their cars after a hit-and-run.

"Is this supposed to mean something to me?"

"Years ago, I was trying to find a little girl. When I did, she was scared and it was dark. There were some bad men trying to find us, so I had to leave her and find them before they found us. There was the chance that I might not make it back." I motioned to our hands. "When I returned in the dark, I stretched out my hand. Speaking without opening my mouth. Over the years, it's become a thing."

She let go and wiped her hand on her jeans. "Now that we've had our little moment, if you don't come back, I'm keeping the watch." Admiring my several-thousand-dollar dive watch, she walked through the automatic doors and disappeared inside the hospital.

I deliberated taking a car to get there faster, but that brought about two problems. First, I didn't have one. Second, if *Fire and Rain* cast off from her mooring, I'd need *Gone Fiction* to follow.

We returned to the dock where *Gone Fiction* floated expectantly. Feeling somewhat guilty for how I'd neglected him, I lashed Fingers' orange lunch box to the underside of the T-top so he could look down on the world. Given that you couldn't really see him unless you were looking for him, I thought maybe I'd just leave him there for the duration. Directly above my head. Three minutes later, we idled out of the yacht club and into the no-wake zone.

Summer stood close, biting what remained of her fingernails. She'd start to say something, then swallow it. She did this several times before I looked at her, inviting the question.

She whispered, "Priest?"

Her face betrayed both disappointment and curiosity. I wasn't sure where she was going with this, so I dodged it. "I don't follow you."

"The morgue. Your wallet. That guy took one look and—"

"Oh." I couldn't tell if she was irritated or amused, so I downplayed it. "Short question. Long answer."

She waited.

"It was a long time ago."

She thumbed over her shoulder toward the morgue. "Evidently not."

She wrapped an arm around my waist. I answered while not answering. "I'm also a priest. Or . . . I was."

"I thought once a priest always a priest."

I shrugged. "I'm in a bit of a gray area."

"Why?"

"Priests don't do what I've done."

"You want to talk about it?"

"Not really."

"Why?"

This conversation was moving fast. "You ask a lot of questions."

"Well . . . ?"

"You won't like the answer or me."

"Why?"

"It's painful."

She stared out across the water. "In case you haven't noticed, we're swimming in pain right now."

She was right, and maybe none more so than herself. "Maybe some other time."

She smiled. "There it is again."

"What?"

"That thing you do where you avoid the tough questions I'm asking you."

She leaned against me, pressing her heart to my shoulder. Not speaking as the keel sliced the water. Still not satisfied, she turned to me and held up her hand, a single finger extended—just like I'd done with Ellie. Then, with her palm facing outward, she extended all five fingers, eventually resting them on my chest. Having mimicked the hand motion, she stood with her index finger extended like E.T. Waiting. "There's more to this, isn't there?"

"Yes."

"What's it mean?"

I spoke as our fingertips touched. "The needs of the one . . ." When all five fingertips touched, I pressed my palm to hers and our fingers interlocked. Her hand felt strong. "Outweigh the needs of the many."

She waited. Baiting me for more. She leaned closer, her face inches from mine. Breath on my face. She had yet to let go of my hand, and I could tell she liked being in my space. She found comfort there. "Are you?"

"Am I what?"

"Going to find the one."

"Working on it."

She shook her head but didn't back up. Still bathing me in breath. Sweat. And the smell of woman. "Why? Why you? Why not—" She waved her hand across the earth. "Some other schmuck out there?"

The no-wake zone ended. I turned to her and spoke as the names flashed across the backs of my eyelids and I pressed the throttle forward. "I don't know that I have an answer for that. Maybe I got tired of waiting."

Sensing that we were now swimming beneath the surface, she didn't speak. Just waited. Finally, she offered, "In my experience, men who say things like that seldom, or never, back them up. They chicken out when it comes time to pay the bill."

A dozen or so places on my body began hurting simultaneously. I turned the wheel slightly. "It can be costly."

She was playing with me now. Still invading my personal space. "What's it cost you?"

I slid my shirtsleeve to the elbow and exposed a long scar that traveled nearly to my wrist. "Knife." I lifted my pant leg and pointed to a scar mid-shin. "Sudden impact with the ground after I jumped out of a third-story window and my shinbone poked through the skin after it snapped." I pressed my left ear forward, allowing her to see the long scar behind my ear. "Jumper cables." Those were probably enough, so I fell quiet. The complexion of her eyes changed as she looked at me.

She glanced at my ear. "Jumper cables?"

I nodded.

"You're serious?"

"Yes."

"What? How?"

I chuckle. "Somebody was attempting to jump-start the truth out of me."

"You're playing with me, aren't you?"

"No, I'm trying to talk about something I don't want to talk about."

She nodded. "I guess I had that coming."

Hidden in the safety of the eye of the hurricane, Summer wrapped both hands around my waist, pressed her chest to mine, and kissed my cheek. Then the corner of my mouth. Her lips were tender. While my heart fluttered, fear flooded me. I'd been down this road. I'd seen what we were about to see. Angel could be dead. Or worse, about to be dead after having been violated by God knows how many men. To Summer, Angel was her daughter. The product of her womb. Bone of her bone. To the men who held her, she was property. Worth about as much as the wrapper on a candy bar. And while Summer was hopeful, sometimes the end of this road was real bad. Sometimes where we were headed and what we were about to see were the two most awful things any human would ever witness.

CHAPTER 20

With one no-wake zone following another, the trip south took an hour. We passed through Juno Beach and under US1 and were about to turn into the northern tip of Lake Worth when we saw *Fire and Rain* moored inside the Old Port Cove Marina. She was in a slip at the end of the dock made for hundred-plus-foot yachts. We circled around her, but I didn't like it.

The marina was a safe-harbor marina, meaning the water was calm and protected. It also meant one way in and one way out, so I returned to the IC, cut the wheel north, and then slipped into the narrow channel leading into a cul-de-sac of sorts that gave water access to about a dozen homes. I docked on the bulkhead but knew it wouldn't last long. The first homeowner to catch us would have us towed. My hope was that we could get in and get out before somebody noticed, but this was West Palm. I had my doubts.

We tied up, walked around a pool, over a chain-link fence, through a parking lot, across Lakeshore Drive, and into the parking lot of the marina. Fortunately, the dock was empty of people save a few crew members washing various boats. We walked past the harbormaster's office, alongside the dock house, and onto the dock for about two hundred feet before ending at a ninety-degree corner. The dock was wide enough for a golf cart, which is the case with most high-end marinas. We turned right, walking in between boats ranging from fifty feet to well over a hundred.

Her bow pointed south. An ominous compass needle. The Intracoastal Waterway south of Jupiter Island is where the wealthy bring out their toys. They may invest in homes, but their boats are where they brag. And *Fire and Rain* was no different. She was on display for all the world to see, which suggested she was empty.

Summer and I started making our way down the boardwalk. In order to minimize suspicion, I held her hand—just two lovers on a walk. She adopted the ruse and leaned into me—although I wondered if the leaning was ruse or need. We stopped at a waterside café and bought two coffees, giving ourselves a few moments to study the decks. The boat was quiet, but its tinted windows made it impossible to determine who, if anyone, stirred inside.

Walking alone and blind into a boat manned by bad men was one thing. Walking into the same boat with an unsuspecting woman was something else entirely. I gave her one last chance. "You can stay here."

She gritted her teeth. "Not a chance."

We stepped onto the aft deck and walked up the stairs and into the main salon. She was nicely appointed. Mahogany. Marble. Granite. China. Crystal. No expense spared. Unlike the first boat, this one was a bit cleaner. Not clean, of course; just cleaner. There had been a party here but with some restraint. Which possibly suggested wealthier clientele.

Summer followed me as we began searching the staterooms, galley, lower level, crew cabins, guest cabins, upper level, and helm. Finding the boat empty, I began filtering through drawers. Turned out, *Fire and Rain* was owned by a company out of Australia and rented for $42,500 per week. Sifting back through the bedrooms, I turned on every electronic screen I could find. My guess was that these guys were paying that bill by bringing paying customers aboard in one port and dropping them off at the next— allowing them time and freedom to purchase what they wanted while aboard. A flesh buffet. One swipe with Amex Black. In my experience, men who did what these men were doing liked to have a record of it. Which meant video. Most men were careful to take the evidence with them as a memento when they disembarked, but copies were often made, and copies had a way of multiplying. I also took note of the multiple closed-circuit television cameras pointed at us. Every room, every hallway contained a camera. All of that data had to be going somewhere. I had a feeling it was live-streaming off the ship at that very moment, but every camera had a backup. It's just the nature of electronics.

I returned to the main stateroom. Decadence defined. I turned on the TV and then rummaged through the external inputs—one of which was labeled "Library." Didn't take long to find the list of last week's videos.

I turned to Summer. "I'm pretty sure you don't want to watch these." I was certain I didn't either.

She crossed her arms.

There were sixty-some videos in just this one library. I did not like this aspect of my life. No matter how many times I had come upon just such a cache, I still had a tough time removing these images from my mind. They didn't titillate me. Didn't entertain me. Didn't excite me. They made me want to vomit. I didn't want to see them. Ever. And these men were the sickest among us. Animals. While the slave trade was abolished in England in the nineteenth century, it was alive and kicking in the twenty-first.

The only help I had was the fast-forward feature or the 4x scan. I began scanning through the videos, which were a wealth of information. The traders—the guys who ran this ship of flesh—cycled the men through the girls at one-, two-, or three-hour intervals. Depending on how much time they bought. For one girl they would charge fifteen hundred to three thousand an hour. Sometimes more. And the girls worked round the clock. Often twelve to fifteen hours a day. Or longer. Multiply that by a dozen or more girls and it's easy math. And that doesn't include the fee just to get on the ship. The buy-in was often several thousand. Ships like this were cash cows. As a result, video quality was high and the length varied.

With each video, Summer's face became more disgusted. Fortunately, Angel's face did not appear in the bedroom videos. We did find her in the hot tub, on the pool deck, on the jet skis, and in the common areas. Upon first glimpse, Summer sucked in a deep breath and covered her mouth. The transformation in her daughter was striking. Angel was noticeably skinnier, the circles beneath her eyes darker. She was living the high life, but for some reason she didn't appear in any of the hourly videos, which meant she hadn't been sold as of yet. Or they were saving her because she had been bought on the black web, and they were waiting for transfer at a safer location. Like a dock in Cuba. Or the Bahamas. Or some other vessel in international waters.

I rummaged through each room, each screen, but found no thumb or hard drives or laptops left behind. In terms of electronic evidence, the boat had been bleached. I climbed down into the engine room, finding nothing of interest there except a lot of cables and wires, including ethernet, routed from the different levels above us into another small room just outside the engine room. The door was locked.

I lifted an ax from the engine room but hesitated. I knew breaking this door meant an alarm would sound, and whoever placed these cameras would probably begin looking at us on a live-feed screen somewhere around the world. I also thought through the process of covering our faces with pillowcases like Casper the ghost, but they'd had us from the moment we'd stepped foot on the aft deck. It was too late for that. Summer, and maybe more importantly Summer and I were now on somebody's radar. Breaking down this door did little to affect that. The only advantage I had was that they didn't know who I was and wouldn't be able to figure that out apart from high-level security clearance. What they would know was that I'd done this before and I was nobody's dummy. They'd be less inclined to leave the boat unattended in the future, which meant life was about to become more difficult.

I swung through the door, splintering the area around the knob. Two more swings and I'd loosened it from its hinges. A few more and it swung open. The electronics room was ventilated and cooled and humming with expensive and sophisticated equipment. This was no weekly rental. Two computer processors and four hard drives were hardwired and mounted to a frame that traveled from floor to ceiling. They were not large but they were bolted in, which meant they'd survive rough seas or somebody wanting to steal them. Which I did. Fortunately, I'd seen tools in the engine room that allowed me to unscrew the mounting hardware and place the drives into the tool bag.

It took five minutes.

The moment I finished, footsteps sounded above us. Followed by voices. I turned to Summer. "Stay behind me. Do what I do. And don't hesitate."

She nodded, but the fear had crept in.

I climbed the stairwell and was met by a smaller man with a loud mouth and a lot of hand motions. He was screaming at me. Behind him, two more men appeared. They were not small. Nor were they loud. Bears wearing suits. If he was the brains, they were the wrecking crew.

I smiled and played the idiot card. "You guys are all finished up, but you might think about replacing it in the next year. Salt water and satellites don't really mix." I kept walking toward the aft deck while Summer followed me. Little Man stepped in front of me, and I continued the ruse by handing the tool bag to Summer. "Put that in the truck and I'll finish the paperwork." She walked through the sliding-glass door, where a fourth man stood. She skirted around him, but he put a hand on her arm.

Time was short now. Measured in seconds. The chances that one or all four had weaponry were near one hundred percent. Chances they knew how to use it were higher. With no desire to be a hero, I raised a finger to the fourth guy, who was looking at me through the glass.

Flesh is serious business, and Summer was about to learn. Fights are never fun and seldom does anyone win. Even when you win. I would have the element of surprise, but that was about it.

I stepped around Little Man, who didn't like me dissing him—but the fourth man had one hand inside his jacket. I slid out the door with an ear-to-ear smile on my face and said with a stutter, "H-h-h-hey, you s-s-sign this paperwork for me?"

A Glock 17 is not a fancy or flashy weapon, but it is effective. Maybe one of the most effective. Ever. Somewhere around sixty percent of all law enforcement agencies on the planet use it. And while the 9x19mm Parabellum projectile is a deterrent in its own right, so is looking down the barrel. Of any weapon. Especially if you've been shot by one.

He aimed it at me but he still had one hand on Summer, so his grip was weak. I broke his elbow and then his wrist. The pain of that breaking caused an accidental discharge, sending the chambered round through the floor and into the engine room. Whether it continued through the hull and into the water was anybody's guess, but I doubted it. With a broken wing, the goon wasn't much of a threat, so I took the Glock and beat him in the face with it.

Both the sound of the shot and the speed with which I moved stunned little Napoleon, who paused. Asking himself who I thought I was. His hesitation gave me the second I needed to slide in underneath and hip-toss him overboard. This dramatic movement brought the two circus bears running, and they weren't as stupid.

When the first charged me, I slid the glass door more toward the closed position. With as much mass as he was carrying, it was tough to slow down, so his head went through the glass—which was good for me and not so good for him. While he bled across the aft deck and cussed my entire lineage, starting with my mother, the remaining muscle, who looked more like a block of granite than a human, saw that the commotion had gained the attention of some deckhands walking our direction. Figuring gunplay was not wise, he pulled a knife.

I hate knives.

Almost as much as guns.

Sixty seconds later, we were still standing. I was bleeding, but he was both bleeding and broken. I finally shattered his left knee, he dropped the knife, and I hopped off the aft deck and onto the boardwalk where Summer waited. Shaking. Sirens sounded in the distance. Incidentally, the man I threw overboard had not landed in the water. He'd landed on a smaller boat. Somewhere between the T-top and the polling platform. He had yet to move, but judging from the twisted look of his legs, plus the unnatural sight of bone sticking through his pant leg, moving wouldn't be fun.

The whole mess would be reported. If we weren't on their radar before, we were certainly on it now.

I grabbed Summer's hand and started to return up the dock when we saw that our four friends had driven a golf cart. Which we stole. The last thing I wanted was for any of them to see us getting into *Gone Fiction*, so I drove past the dock house, under the nose of the harbormaster, and out into the parking lot while Summer clutched both the tool bag and me. We crossed Lakeshore Drive, sped through another parking lot, and abandoned the cart next to the fence, which Summer hopped and I fell over. I made it through the grass and into *Gone Fiction* about the time my adrenaline dump ended.

Over the last few minutes, I'd paid little attention to my body, but apparently the guy with the knife had been a surgeon in a former life. I was swiss cheese, bleeding everywhere. I cranked the engine, turned the wheel, and we pulled out of the cul-de-sac and back under US1. A glance behind us showed no one, but I had to assume someone was watching us leave.

Fortunately, the marina had been positioned at the end of a no-wake zone, so I put *Gone Fiction* up on plane—and only then took a look at myself. He had cut me six times that I could count, and I wasn't sure about my back. The deck of *Gone Fiction* was running red. Summer was about to hyperventilate when I asked her to hold pressure on two gushers as we made our way north.

In the delirium of moments of high stress, I often focus on the comical. I can't explain that, but it's how my body deals with stress. As Summer held pressure on my wounds, I had an odd sensation that she was playing whack-a-mole. Every time she stopped the bleeding at one spot, it would surface at another.

We passed under PGA Boulevard and around Seminole Marina and then wound our way a few miles north to the Jupiter Yacht Club and Best Western Intracoastal Inn. I pulled on my Gore-Tex rain jacket so I wouldn't scare people, and we walked to the office. Summer paid, got two room keys, and, carrying my first aid kit, led me to a room facing the Intracoastal. Had I not been leaking like a sieve, it would have been a nice room. We could step out our door and right into the IC.

CHAPTER 21

Standing in the shower, I pulled off my jacket and shirt and let the warm water wash the red off me while Summer found the source of each wound. Then she began pouring hydrogen peroxide on my hands, forearms, biceps, and chest. Evidently I had more than six cuts. When I turned my back to her, she gasped, covered her mouth, and recoiled in both horror and surprise.

In the several days we'd known each other, she'd never seen me without a shirt. I had some explaining to do.

She was crying, so I turned and held her hands with mine while I bled into the drain.

Her eyes were darting, tears were falling, and she was shaking her head slowly from side to side. On the verge of cracking. I cupped her hands in mine, took the bloody rag from her, and said, "Hey."

She looked at me, but she wasn't really looking.

"It would be really nice, before I bleed to death in this hotel room, if you could help me out."

Her eyes were wide and she made no response.

"If I turn back around, do you think you could try to stop the bleeding?"

She bit her lip and nodded. When I turned, she sucked in another involuntary breath of air and attempted to compose herself. After a moment, I felt her touching my back. Moving from point of pain to point of pain. "Did I do this?"

I shook my head and smiled, "No, the guy with the knife did." I rinsed the rag and handed it to her. She whispered, "And the scars?"

A forced laugh. "They were there before. It's the nature of a scar."

She washed over them with the rag. "What caused them?"

I weighed my head side to side, trying to decide how to answer. "Remember that price we were talking about?"

She nodded, slowly touching each of the scars. "But . . . ?"

I spoke slowly. "Bullets . . . exiting my body."

I could feel her fingers tracing the lines on my back. "And . . . the tattoos?"

Over the last twenty years, my back had been tattooed with a long list of names in paragraph form stretching from the edge of my left shoulder blade to the edge of my right shoulder blade. By now the paragraph was thirty lines and eight inches long. An ink column down my spine.

Her lips moved as she read each name out loud. One after another. "There must be a hundred . . ."

I spoke without looking at her. I knew them by heart and in order. "Two hundred and twelve."

"Who are they?"

When I answered, the remaining stones of a wall she'd erected to protect herself from me shattered in a pile of rubble at our feet. If we'd been staring through the window at the table set before us, we were now seated. White tablecloth. Buffet before us. The faces attached to each of the names flashed across my mind's eye. Each distinct. Each anchored in time and place. The pain returned beneath the scars. As did the laughter, the screams, and the silence. I shifted beneath their weight. "Daughters. Friends. Moms. Broken children like . . ."

She stood, holding one hand over her mouth, tears streaming down her face. "Angel?"

I shook my head. "Like you and me."

She dropped her hands and wrapped her arms around my stomach, pressing her chest to my back. Holding me and wanting to be held. She spoke with her face to my back while I bled. "Tell me about them?"

"What do you want to know?"

She read the sixth name on the third line. "Fran McPherson."

"Number thirty-six. Fourteen at the time of her disappearance. Taken from a Boston school bus stop. Sold in southwest Texas. We stole her back in Mexico. She's now married with two boys. Husband is an architect."

"Blythe Simpson."

"Fifty-eighth. Seventeen at the time. Not real compliant until it got real bad because she was having too much fun. Last seen in Chicago. We found her in New Orleans. Spent a couple years in rehab. Talented artist. Overdosed eleven years ago. Opioids."

She dragged her finger gently up my back and whispered, "Melody Baker."

"Number seven. Twelve years old. New York City. Taken out through the window of a movie theater bathroom while her parents shared a bucket of popcorn. We lost the trail in Managua, Nicaragua. Her body was found on the shoreline by fishermen a hundred miles away."

Summer swallowed and said, "Kim Blackman."

"One hundred and eighty-third. Eight years old. Taken in Dallas. Day care. Flown to Seattle. Later to Brazil. A year later, I found her in a hospital in South Africa. She died six hours later."

I felt her finger move across my skin. "Amanda Childs."

"Two hundred and fifth. Thirteen at the time, which was three years ago. Still missing."

Summer stood crying. Finally, she moved her finger to a single name, tattooed at the base of my neck, above the paragraph. While the names had been tattooed in script, this word had been etched in small, bold block letters. Her question fell to a broken whisper. "Apollumi?"

"It's a Greek word. It means 'that which was lost.' Or 'to perish . . . die.'"

"Why?"

"It's a reminder."

"Of?"

"The consequences."

"Of what?"

"Not going."

Summer hugged me from behind again. "And Angel? Where will you put her name?"

I turned. "We'll find—"

Her eyes narrowed and she pressed her finger to my lips. "How do you know?"

I wrapped my hands around her arms.

She was shaking her head when she spoke. "She's already gone, isn't she? I'm living in a fairy tale."

"No. She's not."

"She's gone, isn't she?"

I held her by the arms. "Summer."

She wouldn't look at me.

"Summer!"

Her eyes found mine. She was cracking.

"You have to let me do what I do. She's not gone. Not yet. If she were, I'd tell you. It would hurt too much not to." I looked around. "We've got a couple of problems and I need to get to work on them. And I need your help. Starting with not bleeding to death. You standing here crying and me bleeding does no good. Just makes you tired and me weak."

She stared at my back. "How do you live this way? Why not just move on? Forget. Live your life."

I shook my head once. "Once you step foot into this world, there is no moving on. No forgetting." I tapped my back. "No matter what happened to put them on the list, no matter what they might have done or not done, these are people. They laugh. Hurt. Cry. Hope. Dream. Love. I wrote them in ink so I won't ever forget. They go where I go. Always." Blood dripped onto the floor. Dark red, warm, and sticky. A single tear drained out of my eye and mixed with the mess on the floor. "These are the names I carry."

CHAPTER 22

S ummer had sewn her fair share of costumes both on and off Broadway, which proved helpful. Once she had closed all the leaks in my hull—a phrase that had caused her to laugh the most delightful laugh—she brought me some clean clothes from *Gone Fiction* and we returned to the dock. One of our biggest problems had to be addressed quickly.

I couldn't guarantee that no one had seen *Gone Fiction* as we pulled out of that harbor. If the harbormaster had seen us, he'd know what type of boat we were in. A Whaler like mine is easy to spot. The lines of the Dauntless are distinctive. If you know boats, chances are good you can pick mine out of a crowd. If I was smart I would abandon her, walk away, and find another. But I was short on time and we had too much history. I could no more abandon *Gone Fiction* than I could cut out my own heart. Too many miles traveled.

I returned to the marina where I pointed to the "Marine Wrap" sign and asked the guy working, "You do that?" Marine wrapping is something akin to vacuum wrapping really tough plastic wrap around a boat. Most guys do it to advertise a brand name, but it also protects the hull from pretty much anything. It can also affect the speed for the better, at least until something tears the wrap.

He spoke without taking his eyes off the Yamaha he was working on. "Yeah."

I pointed to *Gone Fiction*. "How long would it take you?"

158

"What do you want done?"

"Solid color. Complete wrap. Just something to protect her."

"T-top, motor, hull, everything?"

"You got time?"

"Yeah, but it'll be next week."

I pulled out a wad of hundreds and he quit working on the Yamaha. I licked my thumb and started pulling them off one by one. "Would tonight be too soon?"

He wiped greasy hands on a rag and stared at the money.

I said, "How much you make in a week?"

"A grand." That was probably the truth.

I handed him a thousand dollars. "Another thousand if you can finish her tonight and I can roll out of here tomorrow morning."

He took the money and started studying my boat. "Done."

I pulled out another three hundred dollars. "You got a car I can borrow?"

He pointed at a Tacoma. "Keys are in it."

I gave him the money. "I might be gone a few hours."

"No hurry." He took off his cap, glanced at the coffee maker, and smiled. "I'll be up awhile."

While Summer went to find something to eat, I opened my laptop and began searching the hard drives we'd stolen from *Fire and Rain*. There were hundreds of videos, which mandated a rather sophisticated video monitoring and recording system. All total, I counted fifteen girls, multiple clients, and lots of traffic. In business terms, this was a well-oiled machine, and I felt my anger rise with each new face. I was also careful with the drives, producing backups—both in hard copy and on the cloud. Each video would serve as nails in the coffin of a courtroom conviction, no matter how much power or money these animals once had.

Each of the sick and twisted men I saw on video believed his past lay behind him. Buried. Hidden. Each was currently walking about the earth with a smile on his face. Having gotten away with it. Going about his everyday life as if he'd made a run to the grocery store to buy butter. But in the next few hours, I was going to pass these videos to a group of people who had made a career of putting guys like that in dark cells the rest of their natural lives. And prison is not kind to men who take advantage of young girls.

There is courtroom justice, and then there is prison justice.

Angel appeared often in the common areas of the boat but never with a client. The two men I'd seen on the *Sea Tenderly* when she'd docked at my island were regulars in the videos but never with the girls. Professionals, they didn't sample. Lastly, the cameras had recorded Summer and me as we'd stepped on the boat, following us throughout our journey. I guessed that one of the four men we'd met had been watching a live feed. I doubted the hard drives I now held were the only backup, but with that much video, it would take a long time to upload to the cloud. That meant there was a chance, albeit small, that the flesh drivers did not have a record of Summer and me. Only what the four guys could remember seeing.

As I expected, each video had a GPS signature. I opened Google Maps and began entering the coordinates for the video signatures. The results told me what I already knew: that *Fire and Rain* had motored south down the IC without stopping, which meant they used tenders to ferry customers to and from the moving vessel—which again suggested a well-oiled machine and a rather effective word-of-mouth advertising campaign. It also meant they'd done it before. That the customers knew about the boat and were expecting to be contacted. What I wanted was that list of customers—the names.

While most of the longitudes and latitudes formed a series of satellite bread crumbs moving down the IC, one coordinate stood out. It looked like a house along the water where the vessel had moored for a couple of hours.

I saved the coordinates in my phone.

Summer returned with lunch while I took screen shots and cut the videos into shorter three- and five-second videos that showed clear faces and features. Just enough for identification. I uploaded it all to a Dropbox account, sent my contact the link, and dialed his number. He answered quickly. I put him on speakerphone this time so Summer could hear. There was a ping-pong game in full volley in the background, including the sound of laughing women.

He spoke without waiting on me. "My fun-meter tells me you bumped into some trouble."

"Same stuff. Different day."

"You hurt?"

"Summer closed the leaks in my hull."

Summer laughed again. And the sound was even more delightful. Almost medicinal.

He paused. "Summer?"

"Long story."

"You're good at those."

"You're on speaker. Say hi."

Summer waved at the phone and said, "Hello."

I could hear him smiling. He liked it when I came out of my shell and interacted with other humans. It meant something in me was alive. "Summer, everybody round here calls me Bones. Nice to make your acquaintance. A friend of Murph's is a friend of mine. You need me, you call me. I have two words of caution, and you should listen because I know what I'm talking about." Summer sat upright. He continued, "Don't let him get you on the back of a motorcycle. He's an idiot and can't drive one to save his life. And whatever you do, I don't care how he makes it sound enticing or if it's the end of the world and the last meal on planet earth, don't—under any circumstance—let him cook anything. Ever."

She laughed.

I said, "We're in that uneasy lull when a whole lot can go wrong and a little bit can go right."

He knew what I meant, but he was being cute for Summer. "Meaning?"

"Meaning I just sent you a link. There are fifteen new faces and I think the number is growing. Somebody, somewhere is looking for them."

"We're on it."

"They are not going to take kindly to my busting up their boat and taking their drives. These guys are smart, financed, and they won't sit. They may well move. Possibly even split up. We may have hurt ourselves more than helped."

"The trader's dilemma."

Summer looked confused. "What's he mean?"

I spoke loud enough for Bones to hear. "It means the guys who do this live in this tension: at the first sign of trouble, do they wholesale everything and disappear, ensuring they're not caught and they can live to trade another day? Or do they continue doing what they're doing, shake the money tree for all it's worth, make as much cash as possible, and try to stay one step ahead of us?"

Bones picked up where I left off. "Choosing the latter means doubling, tripling, or even quadrupling their money. And we're not talking chump change."

I continued, "Just do what you do and get back to me. I just uploaded the videos and will FedEx the actual drives to you soon as I eat something. I found nothing on the boat to tell me where they're going, and other than a GPS signature on a couple of the videos that suggest where the boat spent a few hours, my trail is cold. Ask the guys to listen closely to the audio. And bring in Nadia. She speaks Russian."

"I've already forwarded the link. Get me the drives."

Before he hung up, he paused. "Summer?"

She leaned in closer. "Yes?"

He spoke with the gentleness for which he was so well known and loved. "What's your daughter's name?"

Summer's eyes watered. She leaned in close to the phone and whispered, "Angel."

"Ah . . ." I could hear him scratching his chin. "It's a good name. Was she on that boat?"

"Yes."

He must have moved inside, because the background noise grew distant and muted. "How well do you know Murphy?"

She looked at me. "I've known him for about four days."

"Has he let you read his book?"

I stiffened.

"It's etched across his back."

I breathed out.

She glanced at me. "Read? No, but I did glance at it."

"I realize there's not much I can say to make you feel better in this moment, but you might ask him to tell you the stories of 87 and 204."

Her eyes found mine. "Okay."

"And don't let him leave out the good part."

She continued looking at me but spoke to the phone. "What's the good part?"

He chuckled. "You'll know it when you hear it." He paused. This time speaking to me. "You going to check out that GPS location?"

I nodded but not for his benefit. "Shortly."

"Want me to send some help?"

"Maybe when I leave. Let me snoop around first. There's always the chance we get lucky."

"Watch yer top knot."

"Watch your'n."

He hung up. And I unwrapped my Publix sub. One of my simple pleasures in life. I was starving. Summer looked confused. "Top knot?"

I spoke around a ginormous bite of food. "Robert Redford movie. *Jeremiah Johnson.* Something he and I have watched a few dozen times."

"What's it mean?"

"It means don't let somebody with a knife peel the top of your head off while you lie there and scream helplessly."

"Pleasant thought." She pointed at the phone. "Who is he?"

I weighed my head side to side. "Bones is the guy who taught me how to do what I do."

"Where is he?"

"Colorado."

"What exactly does he do?"

"He does a lot, but right this minute he's babysitting."

"You're not going to tell me, are you?"

"Not right now. Sometime. We need to get back to the hospital."

She sat cross-legged, unwrapping her sub. "Eighty-seven?"

"A difficult one. Maybe the most difficult. Teenage daughter of a senator. High profile. We chased her through more states than I can remember.

Then countries. The guy who bought her was wealthy beyond measure and somehow had better intel, so he was always a step ahead of us. But he was also cocky. Which is a bad combination. The trail went cold for weeks, and then one of our guys found a credit card transaction at this remote spa in Switzerland. The receipt included lemonade. We knew it wasn't his. Guy was a health nut and didn't consume sugar. We rented the suite next to his and extracted the girl when he brought in a masseuse."

"How?"

"I was the masseuse."

"And?"

"The little girl and I walked out the front door. She's in college now. Harvard. On the rowing team. Top two or three in her class. Headed to law school. Sends me Snapchat videos."

"And the guy?"

"Confined to a wheelchair. Drinks his meals through a straw. Does not enjoy prison from what I hear."

She chewed silently. "And 204?"

"204 is the mother of 203. Sally Mayfair. She felt somewhat guilty for the circumstances that led to her daughter's disappearance. Felt like she was to blame. She wasn't, but while it's possible to convince the mind, convincing the heart is another thing entirely."

"Why did he suggest I ask you about those?"

"To encourage you. He can't tell you everything will be all right because we don't know. It might not be. It might be really bad. But he was trying, in his honest way, to lift your spirits by telling you that we have found even the most difficult ones."

She raised an eyebrow. "And 204?"

"Most parents feel responsible. Blame themselves. Woulda, coulda, shoulda. He's trying to silence those whispers."

She tilted her head to the side. "You ever going to tell me your real name?"

"It's better for you if I don't."

"And when this is over, will I ever see you again?"

"That's probably more up to you than me."

CHAPTER 23

We overnighted the drives to Colorado and drove the boat mechanic's Tacoma to the hospital, where I heard laughter. Clay was sitting upright in his room. Clear fluids dripping into his left arm. A beautiful nurse taking his blood pressure. He was reclining slightly, legs crossed, a plate of hot food in his lap. Living the good life while entertaining Ellie and his new girlfriend with stories from prison. He looked better. And his laughter was not accompanied by a cough, which meant the steroids had reduced the swelling. Hopefully the antibiotics would work next.

Gunner saw me and launched himself off the ground where he'd lay in vigil next to Clay. The old man looked at the bruising on my face and the stitches on my neck and arms. He sat upright and actually set one foot on the floor as if he were going to a fight. "Looks like you been tangling with some of my friends."

"They had definitely done time." I patted his shoulder and he relaxed. I asked him, "You good?"

At this moment, his twentysomething nurse walked back in carrying another IV bag of fluids. "Yep, I'm about to take my nurse dancing."

I'm not sure of the reason, but people who spend an extended amount of time—and specifically hard time—in prison have an uncanny sense of humor that makes light of even the heavy stuff. It's a beautiful gift. And Clay had it more than any man I'd ever met. Which spoke volumes about the hardness of his time.

I spoke to Clay. "When you finish with your great-granddaughter there, get some sleep. You'll need it. I need to check out an address, but when I return, I'm heading south. You be ready?"

He nodded, laid his head back, and patted the bed next to him where Gunner immediately appeared and curled up into a ball. "I'll be waiting on you."

I look at both Summer and Ellie. "Any way I can convince you two to hang here? I'd better do this alone."

Summer stood. "Not likely."

"How's this going to work if you don't ever do what I ask?"

She put a hand on her hip. "You stop asking and I'll stop telling you no."

Ellie stood next to Summer. "I'm with her."

We returned to the Best Western where my lack of sleep caught up with me. I'd had no rest for a couple of days and been in a pretty good fight, and my body was feeling it. I knew I needed to check that address, but I also knew I'd be no good if I didn't get some sleep. I spoke to the two of them. "I can't keep my eyes open. Maybe sleep an hour or two."

They nodded, but something told me their nodding had less to do with them and a whole lot more to do with me. I rented a second room next to the first, told them good night, and closed the door behind me. I set the thermostat on snow and lay down on the bed. My body hurt, the stitches hurt, and I'd taken more licks in that fight than I cared to admit.

I don't know how long I'd been asleep, but somewhere in the dark someone slid under my sheet and wrapped an arm around my chest, nestled her foot around my leg, and rested her head alongside mine. I woke but didn't stir. I was reminded of that scene in *The Once and Future King* where King Arthur climbs in bed with his wife to celebrate their wedding only to find out the next morning that he'd been tricked by a different woman. My fears were laid to rest when she spoke softly. "Remember how I told you there was more to my and Angel's story?"

I'd had a feeling this was coming. Just not at this moment. "Yes."

"Remember my pharmacist?"

"Yes."

"Over the months, he let me buy on credit. Every three weeks, I'd go through the drive-through, wave, and he just added it to my bill. I told myself I'd do that just until I got my feet back under me. But I'd shredded some ligaments and my pain was high and I needed more than my doctor would prescribe. So one day I said something to him, and he told me he could get me as much as I wanted but the price was a lot higher. And since he was the middleman, he couldn't do anything about that. So the price went from six dollars per pill to sixty dollars per pill, and at this point I'm eating them like Skittles and trying to pay the rent.

"Before I knew it I owed twenty thousand. The interest alone was more than I could service, and his dealer was putting pressure on him. But for months I kept buying. Kept medicating. Kept lying." She made imaginary quotation marks with her fingers. "Just until I get back on my feet. Or my foot." She shook her head. "I was never getting on my feet. That train had left the station.

"To make matters worse, he got transferred and my sweet deal with the pharmacy got noticed, not to mention my bill. Now I owe a lot of money to two people. The pharmacy and the dealer. Neither of which I could pay. The pharmacy passed me off to a collection agency who started calling nonstop and talking about garnishing my wages, and I'm thinking I'm going to lose my studio. And all this time he kept supplying me and never asked me for anything. I mean physical. He was a real gentleman when other guys wouldn't have been. He showed up for his lessons and left the bottle and the payment for his lesson on the counter when he left. Always cash. He was a good bit younger than me, but then he invited me to this get-together with some friends, and when he saw Angel's picture on my desk, he asked if she might like to go. I thought, *Why not?* He was successful, kind, pretty good dancer. Hadn't laid a hand on me. Maybe he had nice friends. What could it hurt?"

She paused as the memory returned. "Pretty soon we were doing dinner, bowling, whatever. Angel would tag along. He was ten or twelve years older than her, and they became friendly but it wasn't like a dating thing. It was more like he became an uncle. Least that's what I told myself. Angel's always had a thing for older men, but I didn't worry too much about him. He was a standup guy. Never laid a hand on me or her. It seemed natural when he started inviting her to parties. He was just including her in a good time. I could tell she was growing to like him, but he looked out for her. She met a lot of his friends. There was always a party. And how could I tell her to lay off the drugs when . . .

"Anyway, he told her about this boat trip he'd been planning for years. He had this rich buddy who had this boat, and they were inviting whoever wanted to come with them. An *Endless Summer* sort of thing. Spend three months in the islands. Scuba. Sun. Sail. Bahamas. Cuba. Wherever the wind blew. I thought it sounded like a great adventure, and I certainly couldn't afford to pay for her to do anything like that.

"They kept hanging out, but then some strange things started to happen. Like she had a personality transplant or something. I couldn't seem to find my daughter. I mean, there was somebody who looked like her living in my house, but her heart was someplace else. Half the time Angel was screaming at me and it was almost as if something had turned her against me. I couldn't put my finger on it. I was telling her to be careful and she was accusing me of being a helicopter mom. Then we had a fight 'cause I was getting cold feet about her boat trip and she'd made plans to go and these new friends were expecting her—and then the next week, without explanation, this guy, he just canceled my bill. All of it. Zero. Problem disappeared. With both his dealer and the pharmacy. Told me he had several friends who were in the same boat, and this wealthy friend of his didn't want any of the parents of the kids on his boat to worry about their kids while they were gone—that somebody had done him a favor one time and he just 'took care of it.' Called it 'debt forgiveness.'"

"How much?"

"Not quite forty."

Her hand was trembling. I let her talk. "And if I'm being honest . . ." A moment passed. "I knew when he came to me and said he'd canceled my bill that it was payment. Payment for Angel and the summer and the boat trip."

She whispered, "I sold her." She waited a second, then said it again. Punishing herself even more. "I sold my own daughter." She was quiet for several minutes before she continued. "Can you believe a mother would do that? That I'm so demented and desperate that I'd sell my own daughter to pay my drug bill?"

I lay on my back and put my arm around her while she sobbed on my chest. After several minutes, she sat up cross-legged. She wiped her face and turned to me. "Is there a special place in hell for people like me?"

I turned on a light. "Tell me how you hurt your ankle."

She looked surprised. "I was getting in my car at the grocery store. Sitting in the driver's seat, one leg sort of hanging out the door while I set the bags on the passenger seat. A lady's cart got away from her, slammed into my door, and the door closed hard on my ankle. It swelled up like a cantaloupe."

"And when did this guy come to your studio for lessons?"

"That afternoon."

"And when did he happen to mention that he worked for a pharmaceutical company? That his area of specialty was pain management?"

She nodded. "Said he had worked in physical therapy before going back to pharmacy school. He looked at my ankle. Gentle. Caring. Gave me something for the pain. Didn't charge me."

"Does any of this strike you as coincidence?"

She thought about it. "Not really."

"That's why people like them prey on people like you. 'Cause you don't think like them. You believe people are good and so are their intentions. Let me ask you this—if you were a bad person, looking to lift little girls, and you wanted to reduce the number of parents who were looking for them, would you do what he did? Remove suspicion and cause them to feel somehow indebted? Guilty even?"

"You think—"

"You were set up. Happens all the time. It's all part of the emotional warfare that takes place prior to the abduction."

For the first time, anger swept across her face. "You mean—"

"It was never about you. It's always been about Angel. You just fit the profile. They'd probably been studying you for weeks. And they sure as shooting slammed the car door on your ankle when the opportunity presented itself."

She sat back as the pieces of the puzzle fell into place. She shook her head. "What kind of sicko—"

"The kind that trades in people."

Moments passed. "Why?"

"There is no good answer to that. They're just evil."

She was quiet for a moment. "I need to know if you think worse of me. Am I defective goods?"

The question did not surprise me. I'd heard it before. More than once. "Why?"

"'Cause I'm a good mom. Not perfect, but I love my daughter and—"

"My answer will only convince your mind. Not your heart. And that's the answer that matters. So give it time . . ."

"What happens when we find her?"

"That will go one of two ways. We snatch her back, which will be more difficult now that they know we're looking. Or we are willing to pay more than someone else."

"You mean like actually pay money?"

I nodded.

"What will that cost?"

I stared at her. Then out the window. "Everything."

CHAPTER 24

My phone rang. My faceplate read "1:47 a.m." I tried to answer it, but even though it was ringing, no one was calling. That's when it occurred to my foggy brain that my other phone was ringing. I answered the sat phone. "Hello?"

Her voice was loud, obnoxious and slurred. "Padre! Whussup?!"

Summer heard Angel's unmistakable voice and sat upright. Eyes wide. I tried to get her talking. "I was hoping you'd call. You having fun?"

"You should see this place. It's off the . . . off the train."

Evidently the pharmacist was keeping her highly medicated. "I'd love to see it."

"You should come join us. I'm a good kiss . . ." She trailed off.

With my other hand, I dialed my cell phone, and when he answered in Colorado, Summer gave him the number Angel was currently using to call me. I tried to keep her talking while he located it. "Tell me about it."

"It's this cabin."

"You're not on a boat?"

"No. We got off the boat."

"When?"

"I don't know. What is this? Twenty Questions?"

"No, I just thought the boat was the place to be. You know, the bomb."

"No, no, no. Thiz place is the bomb. Out here in the Neverglazed. We rode an airboat with a big-a— Oops. Sorry. Forgot you wear the collar.

Gotta clean up my mouth. Anyway, this boat had a huge plane propeller on the back. Looked like something out of *Indiana Jones*. Then we saw some alligators with some big fri— I mean big teeth, and then we rode on a truck, like the monster kind, tires bigger than me. This is the party of all parties."

"Sounds like it."

I could hear her making noises with her mouth again. "You should meet my momma. She's one he—" She swallowed. "She's a good dancer, but you might have to wait 'til her ankle heals 'cause it's been hurting for a while and she tried to hide it from me. I said some things to her I shouldn't have said." She paused. "Padre? You ever said stuff you wish you hadn't?"

The words returned. "Yes."

Summer covered her mouth to prevent herself from crying out. My cell phone dinged with a text message showing coordinates and a location pin. The text read, "Tough to get to, but it can be done. A little over two hours from where you are now."

I returned to Angel. "Sounds like you've had quite the adventure. Where are you headed next?"

"I don't know. Keys. Islands. Wherever. Why do you care?"

"You called me, remember?"

More mouth noises. "Padre, I'm a good . . ."

Her voice trailed off but the connection stayed live for another few minutes. I could hear her snoring. Other people talking in the background. Music. Laughter. This young girl was in a bad way, and as much as she didn't want to admit it, I think something in her knew she was in over her head.

My friend the mechanic was asleep on a cot in his office. When I walked in, he sat up and wiped his eyes. His hands were paws with layers of muscle. He stood, and I followed him to an enclosed boathouse. *Gone Fiction* sat floating beautifully. An aqua teal color. He had yet to wrap the T-top and motor, but he was close. He'd be finished by morning.

I pointed at his truck. "I need another lift."

He tossed me the keys to his Tacoma. "It's yours. Take it."

"Not sure when I'm getting back. And I don't want to hold you up. You mind chauffeuring? I'll pay."

He laid down a box cutter he'd been using to cut the wrap around the motor housing, rubbed his eyes, and smiled. "You've paid me enough. I'll drive."

He drove us five miles and dropped us off at a secure storage building. The kind where you plug in your code to get in, another to get through a second door, and a third to ride the elevator. Summer watched me punch in the numbers at three different points of entry, and then a fourth as I entered the combination to my climate-controlled unit. I swung the door open, she walked inside, and I clicked on the light, locking the door behind me.

Summer stared at the contents with an open mouth.

Scuba gear, clothing, costumes, weapons, ammunition, fishing gear, medical and trauma supplies, a couple paddle boards, two motorcycles, a Toyota truck, a mountain of tools, and a small skiff called a Hell's Bay. I also kept a cot. Having a safe place to sleep could be a comfort sometimes.

She slowly scanned the inside. When her eyes came to rest on the weapons hanging on the wall, she asked, "What are you doing with all this?"

"For a multitude of reasons, South Florida is a launching point for both human and sex trafficking. Water ports, international airports, density of population, and otherworldly wealth are just a few. Because of this, I've worked a lot down here. Hence the storage unit." I paused. "I have five others scattered up the East Coast. A couple more dotted around the country."

She turned in a circle and said nothing.

The BMW 1250 GS is an adventure bike, made famous in several extreme documentaries for its abilities under any condition. Bikes such as this one have crossed continents, mountains, deserts, and rivers—all under the worst conditions possible. A chameleon on two wheels, it's meant for both highway and off-road use—which I had a feeling would come in handy. Truth be told, I'm not a big fan of motorcycles, but they do serve a purpose. If we found Angel, we would need the truck, but I had a feeling that to get where we might need to get, we'd need the motorcycle.

I rolled the bike outside and gave her a helmet. She pointed at my phone. "What about . . . ?"

"You should probably listen to him."

She strapped on the helmet and swung a leg over. "Not likely."

Five minutes later we were rolling west on 98 to the southern tip of Lake Okeechobee. Just south of the lake, we turned due south on 27 to the Miccosukee Casino and then west on 41. The road is bordered on either side by canals, which are part of the intricate network of the more than eight hundred square miles called the Everglades.

Had it not been so dark, Summer would have seen some of the thousands of alligators floating at surface level, or possibly a few of the hundreds of thousands of pythons and boa constrictors that now fill the Glades. The alligators are native; the snakes not so much. In the last few decades, a couple of hurricanes have leveled parts of Miami and the surrounding areas. Including pet shops. When rising storm waters filled the shops, the snakes slithered out and found a natural home in the Glades' eternal sea of grass, where they have repopulated with a vengeance. Some are now large enough to eat an entire deer. Whole.

We passed Everglades Safari Park, and then the somber reminder of the ValuJet Flight 592 Memorial. We passed through the Miccosukee Indian Village and then north onto the limestone road paralleling the L-28 Canal Eden Station. We traveled on the limestone-dusted road for nearly thirty minutes when both the road and the canal abruptly ended. A thin trail with fresh four-wheel drive tracks continued northeast. In winter, the Glades are a markedly different place than spring or summer. The normally wet ground dries up to a hardpack surface. Much of the actual surface is limestone. It's tough, unforgiving, and will cut right through a shoe or a motorcycle tire. Winter also means the mosquitoes have taken a nap. Albeit brief. They don't really go anywhere; they're just not as angry as in the summer months when it is literally impossible to stand outside at sundown.

We followed the trail as indicated by my GPS and the coordinates of Angel's phone. It ended on a dirt road with no name. This area of South Florida forms the northern boundary of the Everglades, and it does so through a series of hundreds of man-made canals that literally drain the state. On a map, it looks like a sheet of graph paper with the lines being the canals. That allows it to drain effectively but makes it tough to navigate if you don't know which roads cross which canals via bridges and which roads end in cul-de-sacs. It's like one giant corn maze.

And I didn't know the secret.

Which meant I had wasted a lot of time trying to figure it out.

I cut the engine and the lights and allowed my eyes and ears to adjust. In the distance, maybe a mile away, I saw lights flickering. I motioned and Summer and I advanced at an idle up the limestone path, making me thankful for the motorcycle. Canals lined both sides, teeming with reptiles of every shape and size. I was careful to keep my light shining downward and not let it venture toward the water's edge. The moment it lit on the eyes staring back at us—there were probably a hundred pairs watching our approach—I knew I'd be wearing Summer like a backpack. Some things are better left unknown.

We closed to within a half mile and I heard singing. I killed the engine and the lights, and we continued on foot. Careful to walk the middle line between the two canals. We closed within two hundred yards of the cabin. Given the amount of money these guys were spending, the clientele they catered to, and the proficiency with which they did so, I was pretty sure they'd station armed guards, even in a place like this. Thirty seconds later, my ears told me I was correct.

CHAPTER 25

The moon wasn't overly bright, but it wasn't pitch black either. I could see well enough. Summer squatted behind me, one hand clutching my shirt. An alligator bellowed off to our right, only to be answered by one on our left. Her hand tightened and her arm stiffened, but she had yet to stand atop my shoulders.

Footsteps advanced, crunching limestone and grass. He was quiet. Purposeful. He'd done this before. Chances were good he'd seen the motorcycle. Or at the least the headlamp. I had to assume he was looking for us the same way we were looking for him. He approached within ten feet and I heard someone speak through his earpiece. I couldn't hear what they said. He responded in a professional whisper, saying no more than was needed as he continued his walk along the perimeter. The only camouflage we had was the grass, of which there was plenty. Chest high, it formed a sea, and we were crouched beneath the level of it. The guy would need night vision or thermals to detect us. I was hoping he had neither.

When he stopped within five feet, I felt Summer's hand trembling behind me. He took another step, and I launched from my perch. When I returned some ten seconds later, Summer's entire body was shaking. I shined the light on myself and held out my hand, and she pressed her fingertips to mine. Then locked her fingers inside mine. In the distance, I heard the crank of an engine and then the signature sound of helicopter blades beginning to whip the air.

We moved more quickly. I counted ten people dancing around a bonfire a hundred fifty yards in the distance. Summer pointed at a lone figure dancing by herself. Hands in the air. Lit by firelight. She was swaying. Stumbling. I judged the distance. Between us and them stood another man. Looked like another block of granite. He was speaking into a microphone. If he was armed, and I was certain he was, I'd never make it. He spoke again into the mic. This time louder. Given that I was currently wearing the earpiece and carrying the radio, I heard him loud and clear. Not getting the response he wanted, he herded the group into the helicopter.

A minute later, at 3:00 a.m., one helicopter lifted off the ground, hovered, and then shot up and east toward the coast. Followed closely by a second I had not seen or heard given the noise from the first. We watched in silence, knowing full well that Angel was on one of those birds. And that we'd missed our chance.

We were late. Again.

The sound of the helicopters faded, silence returned, and we stood alone in the darkness. I grabbed the bike and returned to the end of the road and the cabin. The bonfire still burned. The power grid doesn't reach this far, so we circled the cabin on the bike to use its lights. In the Everglades, little islands or rises in the limestone emerge above the surface of the grass. Sometimes a foot. Sometimes two. They rise enough to form dry land given normal water levels. Indians used to call this home, which explained the presence of citrus trees.

Whoever had built this cabin had done so on a small island. Maybe a hundred yards square. An island in a sea of grass. My kind of place.

I found the generator, still hot from use. Which meant they'd been here long enough to need it. Fifteen feet away, a water hole shimmered in the moonlight. Summer began walking toward the water when I gently grabbed her arm, clicked on my flashlight, and exposed a ten- to eleven-foot alligator floating inches from the water's edge. Summer covered her mouth and backed up slowly.

The cabin wasn't locked, but it was well-appointed. I wanted a look inside for any sign, any clue. True to form, this cabin had housed a party in much the same fashion as the yachts. Empty bottles. Furniture scattered about. Articles of clothing. Darts thrown at a dartboard. In comparison to others I'd witnessed, this scene was relatively tame. And given that we saw only two helicopters leave, rather than a long line of cars, this party must have involved few in number. More exclusive. Invite only.

I swore beneath my breath. We had missed her by two, three minutes max.

Finding nothing, I swung one leg over the bike, Summer did likewise, and I cranked the engine. Taking one last look over my shoulder, I pushed the gearshift down and into first gear. In that momentary pause, I saw it. A small red light coming from a fruit tree nearby. I said nothing, pretended not to see it, and eased off the clutch, circling around and behind the cabin. Then, leaving the bike running, I motioned to Summer to follow and pressed a single finger to my lips. She did, and when I pointed to the item duct-taped to the branch of a lemon tree, the space between her eyes narrowed. Followed by a wrinkle. I again pressed my finger to my lips and shook my head. We backed up quietly, climbed on the bike, and eased down the road that led back to civilization. A mile away, I stopped and turned, and even with the helmet on and face mask down, I could see Summer's fear.

She lifted the face mask. Her voice cracked. "Was that an iPhone?"

"Yes."

"Why was it in the tree?"

"Someone was watching us. An instant video feed."

"Do you think they saw us?"

"Yes."

"But why?"

"They wanted to know if she was being followed. And by whom. It's why they let her make the call. They baited us. I never saw it coming, but I should have."

She wrapped her arms tighter around my waist. She whispered, I think because the sound of the words hurt too much: "That's bad, right?"

I didn't sugarcoat it. "It's not good."

By leaving the way we did, we had convinced whoever was watching that we didn't know about the phone. Given that, they'd probably hung up and chalked up the loss of an iPhone to necessary intel. But I knew we needed that phone. "Wait here."

Summer grabbed my hand. "You coming back?"

I nodded.

"You promise?"

I laughed. "Unless . . ." I shined my light out across the water at nearly fifty pairs of eyes staring back at us. "One of them gets hungry."

She climbed up on the bike and sat on her haunches.

I ran back for the phone, circling the tree from a distance. The light was off. Call disconnected. But the owner had still sent me a message. When I cut the duct tape, the vibration buzzed the phone on, waking the home screen. One text waited. I opened it, knowing it had been sent for me. It was direct and to the point. There was a picture of Angel. Taken over her shoulder as she sat lounging on a couch. Drink in hand. Sunglasses. Bikini. Whoever held the camera also held one end of the strap to her bikini. It draped over his finger, which was resting on her neck. She was laughing. Oblivious. The suggestion was clear. The text read, "Now accepting bids."

I powered it off. Removed the SIM card and placed both in my pocket. I didn't want them tracking me. I'd already been baited once. Didn't want it to happen again.

We rode in silence back to the hotel. Over that hour, Summer didn't say a word. One hand wrapped around my waist, while the other had climbed higher, inside my shirt and lying flat across my heart. Ever since Angel had left my chapel, the clock had been ticking. Now it was ticking much faster.

At the hotel, I scanned the phone's contents. No surprise, it was empty. No videos. No pics. No apps. No history. It hadn't been wiped; it simply hadn't been used. It was a sacrificial phone. Probably one of many. The only data showed that the phone had called or been called by two numbers. Multiple times. Over the course of a week. Which meant the phone had had a one-week life span. Summer looked over my shoulder. "Any luck?"

I deliberated. The text and picture would not encourage her. They would worry her. A lot. But this was her daughter and she had a right to know what she was up against. I clicked on the text. The picture opened. Summer read the words, then chewed on her lip. She wanted to ask but didn't, so I explained. "Somewhere on the black web, Angel has her own page. They've taken pictures, maybe movies. And they've started an auction."

Summer stared at the picture.

"My guess is that they'll give it a couple of days, then close the auction and arrange for transfer. Along with several other girls."

Summer sat with her knees against her chest, chewing a fingernail.

I called Colorado and gave him the numbers. He called back five minutes later. Both numbers were no longer in service, telling me these guys were no amateurs. I already knew that. He also told me that the number tied to the SIM card was the same number Angel had last used to call me.

It was another message. And Angel had not sent it.

CHAPTER 26

My guess was that whoever was moving these girls had found a new yacht and would move them there for the last push down the IC toward Key West and parts south. Or they'd take off east out of Miami and cross forty-four miles of open water to Bimini—the gateway to the Bahamas. I doubted the latter, as the winds were too high. So I was betting on Key West.

But I also knew I was dealing with a captain who would think things through in the same way I had, and he was probably as savvy as me. Maybe more so. He might venture out into the open water just because he thought I thought he wouldn't. We'd ventured into mind games here, and I knew it. He probably knew it too.

I was a batter trying to guess the next pitch. Never easy.

I stuck with my gut, which said Key West. It gave him more options. And I said none of this to Summer. We were in a bit of a lull before the storm. I knew he had to move his party onto another vessel. Probably a large vessel. Continue to service clients to pay for everything and continue to lure more and new clients through word of mouth. For the uber-wealthy, this entire world was little more than a game. These were not girls with faces and hearts and emotions and the desire to wear a white dress and press the face of their firstborn to their bosom.

This was flesh. Period. Nothing more.

This captain would keep his inventory available for sale all the way down the inside of the coast, using the Keys to protect him from the northeast winds. I was betting he would continue to post provocative videos and milk his current system for all it was worth, still taking on girls and monitoring his online auctions on the black web. Once he'd reached Key West, he'd dump his used inventory, sell his unused girls to the highest bidder or bidders, and fly out on a jet sipping champagne before moving his operation to some other coast in some other unsuspecting country.

The phone in the tree told him, I hoped, that he was dealing with a single individual or two. Not an agency. Which would probably embolden him. I'd seen it before. First sign of guns and badges and radios and tactical vests and night vision, and party's over. Inventory sold in a flash sale to the highest bidder or dumped in international waters for sharks. But Summer and I had not shown him that. We'd shown him two people curious about a party. We looked small. Insignificant. Naïve even. A couple of overeager parents or private investigators sent to take pictures. My guess was that he wasn't too worried about us. Which was good. I didn't want him worried. I wanted him comfortable. I wanted him doing business as usual. I wanted him cocky. I wanted him thinking about quadrupling his money.

But in order to do anything, we needed a break. Thank God for old men who pretend to be hard of hearing but aren't.

Ellie was awake when we walked in. I doubted she'd slept. She was sitting at the table spinning the lockbox key like a top. We asked my mechanic friend to look after the motorcycle, and ten minutes later we were headed southbound in the ditch. Ellie stood beside me and showed me the map on her phone. She pointed. "We'll pass right by it. They open at nine. Won't take but a second. Then you can be rid of me."

She was right. We would. Since our return to the hospital, I'd not asked for my Rolex back but let her continue to wear it. Figured it gave her a sense of peace that as long as she wore it, chances were good I wouldn't run out on her.

I glanced at my watch on her wrist. "What time is it?"

She checked the time but made no attempt to give me back my watch. "Quarter 'til."

I stared at the sun making its way higher. What would twenty minutes hurt? She'd waited her whole life. A tortured creature who—despite her crusty exterior and like the rest of the human race—had been and was continually asking two questions: Who am I? And more importantly, whose am I?

In my life, in my strange line of work, I'd discovered that we as people can't answer the first until someone else answers the second. It's a function of design. Belonging comes before identity. Ownership births purpose. Someone speaks whose we are, and out of that we become who we are. It's just the way the heart works.

In Eden, we walked in the cool of the evening with a Father who, by the very nature of the conversations and time spent together, answered our heart's cry. It was the product of relationship. But out here, somewhere east or west of the Garden, beyond the shadow of the fiery walls, we have trouble hearing what He's saying. And even when we do, we have trouble believing Him. So we wrestle and search. But regardless of where we search and how we try to answer the question or what we ingest, inject, or swallow to numb the nagging, only the Father gets to tell us who we are. Period. This is why fatherless boys gravitate toward gangs. No, it's not the only reason, but it plays a big part.

In the absence of a dad, can the mom answer it? Sure. Happens all the time. I've met many a mom who has more gumption and guts than the weasel of a man she married. Truth is, ninety-nine percent of broken homes are caused by dads leaving. Not moms. The problem seldom lies at the feet of the mom. They're stuck cleaning up the mess. Although there are exceptions. And maybe those exceptions are the most painful of all. But whatever the cause and however it is answered, and regardless of who answers it, we—as broken children—forever ask, "Whose am I?"

This is *the* cry of the human heart.

And as I looked down at Ellie, her eyes were screaming both questions. And I couldn't answer either one. "Okay."

Her feet moved nervously. As if she stood on the precipice of some great discovery. And while it was tough to tell because she wore a practiced poker face, I almost thought she was smiling.

We returned down the narrow IC, past the North Palm Beach Marina and beyond the Old Port Cove Marina where we'd boarded *Fire and Rain* the day before. As I'd figured, she was gone. Slip empty.

A few miles farther south, we tied up at the boardwalk, lining the side of *Gone Fiction* with bumpers. The security agent at the bank opened the door for us and said, "Welcome." Ellie, Summer, and I approached the teller.

"May I help you?" she asked.

I held out the key. "We'd like to open this box."

She eyed the key and nodded. "Follow me, please."

We did, winding through a door and down into a basement. The old, damp bowels of the bank. Another security guard unlocked a door that led into a room of what looked like a thousand lockboxes. The teller wound her way through the aisles, reading numbers, leading us to 27. Finally, her eyes came to rest on the one. She inserted her key into one of the two keyholes and asked me to insert mine—or Ellie's—into the second. I did. She turned both, unlocking them with a clink, swung open the door, and allowed me to slide the box out. She then led us to a room, pointed at the desk, and closed the door behind her, saying, "Take your time."

Ellie sat opposite me, staring at the tarnished box. It wasn't mine, so I spun it clockwise, facing her. Then Summer and I sat waiting.

For Ellie, all her life and every point on the compass had led to this moment. When she reached for the knob, her hand was shaking. A tear had puddled in one eye. Embarrassed, she palmed away the tear and stuck her hand in her lap. Looking away, she recovered, and her eyes narrowed. For a minute, she sat rubbing one thumb over the top of the other. Finally, she looked from the box to me and back to the box. "You mind?"

I walked around beside her, knelt, and lifted the lid of the box, allowing her to see the contents. Inside was a sealed manila envelope.

I spoke softly. "You want me to open it?"

She lifted it out of the box, stared at it, and then shook her head. The only writing on the outside of the envelope was a date thirteen years in the past.

She clutched the envelope to her chest and stared nervously around the room. It was the first time I'd seen a crack in her tough exterior. I sat opposite her. "We have time."

She laid it flat across her lap. Touching it gently. Tracing the numbers. Finally, she looked at me and shook her head. "I'll wait."

"You sure?"

She nodded.

We walked out of the bank and stood on the boardwalk. Staring around. *Gone Fiction* floated alongside. Calling to me. The look on Ellie's face said she was wondering what to do next. Stoically, she took off my Rolex and held it out to me. As if I'd fulfilled my end of our bargain and our time had come to an end. She spoke without looking at me. "Thank you."

I wasn't about to just let her walk off, but I couldn't make her stay. I had to make it seem as though the idea were hers. "Give me an hour. I'll get you to the airport. Fly you back to school or—" I pointed at the envelope. "Wherever."

Summer nodded in agreement, then lowered her arm. I had a feeling Ellie was short on money, which explained why she considered my option. She pressed the envelope to her chest with crossed arms. She stared west, then down at the boat. Then at me. Finally, she nodded and climbed down, taking her seat on the bench in the stern.

I cast off the lines and followed my map, trying not to pay attention to the hair standing up on my neck.

We drove south, the engine turning at less than a thousand rpm's for the better part of an hour. Given their wealth and influence, the folks in South Florida have swayed their representatives to declare most of the IC in their area as a no-wake zone. It deters fast-boat traffic, which means most people who want to go fast opt for the unregulated Atlantic. I understood the reasoning. Without the restrictions, you'd have go-fast boats scorching down the ditch at over a hundred miles per hour and kids dying on jet skis all the time. If you want to go fast, take it out in the ocean. But given the steady thirty-knot wind currently blowing out of the northeast, we were stuck idling down the IC at a snail's pace.

We turned farther south into Lake Worth, with Peanut Island and Lake Worth Inlet just off our bow. We passed under the Blue Heron Boulevard Bridge, where the water on our port side was dangerously low. As in shin deep. During the daytime, this half-mile-square area would be log-jammed with two hundred boats and a thousand people. Locals call it the Low Tide Bar, because at low tide it's where the locals go to drink. It's one of the most popular places in this part of the world where the kids come out to play and show off their toys—the living, the sculpted, the siliconed, and the motorized.

We passed the Port of Palm Beach and soon saw the headlights of cars moving slowly north and south along North Flagler Drive and beneath the Flagler Memorial Bridge and A1A. On our port side was one of the wealthiest zip codes on the planet. Palm Beach proper. It's the home of The Breakers and Mar-a-Lago. Folks over there don't mess around. They have their own police force and their own speed limits, and you've never seen immaculate landscaping until you've driven North County Road. Landscape companies are interviewed and vetted for the unique opportunity to pick up blades of grass by hand.

With the Royal Park Bridge overhead and Palm Beach Atlantic University on our starboard side, we began running parallel to Everglades Island and Worth Avenue off our port side. Everglades Island is a smaller man-made island attached by a single road to the intracoastal side of Palm Beach. The only road runs due north and south and splits the island down the middle. Ginormous single homes sit on either side. The entire island might contain fifty homes. It's an exclusive situation inside an exclusive situation. Sort of like a gated community within a gated community—situated on an island that juts off an island.

Google Maps led me to a massive compound of a house on the southern tip of Everglades Island. I turned 180 degrees north and tied up at a deserted, unlit, and unwelcoming dock capable of harboring an eighty- to hundred-foot yacht, plus several slips for tenders that were also empty.

Despite the daylight, motion lights flicked on the moment I stepped foot on the dock. Ground-level lights lit up the marble walk to the house, which was fifteen thousand square feet and stretched even wider with two wings that looked to be two or three thousand square feet each. The entire thing was surrounded by a ten-foot wall covered in some sort of flowering vine. And maybe fifty cameras.

CHAPTER 27

Beer, wine, and liquor bottles lay scattered across the lawn, sparkling like discarded rubies, emeralds, and diamonds in the bright sunlight. The once-meticulous landscape had been trampled in random places in what looked like the mob movements of a herd of animals wearing high heels. Exotic bushes and shrubs had been broken off near the roots, and forty or fifty rosebushes had been broken at dirt level by one or more golf clubs. I know this because someone had emptied an entire bag of clubs, each shaft broken in half, and left them scattered like pick-up sticks among the dead and decapitated roses.

The remains of an enormous bonfire smoldered in the middle of the grass. Odd pieces of wood and debris lay half burned in a circle around the epicenter where the fire once consumed its contents. Absent their pedestals, several naked marble statues rested quietly on the floor of the pool, each striking some strange and no longer erotic pose made even more ridiculous by the green-tinted water. Four dented and evidently empty beer kegs pivoted about the pool's surface like bumper cars. At least, I guessed they were empty given the ease with which they floated. Lying on its side in the deep end, which according to the tile at water level read twelve feet, was what looked like a BMW motorcycle.

Across the pool deck, every manner of shirt, pants, dress, shoe, sock, underwear, bra, and any other item of clothing once worn by someone lay crumpled where it had been removed. The grill in the outdoor kitchen still smoldered with the charred remains of something. Steak, maybe. Hard to tell. It was ready to eat a few days ago. The eight ceiling fans were each missing at least one blade. Some two. Most were still spinning, wobbling wildly. Five television screens flashed some sort of input problem. Two of the screens had cracked when someone threw a bottle—which now lay in shards on the ground—at them. One of the grills, possibly a smoker of some sort, had been moved to the pool, turned on its side, and appeared to be the ramp Evel Knievel had used to submerge the BMW.

As Summer, Ellie, and I carefully made our way up the walkway from the dock, movement to my left caught my eye. Camouflaged against the backdrop of what was once a Japanese garden now lying in ruins, I spotted a huge lizard, at least six feet long, leashed to a palm tree. Yes, six feet. And leashed.

Closer to the house, more movement caught my eye. A monkey, also leashed, had climbed into the gazebo, but fighting the tether, he'd inadvertently wrapped himself tightly around one of the two-by-sixes. Afraid, he continued to pull wildly against the cord and emitted an ear-piercing shriek when we appeared on the pool deck. Not wanting him to choke, I cut the end of the leash, loosing him. Sensing himself free, he made a final chirp, circled the pool, ran over to the lizard, pounced on it, smacked it in the face six or eight times, and then climbed the ten-foot retaining wall and disappeared, dragging his leash, never to be seen again.

I would have slid open the sliding-glass door, but it was missing. Not broken. Not cracked. Not sitting oddly canted on its runner. But missing. Completely gone. We stepped into the house where we were met by a blizzard of cold air blowing from the vents—which immediately escaped out the several missing doors and windows. If the outside of the house was trashed, the inside defied the laws of architecture and engineering.

The interior had once been supported by a colonnade of eight large wooden columns—three of which were now missing, exposing Volkswagen-size holes in the ceiling. A fourth lay at an odd angle with an ax stuck into its side. Two *Gone with the Wind*-style staircases led up to the second and third stories. One of the staircases was totally gone. The shape of the intact staircase helped me recognize the odd pieces of wood circling the ashes of the bonfire.

Both of the faucets in the kitchen were running at full go, which normally would have just meant a waste of water. But given that the drains had been stopped up, the floor of the recessed kitchen was flooded in six inches of water. Summer was about to step in and turn off the faucets when I touched her arm and showed her the myriad of electronics and wires now submerged in water. I walked into the utility room, opened one of several breaker boxes, and flipped everything off. Free from the possibility of electrocution, Summer turned off the faucets. The eerie quiet allowed us to hear water running elsewhere in the house. Probably upstairs.

From the utility room behind the kitchen, I opened a door into the eight-car garage. Two bays were empty, while six cars filled what remained. Two Porsches, a Range Rover, a McLaren, a Bentley, and a Dodge diesel pickup of the 2500 class. Parked in its own outcove was one untouched BMW motorcycle that looked to be twin to the one Knievel took swimming. All of the tires of each vehicle were flat, including the bikes hanging on the wall, save the truck and the motorcycle.

Returning inside the house, Summer and Ellie followed in dumbstruck amazement at the wreckage inflicted upon a once-beautiful home. At the amount of money wasted and the stupidity exhibited. I stood on the staircase and surveyed the landscape, guessing that the house had suffered several hundred thousand dollars of damage.

On the second floor, I counted ten bedrooms. There had evidently been a pillow fight because a million down feathers covered the floor, furniture, and return-air vents. There had also been a paintball war—all the mattresses and box springs had been extracted from the beds and leaned on their sides along the halls, creating a maze of protecting walls now covered in fifty thousand neon pink, red, green, and yellow splotches. Many of the doors had either been ripped off their hinges or had the pins removed, adding to the maze. Similar to the pool deck, clothing and bottles littered the floor.

On the third floor, which once housed the exercise room and theater, someone had greased the marble hallway with some type of oil or Crisco. At the far end, they'd piled empty bottles like bowling pins. I'm not sure what they'd used for a ball unless it was their bodies, which might explain the oil. Although I'm not sure anything could explain anything about this chaos other than extreme and prolonged hallucinogenic drug use by a lot of people.

The fourth floor housed a library and office. It had fared best with only minor violence, which suggested that drunk and high people had tired of walking up stairs. I was about to return downstairs when Summer pointed at a ladder that led out of the library and into what looked like a crow's nest. We climbed the ladder and found a bedroom, bathroom, and small kitchen. Maybe a mother-in-law suite, although I couldn't imagine someone of any age climbing all those stairs on a regular basis. That was until Ellie opened a door to reveal an elevator shaft. I say "shaft" because the elevator itself had been freed from its cable and now lay four floors below in a mangled heap.

Trying to make sense of all this, and staring out the glass toward the dock below, I noticed a helicopter pad atop the dock house. Minus a helicopter. Looking at the mayhem around me and the absence of a helicopter, I guessed this party had taken place prior to the party at the cabin in the Everglades. I figured they'd trashed this place, hopped in the helicopter, and flown west. My guess now was that they'd flown south.

We three were still standing with our jaws open when we heard the sound. A thud.

Turning toward the noise, I saw spewing steam and heard the sound of running water from the bathroom, so I followed both. They led me to a large tub. The walls of the entire bathroom were made of glass blocks, giving warped yet spectacular and unobstructed 360-degree views of the Intracoastal to the west and the Atlantic to the east. Surrounding the tub and scattered on the floor lay thirty or forty plastic bags that, according to the labels, once held twenty pounds of ice each. I could only imagine that the ice was used to fill the tub, but the tub was empty. Moving around it, I stepped into the walk-in shower, which poured steam—it doubled as a steam bath. Umpteen stainless steel taps, all of which were currently spewing, filled the room with steam. Someone's personal car wash. I couldn't see my hand in front of my face.

Staring at the oddity before me, I heard the thud again. A second time. But this time it sounded thinner. More metallic.

Handing Summer my phone, I walked into the steam and through the waterfall and car wash of a dozen or more showerheads shooting cold, pressurized water toward the floor. Hot steam and cold water didn't make sense. Kneeling, I crawled across the floor of the shower, which drained via four drain holes. Reaching the fourth drain on my hands and knees and unable to see six inches in front of me, I reached toward the wall. But my hand didn't touch the wall.

I moved my hand slightly, "reading" the surface. The texture was smooth, then coarse, then stringy, then soft.

Then it moved.

I crawled closer and found the bare foot of what looked to be a woman. Unable to make sense of anything given the barrage of water and steam, I moved my hand to her wrist but couldn't find a pulse, so I traveled up her torso to her neck and carotid artery. The pulse was faint. I sank my arms below her legs and her head. Standing, I lifted her limp body and returned through the fog. When I appeared carrying a naked and limp female frame, both Summer and Ellie sucked in a breath of air and covered their mouths. I glanced quickly at the girl in my arms. Late teens, dark hair, dark circles beneath her eyes, a splattering of tattoos, needle holes at the crease of her elbow, skinny, deathly white, with a trail of vomit caked to her mouth and neck.

Then I looked at her face.

It was not Angel. But it was one of the girls we'd seen on video.

I turned to Summer and spoke as we descended the stairs. "Dial 911 now. Put them on speakerphone."

Summer dialed.

They answered as we reached the fourth floor. "911. What's your emergency?"

The only way this girl would make it was if they landed LifeFlight on the lawn outside and airlifted her to a hospital. Absent that, she was dead. The lady on the other end of the phone received dozens if not hundreds of calls a day. Each claiming the end of the world. To take the burden of decision off of her, the authority to call in a helicopter had been left to first responders once they'd assessed the situation. Although there were situations where the operator, based on his or her knowledge and experience, could override that protocol given what he or she was hearing from the caller.

Knowing all this, I threw everything at her I could think of that might be even remotely true to register on the trauma scale, which I hoped would trigger a LifeFlight takeoff. "This is Murphy Shepherd. I work for the US government. I've got a white female, possibly late teens, limited pulse, shows signs of near drowning with possible hypoxia or altered mental status. Also possible overdose with hemodynamic or neurologic instability, currently exhibiting uncontrolled seizures with possible respiratory failure requiring ventilation. I need LifeFlight on the lawn of this house like five minutes ago or this girl won't make it."

She was quiet for two seconds while I heard typing. "Sir, can you give me an exact location?" the operator asked calmly.

I responded with the longitude and latitude GPS coordinates I'd taken off the video signatures we'd stolen from the boat.

She paused. I knew first responders were en route, but I also knew she was deliberating sending LifeFlight. I spoke softly. "Ma'am, I know your protocol. And I know you don't know me. This girl will die if you don't send the bird. If you want to save her life, send it."

I heard fingers on a keyboard typing at the speed of hummingbird wings. "Is it possible to move her to an open area, maybe the backyard, driveway, or someplace out of interference from overheard wires?"

"Not necessary. There's a helipad atop the dock house."

"LifeFlight is on the way. ETA four minutes."

This girl didn't have four minutes. I turned to Ellie and nodded at *Gone Fiction*. "Inside the head, that red bag you were using for a pillow. Get it."

Ellie ran to the boat and returned with my medic bag. I rifled through the medicines, finding two that I needed. One nasal spray. One injection. Both were naloxone HCL. An opioid inhibitor. I sprayed each nostril, then injected her. The bad news was that I couldn't find a pulse, so I ripped open the AED, turned it on, attached the pads to her chest, told Summer and Ellie to stand clear, and shocked her. After her body convulsed, rising nearly a foot off the ground, I administered CPR. Compressions. Breaths. Compressions. Breaths. When she didn't respond, I shocked her again. Alternating CPR. Then again. After the third shock, her eyes flittered. She sucked in part of a breath and a pulse registered in her carotid.

I laid the girl in the grass. Her body was vomiting again. I say "her body" because she wasn't conscious enough to know it. I turned her head sideways and attempted to clear her airway so she wouldn't aspirate the contents of her stomach. In the distance I heard sirens. Then I heard the signature *whop-whop* of a helicopter. This girl was suffering drug and alcohol poisoning on a level I'd seldom if ever seen. It was possible she'd already suffered brain damage, and I had no idea if she'd ever open her eyes again. Given the limited open ground, I turned to Summer and Ellie and said, "You two should get inside."

As the helicopter hovered and then began to descend to the pad, churning up pieces of debris like a whirlwind, they ran inside. The helicopter touched down, and before the paramedics had time to exit and assess her, I carried her up the dock house steps and to the rear-opening door of the bird and slid her onto the stretcher, which they were in the process of removing. Observing the girl's condition, one paramedic listened to me while the second, a woman, climbed back inside and began working on her. In the fifteen seconds it took to inform the paramedic, the woman had inserted an IV, shot something directly into the girl's heart, and intubated her, giving her oxygen.

In thirty seconds, as the sheriff's deputies appeared in the driveway, the helicopter was airborne again and disappeared over the rooftops. Summer appeared to my left, hanging on my arm. Her face posed a question her lips did not articulate.

I shook my head. "I don't know. We may have been too late."

The sheriff's deputies had been prevented from entering the grounds by a locked front gate. While they worked to open it, I began to focus on the next few minutes. They would want a statement from us, and I knew I didn't want to give it. No time. So I turned Summer and Ellie around and pointed. "Boat. Now."

They understood. We returned down the walkway to the dock, loaded into *Gone Fiction*, and untied her ropes. Reversing quietly, I backed out of the dock and then slid the stick forward. By the time the deputies made it through the house and into the backyard, we had cleared the pilings and were moving back toward the IC. The nearest deputy, some jacked guy wearing shades and SWAT gear, ran to the water's edge and told me not to move any farther. I slid the throttle to full and we shot forward into the ditch and out of his line of sight.

CHAPTER 28

O nce into the open water, I dialed Colorado. He answered after the second ring. I told him what had just happened and asked him to call the local sheriff's office, explain who I was, and tell them we'd be at the hospital if they wanted my statement. I also asked him to find out what he could about the girl in the helicopter and where they were taking her. If she lived, I wanted a few words with her.

He hung up, and I returned to Summer and Ellie, who were both huddled on the back bench, riding in silence with stunned looks on their faces.

Summer sat staring at a silver chain draped over her right hand, at the end of which dangled an odd-shaped piece of honeycomb. One hand was holding the other. Both were shaking. As was she. She was close to cracking. She was holding Angel's Jerusalem cross. The one I'd seen her wearing when we met in the chapel.

"Where'd you find that?"

She spoke through tears while looking in the direction of the helicopter, which was now little more than a speck in the sky. "In the hand of that girl."

I returned north. Ellie appeared on my right side. Hanging on to the T-top with one hand, the envelope with the other. "Did you save that girl's life?"

I shook my head. "I don't know."

She touched her nose. "What did you give her?"

"It's called Narcan. When someone uses heroin or hydrocodone, any kind of opioid, the drug binds to receptors in their brain. It blocks pain. Slows their breathing. Calms them down. In the case of an overdose, it can be fatally calming because they quit breathing. Become unconscious. The drugs I gave her reverse that and kick the drug off the receptors. Waking them up."

She pointed at the AED.

"That allowed me to shock her heart back to work. Sort of like jumper cables for the human body."

Her face spoke of earnestness. "You always carry this stuff in your boat?"

I shrugged. "I have for several years—although the drugs and technology are always changing."

"How many times have you used all this?"

I shrugged. "Some."

"Does it always work?"

I stared across the bow. "No."

She didn't take her eyes off me. "What now?"

I pointed at the now-disappeared helicopter. "You mean for her, or—" I looked straight at Ellie. "You and me?"

"Both."

"If she wakes up and can talk, I'd like a few minutes with her. As for you and me, that's up to you."

She clutched the envelope to her chest. The events of the last hour had shaken her. When she spoke, she turned her face away. "Could we stop for a second?"

Palm Beach lay to the east. West Palm Beach proper to the west. Our cutwater had just entered the Lake Worth Inlet. I cut the throttle, navigated around Peanut Island, and ran the boat aground in the shallows of the low tide sandbar just north of the island. Given the outgoing tide, the water was shin deep. Forty or fifty boats had done likewise. The weekend had started early. The air smelled of suntan oil and rum, and was filled with the sounds of Bob Marley and Kenny Chesney. Off to our left, a dozen college kids floated a Frisbee through the air while one optimistic dog ran back and forth.

I cut the engine. She laid the envelope flat across the console. In front of me. Her hands were shaking again, so she crossed her arms and buried her hands in her armpits. "Will you?" She stared at it. Then me. Her lip quivered. "Please."

While I'd looked at Ellie, I'd not really studied her. Although she tried hard not to be, she was stunningly beautiful. Like, take your breath away. Maybe here and now, having suffered the violence of what she'd just seen, her walls were crumbling. Of if not crumbling, at least the gates were opening.

Summer appeared at my left shoulder. The three of us formed a semicircle around an envelope that as far as I knew had not been opened in thirteen years. I opened the clasp, folded back the top, and emptied the contents onto the seat next to me.

One item appeared. A letter.

I unfolded it. It was printed on official letterhead from the Sisters of Mercy convent in Key West.

Like the envelope, the letter was dated thirteen years prior.

It read:

Dear Florence,

You have been offered provisional acceptance into the Sisters' initiate. We eagerly await your arrival.

Sincerely,
Sister Margaret

Something rattled in the envelope, so I turned it on its end, emptying it completely. A ring fell onto the seat. It spun like a top, wobbled, and then settled.

When it did, it took my breath away.

It could only mean one thing.

CHAPTER 29

I picked up the ring, turning it in my hand. The band was made of three thinner platinum bands woven together. Mounted above the vine-looking band sat a single diamond and two smaller emeralds, both mounted in silver settings on either side. Ellie looked at me. Her head tilted sideways. She stared at the ring as I placed it into the palm of her hand. When I did, something passed from me to her. Something I can't name and never knew was there. But something real, something palpable, left my body and wrapped around hers.

She looked at the ring with incredulity. Shaking her head. Anger rising. She was about to throw the ring in the water when I caught her hand. "Wait."

A vein had popped on the side of her head as she crumpled the letter. Speaking to the wad of paper, she said, "Just say it. You don't want me. Never did. Just throw me out with the trash. Why the riddle? Why all this? Just freaking say the word!"

"Maybe she is."

Ellie shook her head. "What do you mean?"

I straightened the letter. "I don't know any of this for certain, but I think your mom did not intend to have you, and when she found herself pregnant, she gave you up and then went to this convent. Where she might be still. So maybe . . . you . . . we . . . should just go here"—I tapped the letter—"and ask around. Can't hurt."

Her shoulders rolled down at the edges. "I've been waiting my whole life for somebody, anybody, to tell me who I am and where I come from and why nobody wanted me—and all I've got is this stupid letter and this ridiculous ring that's not worth squat."

I stared at it. "It was to her."

"How can you say that? She dumped it in this box thirteen years ago and hasn't looked back since."

I shrugged. "You don't know that."

She cocked her arm again as if to throw it.

"Wait."

She set her hand in her lap.

"You can throw that if you want, but don't let your pain speak louder than your love. Thirteen years ago, pain took that ring off and love put it in that box. The fact that you're holding it now is a message, I think, from your mom. Before you bury her at sea, you might try to figure out what she's saying."

Ellie stared out across the water and shook her head.

I pointed south down the IC, toward the Keys. "Can I tell you a story?"

She did not look impressed.

"I know you see me as this ancient old man with arthritis and bad eyes, but I was actually in love once."

Her complexion altered ever so slightly. "Why would I care about who you loved?"

I ignored her. And while I was working hard to keep her attention, I had all of Summer's. "Sophomore year of high school, we'd all gone to this party. Big house on the river. Ski boats. Jet skis. Parasail rides. The parents even had a helicopter and were taking the kids on rides. Pretty wild party. Entire school was there. Maybe two hundred kids. I was sweet on this girl named Marie. She liked me but I was quiet, kind of a nerd in tenth grade, and not real popular. In my spare time, I fished and looked for stuff. Like sharks' teeth or Indian artifacts.

"Marie and I had been friends longer than most. Childhood. We kind of grew up together. She was my best friend when guys weren't supposed to have a girl as their best friend. We shared secrets. Hopes. Dreams. She knew I had my heart set on the Academy and she was just about the only person who told me I had a chance. That I could do it. Marie believed in me, and as a result, I did too. When I broke forty-eight seconds in the four hundred meters, set the state record, she was cheering me on. Without her, I don't think I'd have broken sixty."

"If Marie had an Achilles' heel, and she did, it was acceptance. I couldn't have cared less, but her identity was inextricably woven into the fabric of the crowd she hung with. She liked the popular guys with letter jackets and college offers. The ones everybody was talking about. I was night shift. Community college. Nobody was talking about me. She also had a thing for fast cars and fast boats, and I had neither.

"It was a Saturday. I worked at a tire store and got off work about nine p.m. When I got home, word of the party had spread. I had one interest in that party, and she wasn't real interested in me. So I grabbed a light, a few poles, hopped in my Gheenoe, and fished a full moon and a flood tide. Big redfish love a full moon, and they were hitting on top of the water, making a loud smack. If you're a fisherman, it's a good sound.

"Midnight found me toward the mouth of the river, where the IC meets the St. Johns. It's big water and no place for a Gheenoe, but the reds were there, so . . . About twelve thirty, I heard a distant helicopter. Then I saw a boat motoring slowly downriver with two large spotlights searching the surface of the water. Never a good sign. A moment later, the helicopter passed overhead, a larger searchlight, and then the boat, which circled through the inlet and sent a wake my way that nearly swamped me. I heard loud, frantic voices. I flagged them down and saw several guys I recognized from school, the guys with letterman jackets and college offers. They told me they'd gone night tubing and one of the girls had been thrown off. They couldn't find her.

"'What's her name?' I asked.

"One of the guys flippantly waved his beer through the air. Shook his head. 'Starts with an M. Mary. Marcia. Something.'

"Three Coast Guard boats appeared soon after. Flashing lights. Sirens. Followed by two helicopters. The water became a choppy mess and no place for my boat. It was also September and the moon was high, which meant there was about twice as much water, so an outgoing tide would be moving about twice as fast as normal in an attempt to get all that water out.

"I asked the guy, 'What time this happen?'

"He swigged his beer and threw the can in the river. 'About eight thirty.'

"That was four hours ago. I looked at those people like they'd lost their ever-loving minds. *Idiots*. They were all looking in the wrong place."

Ellie had softened. While her shoulders pretended to be doing me a favor, her face told me I was getting through that granite exterior. Summer had moved closer. Touching me ever so slightly with her shoulder.

"I cranked the engine, turned the throttle to full, and made my way by moonlight about three miles toward the inlet where the St. Johns River meets the Atlantic Ocean. The Jetties is a narrow, deepwater shipping canal for both commercial and military vessels, including submarines, and the waves rolling between the Volkswagen-size rocks that make up the Jetties can reach six to eight feet on a calm day. Nobody in their right mind would ever take my boat anywhere near it.

"Twenty minutes later, I reached the Jetties. The waves were over my head. Even if I was able to navigate out of the channel, against the waves, when I returned the force and height of the waves would nosedive my boat and sink it like a torpedo. I cut the engine, felt the pull of the current taking me at six to seven knots, and knew that Marie had already passed through here. She was floating in the Atlantic. Out to sea. I cranked the engine and pointed the nose through the waves. My only saving grace was that I was the only passenger and both my weight and the engine weight lifted the bow enough to soften the blow of the waves. Several waves crashed over the bow, but I was able to bail enough water to stay afloat and still push out to sea.

"Once I broke free of the Jetties, the waves calmed and I could make out the surface of the water in the moonlight. I cut the engine, let the current pull me, and listened. I did this every couple of minutes as the lights of the shoreline grew more and more distant. Finally, with land six or seven miles to my west and a whole lot of really big water to my east, I just sat there floating. Listening. Letting the current pull me. Somewhere in there, I heard a voice rise up out of the water. In the middle of that really big dark ocean, I heard my name. Faint. Then louder. I searched frantically but couldn't make it out. So . . ."

I fell quiet, shrugged, and acted like that was the end of the story.

Ellie looked at me like I was loco. "That's it?!"

"Yeah, I just gave up on her because it was hard and I didn't have enough information to go on."

She looked at the ring in her hand, then at me, and rolled her eyes.

I leaned in closer. "Would you like me to finish the story, or would you like to throw that ring in the water?"

She feigned indifference. Crossed her arms. "I'm listening."

"Couple hundred yards south, I saw a disturbance in the water. Could have been anything. But I aimed for it and held the throttle wide open until I reached where I thought it had been, then I cut the engine, coasted, and listened. Marie was screaming at me off my starboard side. That's the right side. I pulled hard on the tiller and found her clutching a piece of driftwood and wearing a life jacket, which probably saved her life. She was cold, in shock, her head barely above water.

"I knew I'd never make it back through the Jetties, and I wasn't sure if I had enough fuel to make it back to land, so I pointed the nose at the lights onshore and hoped. We ran out of gas a couple hundred yards from shore. I paddled the rest. We pulled the Gheenoe up on the beach, I built a fire, and we sat there holding each other until the sun rose. We never told anyone what happened. When they asked her at school, she told everyone she'd hit her head on a dock piling and was only able to climb up before she passed out. When she woke up, she walked home."

I fell quiet again, and Ellie called my bluff. "That's not the end of the story."

"Yes, it is."

She shook her head. "I'm young. Not dumb."

Summer's eyes were boring a hole through me, willing me to tell the rest. I stood, walked to the bow, and spoke out across the water. To the memory.

"That night on the beach, after she'd finished shivering, she held up a single finger, touching mine with the tip of hers. She said, 'You could've died out there tonight.'

"She was right. I nodded.

"'Why'd you leave everyone to find me?'

"Maybe I was trying to impress her and maybe I was telling the truth. Whatever. I said, 'Because the needs of the one outweigh those of the ninety-nine.'"

Ellie frowned. "Seems kind of heavy for a high schooler."

"Looking back, maybe it was."

"Where'd you learn that? Self-help book?"

"A friend of mine. A priest. And until that moment with Marie, I really had no idea what he was talking about."

I continued with my story. "When I said that, her fingers spread and intertwined with mine." I held up my hand, fingers spread. "This silly hand gesture started there. It became the fabric of us. Our thing. It was how we remembered the moment. We could be in a crowd of people, loud music, chatter, and all she had to do was touch my fingertip with hers, and immediately we were back in that water. Sitting on that beach. Her and me. Us against the world. Then it wasn't so silly anymore.

"And that morning as the sun rose, we walked the beach. Hand in hand. Maybe the most perfect sunrise in the history of the sun rising. With the water foaming over our ankles, the sun hit the beach and shone on something at the water's edge. I lifted it. A silver cross. Washed up by the same flood tide that had ripped her seven miles out to sea. It was hanging by a leather lace. I tied the lace in a square knot and hung it around her neck. It came to rest flat across her heart. She leaned against me, pressing her ear to my heart. Beneath the waves rolling gently next to us, she whispered, 'If I ever find myself lost, will you come find me?'

"I nodded. 'Always.'

"She wrapped her arms around me, kissed me—which almost made my heart stop—and said, 'Promise?'

"'I do.'"

When I turned around, Ellie was staring up at me. Summer sat beneath the T-top, wiping tears. Ellie tried to harden her voice, but my story had knocked the edges off of it. "Why're you telling me this?"

"Because finding people is what I do."

"Whatever happened to Marie?"

I was quiet a minute. Shook my head.

She pressed me. "What happened?"

"She died."

Ellie swallowed. Summer held back a sob.

I tried to return us to the moment. "I know it's hard and that I'm asking you to be older than you are, but I think I have some experience with Key West. I know that convent. Least I think I've seen it. Hang in there a few more days. I'll take you there. We'll go together."

Disbelief drained down her face. "Why would you do that?"

"Whoever put that ring in this envelope is trying to send you a message—" Just then, my phone rang. Colorado. I answered, "Hey."

"Your girl is awake. Asking for you."

"Where'd they take her?"

"ICU. Same hospital."

I was about to hang up when I looked at Ellie. I turned, speaking quietly. "Hey . . ."

"Yeah?"

I asked him, "Do you know something I don't? Something about me?" He heard my question in the tone of my voice. I'd seldom used it with him.

"I know a lot you don't."

"I'm asking you something specific. If you knew it, it'd come to mind."

"What I hear in my confessional stays there."

"You're gonna pull that with me? After all we've—"

"Doctors say she's going to need a few months to recover, but she will. The Narcan you injected probably saved her life."

Water lapped against the hull of the boat. For some reason, all I could think of in that moment was Angel. I could hear the clock ticking. "I'll be in touch."

I hung up and turned to Ellie. She was staring at the ring and shaking her head. "What message?"

I knew her world was crumbling and I didn't know how to answer. "Stay. A few days. A week maybe. We'll go together. Maybe we can figure it out. Then if you like, I'll put you on a plane. Deal?"

She took her time considering this, finally nodding. Quietly, she folded the letter and sat on the back bench. Alone. Turning the ring on her finger. Staring at it with each turn. It occurred to me that it might be the first piece of real jewelry she ever owned.

CHAPTER 30

Gunner heard us coming and charged out of the hospital room, his nails scratching the polished floor. He tackled me in the hall. The strength of his excited licking and tail-wagging told me he desperately wanted out of that hospital. Clay was sitting up when I walked in. Whatever they'd given him had worked. He looked ten years younger. He stood up. "If you're waiting on me, you're backing up."

I sat next to him. "How you feeling?"

"Better. I'm good. You?"

"I need a few minutes, but collect your stuff. We'll be on the water in an hour."

"I like the sound of that." He cleared his throat. "I need to talk with you when you get a second."

"Is it urgent?"

"It can wait."

Summer and I exited the elevator on the ICU floor, and I showed my clergy credentials to the nurse. She read them and showed us to the girl's room. A deputy stood guard. The doctor was leaving when we walked up. I told him who I was, and he briefed me on her condition, which was stable but still bad. She'd either ingested, injected, or been given some form of opioid and then a fatal dose of hallucinogenic drugs. He ended by saying, "Nobody takes that recipe or that amount unless they want to check out. Hence—" He glanced at the deputy. He rubbed his hands together. "Although there is a chance someone else gave it to her."

The room was dim. Lit only by screens and little blue, green, and red lights. An IV had been inserted into each arm. Her pulse was slow but steady, and while low, her pressure was stable. Her eyes were heavy. When we came in, her head turned and her right hand flipped over, inviting mine.

I sat, rested my hand in hers, and said, "My name's Murphy. Most folks call me Murph."

Her eyes closed lazily and then opened. She slurred her words. "Pleased to meet you." She swallowed. Another long blink. "Casey."

"How you feeling?"

"Alive."

"You remember anything?"

She shook her head once. Then she spotted Summer and the Jerusalem cross hanging at the base of her neck. She considered it. Tried to shake off the fog. "I had . . . My temperature was getting high. Really high. Somebody put me in a tub and filled it with ice." She shook her head. "Packed me in ice. Armpits. Everywhere. A girl. When I came to, she was gone . . . I made it to the shower."

"You remember her name?"

"Never met her."

I held up my phone, showing her Angel's picture. "This her?"

She nodded. She looked up at Summer. "She yours?"

Summer nodded.

Casey reached for Summer. "When you find her . . ." A tear rolled down her cheek. "Hug her for me."

Summer kissed Casey on the forehead.

Casey spoke without looking at me. "The men were . . ." She turned her head farther. The shame fell like a shadow. "One after another. I lost count. Weeks." She swallowed. "Then they injected me . . ." She looked up at me. "Is my life over?"

This right here was what the men spit out. The residue. When they were finished, this was what was left over. My anger roared. Countless times I'd knelt by similar bedsides and been asked similar questions. I shook my head. "I think you're only just beginning."

"Feels over."

"You have any family?"

"No."

"You up for a little travel?"

She nodded. "Anywhere but here."

"I'm going to talk to these doctors, and when you get well enough to travel, I'm going to request they release you into my custody. Or at least, some folks who work with me. They're going to come get you and fly you on a private plane to Colorado, where they'll nurse you back to health, give you a place to live, and get you in school. You'll meet other girls like you."

"Total losers—"

I laughed. "Don't kid yourself. We all lose our way. Sometimes it just takes somebody else to find us and bring us back. Remind us."

She laughed. "Of what?"

I leaned in close and spoke slowly so my words would register. "That we were made to want and give love. That no matter how dark the night, midnight will pass. No darkness, no matter how dark, can hold back the second hand. Whether you like it or not, whether you want it or not, whether you hope it or not, whether you build a wall around your soul and cut out your eyes, wait a few hours and the sun will crack the skyline and the darkness will roll back like a scroll."

The tears drained. "This place . . . is it really real?"

"Yes."

"Will you be there?"

"I'll come check on you."

"You promise?"

"I do. But first I have to go find someone."

She glanced at the cross. Then back at me. She was shaking her head. "They won't let her leave."

"I know."

"They're saving her. Taking bids. Her and a couple others. An online auction. They take pictures of her. Some when she's passed out. Then they post them. Bids get higher. They're bad men. Guns and . . ."

I nodded. "Any idea where they're going?"

"They're hush-hush. But I heard them say Cuba. They're excited because they're getting a lot of money for her and they don't want to end the auction." She squeezed my hand. Tears rolled down her cheeks. "I'm sorry."

"Shhh." I stood. "Breathe in. Then breathe out. Then"—I smiled—"do it again. Wash. Rinse. Repeat. You'll like Colorado this time of year."

She stared at the window. "I've never flown on a plane."

"Well, this will ruin you for ordinary travel, but it's a great way to start."

She was crying now. A fetal ball. Sobbing silently. Holding it in. Summer sat and cradled her. For a moment, Casey wouldn't let it out, but after it built and she couldn't hold it anymore, it burst forth. I'd heard the same noises before, which made it all the more painful. The deputy poked his head in, but when he saw what was happening, he nodded, backed out, and stood guard.

I knelt next to her bed, my face inches from hers. When she opened her eyes, she was looking beyond me. Into the past. All the ugly stuff. The memories the darkness painted. She tried to make the words, but they wouldn't come. Finally, she whispered, "Who will ever love me after . . . ?" She motioned to herself.

I cradled her hand in mine. Waited until her eyes locked on mine. "Right now there is a man walking this earth who can't wait to meet you. He's been waiting his whole life."

She chuckled. "I thought I was the one on drugs."

"When he meets you, his heart will flutter. His palms will sweat. He'll think somebody stuffed a bag of cotton in his mouth. He won't know what to say, but he'll want to."

"How do you know?"

"It's how we're made."

"You've seen this?"

"I've married these people."

"Are you a priest?"

I shifted my head from side to side. Paused. Then nodded once. "I'm also a priest."

"But—"

"Love is an amazing thing. It takes the brokenness, the scars, the pain, the darkness, everything, and makes it all new."

"You've really seen this?"

"I've lived this. Known it. Know it."

"And all this is in Colorado?"

"Yes." I considered my next question carefully. "You like to read?"

She nodded.

"Okay, I'm going to send you some books. Something to pass the time. Mostly they're just check-your-brain-at-the-door romance novels, but they're entertaining. They might fill your hope bucket and maybe we can talk about them next time I see you."

She nodded. Wanting to believe me but afraid nonetheless. When I turned to leave, she wouldn't let go of my hand.

Walking down the hall, I pressed Redial on my phone.

He answered. "She said yes."

"I'm on it."

"And she's never flown, so—"

"We'll roll out the carpet."

"And she likes to read."

"You asked her that?"

"Yeah."

"You having second thoughts?"

"Just send her some books, will you?"

"You got a favorite in mind?"

"You know better."

"I know." He paused. "The trail on Angel is cold. I got nothing."

I turned so Summer couldn't hear me. "I know. I'm thinking they'll fuel up once more around Miami, maybe take on more girls, then head to Key West and disappear."

"They know by now. That phone in the tree was put there by somebody who knows what he's doing. This is not his first time."

I was about to hang up when I had a thought. "Hey, one more thing."

He waited.

"See what you can dig up about a Sisters of Mercy convent. Somewhere in South Florida. Probably Key West."

"Probably a story there."

"Not sure. That's where you come in."

I hung up and pressed the button for the elevator. Standing there, afraid to look at Summer for fear that she'd read my face, I felt her slide her hand in mine. She inched closer, her body touching mine. She said nothing.

Which said a lot.

Riding down the elevator, I knew I needed to speak. I stared at the numbers above us. "We need to get south. Quickly. Things are . . . I can't—"

She pressed her finger to my lips. "I'm not afraid."

The numbers decreased by one. When I spoke, it was only to myself, and she couldn't hear me.

"I am."

CHAPTER 31

Four thousand rpm's felt good. *Gone Fiction* glided across the top of the water at thirty-one mph. Clay reclined in the beanbag, his feet propped on the front casting deck. Gunner gave his best *Titanic* impression, hovering over the bow. The wind tugging on and flapping his ears. His tongue wagging in rhythm with his tail.

Summer sat alongside me on the helm seat. She was never far, closing the physical distance between us with each new day. I knew that some percentage of her clinging to me had something to do with the very real possibility that she might never see her daughter again. And with each day that passed, it grew more real. Her proximity to me was a self-protective thing—she wanted something or someone to hold on to if there was no one else.

Ellie sat with her knees tucked up into her chest on the back bench, staring east, mindlessly spinning the ring on her finger. She hadn't eaten much breakfast or lunch. Fingers' orange box rested above me, tied into the T-top. Staring down on all of us. Probably laughing. The thought of spreading my friend's ashes on the water where we first met seemed a long way away.

Truth was, we were in a bad way. Trouble piled on top of trouble.

When Bones and I opened the town, we knew we needed a secluded fortress. Drug-addicted women who have been emotionally, physically, and sexually abused need a safe space to unwind all the knots the evil has tied. Getting free is tough enough without looking over your shoulder.

So we built it in a secure place: a deserted town. Literally. What had once flourished in the late 1800s with schools and churches and shops and kids playing games in the streets became a ghost town when the silver ran out. Situated in a high alpine valley, it's one of the more beautiful places I've ever been. And given newer technology and better roads, it's now accessible while also hidden. The altitude takes some getting used to when you're two miles above sea level, but acclimation doesn't take long. Most folks who live around there have no idea we exist. We like it that way.

To guard us, Bones brought in some ex-Delta guys and SEALs and guys retired from Los Angeles SWAT. We let them live rent-free. Educate their kids for free. Free health care. And pay them to stand guard. Which they do. Rather zealously. Not only that, but most are still on some sort of active duty, which requires them to stay current in their training. And because the mountains around us are some of the toughest anywhere, they bring in their military friends and conduct their mountain and cold-weather urban training all around us. Sometimes they even let me play along. We share stories at twelve thousand feet.

While Bones plays the happy-go-lucky grandpa everyone loves to love, he walks those mountains morning and night, and there isn't a footprint or broken twig that gets past him. These are his sheep.

For lack of anything more creative, we used to just call it The Town. But somewhere in our first year of operation, one of the girls said something to change all that. She'd had a rough go. Through no fault of her own, she was taken from her home and sold as a sex slave. For two years she was traded around. Suffered horrors untold. To medicate, she took anything she could get her hands on, numbing the pain of the present and past and future.

Took us a while to find her. When we did, we airlifted her there. She stayed in ICU for two months. Bones took her under his wing, which I thought was amazing when we learned what she had endured. The fact that she would ever get within arm's length of another man surprised me. But

Bones is like that. Everybody's grandfather. Or the grandfather they never had. Four years into her stay here, she'd graduated college—with a nursing degree no less—and taken a job in our hospital. Working with the girls. Nursing them back to life. She'd met a guy. Bones liked him. They'd set a date. She'd asked Bones to walk her down the aisle.

During the early years of The Town, many of the girls wanted to climb to the top of the mountain, which leveled out just above fourteen thousand feet. Problem was, most of them were in such bad shape or they'd been beaten so badly that they were months from being physically able to make the trek. So Bones and I bought a chairlift and had it installed. All the way to the top. It sits four across. We also built a cabin. Roaring fireplace. Espresso machine. We called it the Eagle's Nest.

A few weeks before her wedding, this girl and her fiancé and Bones and I had ridden to the top and were sitting on the porch, sipping coffee, looking out across a view that spanned seventy to a hundred miles in most every direction. And as we sat up there, she started shaking her head. She said, "There was a moment in my life when I was lying in the darkness, a different man every hour, on the hour, day after day after week after month, and I felt my soul leave. Just checked out of me. Because to live inside me was too painful. I let it go because I couldn't understand how anyone, much less me, would ever want to live inside me. Too filthy. Too . . ." She trailed off, just shaking her head.

Finally, she turned and looked at us. "Then you kicked down the door. Lifted me up and carried me. Here. And slowly, I learned to breathe again. To wake up and see daylight. And what I found with every day was that something in me stirred. Something I hadn't known in a long time. Something I thought was long since dead. And that was my hope. Hope that somebody, someday, would see me. Just a girl. Wanting love and willing to give it—to give all of me. I had this hope that somebody would accept me without holding my past against me. Without seeing me as stained. As the horror. As something you just throw away. But somehow . . ."

She sank her hand into the snow resting on the railing. "Like this." For several minutes she just cried in the arms of her fiancé. But it was what she said last that changed the name. Looking from Bones to me, she said, "I never thought I'd walk down an aisle in white. How could I ever deserve that? Not when . . . And yet, I am. I don't really understand it, but somehow, in some impossible way, love reached down inside me, took out all the old and dirty—the scars and the stains that no soap anywhere would ever wash out. And love didn't just clean me but made me new. And maybe the craziest part of that is how I see me."

She held her fiancé's hand. "It's one thing for him to see me as I want to be seen. It's another thing entirely for me to see me, and I want to see me." She laughed. "When I look in the mirror, I don't see the freak. The maggot. The refuse. I see the new. Sparkling. Radiant. And I like her. I have hope for her. I think she's going to make it. She is now what she once was . . . beautiful. A daughter. A wife. Maybe one day, a mom. If you only knew how impossible that seemed not so long ago."

She waved her hand across The Town nestled in the valley below. "I cannot begin—" We sat in silence several more minutes. The temperature was dropping. I stoked the fire. She reached into the air in front of her, made a fist and returned it to her chest. Pounding. "I was there. Now I am here. Love did that." She spoke through gritted teeth. "I am free."

So, while it may seem cheesy if you don't know the story, The Town became Freetown. It worked in West Africa; why can't it work in western Colorado?

Walking into Freetown is a bit of a homecoming for me. It's there and really only there that I possess some sort of celebrity status. These girls know nothing of my artistic career. Sure, they read my books; they just don't know I wrote them. They only know I'm the guy who kicked down the door. Some don't even know that. So walking down Main Street can take a while. I love seeing their faces. Hearing the stories.

Sipping my coffee, the wind whipping around me as *Gone Fiction* split the water, I let my mind wander back to Main Street and the sound of freedom. Which is laughter.

One hand on the wheel, staring at water staring back at me, I needed the sound of that laughter. I would have given most everything I had to teleport all of us to Freetown in that moment. Just lift out of here and leave all this behind.

We motored south out of West Palm Beach into Lake Worth, Delray Beach, and Deerfield Beach. It was slow going but I had a pretty good feeling that whatever captain or captains I was chasing would not venture out into the Atlantic. The wind was blowing out of the northeast at greater than thirty mph. No captain in his right mind would take a pleasure boat out into that. Not if he wanted to keep the people on the boat. And my guess was that he desperately wanted to keep them on the boat and keep the party going. Even if it meant turtling down the IC.

Pompano gave way to Fort Lauderdale, which put Miami off the bow. I'd now come some three hundred miles since my island. Seen a good bit of water beneath the hull. My problem was simple: I had no idea what vessel they were on or where they were going. Every boat was a possibility, and there were ten thousand boats. Fingers' box hung above my head. Staring down. I missed him.

Motoring under the Rickenbacker Causeway en route to Biscayne Bay, Clay stood from his perch on the beanbag and shuffled back toward me. He asked, "You got a minute, Mr. Murphy?"

We were idling at little more than six hundred rpm's. Ellie was asleep on the back bench with her head on Summer's lap. I stood. "Yes, sir."

"Late at night, when the party died down and I was cleaning up my bar, these two fellows would order drinks, stand within whisper distance, and talk in muffled tones. One foreign. One not. I didn't understand much. Caught bits and pieces. They thought I was hard of hearing. Harmless." He laughed. "Maybe I'm not as hard as they think. They'd talk around me as they sipped their drinks, and they'd point at a chart showing the southern end of Florida. Down 'bout where we are now. Kept using phrases like 'picking the coconuts' and 'walking on water to the loading dock.' That make any sense to you?"

I shook my head. "No, sir."

"Last thing I remember them saying was something about 'fruit in the grove,' 'walking on water,' and then 'spending one last night with Mel and his turtles' before they cashed in their chips."

I let the words settle. "None of it rings a bell at the moment."

He looked bothered as he glanced at Summer. "She's a tough momma. But she may have tougher coming. They're bad men." He paused. "And I seen bad."

I watched Summer hug herself against the wind. "Yes, sir."

He put his hand on my shoulder and said, "Sorry I'm not more help." Then he returned to his beanbag.

I studied the chart. The University of Miami sat just a mile or so to the west. So did Coconut Grove. A common hangout for girls from the University of Miami. Maybe that had something to do with it. Walking on water? Not sure. But we would soon be in spitting distance of Stiltsville. The remains of a group of vacation homes built by the most optimistic people on the planet out on the shallow shelf in Biscayne Bay. Most of the forty or so homes had been blown away in hurricanes. Maybe six or seven remained. That wouldn't be a bad place to hide if you wanted to do it in plain sight.

And Mel and his turtles. Mel Fisher found the *Atocha*—the richest underwater shipwreck treasure ever—near the Dry Tortugas. *Tortuga* is the Spanish word for turtle, and the Dry Tortugas is the name of a Civil War fort on a small island some sixty miles west of Key West.

While I knew a little more, I still didn't know much.

Biscayne Bay opened before us. The wind from the Atlantic had churned the water to whitecaps. I tried skirting the edge as close as possible to get a break from the wind, but it was no good. She beat us up pretty good. We gassed up at the Black Point Marina, used the bathrooms, and I tried to cheer up the troops for the remainder of the trip across the bay. Conditions were ugly and worsening. If I could come out of the marina and drive due east-southeast toward Elliott Key, I could come in under the windward side of the key where the waters would be calmer. But getting there would beat most of our teeth out of our heads. Moving due south along the western edge of the bay was asking for more of the same, only longer.

My hope was to get to the Card Sound Bridge and inside the cover of Key Largo, where we could dock for the night at a hotel on the water. After today's beating, they'd need a good night's sleep in a bed.

I chose Elliott Key. We'd pay for it for the first hour, but getting there would be worth it. When we exited the safety of the channel and were back out in open water, Gunner hopped up onto Clay's lap and the two held each other. Summer and Ellie crouched behind me, bracing themselves between the back bench and the seat of my center console.

Me? I held on while the waves broke over the gunnels. I put her up on plane, tried to find a rhythm to the waves with the least amount of water in the boat, and adjusted the tabs. I tried everything I knew, but it was little help. We were getting soaked. Between spray and waves breaking over the bow, I turned on the bilge pump and watched as the ankle-deep water drained out the scuppers. While *Gone Fiction* could handle it, I wasn't too sure about us. Crossing the bay, one thing became apparent: we were the only boat on the water.

Two hours later, we approached Elliott Key. Once inside her shadow, she broke the wind and the water calmed. Almost to glass. Gunner walked around, sniffed my ankle, looked up at me, and then returned to Clay. I think that was his way of telling me I was crazy.

Elliott Key is a national park. Nice cove marina. People camp here for days at a time. Atlantic on one side. Bay on the other. It's idyllic. Right now, the place was empty as the waters and wind from the Atlantic beat the shoreline and campsites. Save one boat.

A nice boat. Forty-plus feet. Five Mercury engines. Two thousand horsepower total. She was a seventy-plus-mile-an-hour boat made to run the islands and back in about the time it takes to eat a sandwich. A million dollars or better. Black hull. Black windows. Black matching engines.

She said, "Don't mess with me." So of course I did.

I tied up behind her and let the troops and Gunner stretch their legs while I made myself look busy. Nobody moved up top, but I heard the faint noise of a stereo beneath. Walking along the boardwalk to the bathroom, I passed her from stern to bow. She was spotless. New. Well maintained.

Somebody's pride. She also had no name and no significant markings. Nothing to set her apart other than the all black.

If I was waiting for a storm to pass or let up, this would be a good place to do it. Nobody in their right mind would attempt to pick up anyone from land or deliver them either to another vessel or—and this got me thinking—a house on stilts. The wind and waves made it impossible. Both people and boats would be crushed. But if the wind abated, I'd stow my boat right about here.

I needed to do some snooping around, and I couldn't do it with a deck full of tired people. We exited the marina and wound through the mangroves en route to Key Largo. Mangroves are one of my favorite trees, and Summer picked up on this as we slipped between them. She, too, was glad to be out of the eggbeater.

The sun was falling, but she chose to say nothing. She just stood there. Next to me. And if I'm honest, I liked it.

CHAPTER 32

K ey Largo loomed on our left, and soon we passed beneath the Card Sound Bridge. A bridge of some reputation. Years ago, some crazy writer with a broken heart drove his Mercedes off the top of the span. His mangled German automobile had been salvaged and erected as a rusty monument on the shore nearby. His body, on the other hand, was never found.

We passed through the relatively calm waters of Barnes Sound, where Clay sat up and began taking notice. Off to our left, an old sailboat, maybe sixty feet or better, lay on her side, taking on water. Had been for years. Her mast was snapped at the waterline. She'd never recover. Lost at sea. Once beautiful. Now, not so much.

We idled beneath US1, and the life of Key Largo opened before us. Waterfront bars, jet skiers, fishing boats—the calm waters were alive with people. Most had come to snorkel or scuba in John Pennekamp Coral Reef State Park, a three-mile by twenty-five-mile underwater haven on the other side of the Key. In the Atlantic. It's Florida's Grand Canyon. Living coral for seventy-five square miles or thereabouts. It's so fragile, and so alive, that boaters aren't allowed to anchor in it for fear of killing it. It's one small part of a larger whole known as Florida's Great Reef, which stretches from Miami to some seventy miles south of Key West. If you really want to "see" Florida, you'd be hard-pressed to do better than Pennekamp. It's an undersea wonderworld. Full of sergeant majors, jack crevalle, pompano, yellow grunts, mangrove snapper, smiling barracudas, sharks, leopard rays—you name it, it's there. Then there's the coral. Every color under the rainbow paints the coral, which waves at you as the current ripples through.

But there'd be no Pennekamp for us. I skirted along the eastern edge and pulled into the marina attached to the Key Largo Bay Marriot Beach Resort. I needed something that attracted the party crowd.

I parked the boat much like you do your car and rented three rooms. As the dark reds and crimson of sundown burst onto the western skyline, I handed each their key and told them, "Don't wait up."

Clay stiffened. So did Summer. Both objected, but I explained, "I've got to do some snooping, and besides, I need your eyes and ears around the pool deck. I need you to listen to what people are saying. I'll be back. Midnight. Maybe after."

Summer tried to convince me otherwise, and I told her, "You can be the most help to me if you'll watch Ellie, drink some drinks with umbrellas sticking out the top, and listen closely to what other people are saying."

Gunner looked at me and pushed his ears forward. I patted my thigh and he stiffened and looked at Clay. Clay said, "Get on," and Gunner hopped down into the boat. I cast off, eased back out into the water, and tried to shake off both the weary and the tired. Behind me, Summer stood on the dock, arms crossed. I turned the wheel and returned, pulling up alongside the bulkhead. She looked down at me. I shifted to neutral.

"I'll be back."

"I know."

"Oh, you do?" I'd missed that completely. "I thought you looked worried that I might not."

She shook her head. "I'm worried about the condition you'll be in when you do."

I laughed. "That's comforting."

I turned the wheel and put the resort in my wake. With daylight fading, I shifted to nighttime mode on my electronics, passed back beneath the Card Sound Bridge and within sight of the Mercedes monument, and began hugging the easternmost coastline. As long as I stayed within cover of the mangroves, I cut through smooth waters. But the moment I ventured too far from the protection of the shoreline, the waves and whitecaps returned. An hour later, shrouded in darkness, I cut all my running lights, running illegally and blind to anything but radar, and continued creeping along the inside. When I reached Elliott Key, I tied up loosely to a mangrove and watched the entrance to the cove through Leica binoculars.

For three hours I studied the cove and the rough waters of the bay. In the distance, silhouetted against the sky, I counted seven houses on stilts. Each was dark. Not a light anywhere. The only lights I could see were those of the Miami shoreline and the lighthouse just north.

At two a.m., a forty-plus-foot vessel cloaked in black and carrying five engines on her transom idled out of the cove without a single running light. Once clear of the shallow water, she throttled up and churned the rough water, having set a vector for what looked like Stiltsville. That boat was far more capable of handling six- to eight-foot seas, which was what we were looking at. I could survive in my Whaler. That boat could navigate. Big difference.

Losing sight, I knew I needed to close the gap. I pulled in my line, set my phone inside a watertight OtterBox, and ventured out where the waves began crashing over the gunnels. Within minutes I was soaked. Between my chart and the physical landmark of the lighthouse, I set a course toward the closest house, knowing I couldn't get near any of the pilings or the waves would split *Gone Fiction* against them. The vessel I was following no doubt had bow thrusters. Given her weight, agility, and power, she could navigate close enough to one of the homes to either take on or offload passengers.

The wind pushed me hard off course, and I had to fight the wheel to keep her aimed north. Gunner whined above the roar of the wind. He didn't like this any more than I did. He retreated from the bow and huddled next to me, eventually bracing himself between my legs. I kept one hand on the wheel, one on the throttle, and every few seconds I'd touch his head and let him know I knew he was there.

In the chaos, I lost sight of the boat, but that did not mean they had lost sight of me. While I couldn't see twenty feet off the bow, chances were good they had radar, which told them both my and their exact locations. My chart told me I was within a thousand feet of the first home, but my electronics worked off of GPS; given the clouds, I doubted my location. And I was right to doubt it. A wave crashed over the bow, flooding the inside. When I looked up, I was nearly beneath the porch or some outcrop of the first home. Above me loomed concrete beams threatening to crush my T-top.

I slammed the throttle forward, digging myself out of the black hole I'd fallen into. My momentum pushed me into and through the next oncoming wave, further flooding the deck. The water had risen above my ankles. More mid-shin. I wasn't worried about *Gone Fiction* sinking as much as I was worried about the engine flooding and leaving me powerless to be bashed against the pilings or tossed at will through the bay.

The next wave brought more water. The boat turned thirty degrees beneath me and Gunner slid out from beneath my legs, slamming into the wall of the gunnel. The impact flipped him and sent him spinning through the air like a caricature from a comic book. While he was a good swimmer, I doubted he was that good. I lunged, grabbed his collar, and dragged him back through the foam and spray. I wedged him between my legs and throttled through the next wave as the water poured over the bow, again threatening to swamp the boat. Conditions had deteriorated, and I needed to get out before I lost the boat. Gunner whined beneath me in agreement.

In the distance, a single running light flashed. Tossing about the water like a bobber. There it was again. At half throttle, I circled, allowing the wind to come in behind me, which meant the waves were no longer coming over the bow. Now the wind was pushing the nose down, threatening to bury the bow in the troughs between the waves.

I used the light like a beacon and moved toward it. Somehow that boat had enough power to remain stationary on the leeward side of one of the homes toward the middle of the cluster. Between her two thousand horsepower, her bow thrusters, and a bow line that threatened to snap the piling in two, she was able to counter the storm and remain stable enough beneath a platform. Stable enough that bodies appeared, walking on the porch above it. Ninety seconds later, a line formed on the edge of the porch, and one by one they began jumping off the platform onto the deck of the boat below. This was roughly akin to jumping off a one-story house into a swimming pool—although the pool was moving and tilting at more than thirty degrees. The figures were female. Save the very last one. He was stocky, in charge, and pointing something at them. Prodding them. One by one, they jumped. Maybe ten in total. Their mouths said they were screaming, but I couldn't hear them.

With two to go, one of the girls mistimed her jump and missed the boat entirely, landing in the water. One of the girls in the boat reached for her while others shined a light, but it was useless. She was gone.

The guy with the gun pushed the last of the girls headfirst into the boat, and then he turned toward me. I knew this because I saw the thing in his hand flash red. Once, twice, then a continual red flash. I did not hear the report of the rifle over the roar of the wind, but in my experience, you never hear the bullets before they hit you. If you're lucky, you hear them after.

I cut the wheel hard north and slammed the throttle to full, shooting me out of one wave trough and immediately into another. Cutting the wheel again hard left, I saw the transport vessel had throttled up and was moving up on plane. Attesting to the power of the engines. All I could see was the white foam of her wake painted against the darkness that had become the ocean.

Whoever had ended up in the water was certainly long gone, but judging by her mistimed landing, she was only a hundred yards or so from the next house. The wind and waves would push her directly into the pilings or the dock. Which would either snap her neck, causing her to drown, or spit her up on the floating dock.

I made one pass. Saw nothing. Then circled again. Still nothing. Gunner whined. The black boat was becoming a speck in the distance. I screamed at the dog. "You see her, boy?" I pointed to the dock, which was appearing and disappearing with every wave. On my third pass, Gunner stood on the console, bringing his eyes near shoulder level with me. As I turned to follow the boat, he barked. Then again. I didn't know if he saw something or he was just angry at the storm, but since he was the smartest dog I'd ever met, I whipped the wheel 180 degrees and pushed the throttle to fifty percent.

A body lay on the dock.

Somehow either the current or a wave had spit her up on the floating dock. She'd wrapped herself in a mooring line and clung to a piling. When I approached, massive waves threatened to rip her from the dock's surface. I knew I had one shot. Gauging the current, the wind, and the time between the waves, I rode down one wave, up another, and throttled up to almost ninety percent, shooting me nearly airborne onto the floating dock. The hull landed hard, and the solid surface of the dock listed the boat violently, nearly tossing me and Gunner overboard.

I saw the girl. Reached. But she wouldn't let go of the piling. A wave crashed over the bow and caught the center console in the middle, catapulting *Gone Fiction* off the dock and back into open water.

The girl was weakening. She wouldn't last another wave. I slammed the throttle forward, broke the bow through the next wave, rode the incoming wave up onto the floating dock, and banked the gunnel off the piling. The girl extended a hand, and I grabbed it as the next wave shot us off the dock and back out into the ocean.

Gunner had squatted below me. Whining. The girl flew across the space between us and I caught her with one arm while turning the wheel with the other. The wave landed over my shoulders and caught Gunner square in the chest, dragging him out from underneath me. I had one hand on the girl and one hand alternating between wheel and throttle as I watched the water drag him out the back of the boat. Water had filled the boat, and I'd lose the engine if I didn't throttle up *right now*.

I screamed, "Gunner!" but there was no response.

He was gone.

With the girl latching on to me with a terrified death grip and another wave towering down on us, I swore, gave it all the throttle it could handle, and cursed myself for bringing him.

CHAPTER 33

We rode southwest. One minute passed. Then another. The water drained out the back as the engine steamed and smoked amid a deluge of salt water. I turned west-southwest and put the wind directly behind us, hoping to use the T-top as a sail. We picked up speed, banging from one wave crest to the next wave trough.

The loss of Gunner cut me deeply. I aimed my anger at the boat.

Ten minutes in, we'd crossed half the bay. In the distance, I could see the lights of the Card Sound Bridge, but there was no sign of the transport vessel. I had to choose. Black Point Marina or bridge. He went one way or the other. Given a boat that powerful and cargo that expensive, I figured he'd race under the bridge, hit the clear waters of Barnes Sound, and turn west for the Gulf, finding a channel through the flats. My guess was that he was either connecting with another larger yacht nearby or making for Key West tonight to make the transfer.

I chose the bridge. Despite the fact that we'd fueled up yesterday, my fuel gauge read less than 10 percent. I'd spent so much time throttling up and down waves, much of the time near full power, I'd burned through much of my fuel. The boat drained but conditions did not improve. Waves tossed us about like a rag doll. Five minutes in and my passenger was vomiting on the deck beneath me. Every time she did so, a wave broke over the gunnel and washed it out. This happened more than I cared to count. Finally, she just knelt on the floor next to me, dry heaving.

What should have taken twenty minutes took closer to forty. When we finally reached the bridge, my hands were cramping on the wheel and the girl lay beneath me, clinging to my legs, screaming. When we passed beneath the bridge, the Key appeared on our left and blocked the wind. The surface of the water changed from violent and full of rage to placid and almost peaceful in less than a quarter of a mile. Soon the water turned to glass.

I pulled the throttle to neutral, turned on my interior LED lights, and helped lift the girl to her feet. She had lost all control of her emotions and was screaming and beating the air wildly. I grabbed her hands, wrapped my arms around her, and held her. "It's okay. It's okay. You're safe. You're going to be okay. I won't hurt you."

After a few minutes, the reality of her situation sank in, and she must have believed me because screaming turned to whimpering to her collapsing in my arms. I set her on the bench, pressed her hair out of her face, and said, "I know you're probably scared out of your mind, but do you know where that transport vessel is going?"

She shook her head.

"You sure? Anything you can tell me? Did you overhear anything?"

Another shake.

We were running on fumes, so I steered to a marina and a fuel pump protected in a cove on the north end of Key Largo. A Mexican restaurant next door. While she sat on the deck of the boat and cried, I filled the tank and studied the dark skyline for any sign of a moving boat. I also glanced behind me, looking for any sign of Gunner. But I knew better. We were seven miles or more from where he'd flown overboard. In a torrential sea.

Gunner was gone.

I tried not to think about the conversation with Clay.

I hugged the coastline. In the distance I could see the lights of the top floor of the resort. I wrapped a towel around the girl, throttled up to plane, and covered the few miles in just a few minutes. Rather than docking in my slip appointed by the check-in clerk, I circled southeast and came up inside the beach area. It was nearing four o'clock in the morning. The beach was lit, and all the lounge chairs were empty save one. I eased the bow up into shallow water, trimmed the engine, and came to a stop when the bow gently touched sand.

Summer stood from the chair, wiped her eyes, and saw me step from the boat carrying a female. She sprinted into the water, but seeing that I wasn't carrying Angel, she grabbed a towel and covered the girl after I set her on a chair.

The girl was blonde. Cheerleader looks. College age. Maybe a sophomore. Doubtful she was a senior. Dressed in Daisy Dukes and a T-shirt, she wore a bathing suit underneath, which suggested she'd been taken from somewhere near the water with the intention of getting into it. A quick examination told me she was unhurt save her emotions and mental capacities, which might take a while to heal.

Once she quit sobbing, I knelt and said, "I need you to tell me what happened, and I need you to do it quickly."

Summer tapped my shoulder. "Where's Gunner?"

I shook my head.

She covered her mouth with her hand.

The girl was unable to speak. I held her hand and waited while her eyes focused on us. When she finally made eye contact, I asked the question differently. "Did you know the other girls?"

She shook her head.

"Sorority? Class?"

A single shake. "We responded to a model call. Photo shoot. First the beach. Then a yacht. Five hundred dollars if they chose you. They chose the ten of us, loaded us onto a small boat, maybe about the size of yours, and then dropped us at that house."

Clever. "How many days have you been there?"

"Five. I think."

"Any idea where they were taking you?"

"No."

I returned to the boat, pulled my dry phone out of the OtterBox, clicked to Angel's picture, and held it up. "Do you recognize her?"

She looked and shook her head.

"You sure? Look closely. Please."

She looked again and shook her head one final time.

I looked at Summer. "Call 911. Tell them what you know. Anything and everything she can tell you." I climbed back into *Gone Fiction*.

Summer grabbed me by the arm and wouldn't let go. When I turned, she didn't speak. She just stood there. Hopelessness screamed at me from behind her eyes.

"Give me a couple hours. I'll be back at daylight. If I don't find anything, we'll be in Key West by lunchtime."

Tears appeared. She wouldn't let go. "Summer. I—"

She pulled me to her and kissed me. When finished, she looked at me, pressed herself to me, and kissed me again. This time longer. Her lips trembled and tasted salty. The tears broke loose, trailed down her cheeks, and hung on to her chin.

I thumbed away each, speaking softly. "I'm coming back. I promise."

She let go and began dialing her phone. From the helm, I glanced in the direction of the bay and Gunner's watery grave. "Better let me tell Clay."

I reversed out of the private beach, turned due west, and began studying the charts for channels that led out into deeper water. While the transport vessel had certain advantages out in the bay, back here, in shallow water, I could navigate easier. She probably needed three to four feet to draft. And at least four to get up on plane. I only needed two. Sometimes less. That meant I could go places she could not.

To my way of thinking, the captain of that transport tender had two options: deliver the girls to a larger yacht anchored somewhere in the Gulf of Mexico and then make a slow overnight to Key West while they took on clients, or make a fast run down the calm waters of the inside en route to Key West, where a larger vessel and clients awaited. Either way, I felt Key West was the destination and that there was some urgency to it; otherwise they never would've risked the Stiltsville pickup.

The Keys of Florida separate the sometimes angry waters of the Atlantic Ocean from the relatively calm waters of the Gulf of Mexico. There are obviously exceptions, such as when hurricanes roll up from the south, but on the whole the Gulf is far calmer than the Atlantic. At times, it's more lake than ocean. The Gulf is also much shallower.

The exposed ocean floor around the Keys is limestone dusted with sand, where depths range from a few inches to a few feet. Safely navigating this to the deeper waters of the Gulf requires local knowledge of channels, or something akin to underground rivers that have been marked over time to allow larger vessels access to deeper water.

These channels are easier to see from the air and tough to find from the waterline. A good chart is a must, as is local knowledge. Whether the black boat transporting nine girls was taking them a short distance to a larger boat or a longer distance to Key West, the captain had to know these waters. Meaning he'd done this before.

I throttled to full, trimmed the engines, and navigated via chart southwest through skinny water past Plantation, Islamorada, Lower Matecumbe Key, Duck Key, and finally Marathon. I thought if I could race down the inside, I could hop in front of him because he would have to divert due west to find safe passage, whereas I could skim over the top. From Marathon, I turned northwest and rode seven miles out into the Gulf, where I anchored and stood on my T-top staring through my Leicas as the sun broke the skyline east of me. Theoretically, this gave me at least fourteen or fifteen miles of perspective—probably farther. If any vessel traveled north or south along the inside, I'd have a good chance of seeing her.

My problem was sleep. Or lack of it. I'd not slept in at least a day, and I couldn't remember when I slept more than four hours in a stretch. I was exhausted and could barely hold my eyes open. Between my stitches, deep bruises, and the stress and pounding of last night's bay crossing, my body hurt everywhere. I knew if I sat down, I'd sleep several hours I could not afford.

I lit my Jetboil and made some coffee. It helped. Coffee can be a comfort when comfort is hard to find. As the sun rose higher, I stood and studied the edge of the world. Boats passed, but not the one I was looking for. I must have missed her.

At noon, I climbed down, pulled up the anchor, and set a course for Key Largo. An hour later, I tied up at my slip. Clay, Summer, and Ellie were sitting on the beach. I knew my conversation with Clay would not be easy.

Summer informed me that the girl we rescued from the water last night had been evaluated by the paramedics and—other than the trauma of being kidnapped and the shock of nearly drowning and the horror of learning she'd almost been a cog in the sex-traffic wheel—she'd be fine. Turned out she was the daughter of a wealthy tech manufacturer out of Miami with friends in government. Summer and Clay had spent all morning talking with agents, and up until a few minutes ago, this place had been crawling with men wearing guns—all of whom wanted to talk with me.

That meant the satellite, radio, and telephone chatter had increased a hundredfold and whoever was currently transporting girls knew it. Guys in that business always had an ear to the track, and they could feel when heat was closer. They paid well for that kind of information, which might explain why we didn't intersect last night or this morning.

Clay listened as I told him the story, his wrinkled face growing more wrinkled as I spoke. When I finished, he nodded and stared north toward the bay. Finally, he sucked through his teeth and put his hand on my shoulder.

I knew we needed to push south, but I was fighting a weariness I'd not known in some time. I told them to grab their bags and we'd shove off. If I quit moving, it'd be some time before I got going again. I was afraid if I closed my eyes I wouldn't open them again for twenty-four hours. Ten minutes later, we were loaded up and shoving off. Everyone was quiet. The loss of Gunner had hit us hard. I thought through the events of last night for the ten thousandth time, wondering what I could have done differently. The only answer was not to bring him, but then he'd been the one who saw her. Without Gunner, I never would've found that girl.

We idled out past the Mexican restaurant, the jet skis, and the sailboats tugging on their mooring lines. I was about to put us up on plane when Summer thought I might be hungry, which I was, so she brought me a sandwich. I paused long enough to open the wrapper and take a bite.

One glorious, magnificent bite. Which gave me just enough time to listen to the world around me.

Clay heard it too. I turned, and there it was again. The sound drew each of us to the gunnel, our eyes searching the waterline. Several hundred yards in the distance, coughing salt water, tired, and barking for all he was worth, paddled Gunner.

Clay stood, slapped his thigh, and swore. "I'll be a suck-egg mule!"

I cut the wheel, throttled up, and closed the distance. When we reached him, Gunner's paws were churning the water like pistons. I reached down, lifted him from the water, and set him on the deck where he shook and began licking my face, his tail waving at six hundred rotations a minute.

It was a bright spot in a dark couple of days. We crowded around while Gunner licked the skin off our faces. He climbed up on Clay, spun around, barked, hopped down, ran once around the boat, then again, then tackled me. I had never been happier to see a dog in my entire life. He smelled my sandwich, sniffed it, and devoured it in one bite, only to tackle me again.

I held him, pulled him to me, and said, "Forgive me?"

He ran to Ellie, climbed up on her lap while she sat there and giggled, then Summer, then back to Clay—who laughed out loud. Finally, he lay down on the front casting deck and rolled onto his back, his tongue hanging out. I returned to the helm and spoke to him over the idle of the engine. "When we get to Key West, the steak is on me."

CHAPTER 34

O ur mood improved immensely. And the trip to Key West passed quickly. Tucked in behind the windshield, I dialed Colorado. He answered, and I updated him about last night, the girl, the investigation, and asked him to make some inquiries. He said he would. I also told him I needed a place for the four of us to stay in Key West. "Someplace that's dog-friendly."

I was about to hang up when he said, "One more thing. Sisters of Mercy."

"Yeah."

"Used to be a convent."

"What do you mean, used to?"

"Women quit joining. Nuns grew older. Started dying off. Only a couple left. If that. They own a compound, couple of blocks on the water. They get to keep it 'til the last one dies, then it reverts back to some entity that's loosely associated with a church."

"Got an address?"

We passed Islamorada, the fishing capital of the world, and then turned due west, putting Lignumvitae Key off the bow—a three-hundred-acre ancient island, accessible only by boat and named after a small, very dense tree that grows in the tropics. So dense, it sinks in water. At seventy-nine pounds per cubic foot, it's strong stuff. In Latin, it means "wood of life."

Lignumvitae Key is Florida before people. Before machines. Before anything, save the breath of God. It's also home to the exceedingly rare black ironwood—the densest and heaviest wood on earth. Eighty-seven pounds per cubic foot. The Calusa Indians once lived here. They fished, grew citrus trees, and swatted the mosquitoes that swarmed in the billions. Which might be why no one lives here now. The swamp angels have taken over.

Despite my affinity for the untouched beauty of Lignumvitae, we would not be stopping there either.

We followed the chart, turned southwest, and skirted around No Name, Big Pine, Middle Torch, Big Torch, Summerland, Cudjoe, and Sugarloaf Keys. All smaller keys connecting the southern tip of Florida to Key West. Finally, we skimmed across the Waltz Key Basin and into the waters surrounding Key West. Colorado had made reservations for us on the southernmost tip. Just north of Mallory Square at Pier House Resort and Spa. The location was strategic in that it gave us a view of every vessel that passed within eyesight.

Two quiet days passed.

I circled the island several times a day. A twenty-six-mile round trip, it took an hour or so. I was looking for anything. A large yacht. A blacked-out tender. Anything either flashy or subdued that caught my eye. Nothing did. The trail was cold.

Clay arrived in Key West and promptly disappeared. Without Gunner. Curious, Gunner and I followed from a distance. Clay walked into a men's shop, got fitted, and returned a day later to walk out wearing a new suit, shiny shoes, and a hat. He bought some flowers and walked eight blocks to the Key West cemetery. He zigzagged through the stones for almost half an hour, finally stopping. When he did, he took off his hat, stared down at the stone, and talked. Out loud. After several minutes, he set the flowers down, pulled out his handkerchief, and wiped his eyes. He stood holding his hat, hands crossed. Looking brilliant in his new suit.

Gunner and I walked up behind him and stood two rows back. He spoke to me without looking. "Mr. Murphy, I'd like you to meet my wife."

I wound around the headstones and stood next to him. He pointed. "Celeste." The stone read "Mary Celeste Pettybone." He spoke softly, as if he were afraid to wake her. "She died ten years ago. Age of seventy." He sucked through his teeth and continued, "Came to see me every week. Drove six hours one way." He wiped his eyes again. "For forty years."

I just looked at him.

He laughed. "I tried to divorce her, tried to tell her to find another man, even stopped coming up to see her for a while when she'd visit, but . . ." He trailed off. "She never quit. Not on me. Not on us." He stared out across the stones. "Forty years." Another shake of his head. "Wrote me letters. Told me 'bout her job at the diner. Cleaning houses. She got hired at a hotel. Good job. Twelve years. Then when the arthritis set in, she . . ."

He stared down. "I wasn't there when she . . ." He wiped his eyes. "They came and told me in my cell. Said she had died. That's all." He snapped his fingers. "Like that, she was gone." He was quiet a long time. "When I was young and full of vinegar, I used to talk about the day my ship would come in. The day I met her, it did. She was my whole world." He shook his head. "Life is hard. Harder than I expected. On both sides of the bars." He knelt down and dusted off her stone. "Celeste, I want to tell you that you're a good woman. The best even. And I'm sorry. Sorry for . . . not being there when you needed me. And for everything in between. I'm . . ."

Clay fell quiet. He leaned on the stone and lifted himself off his knees. Then he unfolded his handkerchief and wiped his eyes. I let him cry. His shoulders shook, suggesting he'd been holding those tears a long time. Finally, he straightened his new suit and donned his hat. He spoke softly. Staring at the earth. He glanced at me and back at the stone.

"Celeste always talked about seeing me in a suit. When I got out. How we'd go to dinner. Dancing. I hope she likes it." Standing in the sun, Clay wobbled. I caught his arm, and he leaned on me. He coughed. A deep, productive cough. I couldn't tell if it was returning or leaving. The only thing apparent to me was that whatever had kept Clay alive until this moment, whatever had gotten him through prison and from prison, was gone.

We stood there over an hour.

Having said his goodbyes, we turned and began walking toward the gate. He was a good bit taller than me, so when he spoke his shadow fell across me. "I want to thank you for getting me here, Mr. Murphy."

"I'm sorry it wasn't a good bit sooner."

He opened the gate, then stared behind us. A long minute passed. "Me too." Another suck through his teeth. "But not nearly as much as her."

Standing in his shadow, I knew I was watching a beautiful love story play out in the air around me.

We walked back to the hotel while Clay leaned on me. More so than usual. A light rain dusted our shoulders. After a couple of blocks, he spoke. "You figured out what you're going to tell Ms. Summer if and when you can't find her daughter?"

"No."

He looked at me but said nothing. His face said plenty.

Summer sat poolside when I returned in the early afternoon. A novel on her knees. Number thirteen. Fumbling with her hands. The sun was falling and the crowds were filling the waterside bars en route to Mallory Square for the sunset ritual. Staring at Summer, two things caught my attention: the book and her bathing suit. A bikini. And it'd been a while since I'd noticed a woman in a bathing suit.

"Nice suit," I said when she caught me looking. Red-handed. A razor cut on her ankle suggested she'd shaved her legs.

Self-conscious, she fiddled with her straps. "Is it too much? It's all I could find. They didn't have a one-piece." She reached for a towel.

"Not too many people trying to cover up in Key West. Down here more clothes come off than on." I sat across from her. "Can I ask you something?"

She waited. Sweat had formed on her top lip, and her bare shoulders showed the remaining effects of the oysters the night we'd first met. They were healing, and it struck me again that she hadn't complained a bit. Not once. "Why do you work so hard to cover up what so many would show the whole world?" I waved my hand across all the shapes and sizes of the pool deck. Most wore suits that were a few sizes too small. Wearing a memory.

She set the towel down. Summer was beautiful. A class all by herself. She just didn't know it. Or, if she had at one time, something or someone had convinced her it was no longer true. When she spoke, her honesty was disarming. "Being known . . ." She raised her knees and pulled her heels closer to her bottom. "Can be painful." She folded the towel and eyed all the sunbathers. "Sometimes it's just easier to be an extra on the stage than the lead."

I glanced at the book. "Any good?"

She smiled and gestured at four women poolside who were reading the same author. Then she pointed at the men who were with the women. "If all these guys knew how to love a woman the way"—she tapped the cover—"this guy does . . ." She leaned back and shook her head. "The world would be a different place. Although"—she set the book aside—"seems wrong to be lost in make-believe when my daughter is . . ." She turned and eyed the Gulf.

I shook my head. "It's not good. We're looking for the proverbial needle."

"Angel's tough. She'll fight."

I chose not to tell her what my experience told me about such girls. "I know." I had an idea. It was a long shot, but I pointed to the sidewalk that led to Mallory Square. "Can I buy you a beer?"

She chuckled. "You flirting with me?"

"While I would like that, I was actually thinking we might use you as bait, if you'll forgive the analogy."

"What?"

"I want you to walk through the square, looking forlorn. A beer in your hand. A woman scorned. Watch the sun go down."

She half smiled. "That's called 'trolling.'"

I nodded.

"Why?"

"Because I think you'll be noticed. And honestly, I need you to be." I weighed my head side to side. "You game?"

She stood and began wrapping the towel around her. "I thought you were asking me to watch the sunset with you."

I placed my hand on the towel. "Maybe some other time."

"I can't go walking up there like this."

"This is Key West. You'll fit right in."

"But I feel naked."

I laughed. "You sure haven't left much to the imagination."

She blushed. "I knew I should have found something else."

I held her hand. "You're going to draw attention like a puppy in the park. Every man out there will notice you, and right now we need that."

"Murph—"

"I'll be close. I just need you to mildly entertain any guy who begins talking with you and asking you questions. Specifically questions as to whether you're alone. Don't be easy, but don't be quick to brush them off. Be—"

She slid on her sunglasses. "Just what is this going to accomplish?"

"Guys who sell flesh like to be in places where they can spot it." I pointed to the hotel rooms with a view of the square and the water. "They rent those rooms for the sole purpose of people-watching. They're pros at spotting the available and the unavailable. So let's go fishing."

Completing the look, she pulled a ball cap down over her eyes and began walking toward the bar, her hips swaying slightly more than usual. "I'm not sure whether to take that as a compliment or not."

She bought herself a beer and walked off barefooted toward the crowds. Sunset was still an hour away, so we had time. Summer sauntered. Walking slowly. Trolling.

She stood at the railing overlooking the water. Leaning. Sipping her beer. Staring out across the waves. Lost in thought while oblivious to every man around her. To her credit, she had all their attention. I'm not sure whether it's design or happenstance, but women's bathing suits have a way of crawling up their backsides the more they move around. Most girls will routinely "fix" the situation so they're not showing their untanned derrieres to the world.

Summer's suit had inched into such a condition, but for whatever reason she didn't fix it. She left it alone. Giving everyone a pretty good look. As I walked behind at a relatively safe distance, I wasn't quite sure if that was for the benefit of the guys who might be watching or for me. I chuckled. You can take the girl off Broadway, but you can't take Broadway out of the girl. She was quite good in the leading role.

Every man in Mallory Square had noticed Summer by now. A few dabbled in conversation with her, but she feigned disinterest. Adding complexity to the perception of a broken heart.

Thirty minutes later, she bought a second beer and moved closer to the point—where the crowds formed large circles around the street performers waiting on the sun. Consumed in her own thoughts, Summer strayed close enough to the crowd to be noticed while not so close as to be involved in the happiness they were selling. She heard the laughter; she just didn't join in. A couple of brave men, lathered in suntan oil, swollen with muscle, and draped in gold chains and more chest hair than silverback gorillas, made attempts at small talk. She responded but initiated nothing. Leaving her to watch the sunset alone.

Which she did. Her act was so convincing, I wondered whether it was an act.

Watching her watch the sunset was difficult. I'd done the same thing from much the same location for nearly a year of my life. The ping and pain of the memory returned.

The sun turned crimson, then pink, followed by purple, then deep blue. Then it disappeared. The crowd toasted the curtain call, applauded, and returned to their tables and blenders. Summer lingered. Choosing a bench and sitting alone. Thirty minutes later, a man appeared. Bearded. White hair. Tattered shorts. Straw hat. Flip-flops. Walking a dog. His forearms were rippled, suggesting more muscle beneath his baggy clothing. He allowed the dog to wander close to Summer. She took the bait and petted the dog, who hopped up on the bench next to her. The man laughed but didn't pressure her. Didn't pull the dog away. They talked, and two minutes turned into five. Which turned into eight. He was good. Finally, he pulled out a pen and wrote something on her hand, which she tenderly allowed. When finished, he tipped his hat and continued on his way.

Summer glanced at me and returned down the boardwalk to the hotel.

When I turned, Clay stood next to me. I had not known he was there. Leaning against a lamppost. His eyes were trained on the man. I asked without looking at him, "You good?"

He scratched his white beard and followed Summer.

CHAPTER 35

T he man walked south and east around the remainder of the board-walk, attempting to look casual, but his route was anything but happenstance. He dictated where the dog went. Not the other way around. He also stood and waited in the shadows several times, watching crowds of people. Especially women. Maybe he was guilty of people-watching and nothing more. Maybe he was an introvert.

I knew better. His method was textbook. Near 11:00 p.m., he grabbed some takeout and returned to a weekly efficiency rental on the water where he watched a soccer game with dinner on his lap.

Summer had changed and was waiting on me at the poolside bar. A guy with a guitar stood at a microphone singing ballad covers. Pretty good too. When I sat, relief drained into her face.

She said the guy with the dog had been kind, not pushy, and did finally get around to the "are you alone" question. But he got to it by making a statement about himself rather than asking directly. "I been alone for twenty years," he said, with the same forlorn look across the water, allowing her to agree with him and offer her understanding. He followed with, "No fun, is it?" She'd shaken her head. He then offered to take her on a moonlit cruise the following night. Said it'd be him and several friends. He had an old sailboat. They would grill fish. Be back around one or so. She had thanked him and said she'd think about it.

I wasn't sure. Either about him or going through with it. Having watched Summer use herself and her body as bait, I discovered I didn't like it. I wished I hadn't done it. She saw me waffling and lifted her hand. "I'll call him tomorrow afternoon. Or evening. Maybe last minute. After I've had time to think about it."

I nodded, but I wasn't sold.

When I returned to my room, Clay was standing in the shadows waiting on me. From his vantage point, he could see Summer and Ellie's rooms. Gunner lay at his feet. He said, "Mr. Murphy?"

I turned and we watched as Summer closed her door.

He continued, "I know that man." He motioned toward the boardwalk. "The one with the dog."

"How so?"

He showed me a picture of the man, taken up close. From just a few feet away.

Both the presence and the perspective of the picture meant that Clay had gotten close. "You take this?"

"I'm not quite as old as you think I am."

The picture had been taken through a crowd of people, slightly tilted, but showed his face and, more importantly, the tattoo on his left arm. Clay expanded the picture. "When I was working on the boat, he brought girls there. Only to. Never from. He used several boats, and he never looked the same twice. His face would change. Costumes and such."

"You sure?"

He tapped the picture. "He can change his face, but it's a little tougher to change a tattoo. And—" He paused. "I've got some experience with evil men." He closed the picture and put the phone in his shirt pocket. "He's evil. A heart black as crude oil."

I woke two hours before daylight and was standing in the shadows studying his efficiency when his light flashed on. I smelled coffee brewing, and then he appeared. This time there was no dog. He was wearing a striped jogging suit and, oddly enough, no beard. He was bald. And when he turned to walk away, I saw a tattoo crawling up his neck. He moved quickly, more catlike, toward a parking garage, hopped into a turbocharged Carrera, and disappeared north.

His exit left me with one impression. I didn't know who he was, only that he wasn't who, or what, he seemed. I dialed Colorado. When he answered, he sounded out of breath. "You've been quiet a few days."

"Not much to report. Check your phone. I just texted you a license tag. Need you to run it. Quickly."

"Got it. Anything else?"

I was quiet a minute. "I'm worried we've missed our window."

He heard my tone of voice and didn't need to say more. "Let me run the plate." He paused a second but didn't hang up. Purposefully. His voice had softened. Like what he had to say hurt more than the rest. "And, Murph?"

"Yeah."

"Check out the convent."

There was more there. "What are you not telling me?"

The line went dead.

I returned to the boardwalk and the efficiency. I found the breaker to his room and cut the power. If he had monitoring electronics, I didn't want them recording me as I let myself in. The dog met me at the door, sniffed me, and rolled over onto his back. The room was sparse. A suitcase. Clothes neatly folded. No booze. No drugs. Bed made. A sweaty towel hanging in the bathroom, probably from a morning workout. In the closet hung three separate changes of clothes. Each different. One striped suit. Black patent leather shoes. One pair of jeans. Running shoes. White linen shirt. One pair of tattered shorts. Hawaiian shirt. Flip-flops. On the bathroom counter sat three wigs and various types of makeup. A finished crossword puzzle—and the handwriting was excessively neat. Printed.

The kitchen was empty. Nothing in the fridge. No food in the pantry save a bag of dog food. A single leash hung on the wall. Oddly, there was a handwritten grocery list stuck to the fridge door, but he had yet to collect the items. The kitchen ceiling was made up of transparent tiles with fluorescent lights above. A cigar humidor sat on the counter. Fifty or so Cubans. And, curiously, a brass Zippo lighter. The lone kitchen chair sat away from the table. Not really at the table or the counter. Like it had been used but not to sit on.

243

I judged him to be about five feet ten inches. I glanced up.

I stood on the chair, slid the tile back, and scanned the area above the tiles, where they met the wall. Lying on the framing sat two Sig Sauer handguns and one AR-15. I knew I was pressing my luck, but I quickly slid the pushpin that held the upper pinned to the lower of the AR-15, slid the bolt back, removed it from the upper, pulled out the bolt, removed the small cotter pin that held the firing pin, and slid out the firing pin. Then I reassembled the rifle. I quickly rendered each Sig equally useless. The only way to know I'd altered any of the three was to disassemble them and look for the firing pin or attempt to fire—which no one would do.

I scratched my head. There had to be more to this guy. He was too slick. Too little footprint. Too few electronics. He struck me as more old school. A pad and paper kind of guy. My eyes landed on the shopping list taped to the fridge. Same handwriting. It contained fourteen items. Three of which had been crossed off the list: vanilla, ramen noodles, and soy sauce. That left eleven: butter, olive oil, salsa, milk, curry, cumin, mint, salt and pepper, chocolate cheesecake, cayenne, and angel food cake. None of which was in his kitchen. And yet next to each of the remaining eleven were check marks. Some of the items had two or three checks marks. Some had nine or ten. Chocolate cheesecake had nineteen. Angel food cake had twenty-seven.

I read the word *Angel* over and over. Then I looked at this sparse apartment. That Carrera. Those guns. Everything around me was a cover. When it hit me, I spoke it out loud. "This guy is a broker." The list caught my eye again. "He's selling people." I studied the names again. My guess was that the check marks represented buyers or bids or both—a growing price tag. No doubt he was conducting the business end of these transactions on a computer. A phone. Something that allowed bids and transfers with no footprint. But a guy his age, a guy who'd learned to think and calculate before smartphones and black webs, had a way of doing things that was ingrained through practice and education. I was betting that way of thinking had to do with writing it down where he could see it. At the bottom of the list, I saw: "Takeout recipe: Loggerhead soup. Serves 11. Pickup only." But there was no recipe.

I had a feeling there was more to it, but it was too cryptic.

Before I exited his apartment, I studied the walkway. I wanted to know if he was watching for me while I watched for him. Three minutes suggested I was alone. I closed the door behind me, flipped his breaker back on, and found Summer and Clay poolside.

"Where's Ellie?"

Clay extended an envelope. "She said to give you this."

The letter read, "Thanks for trying. You're probably a good man."

I flipped the letter over. "That's all she said?"

He extended my Rolex. "She also said to give you this."

Something in my heart hurt. Giving back my Rolex rang of finality. "You know where she went?"

He shook his head. "Wouldn't say."

An airplane lifted off out of Key West International. Flying northwest. I turned to Summer. "She say anything to you?"

Summer shook her head and stood up. "No, but I'm going with you."

"How do you know I'm going somewhere?"

"You have that look in your eye."

I turned slightly. I didn't want her mother's intuition to read my face and know there was something I wasn't telling her. And I wasn't about to tell her that her date was the broker who had sold her daughter. At least not on this side of the date.

The Uber driver dropped us off on the curb at check-in. We walked inside and didn't have to look hard. Ellie sat in a chair studying departure signs. Reading the destinations out loud. Gunner sniffed her out and started licking her hands. I sat next to her. "You found one that looks good?"

She seemed surprised to see me. "I gave Clay your watch."

I lifted my wrist.

"I didn't steal anything from the hotel."

I raised an eyebrow.

"'Cept maybe one towel."

I waited.

"Okay"—she motioned to her backpack—"I took the robe too, but—"

We sat reading departure signs. Somewhere Jimmy Buffet played. She was turning the ring we found in the safety deposit box on her finger. Finally, she turned to me. Her face was angular. Hard. "No such thing as Sisters of Mercy. Least not anymore." She turned her head, looking away. "Guess they ran out of mercy. Who closes a convent? Like, what, is God . . . closed?"

I let her vent.

She wasn't sure what to do with the silence, so she started talking again. "I don't know why you're here. You don't owe me nothing, okay? You did your thing. You're a stand-up guy and all that." She motioned to Summer. "I realize you two have your hands full right now. I am just filling space in the boat."

I waved at the signs. "Do you have a plane to catch?"

"Well, not yet—"

"Can I show you something?"

"What? Now?"

"If you really want to fly out, I'll bring you back, buy you a ticket, send you wherever you like. Even give you some money for your trip. But this is something you need to see."

She looked at Summer. Gunner had settled at her feet and rolled over on his back. Tongue hanging. Waiting.

She didn't look impressed. "They only have a few more departures. If I miss it—"

"I'll make you a deal."

She rolled her eyes. "I'm waiting."

"Hang around another couple of days, then I'll fly you anywhere you want to go inside the continental US on a private plane."

"You're full of sh—"

I raised a hand. "I promise."

Incredulous, she asked, "You really own a plane?"

I nodded.

"I thought you were lying to that girl in the hospital."

"I don't lie. And it's a jet. Flies close to the speed of sound."

Summer looked at me like I'd lost my mind. The word got out before she could filter it. "Really?"

I spoke to both of them. "In truth, I own two planes."

Sometimes you have to show people your cards to keep them in the game. I stood and held out my hand for Ellie.

She looked at Summer, then me, then back at the departure signs. Finally, she stood without taking my hand and dusted herself off. "I don't believe you own a plane. I'm just saying."

CHAPTER 36

The Uber wound through the tight streets. Finally, I tapped his shoulder and he pulled over. We stood on the sidewalk, but Ellie did not look impressed. She said, "What now?"

Summer watched as I held out my hand. "Walk with me?"

She dug her hands in her jeans and nodded me forward. I knew Ellie was protecting herself. I would too. I also knew I could not protect her from what might be coming. I could only lead her to it. Her heart had hoped for so long that one more dead end was killing what little hope remained. I held out my hand, reaching for hers, but she didn't take it. I held it there long enough to make her uncomfortable. Surprisingly, she gave in and took my hand.

The three of us filed out into the street and the growing crowd of people. We walked two blocks, and I bought them both Kino sandals. It's the Key West version of handmade flip-flops. Leather. Iconic. It's a thing.

We passed the bars, the smell of sewer and urine, then crossed into the neighborhoods and the smells of roses and mint. We wound through the island—some fifteen blocks. Much of the way I held Ellie's hand. The better part of forty minutes. Summer was pensive. Ellie distracted. I doubted she'd ever held a man's hand. Every few seconds I caught her looking at our hands. I bought shaved ice and we walked three more blocks to the water. Effectively crossing the island. To the less crowded side.

The gate was overgrown. Vines. No sign. The brick wall was eight feet and ran an entire block. Then another. Inside, opportunistic orchids clung to giant banyan trees. Some sort of brightly colored bird squawked over my head. In the middle of the yard, two peacocks strutted, fanning their seven-foot tail feathers. I lifted the large iron lock and pushed open the gate. A couple of cats scattered. Eight thick-walled, tabby cottages sat silhouetted against the water. Each needed a fresh coat of paint ten years ago. A coquina chapel lay at the far end. Given its relationship with the weather, nothing in the Keys was very old. Looking around, I saw this compound was older than most.

The cottages were one story and one room. Which probably explained why they were still here. I knocked on the door of the first, but no one answered. Same with the second. And the third. When I knocked on the fourth door, an older woman poked her head around from the back porch overlooking the ocean. She looked surprised to see us. "Hello?"

I walked the gravel path between the cottages toward the ocean. She was eighty if she was a day, and given the leathery condition of her skin, she'd spent her fair share of time in the sun. Her short hair was shiny white and her clothes were more gardener than nun. Tattered jeans tucked into rubber boots. Apron with pruning shears. Stained white shirt. Despite her age, she stepped down off the porch with relative agility.

She laughed. "You lost?"

"Maybe."

"You're the first visitors to stumble in here in . . ." She pushed her hat back. "Some time."

"Looking for the Sisters of Mercy."

She waved her hands across the world around us. "Found it. Or rather what's left."

"What happened?"

She chuckled. "Celibacy."

I laughed out loud. So did Summer. I spoke loudly enough for her to hear me. "Ma'am, my name is Murphy, and this is Ellie."

She nodded. Almost bowing. "Sister June."

"You don't happen to know a Sister Margaret, do you?"

"Did." She pointed to a small cemetery. "You can talk to her if you want. Old goat loved to talk when she was here. Never shut up. But might be tough to get much conversation out of her now."

The cemetery was well kept. Fresh flowers lay at the foot of the head-stone. I asked, "How long you been here?"

She considered this. "Sixty-two years."

Behind me, Ellie muttered, "Holy sh—"

The woman looked at Ellie and smiled. "Tell me about it."

I figured I'd just ask what I came for. "You ever know of a Sister Florence? Maybe thirteen years or so ago?"

She put her hands on her hips. Thought. Then shook her head. "No. Never knew a Florence . . ." She studied me. Walked around the porch, her white hair flowing. She took off her gloves. Brushed the dirt off her threadbare jeans. She stood close. Studying me. Her eyes were the bluest I'd ever seen and matched the backdrop of water behind her. "What, or who, are you looking for, son?"

I handed her the letter. She hung reading glasses on the end of her nose and read the letter. Nodding. "Uh-huh. Mmmm. Uh-huh."

Next to me a peacock spread its fan and spun in a circle.

When finished, she looked at Ellie, then Summer, back to Ellie, and finally at me. She folded the letter, inhaled deeply, and said, "We hadn't had anyone join us in over twenty years. The few who did didn't stay too long. Too hot. Too many mosquitoes. Too much water." She tapped the letter. "But . . . I remember her."

Ellie burst out, "You do?"

The woman took a long look at Ellie, then pointed at the gate we'd just walked through. "Thirteen, maybe fourteen years ago. One of the most beautiful people I'd ever seen. Walked in here. Looked like somebody'd kicked her in the stomach. Took a look around. Crossed her arms like she was cold. Said she didn't know what she was thinking. Turned around." The woman shook her head.

Somewhat the skeptic, I asked, "How do you remember?"

"Easy." She held up two fingers. "Had the most aqua blue eyes I'd ever seen. Like the sea at noon. Only time I've ever seen eyes like that—" She looked again at Ellie and pointed. "A lot like yours." She turned toward the ocean, remembering. "I do remember she said the strangest thing. *Apollumi.*" She shrugged. "Not every day somebody walks in here quoting Greek."

I swallowed. "Any idea what happened to her?"

She looked to Ellie and back to me. "I'm sorry, honey." The woman waved her hands across the grounds. "Feel free to look around." She swept a hand toward the blue canvas rolling in waves beyond the cottages. "It's pretty this time of day." With that, she disappeared as quickly as she'd appeared.

When we returned to the sidewalk, Ellie stood staring. Shaking her head. She kicked the gate. Then again. Finally, she shook it, rattling its rusty hinges. She was muttering, cussing. Soon she was screaming. Most was intelligible. The few words I could make out cut me.

The last lead had run dry, and Ellie knew it. From here, there was no trail. No bread crumbs. No cryptic letter. As the space between her eyes narrowed and anger blanketed her pain, I knew I was watching Ellie's hope die. Summer tried to hold her, but she didn't want to be held. She just walked up and down the sidewalk screaming a string of four-letter epithets. After a few minutes, she turned to me and told me what I could do with my boat and that she wanted to be on a plane. "Right now."

I had one card left to play. "Okay."

CHAPTER 37

I untied *Gone Fiction*, and Ellie looked at me suspiciously. "I'm not in the mood for any more of your games."

"I know." I pointed. "Private airport has a dock."

We circled the island. Slowly. The Gulf was glass, and it felt good to be back on the water. I always thought better out here. We tied up at a dock within eyesight off the gaudy and ginormous marker for the southernmost point of the US. It's an eight- or nine-foot concrete marker that looks like a giant Weeble-Wobble. I've never understood the attraction, but people throng here to stand in line to take a picture.

I helped Ellie out of the boat, and she crossed her arms. "I don't see an airport."

"I know you're hurting, but I'm asking you to give me five minutes."

"You have no idea how I feel."

I never took my eyes off her. "Maybe."

We walked up the dock with Gunner on a leash, which he tolerated but didn't like, and walked to the right of the marker. We stood at a tall, black, wrought-iron fence overlooking a bulkhead and waterline of pieces of jagged concrete.

We walked up Whitehead Street past a food truck selling snow cones and piña coladas and slipped through a small door in the fence. I flipped the hidden latch, and we walked across a semi-grassy but mostly weedy beach that led out to the concrete seawall. Once there, we climbed up on the wall and then stood staring almost due south out across the invisible seam where the Atlantic bled into the Gulf of Mexico and vice versa.

I pointed at a large chunk of concrete. About the size of a minivan. Once part of a bridge somewhere, now it lay half buried in the sand. Defense against the storms. "I want to tell you about that rock."

She and Summer both looked like I'd piqued their interest, but disbelief was also there. "I was twenty-three. I'd graduated the Academy near the top of my class. I'd also graduated seminary, which is another story, but it meant I could pass as a priest if needed. And it was needed. I'd taken a job with an agency within the government that didn't really have a name. There were reasons for being covert. I told folks I worked in Washington, but I'd only been there once. On vacation.

"Anyway, my boss sent me undercover to a church on the East Coast that had a history of pretty young girls disappearing. Young priest. Wet behind the ears. But six months in I had followed the bread crumbs. Whispers from people afraid to talk. I walked into this guy's house on the water. Bigwig in the church. Given lots of money. Problem was he had a thing for little girls. I was a bit green then, so I wasn't expecting him to be expecting me, which he was. I got the girls out but turned my back too soon. Felt the bullets enter and exit. Not my best day.

"My boss, Bones, threw me over his shoulder and carried me to a hospital with a trauma unit. Then he called Marie and told her our wedding might get delayed. Twelve hours of surgery. Umpteen units of blood. Flatlined three times. She sat through it all. They moved me to ICU. A month. Then six months in a rehab unit where I couldn't lift a two-pound dumbbell. Couldn't walk two steps. Couldn't go to the bathroom. She bathed me. Cut my hair. Changed my bandages. We slept together for six months before we ever got married, and yet we never 'slept' together, if you know what I mean. She never left my side. Least not when I was awake. Marie is the singular reason I walked out of that hospital.

"While it was delayed almost a year, she would not be denied what she'd always dreamed of. The chapel was small, but that was the way they made them back then. I stood at the altar. The room was full of friends and family, priest to my right, groomsmen and bridesmaids lined up in either direction. My best man and oldest friend, Roger, stood just over my shoulder, and then the music started, and I blinked and there she was. I just remember seeing white, and sunshine, and . . . my knees nearly buckled.

"I wobbled and Roger caught me, bringing a laugh out of the priest and all the attendees. Then she took a step, and I watched in slow motion. It was as if whatever world had been there before just faded, leaving her. Only her. I'd never seen anyone so beautiful. So . . . She made it halfway down the aisle and her best maid was handing me a handkerchief. Evidently I was crying. More laughter. She climbed the steps, and when she took my hand, hers was trembling.

"I had graduated the Academy. I was working a job I couldn't tell her much about—although she had her suspicions because she'd just spent the last six months nursing me back to health. Taught me how to walk again. Bodies don't react well to bullets."

Ellie had pretended not to be paying attention before, but she was locked in now.

I continued, "She had said she felt like the world had been laid out before us. I told her she was my whole world. She stared at her feet, then at me, back at her feet. She was nervous. I was too. We tried to follow the priest, Bones, but he had to back up a few times and start over, and then when he got to the vows, she leaned across and whispered to me, just low enough so no one else could hear, 'You sure you want me?'

"Bones—" I looked at the two of them and held up my phone. "You know him as Colorado. He was clearing his throat, smiling, trying to get my attention. I whispered. Leaned in. My face inches from hers. 'You are my whole world.'

"She shook her head once as tears rained down. A pregnant pause. She looked up, pleading. 'It's not too late.' Marie was trying really hard not to tell me something she really wanted to tell me.

"I smiled and repeated after the priest. 'I, David, take you, Marie—'"

At the mention of my real first name, Summer's face twitched just slightly. She stiffened.

I continued my story. "'To have and to hold . . . 'til death do us part.' I remember my hands sweating. I tried to wipe them on my pants, but she wouldn't let them go. Finally, Bones turned to her and asked her to repeat after him. Her voice was so low, almost a whisper. Then Bones served us communion, we lit the candle, and then he turned us to face the congregation. She had locked her arm in mine. Just the two of us. We could take on anything. As long as it was 'us.' I kissed her, and when she kissed me back, she held me a long time. Her entire body was trembling. Her teeth were chattering. The audience laughed. We almost danced down the aisle. It was November, and the air was cool. The reception was set up beneath a tent on the grass, and when we walked in they introduced us. I remember laughing."

I paused. "I remember laughter. My dreams had all come true. Hands down the happiest day of my life. No question. Nothing even came close."

I paused while the bitterness returned.

"We danced, took pictures. She was never beyond arm's reach. Never let go of me. Then we sat to eat, and my feet were killing me 'cause my tux shoes were two sizes too small 'cause they'd messed up my order, but I didn't care. I wasn't planning on being in them too much longer. Or the tux for that matter. Then the toasts started."

Another pause.

"Several people said a lot of stuff I can't remember, and then Roger, my best man . . . clinked his glass. And I remember that when he did, Marie grabbed my hand and squeezed it hard and her eyes were teary and she was trying to smile and . . . he lifted his glass and . . ."

I faded off. Tried not to look into the memory, but it was too late. It had returned.

"He was smiling when he said, 'David and I have been best friends a long time. I'm honored he would ask me to stand with him. Really. And I have a gift for the bride and groom. It's one of my favorite memories. One of my favorite moments. Something I'll never forget. I've also given each of you a copy.' Something in his tone of voice caught me as just a bit off, but he was already reaching beneath the chair I was sitting in. He pulled out a manila envelope taped to the underside. He lifted it and said, 'Each of you has one as well.' I watched as people began opening their envelopes and their faces changed from smiles to horror. One hundred–plus people sucked in a collective gasp that turned the room into a vacuum. They covered their mouths and looked at me.

"Roger lifted his glass. 'To David and Marie.' Marie opened the envelope, the light drained out of her face, she dropped the photos, and the color of her skin matched her dress. She looked at me. Shook her head. The slow motion returned. I reached down, flipped the photos over, and stared at the first. It took a minute to register. It was a picture of a hotel room where we'd had the rehearsal dinner the night before. On the bedside table was yesterday's newspaper, and in the bed were two naked figures."

I swallowed as my voice broke down to a whisper. "The next four pictures were variations of the first. Just different positions." I stared out across the water. "My best man and my wife. And—on her hand was the ring I'd given her."

Summer and Ellie stared at me dumbstruck. Jaws resting on the ground.

CHAPTER 38

I kept going. In the middle of it now.

"It took a minute for the images to register. For the meaning to register. People began quietly leaving the reception. Walking out. When I looked at where Marie had been sitting, her chair was empty. She was gone. I stood, and my best man was standing there with a content and satisfied 'What are you going to do about it?' look on his face. I still couldn't believe it. I tried to run after Marie, but he caught my arm and whispered, 'I'll always be her first. And she'll always be mine.' For some reason, it struck me then that he'd done this intentionally. Like, to harm me. Get back at me for something. I stared at him as the difference between what was real and what was not blurred inside my head, and then he smiled. Nodded. Laughed. His coup d'état complete.

"While I'd been laid up, he'd moved in and convinced her I wouldn't make it. That she needed to prepare herself. Psychological warfare. Emotional terrorism. Preying on the weak."

I paused again. Summer swallowed. Ellie didn't move.

"Bones pulled me off him as I was doing my best to kill him. Roger was unconscious, several of the bones in his face broken, teeth shattered. He spent the next couple months in the hospital, but as he lay there, crumpled like a broken pretzel, I could still see that smug smile on his face.

"I ran after Marie, but by then she was gone. She'd taken one of the boats and left the island. A tattered white wedding dress floating in her wake. I took a leave of absence from work and started looking. I used every available technology at my disposal, and given my job with the government and the fact that Bones was still shepherding me, I had access to a lot. I chased her for months. Months turned into a year. I'd find a clue, get close, and she'd disappear. I learned how to live out of a backpack and with very little. How to not eat for days. Sometimes a week. I went days and even weeks in the same clothes. Watching. Waiting. Sifting through receipts or video footage or a hotel dumpster where the nastiest stuff on earth is thrown—stuff that would gag a maggot. I was reading every piece. Every scrap."

"Then one day I got lucky, or she got tired of running, and I caught up to her. Staying at a high-rise hotel. Thing must have been sixty or seventy stories. The porch of each room hung over the water. In the guest book, she'd signed a fake name. I convinced the attendant I was her husband and he gave me a key. Before I walked in, I watched a couple of pigeons fight over some bird seed, and then I unlocked the door and walked in. The room was neat, bed made, her bag and clothes on the floor. There was a letter addressed to me on the bed and the patio door had been swung wide open. I picked up the letter, walked out on the patio, and saw where she'd taken off her shoes and socks before she'd climbed up on the railing. I saw where her feet had stood in the morning dew maybe sixty seconds before. Then I read the letter."

I stood quietly a long time.

"They never found her body. Deep water and a rip current. Several guests in the rooms below us reported having seen something like a person fly past their window heading to the water below. I returned home, numb, and told Bones to send me somewhere. Anywhere.

"He did. Evil doesn't care what pain you're in. We had plenty to do. I thought if I worked hard enough I could forget. Problem was, in chasing her I'd gotten very good at finding people who didn't want to be found or whom others didn't want me to find. So I medicated the pain myself, thinking that somehow finding all these other people would make up for not having found her ninety seconds sooner." A group of pelicans flying in formation flew low across the horizon. "For years, I had this recurring dream. I'd barge in the door. She'd be standing on the railing. Wearing her wedding dress. Holding a bouquet. Smiling down at me. I'd lunge. But I never did reach her. I'd wake up sweating, unable to breathe, my arm cramped from reaching."

Summer and Ellie looked cold.

"In the years following, I found eighty-one people. Girls. Women. Children. Victims all. In each one, I'd look for Marie's face but I never saw it. I worked ninety or a hundred and twenty hours a week. I wasn't human. Wasn't anything. I didn't feel cold. Heat. Hunger. Didn't love. Didn't sleep. I just was.

"Six years later, I was in West Palm at The Breakers. Studying the movements of this hedge fund guy who liked little girls. Paid handsomely for what he liked. Anyway, they brought in these three Asian girls. Eight, nine, and ten. One wore braces. Other two wore pigtails. So we arrested him. Which he didn't like. Offered me a lot of money to forget I'd ever seen him. I broke one arm, shattered his jaw, dislocated both elbows, slammed his hand through a sliding-glass door, and told him to enjoy prison.

"While he rode the elevator to the ambulance, I walked back to my room. The seven-year anniversary of my almost wedding. I was tired. My soul was tired. I was sitting there staring out across the water when there was this light knock at my door. I thought maybe they'd come to clean the room. I opened it and Marie was staring at me. I thought I was hallucinating. Then she touched me. Trembling fingers . . ."

Ellie and Summer stared dumbstruck. I just tried to breathe. Gunner sat next to me. My voice softened.

"Seven years prior, Marie had tired of running so she faked her death to throw me off. Which she had. Obviously, I'd stopped looking. The years since had not been kind to her. She was thinner. More tortured. There was a tiredness behind her eyes that sleep wouldn't cure. Needle scars dotted the inside of her elbows. Over the next several hours, she circled around me. Never crossing a four-foot bubble between us. Four feet might as well have been a million miles. She told me the truth about our wedding,

Roger, and how it had started after I'd been shot. How she was afraid I was going to die. How often she'd wanted to tell me. And how she was sorry. I sat in disbelief. Stunned. Sometime around two or three a.m., I cracked and cried like a baby. I let out all the tears and anger that had been seven years in the making. She didn't say much. She just sat there. A cold breeze. When I woke at daylight, she was gone. Another note."

Ellie sat quietly a long time. Shaking her head. As the sun fell over our shoulders and people continued lining up to take their picture at the marker just on the other side of the fence, we sat in silence.

Finally, Ellie spoke. "Why are you telling me this?"

"Because sometimes it helps to know you're not alone. That you're not the only person on this planet who's been betrayed by someone you love. You wear your wound out where the whole world can see it. As if the world owes you something."

She stiffened. "Doesn't it?"

"It won't satisfy. You'll still be empty."

She dismissed me with a hand. "Oh, as if you're an expert because one woman crapped on you. You're no better than me. You're just a bitter old man trying to understand why some hoozie didn't love you. Earth to whatever-your-name-is." She was screaming now. "Sometimes people don't love you back!"

She hung her head in her hands. The ring from the envelope dangled from a chain around her neck. Summer sat, knees tucked to her chest, staring at me. She looked cold and in pain.

I debated with myself. I knew I needed to tell her the rest; I just didn't want to. This hadn't really gone the way I'd hoped. And given Ellie's reaction, my next words could make it worse. But I figured she had a right to know. I pointed at the ring. "May I see that?"

She lifted it from around her head and threw it at me. I caught it and then sat next to her.

On my rock.

CHAPTER 39

The ring sat in my palm, glistening. "Twenty-two years ago, I was a junior at the Academy. I'd flown home for break. And without telling Marie, I went to see this jeweler in downtown Jacksonville. Had this office on the river. Harby was his name. By appointment only. One of those places where they buzz you in the front door. I told him what I was looking for, he sketched it, and when I nodded, he made it. Maybe one in ten thousand could do what he did. Took him a couple weeks. A one-in-a-million ring."

I stared into the memory and laughed. "Cost me two years of savings plus my skiff. My Gheenoe." A shake of my head. "She knew I was all in when I sold my boat. When I offered her the ring, she couldn't believe it. Couldn't believe I'd done it on my own. With no help from her. She slipped it on her finger, cried, and in that moment, I gave her all of me. And from that moment to this, I never asked for any of me back."

I lifted Ellie's hand, uncurled her fingers, and set the ring in her sweaty palm. "That ring is this ring."

The disbelief drained deeper. She looked from it to me and back to it, finally shaking her head. "This was your wife's?"

I nodded.

She looked up at me. "Does that mean . . . ?"

I shook my head. "She died. A year before you were born."

"How do you know? With everything, how are you certain?"

The air smelled of charcoal and lavender. Somewhere seagulls were filling the air with noise. I swallowed. "I woke in the hotel room. Alone. A note on the pillow. And unlike the first time, she left nothing to chance with this one. This time she would pull it off for real. She rented a boat, took it out a few miles offshore, floating in about ninety-five feet of water. She turned on a video camera, tied a five-gallon bucket filled with dried cement to her feet, tossed it overboard, then stared at the camera a long time. Finally, she wiped tears, mouthed the words, 'I love you,' waved a final time, and followed the bucket. The Coast Guard found the boat and played the video for me in the hotel manager's office. That was a year before you were born."

The three of us sat quietly for a long time.

"After that . . . I checked out. Got drunk. For the better part of a year. Found myself on various beaches in the Keys, and then as if some giant hand lifted me up and set me down, I found myself here, on this rock, an empty bottle in my hand, staring up at that sun, asking myself some hard questions. I don't think I smelled too great, since I hadn't showered in a couple of weeks. And as I'm sitting about where you are, I hear this voice." I chuckled at the memory. "At first I thought I was hallucinating. Hearing voices. Then he said it again."

She turned sideways and looked at me. Asking without asking.

"He leaned down, casting a shadow across my face, and said, 'Tell me what you know about sheep.'

"I didn't know if the voice I heard was in my head and I was going crazy, or if it was real. When I responded, I spoke to the voice in my head. 'I know they are the dumbest animals on the face of the earth and they have a tendency to wander and get lost.'

"Then he leaned in, so I could see him, and he smiled. 'And,' he said, 'they need a shepherd.'

"I stood. Shoved my hands in my pockets and stared through my sunglasses out across gin-clear water. Then I fell in the water. To this day I don't know how he found me, but he did. He lifted me out of the water so I didn't drown, put me in a little flat about three blocks that way, and nursed me back to life. Again. Feeding me. Getting me sober."

Summer whispered, "Colorado?"

I nodded. "Then one day I'm sitting on the front porch of this little efficiency roach motel where he had me sequestered. He was sipping wine. I was sipping iced tea. And he set a pad and paper in front of me. I looked up at him. I was not impressed. I was just angry. The more sober I got, the angrier I got. Which was the reason I drank. To drown the anger. I couldn't have been any more unhappy or angry. I could have ripped someone's head off with my bare hands. I knew I was about two seconds from choking the life out of somebody. Anybody. I was a walking time bomb and I didn't need much to go off. He knew it too, so he set this pad in front of me and he said, 'Tell me who you love.'

"I looked at him like he'd lost his ever-loving mind. I said, 'Love?' I shook my head. 'I'll never love again.' He sat back, shrugged, sipped, and said, 'You can choose that if you want, or you can realize that we are all just broken, and sometimes no matter how hard we try and no matter what we do, people just don't love us back.' He scooted closer, his breath on my face. 'And when they don't, we have a choice. We can hold on to that, let it fester and live out of that puss-filled bitterness, or . . .' He tapped the pad of paper. 'We can learn to love again.'

"He sipped some more wine and poked me hard in the chest. 'Every heart is made to pour out. But sometimes we're wounded and what we pour has soured and turned to poison. You get to choose. Poison or antidote? Life or death? You choose. So what's it gonna be, David Bishop?'"

Summer gave a little start, followed by a low moaning sound of which it seemed she was not entirely conscious.

I shrugged. "I guess maybe that was my moment. Maybe that's when I came to. When I saw more than just my own pain. Maybe I saw his too. The fact that I was hurting had hurt him. Deeply. Somewhere in there it struck me that love is what we're made to do. It is the thing our hearts are made to pour. I would later learn it was his own wound surfacing when he told me, 'We don't love because people love us back. We love because we can. Because we were made to. Because it's all we have. Because, at the end of the day, evil can take everything save one thing: your love. And when you come to realize that, that the only thing you really control in this life is your love, you'll see, maybe for the first time, that we're all just lost.'

"He leaned in and whispered, '*Apollumi*. And the needs of the *apollumi* outweigh the needs of the ninety-nine. So . . .' He tapped the pad again. 'Tell me who you love.'"

CHAPTER 40

I stared down at the water. Remembering.

"I used to come here every day. And I'd write. I didn't know anything about writing. I just knew that when I did, it was like letting pressure out of the cooker. I'd dig the pen into the paper, scarring it more than marking it, but pretty soon I'm remembering the beautiful and not the painful. And I'm wanting to look into those memories where we shared laughter and hope and tenderness, so I wrote them down. Pretty soon I'm talking through the mouths of these characters I created."

Summer stiffened and her head tilted. "The older mentor I named Fingers, modeled after Bones." Summer's jaw dropped open, but I kept talking. "The younger I gave my name. Because I didn't want it anymore. Because I thought maybe I could rewrite the life he lived. Bones gave me a leave of absence from my government job. He came down once a month to check on me, and every time he found me writing. I took a job tending bar"—I pointed—"down there. An oceanfront watering hole. Lots of singles. Looking for love in all the wrong places.

"I'd been sober and writing a year when this woman, this lady who didn't really fit in, sat at my bar and studied me. She wasn't like the usual customer. This lady held power somewhere else and she was just here alone, letting her mind unwind. I'd cleaned my bar and nobody was ordering, so I was sitting down there with a pencil and pad, continuing my story, and she says to me, 'What're you writing?' And I thought about her question.

"When I answered, I said, 'The me I wish I was.'

"She looked curious and asked, 'Who do you wish you were?'

"I said, 'Not broken.'

"She smiled, nodded, slid closer, lit a cigarette, and eyed the paper. 'Tell me about him?' I tapped my pencil and glanced at my words. *A love I once knew.* She held out a hand. 'May I?' Maybe the most dangerous question I'd ever been asked. But I figured, what do I have to lose? So I slid her the pad. She read a few minutes and lit another cigarette. 'You got any more of this?'

"I answered honestly. 'Sixty-seven more pads.'

"She smiled. 'You let me see those?'

"I couldn't tell if she was hitting on me or just passing time, but I said, 'I'll be here tomorrow. If you are, you can see them.' So tomorrow rolled around, I went for a long swim in the ocean, and she was sitting at the bar when we opened. I set the mountain of pads in front of her, and she sat and read and sipped coffee and smoked cigarettes until two the next morning.

"When she closed the last pad, she took off her glasses, wiped her eyes, and stared at me. She said, 'You know who I am?' I shook my head. Had no idea. She placed one hand on the mound of paper. 'Will you let me publish this?'

"That struck me as strange. 'Why?' I asked.

"She stamped out a cigarette. 'Because I've been publishing books for thirty-eight years, and I have yet to come across one that will heal broken hearts like this.'

"I poured myself some club soda and sipped. 'You really believe that?'

"She nodded once. 'I do.'

"So we talked an hour while she tried to convince me. I took her number. She said she'd be down here a week. I could call anytime. Before she flew out, she swung by the bar. I was sitting there writing. I handed her a plastic grocery bag stuffed with all my notebooks. I raised a finger. 'Nobody but you ever knows me. We don't use my real name, don't put my face on the cover, and I'm never doing a single interview. I am a ghost.'

"She smiled. 'Even better.'"

I tried not to look at Summer, whose jaw was hanging down in the water.

"So we concocted this plan to let my character continue to write his own stories. This weird twist on autobiographical fiction. Like if Indiana Jones had written his own books and published them under his own name. We used my name. David Bishop." I shrugged. "My real name is David Bishop Murphy. 'Murph' or 'Murphy' was my nickname. 'Shepherd' we added. Or rather, Bones did.

"The publisher took my bag back to New York and broke those sixty-eight pads into four stories, which she published systematically every six months. By the time the second installment was slated to release, people were champing at the bit and news organizations had hired private investigators to determine my identity. The book stayed at number one for weeks before it ever hit the shelf. Numbers three and four set publishing records I knew nothing about. Seems women readers had a thing for a guy like David Bishop. So while I tended bar for tips, I made more money than I could spend in ten lifetimes.

"I called Colorado and told him I wanted to go back to work but I wanted to do it a little differently. I wanted to create a place where we could help folks once we found them—help them walk the road from broken to not. So we did. I bought a ghost town. A literal town that had been abandoned when the silver ran out, and we brought it back to life. Now we have a school, a hospital, all-female sports teams, and really good security. It's a community of people all wrapping their arms around girls who thought they'd never hear the sound of their own laughter again. Whose lives have been a thousand times worse than anything I can imagine. We've built condos. Homes. If they don't want to go to school, we train them in a skill or trade. We also partner, silently, with Fortune 500 companies, since many of them are run by the moms and dads of the children we've found. They ski on the weekends. Raft and mountain bike in the summer.

"Colorado, or Bones, runs our little secret town, while I find people who need finding." I shrugged. "And at night, to remind myself that I once knew love, I write. Or at least I did."

Summer whispered, "What do you mean?"

I pointed to *Gone Fiction*. At Fingers' orange box. "I wrote the final installment, due out in a couple weeks." I shook my head. "Thanks to readers like you, it, too, sits at number one. Has for over a month. In the story, Fingers dies. As does Marie. Writing just hurts too much. I had to kill them and the series because writing the life of David Bishop was killing me. So before I started out on this trip, I took all fourteen novels, burned them, collected their ashes in that orange box, and strapped it to my boat so that when I got here—to the end of the world—I could spread those words out across the water where I first heard them. So I could say goodbye to Fingers. And when I get home, I'll say goodbye to Marie."

Summer sat shaking her head. She spoke softly. "What about David?"

"You were right. I am wounded. Some days I write to remember. And some days I write to forget."

Ellie was white as a sheet. Gunner lay unmoving with his head flat up the rock. "If by writing about my love for her, I've given Marie a life beyond her watery grave, then I'm glad. If that life has spoken to broken people and helped them walk from broken to not, then I don't even know what to say. I'm beyond glad. I didn't expect that. Somewhere around here, Bones convinced me that maybe I could write my way out of brokenness . . . but with every year and every book and every written word I open up and look inside, I find that the writing is breaking me. Because no matter what I say or how I say it, I can't bring her back. Marie is gone, and no amount of writing will fix her or my shattered heart."

I wiped my own tears. "One time, I loved. With all of me. Emptied myself unselfishly. And then she was gone, and I never got to tell her. Anything. I've published over a million words, spread my soul upon the page. I am known by millions and yet I am wholly unknown. And when I wake and walk about this earth, breathing in and breathing out, I try to give my love away . . . and I can't. Can't carry her anymore."

We sat in silence as the breeze washed over us. Gunner stood and walked around me, finally coming to rest, just leaning against me. I spoke into the wind. Not really to them but loud enough for them to hear me. I was speaking to someone else, but she couldn't hear me. "Every name on my back—" I shook my head once. "I wasn't looking for them. I was looking for Marie. Trying to find the one girl I lost. And I have searched the world over."

Summer sat sobbing. Ellie stared blankly, not knowing what to say. Nobody said anything for several moments. The water around us was only one to three feet deep.

I climbed down off the rock and waded out into the water. Gunner followed, swimming alongside. I walked out to *Gone Fiction*, unlashed the box, and kept walking. Several hundred yards from shore. The water pressing against me. I stood a long time, holding that orange box. The memories returned. The laughter. The fun. Mentor and friend. As I stood in that water, it all flooded back. I would miss him. I would miss the sound of his voice in my mind. But that's all it was. It was just make-believe medication, and I couldn't cope anymore. My drug, writing, had lost its efficacy. The pain in me was deeper than the writing could root out.

I opened the box, pulled out the bottle of wine, pulled the cork with my teeth, and stood there, wine in one hand, ashes in the other. Crumbling under the weight, I turned both upside down. The wine tinted the water while the ashes floated around me, encircling me. Amused, Gunner swam in circles. The wind lifted some of the ash and sent a cloud south. To parts unknown. Waves rippled across me, the incoming tide pulled at my feet, and within three minutes, the red cloud on the water had been washed out to sea. Somewhere out in the seam where the Gulf sews itself into the Atlantic. That tapestry we call an ocean. One man amid a mosaic we call the human heart.

When I turned around, Ellie and Summer stood just a few feet behind me. Summer's hands were clutched to her mouth. Ellie stood with one arm locked inside Summer's.

The pain in my chest was piercing. It was the most pain I'd ever felt. My breath was shallow and the crack in my soul had widened, fractured. Splitting me. Sending the two halves of me spinning off in opposite directions. I'd spent my life searching for and finding the lost. Returning the one to the ninety-nine.

But who would rescue me? Who would return the pieces of me to me?

CHAPTER 41

We climbed into *Gone Fiction* and motored slowly back to the hotel. Ellie kept looking over her shoulder at the rock. Summer kept looking at me. After we tied up, Summer sat staring west, rubbing one thumb with the other. Nervous energy working its way out. She wanted to say something, but time had gotten away from us. And Angel was still out there somewhere. I needed to bring her back to her reality. I tapped my Rolex. "I know you have questions, but you need to call your date."

She gathered herself and placed a call to the mystery man, who was glad to hear from her and told her where to meet him. She changed into her bikini and complemented the costume with a chiffon wrap around her waist. She was putting herself into danger. I said, "You don't have to do this."

"You're one to talk."

"I've been doing it a long time."

"I have to do something."

"There is risk here."

"You'll be close, won't you?"

I hung a necklace around her neck. A silver shark's tooth on a chain. I tapped the tooth. "It allows me to track you."

She asked again, revealing her fear. "You'll be close?"

"As close as I can get without spooking him."

She blinked and pushed out a tear. "Murph—"

I smiled. "My mother called me Bishop."

A weak smile. "Is Angel . . . ?"

I held her hands in mine. "I don't think so, but"—I tried to find the words—"time is not on our side. And . . ."

"What?"

"Time is winding down."

She swallowed and nodded while the sun bathed her face. Summer was innately beautiful. She slid her phone into the side of her bikini and kissed me on the corner of the mouth, then kissed me again. Then she gently placed her hand on my face, turned me, and held her trembling and salty lips to mine. Without another word, she kicked off her flip-flops and carried them in her hand. Adding the final brushstrokes to the forlorn look. Before she turned the corner, she stopped, looked at me, closed her eyes, twirled once, then again, and disappeared.

I walked the dock to the slip where I'd moored *Gone Fiction* and found Ellie sitting on the bow, Fingers' box open and empty in her lap. She hadn't said much since we left the southernmost point. I cranked the engine and began pulling in the lines when I turned and found her staring up at me, Marie's ring sitting in the palm of her hand. An offering. I shook my head. "You were meant to have that." I glanced at my watch. "I told you I'd fly you anywhere." I offered my cell phone.

She looked from me down to Gunner. Then toward the sunset. "Could I . . . would you . . . ever take me to see Colorado?"

"Just say the word."

Finally, she touched my arm. An olive branch. "I'd like that."

I looked out to see Summer lean against the railing of the boardwalk, spending nervous energy. "Won't be long. Day or two."

When Ellie spoke, there was a kindness in her voice I'd never heard. "I can wait."

Summer's date had promised to call once he got the boat loaded and ready. Said he'd pick her up at the marina a few blocks away. This right here, this was the hard part. The waiting. Where each second was a minute. And each minute a day. I did a lot better at full throttle with my hair on fire, but this was not that. This was agonizing.

Once she stepped on the boat, or as soon as she was able to without raising suspicion, Summer was to text me the name he gave her and the number of people on the boat. I also asked her to send me the name and description of the boat. A picture if she was able.

Summer's shark's tooth wasn't much good beyond line of sight. On the ocean that means six or seven miles. Less if conditions break down. I could track her phone as long as she remained within cell coverage. The key there was coverage. No service, no tracking. My ace in the hole was Bones. If the name turned up nothing, he should be able to grab a heat signature from the boat and link it to my satellite phone. That meant I could track him anywhere and he'd never see me—provided he kept the engines running.

I'd told Summer not to ingest anything under any circumstance. Even if he gave her an unopened water bottle, fake it. Let it touch her lips. Don't swallow. Pour it out when he's not looking. If he had anything to do with the guys who'd taken Angel, he'd drug her. Knock her out. She'd wake up in a shipping container in Australia. We'd also changed my name in her contacts to "Amber." Creative, I know.

Our story and code were simple. Summer was a designer from Los Angeles. On a long-needed break. A workaholic with a painful breakup. Amber was her assistant, holding down the fort while they readied some line of clothing for next month's release. So she would text me instructions about pretty much nothing, but she would use color words to let me know she was okay. Any color was a good sign. But the moment she used either *black* or *white*, then things had gone badly and she needed immediate evac. Bring the cavalry. If at any time she sensed Angel's presence or had any information about Angel, she would tell me the stars were beautiful last night. If he brought her somewhere and there were other armed men, she would tell me not to worry, that she'd be home in that many days, and we'd talk about it then. So three men meant she'd be home in three days. Four men, four days, and so on. Lastly, if he brought her to a place where there were other women, and Summer believed those girls or women to be there against their will, then she would tell me their number in relation to the number of days before the clothing release.

So "Use the red silk and turquoise belt" meant all was well. "You should have seen the stars last night" meant Angel was in play. "I leave in three days and we'll have five days to get ready for the show" meant three more bad guys, a total of four, and five girls. And any mention of black or white meant things were not good. Come running.

Lastly, the nuclear option was one word: *ballet*. No particular reason other than it was so different from anything else. *Ballet* meant things were bad and he knew about her. And absolutely every bit of this was dependent on cell coverage. No cell, no communication. I was flying blind.

When we finished with our code debriefing, Ellie shook her head and asked, "Is all that NCIS stuff really necessary?"

I spoke more to myself than her. "I hope not."

"So what's the worst thing she could say to you? Like the world has come to an end . . ."

"Midnight ballet."

She waved me off. "Catchy."

I didn't like the thought of Summer leaving without me. I felt helpless. Responsible even. What if I was wrong? What if . . . ? The questions surfaced. Summer was tough, courageous even, but she was nothing against these guys. There comes a point in every search where you lean out a little too far. Where you hear the clock ticking and your thinking gets muddled and you do things you wouldn't ordinarily do. Stupid stuff. Problem is, you can't see it at the time. Like asking a fish to describe water.

I wondered how blind I'd become.

CHAPTER 42

S itting by the pool, I turned my phone in my hands, fingers tapping. Ellie and Clay sat nearby. Gunner lay on the end of Ellie's lounger, her hand rubbing his stomach.

Clay broke the silence. "You know, someone has to dial a number for that thing to actually ring."

I dropped the phone in my pocket and ordered a coffee. A shadow appeared over my shoulder. Clay and Ellie looked up, surprise spreading across both faces. I turned to find Sister June wearing her habit and staring down at me. Her hands were folded. Her kind face had been replaced by one much more serious.

I stood. "Sister June."

She turned to one side and gestured to me and Ellie. "Would you two come with me, please?"

"What's this about?"

Sister June considered her words. "I have some information for you. Or—" She rubbed her hands together. "I wasn't entirely truthful with you."

Ellie rose to her feet. "You weren't?"

She gestured again. "Please."

I stared at my phone. Then out across the water. Finally at Sister June. "Can it wait? We're a bit busy here."

She shook her head. "I'm afraid not."

"Go ahead." Clay stood, nodded to Sister June, and whispered, "I'll hold down the fort."

I was afraid to look at Ellie. When I did, her eyes were pleading.

We drove *Gone Fiction.* Sister June smiled when I suggested it but said nothing. We launched, circled south, then headed east and along the southern side of Key West. We passed my rock and the southernmost marker, then Smathers Beach, the airport, and the little cut leading to Stock Island Marina. Finally, we slowed in the waters leading into Boca Chica Beach. The cottages of Sisters of Mercy sat beneath the trees directly in front of us.

Idling into shallow waters, I felt my phone pulsate in my pocket. I opened the text to find that Summer had sent a picture of the boat. Which meant he had called. Which meant she was now in play. And something in me did not like that.

Not at all.

The picture had been taken from an odd angle, maybe thigh high, which meant she'd taken it without him knowing. Or attempted to. When I saw it, I scratched my head. I knew that type of boat.

Custom-made in collaboration with Mercedes, they are the crème de la crème of boats in this class. The 515 Project One is over fifty feet long, almost ten feet wide, and boasts a rum runner's pedigree that goes back to Prohibition. Once used to smuggle rum and drugs, they were popular with the offshore racing guys from the islands to the mainland. Boats like this have a deep V shape, making them remarkably comfortable in rough water. This particular version was custom-made from bow to stern light and powered by a pair of Mercury racing engines producing 1350 horsepower apiece. When racing fuel was used, that horsepower rose to 3100, pushing the boat to 140 mph. A waterborne rocket. From Key West, it could be in Cuba or Bimini in less than an hour. Even worse, it could be there and back in under two. His problem, which was also my problem, was the thirty-plus mph wind and eight-foot waves in the Atlantic. None of which currently existed in the glass-calm waters of the Gulf.

As I stared at the picture, my heart sank. If he decided to take off, all I could do was watch. To add insult to injury, the name painted across the back was *Daemon.*

Summer followed the pic with his name. Michael Detangelo. I doubted it was real but forwarded the name and the pic to Bones, who would run a check on both. Bones, my eyes in the sky, had been and was tracking Summer's cell phone, but he'd only be able to keep it up as long as she had cell coverage. Still, even a short amount of time should allow him to identify the heat signature of the boat and follow it with satellite. Which allowed us to track him anywhere he went as long as the engines remained hot.

A few seconds later, Bones replied, "Locked on."

On the beach, under the glow of the moon, a peacock marched. I was conflicted. Summer or Sisters of Mercy. I wanted to help Ellie, but my mind would not let go of Summer, alone in a boat with a bad man. I swore.

Sister June turned and found me staring at my phone. I gently beached *Gone Fiction* in a foot of water. Enough to hold her against the tide while not enough to hold her against the Mercury in the event I needed to leave quickly. As we hopped down, I turned to Gunner. "Stay." He didn't like it, but he lay on his stomach, hung his front paws over the edge of the bow, and rested his head on his front legs. Whining. His ears trained toward me. I spoke softly. "I'll be back."

Sister June, rather nimble at eighty-plus years, led us up the beach beneath the canopy of trees and turned north, walking in the soft sand. Scattered above and around us, leeching to the tree limbs, were more orchids than I could count. Dozens. Maybe a hundred. Orchids are opportunistic so they grab on where they can, whether placed by the hand of God or the hand of man. Such a dense collection meant that somebody here had to love orchids. The water lapped on our right; the cottages stood stoically on our left. Toy soldiers. Under the shadows of the orchids, we paraded up the beach. Sister June, Ellie, and me.

At the last cottage, Sister June turned and began winding her way toward the back porch. This cottage had been better maintained than the others. Fresh paint, roof not caved in, and from the sound of the A/C unit, the air was conditioned.

Sister June climbed the few steps, stood on the back porch, and knocked the sand off her feet. She knocked quietly, opened the door, and said, "Just me." Swinging wide the door, she ushered us in and closed it quietly behind us. The room smelled of lavender, and a single lamp lit the far end where someone with a very small frame lay in a bed. The sheets were ironed, folded back neatly, and tucked, making a cocoon of sorts. Next to the bed sat a single bookshelf. The person was sitting upright in the bed, and a green, cylindrical oxygen tank stood next to it. A clear plastic tube led from the tank. The sound of rhythmic breathing filled the room.

A bedside lamp shone on the bed and cast a shadow across the person's face. Sister June shooed us into the room, then unfolded a blanket at the end of the bed and spread it across the person's bottom half. Having straightened it, she patted the person's foot and said, "I'll check on you in a bit." As she left, she touched my arm and whispered, "Be gentle." Sister June closed the door behind us and left us alone. Ellie looked down at the woman shrouded in shadow, up at me, and then in the general direction of Sister June. She looked confused.

The woman in bed slowly extended her right hand across the space between us. Her arm was thin, almost emaciated, and spiderwebbed with veins. A silent pause sounded between the time her arm came to rest and her speaking. In between, she inhaled and exhaled purposefully and with some labor, drawing a thin life from the line that draped over her ears and the two small prongs that protruded into her nose.

She whispered, "You must be Ellie."

When I heard the whisper, I hit my knees.

CHAPTER 43

T he lamp had thrown a shadow across her face. I rotated the base of the reading lamp, and the light climbed up her chest, neck, and face. She was skin stretched across fragile bones. A tattered canvas sail. Nostrils flaring, she struggled to breathe. I inched forward, leaning in. Her face was nearly unrecognizable. Her eyes were not.

I tried to speak, but no voice came. She tilted her head and her palm brushed my cheek. I whispered, "Marie?"

She pulled me to her. Smiling. And trembling lips reached across time and space and heaven and hell and kissed me, drawing my heart up and out of a watery grave fourteen years in the making.

Moments passed. Years. I struggled to breathe. How? What? When? The pain in my chest exploded, and I cried. I held her, strained to see her, shook my head and tried to speak, but words, like time, had retreated with the tide. Pulled out to sea by a lover's moon.

Ellie stood, a wrinkle between her eyes. Marie reached a second time. Ellie held her hand and sat in the chair next to the bed. Marie sat and cried and focused on her breathing. Finally, she spoke. "I need to tell you a story." A purposeful breath. "I need to tell you about you."

Only the pulsating ding from my pocket brought me back from the other side of the Milky Way. Marie smiled and her head tilted. "You working?"

She remembered. How could she forget? I nodded and stared at the phone. The text was a five-second video. Taken from the helm. It showed the steering wheel and a corner of the Garmin electronic chart. The chart showed their speed. Currently, sixty-two miles an hour. When the camera focused, the speed rose rapidly to eighty-seven. Then ninety-four. Having established the speed of the boat, the video turned 180 degrees and showed a body lying across the three rear seats. Limp limbs bouncing with the rhythmic rocking of the boat.

Summer.

The video closed in on her face. The expression and the drool exiting her mouth suggested she'd been drugged. The video moved in closer to her waist and hips, where the hand not holding the phone moved gently up and down her leg.

Just before the video ended, he laughed.

I wanted to throw up. I stood. My phone was ringing. It was Bones.

Marie held my hand. Inside, my anger was bubbling. She read the uncertainty on my face. I shook my head. "I—"

She pulled me to her, placed her hand flat across my heart, and kissed me. Holding it several seconds. Then again. "Nobody is better at finding the one . . . than you." She looked at Ellie and patted the bed next to her. The image of Summer tugged at me. Marie sensed it. "We'll be here. We have a lot to talk about."

I shook my head. "I—"

She glanced at her bookshelf. My books stood stacked in order. Yellowed. Dog-eared pages. Taped covers. She laid her head against her pillow and smiled a satisfied smile. "I've heard every word."

"How?"

She held Ellie's hand with both of hers. She spoke to Ellie while looking at me. "I want to tell you about your father—and how he saved me."

Ellie looked at me. Eyes wide.

I crumbled. Shaking my head. My phone rang incessantly in my pocket. Marie said, "Go. Just—" A smile. "Come back to us. There is so much we left unsaid."

I could only muster one word. "Father?"

She smiled and held my face in both of her hands. "We did one thing right. And she's standing right here."

I looked at Ellie. I looked at my daughter. My phone rang again. And again.

I stood, kissed Marie's forehead, then her lips, then bolted out the door, running through the soft sand. I hit *Gone Fiction* in stride, slammed the throttle in reverse, and dialed Bones. The slideshow in my mind played two competing images. Marie. Melting into the bed. Death staring down over her shoulder. How long had she been there? How long had she held on? What pain had she known? How did she get there? What about the video and the concrete bucket? Where did she . . . My mind fired ten thousand questions a second. The image flipped and Summer appeared. Drugged and unconscious. Limp body rocking in rhythm with the boat. A hand sliding up her thigh. The sound of evil laughter.

Bones texted me their current latitude and longitude. He was heading due west toward the Tortugas. I slammed the throttle forward. *Gone Fiction* shot out of the water. I lifted the engine slightly on the jack plate, listening for the prop to hit the sweet spot, and trimmed the engines. Five seconds later, I was gliding across the water. Fifty-three. Fifty-four. A little more trim and the GPS read fifty-six mph.

Gone Fiction was screaming.

And yet he was outrunning us by nearly forty miles an hour. I might be too late. Bones talked while I steered. "When he picked her up, he circled the island once, all twenty-six miles, but given his course and erratic speed, I gathered that he's pretty good at looking behind him. Proving—"

I interrupted him. "This is not his first rodeo."

He continued, "Always moving within sight of the island. I think he was giving Summer time to get comfortable with him. Putting her at ease. Given his movements, he's done this before. Whatever 'this' is."

The signal was breaking up. I was losing every other word. It would be useless at the Tortugas. If Bones needed me, he'd call my sat phone. "I'm losing service."

"Roger. Watch your top—"

The phone went dead.

CHAPTER 44

The Tortugas were sixty miles off Key West. He'd be there in thirty minutes. It'd take me an hour. I also knew I couldn't come in directly behind him, so I charted a course that came in from the side. If they sat at the center of the clock face, I hovered around four thirty. Bones called the sat phone. "Careful. A guy like that may have someone watching his six."

Gunner stood nervously sniffing the air. Given our speed, he was hunkered between my knees. Whining. Looking for safe purchase in a boat where it didn't exist for an animal with paws.

A full moon had risen, casting *Gone Fiction*'s shadow on the water. Twenty miles off Key West, he circled the Marquesas. A cluster of small islands west of Key West. A few of which were privately owned. Lifestyles of the ultrawealthy. Doing this suggested he did not have eyes in the sky like I did. He wanted to know if anyone was on his tail. Weaving through the islands like a serpent, he was trying to throw them off.

Fear gripped me.

My white knuckles gripped the throttle, trying to push it farther, but it wouldn't budge. My speed read fifty-eight. My oil pressure was rising, as was my engine temperature. The moon glistened off the sheet of glass in front of me. Below my feet I'd installed a sealed hatch. Situated above the gas tank and below the deck. I unlocked it and swung the lid open on its hinge. Below lay my weapons locker.

I pulled on a fitted black shirt and face mask, then swung my arms through my tactical vest and Velcroed it tight about my chest. I press-checked my Sig 226 and used my fingers to count four eighteen-round magazines in the MOLLE carriers on my chest. Each had been fitted with a plus-two cap, bringing each magazine capacity to twenty rounds. I turned on my RMR, or rigid mounted reflex. It's a red dot for pistols—a comfort when under duress. I pressed the thumb button on my Streamlight flashlight, making sure it lit up the world around me. It did. I slid the Benelli M4 out of its cradle and Velcroed it barrel down alongside the T-top supports. It held nine mayhem-causing rounds. Before closing the locker, I lifted my AR from the rack and swung it across my shoulder. I counted the six thirty-round AR magazines fitted to my vest and unclicked the night vision goggles.

The vest felt familiar while also heavy. A testimony to the quarter-inch plates covering my chest and back. In the forward locker, I'd stowed my crossbow. It was quiet and accurate out to a hundred yards.

The problem with stepping into the ring with someone bent on evil is just that. Evil. And there's no way to get around it. You don't talk with it. Don't reason with it. Don't negotiate. Land for peace never works. Never has. If they step into the ring with a baseball bat, you don't meet them with a spoon. Evil is not interested in peace, and no amount of conversation will lessen its intent.

Gunner looked up at me and whined. I placed my hand on his head and tried to comfort him, but comfort was hard to find. We skimmed across the water, chasing the demon boat. After fifty minutes, the Dry Tortugas came into view in the distance. I'd been looking at them on my chart since I'd left the beach, but now I was laying eyes on them in reality. The fort rose in the distance. Farther west, a large yacht sat parked. Well lit. A hundred fifty–plus feet in length. Probably closer to two hundred. A party on the fore and aft decks.

I studied it through my binoculars. Several tender yachts were anchored nearby. The demon boat idled up to the larger yacht's stern. Two men from the yacht carried something about the size of a human body off the smaller boat. Then somebody hopped off and onto the stern, shaking hands with someone on board. Interestingly, they kept the two engines running.

They didn't intend to stay. I didn't have long.

Just then my satellite phone rang. I didn't have time to talk to Bones, but caller ID read "Unknown." Below that, the description read "Wi-Fi call." I answered. Her voice was shaking, and when she spoke I knew she was struggling to find clarity. "Padre—" Fear echoed across the line. "I want off this boat."

Angel. "Where are you?"

She whispered. I could hear commotion in the background. "I . . . I don't know."

"Can you see out?"

I heard movement. She whispered, "Blindfolded. Siri dialed for me."

"Where are you in the boat?"

"My hands and feet are tied. We're not moving. Boat's not rocking."

"How long have you been there?"

"I don't . . . don't know how long."

"Can you hear anything?"

"Men talking. They . . . Padre, I'm pretty messed up—"

"Hear anything else? Anything at all?"

"I think another boat just swung around us. I can hear the engine."

That might have been the demon boat. "Make yourself invisible." I heard commotion in the background. "Angel?"

Her voice was shaking. Her whisper lower. "Padre?"

"Yes."

Her next words sounded with finality. "Tell my mom I'm sorry. Tell her—" She whimpered and the line went dead.

CHAPTER 45

Time was growing short. I guessed the demon boat had come to pick up Angel and deliver her to the buyer. Cuba or Bimini. Maybe somewhere in the Gulf. I circled behind the island, putting the fort between the yacht and me. I tied off at the wall, and Gunner and I crept around the seawall, staring at the yacht anchored about a half mile in the distance. I pulled on my fins and locked my phone in a watertight Pelican case just big enough to hold it.

I climbed down into the water and looked at Gunner. "Come on." Gunner launched himself in the water, and we began swimming. My plate carrier and all the weight attached to it, not to mention the AR slung across my back, pulled me down. The thought of Summer and Angel pulled me up. But it did little to alleviate the drag. We swam a hundred yards. Then two. Then two more. I could hear voices on the decks. We swam within a hundred yards and clung to a thirty-six-foot Yellowfin anchored in about six feet of water. Possibly a client's boat. I held the ladder with one hand and slid the other beneath Gunner, giving him a break. His eyes were trained on the yacht. The name on the back read *Pluto*.

Most would read that and think of a cute Disney character. But Pluto was the adopted Roman name for the Greek god Hades, god of the underworld. The message was clear. "Welcome to hell."

I dove to the bottom and disconnected the quick-connect of the Yellowfin's anchor chain. The quick-connect would hold some twenty or thirty thousand pounds, but it was designed with a pin that unscrewed relatively easily on the off chance that the anchor became hung up and needed to be sacrificed to free the boat. We swam quietly. With the current flowing in our favor, I let it drift us toward *Pluto*. I dove again, secured the quick-connect to the larger yacht's anchor, and watched as the thirty-six-foot Yellowfin settled into place. The captain would never know he had a problem until he tried to leave and started dragging the smaller boat with him.

I swam around the starboard side, in the shadows, and snaked a three-quarter-inch stern line toward the stern of the demon boat, securing it to the U-bolt just above the surface of the water. The stern was dark, so I lifted Gunner and placed his feet on the aft deck. He shook and stood looking at me. I climbed up and tilted my AR to drain the water out of the gas tube. If I did have to depress the trigger, I didn't want it to blow up in my hands.

Inside, music thumped, lights flashed, and voices sounded. If I charged in through the back door, things would get loud quickly and I'd risk hurting innocent people. Not good. I told Gunner to stay, and he looked at me like I was crazy. "Okay, but keep your eyes open." He made no response. Other than his eyes were already open.

We crept up the side walkway and climbed the steps to the third story and the captain's deck, which was empty. I guesstimated there might have been fifty or more people aboard. I'm no expert at making things go boom, but I needed a diversion. A loud noise accompanied with enough damage to cause these people to want to get off this boat.

Below me, on the second level, was what I like to call the frolic deck, where two dozen men and women either swam in the pool, soaked in the Jacuzzi, or reclined on one of the loungers displaying various degrees of public affection. Some were clothed. Most were not. Many smoked. Everyone drank. In one corner stood a group of men smoking cigars. The red glow plugs sticking out of their mouths matched the intent in their eyes. Given their body language, I judged them to be customers and not crew. Directly below me, the DJ was working to create some sort of mood.

I saw no sign of Summer or her date. Off to one side stood the outdoor kitchen. Complete with an eight-burner gas stove. Given that no one seemed focused on food, the kitchen was cold and dark. Gunner and I climbed down, and I began looking for a spare propane tank. I found one in the gas grill on the aft deck. I carried it back to the stove, clicked it on, and set the tank on the burner. I didn't know how long it would take a propane tank to get too hot, but I wasn't going to hang around to find out. I knew this wouldn't sink the ship, but I didn't need to sink it. I needed to make people want to get off it. My plan was about like sending a large rat or snake into a dance hall full of people. Wouldn't take them long to file out.

Gunner and I made it around the port side of *Pluto* when I got my answer. The explosion cut the tank into pieces of razor-edged shrapnel and was followed by a loud *boom* and fireball that, although unintentional, lit the gas lines leading through the galley and down into the internal tank in the belly below. The second explosion sounded as if the fire hit the internal tank, which, given a vessel this size, could have been close to five hundred gallons.

The first explosion blew off a chunk of the second story, sending the DJ and all his equipment into the waters around the Tortugas. The five men smoking cigars were next to join him, and based on their vocal dissent, they weren't too happy about it. The second explosion occurred about two seconds later and sounded more like a muted *thud* than *boom* as the resulting force shot down and out of the hull and into the noise-canceling water. Fire exploded from beneath the waterline, scattering debris and people. Immediately the ship began listing to one side. Given a depth of only ten to twelve feet, it couldn't go far.

Chaos ensued. Flames rose out of the galley and began filling other parts of the ship with smoke. Screams sounded fore to aft. Half-dressed and undressed partygoers began exiting the boat in swan dives off the upper decks, swimming to one of the dozen boats anchored around us. The rising heat triggered the ship's fire sprinkler system, which began dousing us in water. The owner of the Yellowfin climbed into the helm and attempted to lift the anchor. Doing so revealed his problem. The captain of *Pluto* simultaneously engaged the larger ship's twin diesels and attempted to move the listing vessel to one of the larger docking sites next to the fort, but the sudden lurch suggested that while he was taking on water, he was also playing tug-o'-war with a Yellowfin. The wrestling match was forcing him to spin in a circle. The interaction between the two captains was almost comical as they yelled obscenities and revved their engines. The Yellowfin looked like a dog chained to a tree and pulling against its collar.

Gunner and I watched in the shadows as Summer's date, the tattooed driver of the demon boat, came running out with a screaming and kicking body draped over his shoulder. I met him in stride and caught the body as it was falling to the deck. The man, who was faster than I'd given him credit for, sent his boot into my rib cage, pulled his Sig, held it a foot from my head, and pressed the trigger. His face changed just slightly when he heard a click. He cycled the slide and pressed the trigger again. I was regaining my ability to breathe when he kicked me again and smashed an iron fist into my face. By the time I stood, he was in the demon boat, gunning the engine so that he, too, found himself in a tug-of-war with *Pluto*. Now all three captains were screaming at each other.

Despite the fact that I'd dismantled his Sig, the captain of the demon boat reached below him and pointed something in my general direction that started spitting fire and bullets. I pulled both the girl and Gunner down beneath me and crawled below into what looked like a theater room connected to the galley. Outside, there was a momentary pause, followed by the revving of the powerful engines. I poked my head above the sill only to watch as the demon boat shot eastward. In eight seconds, he was gone from view.

CHAPTER 46

I shined my light on the screaming girl pounding me with her fists, but it was not Angel or Summer. I'd never seen her before. Above me, the sprinklers doused the fire but did little to lessen the smell of burning rubber or rid the cabins of the smoke. The boats anchored around us began disappearing, one by one, into the darkness.

I grabbed the girl's hands. "Hey . . . hey . . . I'm not going to hurt you. How many girls are on this boat?"

Her face was swollen. Purple. Eyes little more than slits. Lips bloody. "Maybe fifteen."

"Where?"

"Downstairs."

"Can you swim?"

She shook her head, suggesting she was hurt more badly than I'd thought.

The captain of the Yellowfin recognized his problem and cut the line, freeing himself from *Pluto*. He, too, disappeared in an obscenity-laced roar of engines and frothy wake. I grabbed a life vest and fed her arms through it. She whimpered. "If anybody but me comes back through that door in the next five minutes, slide down in the water and make your way to the island. Park rangers live there." I glanced at the dark island. "I'm hoping they just heard the boom and they're headed this way."

She nodded, crying.

I stood, realizing one of my ribs was causing a piercing pain in my lungs, and stepped into the clearing smoke.

Given that most bullets travel faster than sound, I felt the sledge-hammer pick me up and slam me against the far wall before I heard the report of the gun. While the chest plate saved my life, it also knocked every ounce of air out of my chest. I sat there retching, attempting to fill my already-damaged lungs, while Gunner launched himself through the air and began chewing on the shooter. Through the smoke, I heard Gunner growling and snapping, and the man screaming.

I had climbed to my feet and was on the way to help when a single gun-shot sounded. Gunner tumbled to the floor, only to try to rise but then fall again. One leg was limp, cocked at a weird angle, and he winced and fell over when he tried to place weight on it. When he stood up a third time, his white chest was painted red. He tried to crawl his way over to me but couldn't. The man stood and kicked Gunner's body, then his pistol flashed again, sending something piercing hot into my hip.

Looking at the man, I had a singular thought: *You killed my dog.*

Two seconds later, I stepped over the man, stared down at Gunner's unmoving body, and moved farther inside toward the main deck lounge, where three men were coming toward me. I wasn't in the mood for con-versation, so our interaction was short. Having stepped over them, I climbed the spiral staircase up one level to the bridge-deck lounge, finding two more men. After another short conversation, I kicked open the ship's office door, tripped over a sixth man, and ran into the bridge, which was deserted because of the fire. Either the fire or the tank explosion had blown out the front glass, and a gentle breeze of salt spray cooled my face—which sug-gested I might have earned some burns from the blast.

I climbed to the top floor and onto the owner's-deck lounge, where I was met by a large man with an enormous belly and a foul mouth wearing only his underwear. As he screamed at me, I almost laughed at the enor-mous tattoo of a hundred-dollar bill across his hairy chest. Below the bill, the words "Cash Money" had been tattooed in script. I laid him out, used the curtain cords to hog-tie him, and was able to learn that Cash Money was a frequent customer from Cuba. Owned an oil company. He offered me a lot of money to cut him loose. I told him to hush or I'd cut off his masculinity. When he didn't hush, I broke his jaw.

A young girl lay on the bed, unconscious but breathing. I pulled an ax off the wall and cut through the Honduran mahogany doors and into the larger stateroom where I found another man holding a knife to another girl's throat. He was skinny, not dressed, his face smeared with white powder, and he was screaming nonsense.

The amazing thing about the cerebral cortex is how quickly and immediately it controls our movements. It's the area of our body where we think something and our body moves as a result of that thought. It's also amazing how quickly it ceases to function when a hard copper object passes through it traveling over three thousand feet per second. With his lights turned out, he dropped the knife and let go of the girl, who stood screaming at the top of her lungs.

Beneath us, *Pluto* rocked forward suddenly, telling me she was taking on more water than I'd initially thought. She was, in fact, sinking. That told me I had only moments to find Summer, Angel, and anyone else held here against their will, and get off this thing before we all drowned. In the air, I smelled smoke, suggesting the fire had restarted, probably in the engine room because something had disabled the sprinklers. I descended the stairs and turned aft into the engine room, but the bottom half was flooded and the top half was engulfed in flames and the smell of burning diesel fuel, so I waded fore through waist-deep water into the crew cabins, past some sort of prayer shrine, and toward the door of the anchor room, where the water had turned red.

And there I found Summer.

I was in the process of reaching for her when I felt the familiar impact of the sledgehammer lifting and slamming me into the wall in front of me. I tried to lift myself off the floor, but whoever had just shot me in the back did so again. This time the bullet missed the plate but passed back to front through my shoulder—then another passed through the flesh on the outside of my left thigh.

He was coming at me when I heard myself say, "Front sight, front sight, press." He dropped in a pile in front of me and Summer, who had completely lost her mind. She was alive, awake, and screaming at the top of her lungs.

The water around us had turned red, and I wasn't sure if I was the cause or something beyond the door. Water poured through the crack beneath the door, proving the room had flooded. I pulled on the latch, but pressure from inside made opening the door impossible. I waded back into the engine room, ducked beneath the flames, and swam to the far side, trying not to breathe the smoke. I lifted a wedge bar off the wall and returned to the anchor hold. I slid the tip in against the lock mechanism and pulled, using my legs as leverage. Or at least one leg. The leg that had been shot wasn't working right. Fearing her daughter was drowning as I fumbled with the pry bar, Summer stood alongside me and pulled, screaming something incoherent. I felt myself growing faint and knew if I didn't stop the blood running out of me, I'd bleed out in the bottom of this boat.

With one last effort, I pulled with everything Fingers once had. When the pressure from the inside and my leverage on the outside broke the lock, the door slammed open, pinning Summer and me against the wall until the water levels balanced out. I could hear girls screaming, but the sound was muted by the water. My eyes fell on a scuba tank hanging just inside the door. Next to it hung an assortment of weights and gear, including an underwater spotlight. I checked the regulator, fed my arms through the straps of the tank, clicked on the light, and swam down the stairs leading into the dark belly of the ship.

There I found eleven scared girls in a tight group breathing the last of a trapped air bubble. With a little prompting and a quick comment about the *Titanic*, we formed a daisy chain, and I led them through the dark water and up the stairs. When they saw the flashing orange emergency lights of the yacht above, the girls swam out and started climbing up the now-inclining keel toward the main-deck lounge. My problem was how to get them off this boat and over to *Gone Fiction*, which was more than a half mile away. I needed the Tortuga park ranger.

Each girl was scared, shaking, and mostly naked. Angel was not one of them. I swam down one more time into the dark hole, but Angel was nowhere to be found. I checked the other three rooms, but each was empty. Finally, I checked the electronics room and scoured back through the rooms upstairs. Everything inside was filling with smoke.

Angel was not on this boat.

On the aft deck, Summer had corralled fifteen girls. They kept coming out of the woodwork. Thankfully, two park rangers appeared in some sort of dual-engine utility boat used for moving heavy loads from larger boats through the shallow water and onto the island. Seeing the flames rise out of the engine room and the smoke pour from the windows, they knew we had only seconds to spare. The girls, followed by Summer, climbed into the rangers' boat and stood in a tight huddle. Summer pulled out her phone, opened the picture I'd sent her of Angel, and showed it to the girls. None of them had ever seen her before.

We were on the wrong boat.

Where was Angel?

One of the rangers saw me and offered to help me into his boat. I limped back inside, knelt, slid my arms beneath Gunner's body, and lifted him off the blood-soaked carpet. As I did, the dog moaned.

I could have kissed him.

Gunner and I made it to the boat, but I wasn't sure which of us was in worse shape. The walls of my world were closing in, and I was having a tough time focusing. I laid Gunner on the deck of the boat.

The ranger asked, "Is that everyone?"

I asked the girls, "Is this all of you?"

They shook their heads. That's when I remembered the unconscious girl upstairs. I dragged myself up the spiral staircase and back into the stateroom. Cash Money, realizing he was about to burn to death, begged me to cut him loose. I did, lifted the unconscious girl off the bed, pointed my empty Sig in Cash Money's face, and told him to move his expansive derriere. Coughing from the smoke and unaware that my nine-millimeter was empty, he did.

On the aft deck, Cash Money climbed down into the ranger's boat.

Whimpering. I stepped onto the deck, holding the unconscious girl, and asked again, "That all?"

They nodded in unison.

The ranger gunned it, and we had cleared only a hundred yards when the explosion sounded. Summer turned as the fireball engulfed *Pluto* and a zillion pieces of super-luxury yacht rained down on the Gulf of Mexico. I stood in the bow, smiling at the sight behind us, unaware that I was leaking from multiple holes. The ranger cut the wheel toward shore, gunned it, beached the keel on sand, killed the engine, and began helping each of us off the boat.

Still holding the girl, I asked, "You got an infirmary?"

CHAPTER 47

T he ranger nodded. "Follow me." Given that they're sixty miles from Key West and even farther from medical care, the rangers had a well-supplied medical room. While his partner, whom I later learned was his wife, worked on the girl, I ripped off my vest and shirt. He took one look at me and started rifling through drawers and cabinets. Over my shoulder, his wife checked the girl's pulse and then her pupils, stating, "She'll be all right."

My ranger wasn't so optimistic. Seeing that I had pretty much blown a gasket, he kicked things into high gear. Within four minutes, George Stallworth, a fifty-eight-year-old park ranger who'd spent twenty years in the Coast Guard as a medic, plugged my holes while Summer assisted in stitching me up. Her hands were shaking and her face was puffy and swollen. She was trying to focus on me, but her lips whispered, "She wasn't on the boat."

I put my hand on hers. "It's not over." Once he'd stopped the bleeding, George started an IV and began putting physical pressure on the bag with his hands, forcing the contents into my blood supply in an attempt to raise my blood pressure, which had dropped dangerously low. Finally, he popped open a Coca-Cola and said, "Drink this. Quickly."

It was the best Coke I'd ever had in my life.

Within seven minutes, he had patched me up and had me feeling more alive than dead. While life flowed back into my veins, I stared down at my vest and realized there was much I didn't remember. All the magazines were gone. As in, I'd run through them all. My Sig rested in the holster attached to my vest but the slide was locked back, proclaiming even to the near blind that it was empty. Evidently Cash Money didn't have much experience with weapons or he never would have been so compliant. My AR was gone and I had no recollection of where it and I had disconnected. My front and back plates had stopped at least six rounds.

I was lucky. Again.

We walked out of the infirmary to where the fifteen girls had surrounded Cash Money, who had dropped into a fetal ball and lay squealing on the ground. One of the girls was holding a piece of wood; three others were holding bricks. All of them were screaming at him.

I turned to George. "Can you hold him here 'til help arrives?"

"Gladly." He looked at me. "You going somewhere?"

I waved my hand across the darkness that stretched between us and Key West. "Got one more to find."

"Anything I can do to help you?"

"Get these girls some clothes and food. They've had a rough go. I'm afraid some of them have been on that boat for quite some time, and there's no telling what manner of evil they've endured."

"Got it."

I stared down at Gunner's body. I knew that when help arrived, he'd be last on their priority list, which meant he'd die if I left him on the island. I also knew that putting him in a boat with me and riding back to Key West would probably kill him. In the end, I couldn't leave him. So I slid my arms beneath his limp body and lifted him, causing him to wince. He was having trouble breathing and a gurgle had set in.

I walked to the bulkhead, set Gunner on the back bench of *Gone Fiction*, wrapped him in a blanket, and was in the process of cranking the engine when Summer grabbed my arm and wrapped a blanket around me. Her face told me she was not open for conversation. "Don't even think about telling me to stay here."

I loosed the anchor line, threw the throttle forward, and a minute later we were gliding back toward Key West at fifty-eight miles an hour. When

I'd trimmed the engine and tabs, I dialed Bones on the sat phone. "Bones, Angel wasn't on the yacht." Silence followed. I thought back through the last few hours. I said, "When he left Key West and circled the Marquesas, did he stop?"

A few seconds passed. "Briefly. Two minutes maybe. Nothing more."

"Long enough for someone to get off or on?"

"Yes."

"Could you see a home or outbuildings on the island?"

"Yes."

"Can you get me back there?"

"Yeah, but why?"

"'Cause he's gone."

"No, he's not."

"Yes, he is. I saw him leave."

"He may have left. But he's back. I'm staring at him."

He'd circled back around! "Where?"

"Loggerhead."

Loggerhead Key is a forty-nine-acre key three miles due west of Dry Tortugas National Park. Its most noticeable feature is a 157-foot-tall lighthouse, which can be seen for twenty nautical miles. I glanced over my shoulder. The lantern rotated like a giant eye scanning the surface of the ocean.

I turned hard 180 degrees. The wind was picking up.

He prodded. "Is Summer with you?"

I gave him the ten-second version of the events.

"And you?"

"I'll live." I glanced at Gunner. "Find the best vet south of Miami. I need him waiting on me when I dock."

"Done."

"And, Bones?" I needed to tell him about Marie.

"Yeah, Bish—"

"Marie is alive." Silence echoed as the words settled. When he didn't respond, I said, "You hear me?"

His tone of voice changed. "I heard."

The change betrayed him. I fought to understand. "You knew?"

A pause.

"Bones—"

"I'm sorry."

"Sorry? You're sorry?"

"Bishop—"

"How long?"

He didn't answer.

"Bones, how long?"

Regret in his voice. "She faked the video."

"You've known for fourteen years? How?"

"The confessional."

I was screaming now. "And you think that justifies it?"

His voice fell to a whisper. "Nothing justifies this." He swallowed.

I hung up and let the wind dry my tears.

CHAPTER 48

I had grown stiff. My leg and my shoulder were screaming, not to mention one of my ribs. I was in a bad way. I drove straight at the light. Four minutes later, we circled the island. Loggerhead Key. The picture of the shopping list taped to the refrigerator returned to my mind's eye. *Loggerhead soup. Serves 11.* When he left *Pluto*, the demon boat had gone in the direction of Key West. Making me think he was headed for the mainland. But he wasn't. He'd made a giant circle.

The cigarette boat lay dark and sleek against the horizon, tied up at the long dock that served the lighthouse keeper's house—right next to a sea plane floating on its two pontoons. I throttled down, killed the engine, and glided onto the beach just north of the lighthouse. My body begged me not to get off the boat.

I stared at the lighthouse and knew I needed weapons, but I'd lost my AR, and my Sig was empty, as was the Benelli. That left the crossbow. I stepped into the sand, grabbed my crossbow from the forward hatch, cocked it, and slid an arrow onto the rest. If I was lucky I'd get one shot with this, and then things would turn ugly. The only good news was that it was quiet, and whoever I hit with it wouldn't know my location. But once empty, it would serve little purpose other than to beat somebody off me.

Summer was climbing out when I stopped her. "No. And don't argue with me. If I'm not back in five minutes, head east." I handed her the sat phone. "Bones will get you home."

She swung a leg over. "I'm not about to—"

I put my hand on hers. "Summer, this is not a dance." I held up my hand. "Five minutes."

She extended hers and pressed her fingertips to mine. I nodded and crept across the beach.

The lighthouse scanned the sea above me while solar LEDs lit the dock and sidewalk that led from the water's edge to the lighthouse and surrounding buildings. I heard screaming coming from somewhere near the lighthouse. The dunes were low, which didn't grant me much cover, so I knelt and watched as a man tried to drag a body out of the base of the lighthouse. The voice suggested the body belonged to a female. She was kicking and screaming. Wildly.

Having trouble holding on, he let her go. Momentarily, bending double at the waist, giving me a split second to make a decision and send the bolt. I did. The arrow entered his right buttock and exited out his groin. I know this because I heard the scream. It was higher pitched than hers.

I ran up the lit walkway where Angel lay fighting against zip ties that bound her hands and ankles. She had pulled off her blindfold, but that did little to help her recognize me in the darkness. I tried to cut her bands and she kicked me in the face. I rolled onto the man who was screaming and bleeding beneath me. When I climbed off him, I got a good look at his face. Only then did I realize he wasn't the driver of the demon boat.

I started to ask myself where he could be when he spoke behind me. "Figures."

I turned slowly. He stood like a cat. Holding a knife. I waved my hand across the island. "Pickup only."

He smiled but said nothing.

I pointed at the lighthouse. "I bet if I open that door, I'll find ten girls just like this one."

He smiled again. But there was no humor in it.

Given my condition and the fact that he was faster than me, I had a pretty good idea I couldn't beat him in a fight. So I tried to appeal to his greedy side. "You're a businessman. What if I offer you more money?"

He paused. His accent surfaced when he spoke. European. "You can't afford them."

"I might surprise you."

"What will you pay?"

I paused. I figured we were finished talking about money. "Whatever it costs."

He understood. "I gave my word."

"An honorable thief."

Another smile. "Thief, yes. Honorable, not so much." He pointed at me. "I've heard of you." He motioned toward his back. "You're the guy with the names."

I nodded.

"You've cost us some money." He waved the knife at me. Circling. "Why you do that?"

"Because I know what it is to love someone and lose them." I paused for effect. "'Course, a maggot like you wouldn't understand that."

He shook his head and laughed, his eyes flashing red. "Flesh. A place to put something. That's all." He switched the knife to his other hand. "We have a nickname for you."

"Yeah?"

"Mercury."

Mercury was the fabled messenger of the gods, sent to rescue prisoners from Hades. "Fitting."

He smiled again. Mirthless.

He was older than me but faster. And given the holes in my shoulder and leg, plus what was probably a broken rib, he was currently stronger. The most I could hope for was to slow him down. Hope I got lucky. He crossed the distance between us in a blur and rolled head over heels. I reached but he was gone. Before I could turn, he stabbed that knife into my thigh. The searing heat and pain brought my attention to the fact that he was on top of me. His hands were paws and his forehead a sledgehammer. His grip crushed down on my esophagus.

I struggled but I was played out. He was too much. I made one last attempt but he blocked it. As if he could read my mind. He knew what he was doing. As the walls closed in, he leaned in, laughing. The vessels of his eyes were red and bulging. He rammed a fist into the hole in my shoulder that Summer had just sewn shut and sent a pain-train to my brain.

Next to me, Angel screamed, kicked at him, and pounded his back with her fist. He swung a powerful arm and sent her rolling. Watching my world come to an end, I felt an odd calm rain down over me. I tried to pry his hand off me, but it was no use. It was a vise. Just before the world went dark, a shadow passed through the air behind him. A snarling, growling, angry shadow. The man screamed, let go of me, and turned his attention to the thing that was threatening to rip off his leg.

Having escaped Summer's grasp, three-legged Gunner had run across the beach, up the sidewalk, and launched himself at my executioner. He landed on the man's back and sank his teeth into his hamstring. The man immediately let go of me and swung violently with his knife, catching Gunner in the same shoulder where the bullet had entered. The dog whined, winced, rolled, and didn't move while blood poured from his shoulder and mouth.

The man rose, glanced at the steady stream of blood draining out of the back of his leg, and took one step toward me with his knife before a boat paddle crashed down across his head. The paddle snapped and he staggered, turning his attention to Summer, who stood holding what was left of the paddle.

The man took a swipe at Summer but she dodged it, distracting him just long enough for me to climb to my feet. I sent one fist down through the man's face, feeling something break. But I knew I couldn't manage a second swing. If he came at me again, Summer and Angel would watch me die.

For some reason, he did not. He staggered, dropped his knife, wiped one hand across the back of his thigh, assessed his own wound, and then stared at me. Spitting, he smiled and said one word: "Ellie." Then he began shuffling toward his boat. Unable to chase, the three of us watched him leave.

When he reached the end of the dock, he threw the lines off the seaplane, climbed inside, cranked the engine, and throttled into the wind. When he'd turned ninety degrees, putting the wind in his face, he revved the engine, skimmed across the face of the water, then lifted heavenward, circling eastward. In less than two minutes, he was gone from sight and sound.

While Summer sobbed and held her daughter, I stared at the end of the dock. The demon boat. I turned to Angel and directed her attention to the lighthouse. "They in there?"

She was clinging to her mom. Crying, but no sound came. She nodded and loosed the dam that held back the sound. The cry echoed out across the island. I shined my light into the base of the lighthouse and saw ten beautiful young girls, each blindfolded and zip-tied. I began lifting blindfolds. "Can you walk?" They were young. Not yet sixteen. "Come on. We're going home." Each nodded. With the knife from the sidewalk, I cut them loose, then knelt next to Gunner. His breathing was labored, gurgling. His heavy eyes were having trouble focusing on me. "Easy, boy."

He tried to lick my face, but there was too much blood. I slid my arms beneath him and limped my way to the two-million-dollar racing boat.

I had to get to Ellie before he did.

CHAPTER 49

Summer and Angel leaned on each other down the sidewalk as Gunner and I painted our own path to the boat. The ten girls followed, huddling against one another. I set him on the deck below the back seat. The girls climbed in and began strapping on seat belts. Summer helped me loosen the lines, and I throttled away from the dock. Then she handed me the sat phone.

I circled west, then south, slowly routing through shallow water. When we reached four feet, enough to plane, I shot the throttle forward, rocketing us up and out of our lighthouse grave. Within seconds, we were traveling ninety-seven miles an hour. The boat is equipped with a key fob of sorts, which—when engaged—allows the captain to make use of all the power the motors possess. The fob dangled in front of me across a dash that looked more fighter jet than boat. I clicked the button, and the engines roared like an F-16. Given the glass-like conditions, we nearly took flight. When I looked down, I saw we were traveling at 122 mph.

The keys were slippery with blood as I dialed Bones. He answered with, "I'm sorry."

I didn't have time for him and me. "You see a plane flying east?"

"No, but your demon boat is traveling east at a hundred thirty-seven miles an hour."

"That's us."

"What?"

"No time. Find the plane. It's small. Like a bush plane."

A pause while he checked the satellite. "Got it."

"Tell me where it lands."

Twenty minutes later, he called back. "He just landed."

"Where?"

"The shoreline at your hotel."

"Where's the vet?"

"Where do you want him?"

"Sisters of Mercy."

"He can be there in five."

I hung up and charted a course for the south side of the island and Sisters of Mercy. Five minutes later, I beached the demon boat on the sand in front of Marie's cottage. I grabbed Gunner, stumbled out of the boat, fell into the water, and hobbled our way up onto the beach. He wasn't breathing.

I turned to Summer. "You sit with him?" Rewrapping the tourniquet around my leg, I limped my way up Marie's back steps. I threw open the door and found Sister June spoon-feeding soup to Marie. When she saw me, her eyes grew wide and she began breathing fast and shallow, willing the oxygen to fill her lungs. I scanned the room. Ellie was nowhere to be found. I spoke through the pain as I stood there bleeding. "Where's Ellie?"

"Went to get some pictures."

"From where?"

"Your hotel."

The words were registering in my brain when my phone dinged. A text. From Ellie. It read, "Midnight Ballet."

I jumped off the back steps, rolled in the sand, stood, fell again, and climbed my way back to the demon boat. Summer sat cradling Gunner while Angel and the ten other girls huddled on the beach. Sirens and flashing lights told me Bones had brought the cavalry.

I couldn't do anything more here and there would be time for conversation later. I climbed inside the boat, slammed the throttle into reverse, and dragged the fifty-foot boat off the beach while digging through the sand with the powerful propellers. Free of the beach, I turned east toward the resort. When I passed Sunset Point, I was traveling above a hundred miles an hour.

Seeing the resort, I turned ninety degrees right, aimed for the tail of the seaplane, and gunned it. The boat skimmed across the water and cut the plane in half, sending it spinning. With way too much speed, I glided up onto the beach, and the demon boat came to rest on dry ground in between the pool and the tiki hut where a guy stood singing cover tunes. I fell out of the boat and began limping to Ellie's room amid the screams and angry hollers rising up out of the bar.

When I reached her and Summer's room, the door was open. Handle busted. I walked in and found the room in disarray. Table upturned. Lamps broken. A trail of blood led in and out. In the corner I heard moaning. I clicked on the light.

Clay was on the floor behind the door. Blood pouring off his face. He shook his head. "He got her."

"Which way they go?"

He pointed toward the boardwalk and Sunset Point. Once there, he could skirt around the crowds, get to his apartment, his Porsche, and he'd be gone. I started running.

Or hobbling.

I rounded the corner where a crowd had gathered to gawk at my boat-driving skills. The pool had emptied. As had the bar. Fifty people stood staring and holding drinks with umbrellas sticking out the top. The sea-plane listed in the water, looking scalped without its tail wing. I circled around the crowd and ran along the waterside in the dark. Streetlamps lit what would otherwise be a romantic stroll along the shore. I hobbled, feeling warmth drain down my leg. I'd bled a lot. I didn't know how long I had left. Not long. I clutched my rib because every breath sent a knife through my lungs.

Ahead of me, I heard a commotion among the people on the boardwalk and heard a muffled cry. I screamed, "Ellie!"

A crash sounded. Followed by a woman yelling and another scream.

This time it wasn't so muffled. I willed my legs to move faster and screamed again. "Ellie! Ellie!"

The first time the reply was muffled and difficult to make out. The second time it was not and I heard exactly what she said. "Daddy!"

Daddy.

There it was again. The word circled inside my head, taking laps around my brain, finally coming to rest in my heart. The meaning registered, and it finally struck me that Ellie was calling to me.

She called me Daddy.

He was less than a block from his apartment garage and his Porsche. If he got her in the car, I'd never see either one again. A table crashed, a bottle broke, and more screams erupted from a waterside bar. Seeing my last chance, I slipped behind an office building, through a garden, around two people in a Jacuzzi, through a carport, and finally across the street and into the shadows at the entrance of his garage.

I watched helplessly as he shoved Ellie inside the Porsche and then fell into the driver's side. I closed the distance. He slammed the door shut, reversed, and shifted into first—which was when I punched through the driver's side glass and grabbed him by both his hair and his leg. Gunner had turned the back of his hamstring into hamburger, so when I squeezed it, he gave out a yelp.

I pulled harder and extracted him from the Porsche, where we spilled onto the asphalt in the garage. He kicked into my leg, sending me to my knees. I stood, and we traded blows. Behind him stood his freedom. Behind me stood my daughter. When I caught him in the jaw, he caught me in the throat, temporarily stunning me. I shook it off but he was on me. Trying to remove my head from my shoulders. I just could not do anything to best this guy. With one final burst of energy, I stood to my feet, jumped for all I was worth, and arched my back. We pivoted in the air and came crashing down. Me on top of him on top of a cement parking stop. He grunted, let go of my neck, rolled, and was on his feet before I could climb to my knees.

Sirens sounded in the distance.

He turned to Ellie. "Every day, whenever you turn around, I'll be standing over your shoulder." He swung, caught me in the chin, and nearly turned out my lights. I spun and watched him limp through the alleyway that led back onto the boardwalk along Sunset Point. As he receded into the darkness, I knew I'd have to spend the rest of my life keeping Ellie safe. Watching over her. My singular mission would be making sure she never lived a single day in fear of that man.

I'd protect her.

As the light of the lampposts showered down on him and his freedom, he turned a corner and disappeared. He was gone. I knew the focus of my life had changed.

As that thought was making its way into my brain, a shadow appeared where the man had disappeared. A taller shadow. The shadow swung, and the flesh-broker reappeared just as quickly as he'd left. Only this time he was airborne. Flying backward, head leading his feet. His head rocked unnaturally on his shoulders and his feet wrapped up with each other like a pretzel. He flew through the air in a perfect arc, coming to rest on his head and shoulders while the rest of his body piled up on top of him like noodles. Above him stood a man. A man with an angry face etched with a road map of wrinkles and scars written by a lifetime of pain. That man was sweating, and blood had stained his white hair and white beard.

Clay.

I pulled myself to the sidewalk, where a crowd had gathered. Clay stood over the man like Ali. I stared in dumbstruck amazement. I'll never know how, given his condition, not to mention his age, he managed to get from Ellie's hotel room to there.

I stared at him. He glanced down at the unconscious man at his feet. Then smiled at me. His teeth were red. Wobbling slightly, he shuffled to a park bench, sat down, crossed his legs, and folded his hands across his lap. He assessed his fingernails like a man getting a manicure, then eyed the split skin above his middle knuckle as if he were glancing at his watch to determine the time. Finally, he looked up at me again and nodded.

I looked at the man and knew I could kill him. Maybe I should. I also knew prison was not kind to men who dealt in flesh. In prison, your sins have a way of returning on you, and his would return with interest. When he woke, mine was the first face he saw. I flipped him, drove my knee into his kidney, drove my other knee into the hamburger that was once his thigh, and torqued his shoulder far enough upward to tear his rotator cuff and dislocate it from its socket.

He yielded.

An hour later, the paramedics had cut off my shirt and turned my pants into shorts in an effort to plug my holes and sew me up. Again. I was in pretty bad shape, and all I wanted to do was sleep.

But as the paramedics were lifting me onto a stretcher to transport me to the hospital, Sister June appeared. She reached for my hand. Her face was taut. "Sister Marie." She pointed to an older Cadillac in the street. I limped to the car as the first rays of sunlight began breaking across the skyline and fell into the front seat. Ellie climbed quietly into the back.

CHAPTER 50

T he ride across town was short. And quiet. Sister June spoke not a word. We parked at the gate and wound through the trees, but there were no peacocks this time. Just silence. Sister June climbed the steps to Marie's cottage and held the door for me. Marie lay in bed. A single light shone down on her. My last book on her chest. The rest were stacked neatly on the bookshelf next to her bed. Each one dog-eared, cover tattered, pages worn. I was tired and couldn't differentiate between delirium and euphoria. When I knelt, she smiled. I slid my hand beneath hers.

She tapped the book. "I like this one." She was pale. Struggling. These were the last words of a dying woman. "My favorite."

I nodded. So many questions. Struggling to breathe, she forced her lungs to expand, inhaled, and let it out. Slowly. She eyed the water in front of us where the sun was just breaking the skyline. She leaned sideways, pressing her forehead to mine. She spoke without struggle and without fear. "Walk me home?"

I shook my head. "I have so much I want to tell you."

She waved her hand across the bookshelf. "You already did." A smile. "Ten thousand times over. I used to lie here and wonder if you would ever walk in that door."

I nodded and opened my mouth, but no words sounded.

She chuckled. "You were here every day. Every sunrise. Sunset. I've never been alone." She paused. Breathing. The vein on her temple pounding, depicting the load her heart was under and how it was struggling to keep up. She placed her palm on my cheek. We didn't have much time. She

309

struggled. "I ran . . . because I didn't feel worthy of your love. The more I tried to push you away, the harder you looked and the more you proved me wrong." She tried to smile. "So many times I stared out the window. You had come within the sound of my voice. And yet I couldn't let myself cry out, knowing what I'd done."

"Marie—"

She stopped me. "I don't deserve it, but I need a favor."

"Name it."

She breathed slowly. In. Out. The end had come. She pulled the clear tube away from her face and lay waiting. She pointed to the beach. Squeezed my hand. "Be my priest . . . and walk me home."

I swallowed. I knew what she was asking. And the pain of it was killing me. "Only if you'll let me be your husband first."

She blinked and smiled, unable to speak. I slid my hands beneath her legs and lifted her frail and thin body. She hung her arms around my neck and pressed her nose to my cheek, breathing in. She weighed nothing. What little she did weigh was crushing me.

Without oxygen, Marie was having trouble focusing, so I called her back. "Marie . . ."

In all my wanderings, all my dreaming, all the slideshows across my mind's eye, I'd never seen us end this way. My lip trembled. Mind raced. I couldn't put the words together. I just pulled her to my chest, descended the steps onto the beach, and held her while the life drained out and the darkness seeped in.

While I carried her, she smiled and whispered in my ear. "Bread first. Then wine." Before us, Sister June had set a table.

We waded into the water.

Her faded gown sucked to her skin. She had become a shadow. Only seconds now. Waist deep, I held her. I tore off a small piece of bread, mumbled something no one could hear, and managed a whisper that mimicked the words I'd written in my books a hundred times: ". . . the body, broken for . . ." Then I laid the bread on her tongue.

She pushed it around her mouth and tried to swallow, which brought a spasm of fear. Of the inability to get oxygen to her lungs. Her body tensed, eyes rolled back, and I just held her. Ellie stood crying just feet away. Around us, the water had begun washing the blood off me, causing a tint. First pink. Then Cabernet. Merlot.

Marie settled and placed her palm flat against my chest where she could feel my heart pounding. I pulled the cork, tilted the bottle, and rolled the wine up against her lips. "The blood, shed for . . ." My voice cracked again. "Whenever you do this, you proclaim the . . ." I trailed off.

She spoke before letting the wine enter her mouth. The smile on her lips matched that in her eyes. I'd known that smile since our youth. Since the beach where we played as kids. I would miss that smile. The look behind her eyes. The window to her soul. It spoke to the deepest places in me. Always had. The wine filled the back of her mouth and drained out the sides.

Blood with blood.

Another spasm. More struggling to breathe. I clung to Marie as the waves rocked her body. One breath. Then two. Mustering her strength, she pointed. Deeper water.

I hesitated.

Marie's eyes rolled back, but she forced their return and they narrowed on me. "Please."

I waded deeper. Her breathing was shallower. Less frequent. Her eyes opened and closed. Sleep was heavy. I spoke the only words I knew. "If I could stop the sun or ask God to take me and not you, I would."

She placed a hand behind my neck and pulled my face close to hers. "I've . . . always . . . loved . . . you." She swallowed and fought for air. "Still do."

I kissed her, trying to imprint the feel and taste of her into me.

I walked farther into the gin-clear water, above my waist, while Marie's body floated beneath the cradle of my arms. A trail of red painted the water downcurrent. Marie tapped me in the chest and used one hand to make the numbers. She tucked three, leaving two. Without pausing, she held up all five. Then she started over. Extending five only to tuck three, leaving two. Making a seven. Her cryptic motions meant 25–7. *Do not remember the sins of my youth, nor my transgressions; according to Your mercy remember me.*

I nodded, and the tears pushed through the dam. I could hold them no more.

Her head fell to one side. Her lips made the words, then the sound came. "Forgive me?"

I kept shaking my head. "There's nothing to—"

She pressed her fingers to my lips and tried to nod. "Please. Forgive—" She tensed. Her lips were turning blue.

The tears drained off my face. She thumbed each away. I managed, "I love you with all of me. I—"

"I know. You told me . . ."

As Marie's life drained into the ocean and her lungs held less air, she pulled me toward her. She was cutting me free. "Tell me what you know about sheep."

We had started this way, and we would end this way. It hurt too much. I shook my head.

"Tell me."

"The needs of the one . . ."

She closed her eyes.

"Outweigh those of the ninety-nine."

She laid her hand flat across my chest. Just two kids on a beach. She pulled herself toward me. "One more thing . . ."

Her pulse had slowed to almost nothing. I waited.

"Spread my ashes where we started . . . that shallow water near the north end of the island."

I stared six hundred miles north. Past my mind's eye. To the beach where we played as kids. I shook my head. "I—"

Blood spilled out the corner of her mouth. "Where we fell in love." The flow was deep red. Then frothy. She was choking now. Rather than fight for air, she chose to speak. "Did then . . . do now. Always will."

She wrapped her fingers around the thin leather necklace hanging around her neck and lifted it off. The years had worn it thin. Tarnished the outside. The side that lay next to her chest had been polished to a shine. She set it in my hand and closed her fingers around mine.

Marie stared at Ellie and then at me. She lifted her hand, extending her fingertips and waiting for mine. I rested her in the water, and we wove our fingers around each other like vines. She tried to breathe but couldn't catch it. That was it. Marie's life would end in my hands. I didn't want to let her go. I couldn't. Seeing my pain, she pressed her palm to my chest, flat. Then pulled me to her and pressed her lips to mine. There she held me. A moment. A year. Forever.

She crossed her arms, smiling slightly. I stared out across the water, but my heart had blurred my eyes and I couldn't see a thing. I nodded for the last time. She let go, and her body lay limp in my arms. Her words were gone. She'd spoken her last. Only the exhale remained. The light in her eyes was fading.

I leaned in. Forcing her eyes to focus. I managed a broken, "I'll miss you." She blinked, telling me that singular muscle movement was all that remained. I rallied what little strength remained in me. "You ready?"

Her eyes rolled back, then she drew a surge of energy from the depths and focused on me. One last time.

While she may have been ready, I was not. The words of her life were draining off the page, black to white. From somewhere, she mustered a final word. Although she didn't speak it. With her eyes closed, I felt her fingertips on my chest. She was writing her name over my heart.

With one hand beneath her neck and one hand covering her chest, I spoke out across the surface of the water. "In the name of the Father . . . the Son . . . and the . . ." My mouth finished the words but my voice did not.

She blinked, cutting a tear loose, and I pushed her beneath the surface.

In that second, her body fell limp, the last of the air bubbles escaped the corner of her mouth, and the water turned red.

Her body felt light as I lifted her. As if her soul had already gone. When she surfaced, her eyes were open but she wasn't looking at me. At least, not in this world. And the voice I'd once heard I could hear no more. I carried her to shore and set her on the sand, where the waves washed over her ankles. Her arms lay flat across her chest—yet even in death her fingers were screaming at the top of their lungs: "23."

I pulled her to me and cried like a baby.

CHAPTER 51

B ones rented a house on the water where they tell me I spent the first three days sleeping. He brought in doctors and nurses to tend to each of us. My physical wounds would heal. I just needed time. The wounds on my heart were another matter. Angel's wounds were deeper than skin. Hers, too, would take time. Fortunately, she had a good bit of that. She and Summer were never far. Arm in arm, Summer and Angel walked up and down the beach to sweat out the toxins in Angel's body.

When I woke, it was to the rhythmic sound of a chair moving under the lazy weight of someone enjoying the moment. I cracked open my eyes to find Clay sitting in a rocking chair, an IV bag hanging above him from a stainless pole on wheels. I found myself in a hammock swung between two posts on the porch. Sea breeze cooling the sweat on my skin. In the distance I heard the sound of small waves rolling onto shore. And women's laughter.

Clay looked good. Whatever was dripping into him was helping. I sat up and tried to climb my way out of the hammock, but I was still too tired. I closed my eyes, and when I opened them again, it was dark and I smelled a campfire and heard soft conversation. I watched as the girls roasted marshmallows on sticks around a fire on the beach. Staring into the firelight, I felt Summer's hand on my shoulder. Then a kiss on my forehead.

When I woke again, it was still dark, the fire had burned out, and the beach was quiet. Only the stars spoke above me. I looked to the rocking chair, but instead of Clay, I found Summer. I wriggled myself out of the hammock, laid a blanket across Summer, and walked barefoot onto the beach where the moon shone down. Gunner limped up alongside me, licked my leg, and stood staring up at me. I rubbed his head but was too sore to bend over. I walked out on the beach, let the waves wash over my feet, and then waded out into the water. When the water reached my thigh, I squatted, sat on my butt—or rather fell backward—and soaked. An hour later, that's where the sun found me when it broke the skyline.

A week passed. We cooked our own meals, walked on the beach, swung in hammocks, and swam often. Despite his own wounds and a painful limp, Gunner was never far off. When I slept, I heard him breathing alongside me or felt his tail wagging and thumping the floor below me. And when I woke, his eyes followed my every move. He had become my protector.

My keeper.

A week later, we gathered on the runway. Ellie stood on steps leading into the jet. Her hard shell had cracked and the softer side had risen to the surface. I liked it. A lot. She looked down at me. "Come see me?"

We had some catching up to do, and I owed her years, not moments. She would love Freetown. "Yes."

"When?"

"Soon."

"You promise?"

I nodded.

She turned and took one step but then stopped and returned. "I don't have a good history with people keeping their promises to me."

I clicked open the clasp on my Rolex, fed it over her hand and onto her wrist, and said, "I want that back."

She smiled and checked the time. "Unlikely." Then she stared at me. A full minute. Her head tilted sideways. She lifted my Costas off my eyes and said, "All my life I've wondered what you looked like." Then she kissed me and hugged me. And when she did I thought I noticed her arms shaking. She lifted one hand, spread her fingers, and waited for mine to touch them. When I did, she folded her fingers around mine, and we made the fabric of us.

Angel was next. Detox had been tough and she was in the middle of it. She was having a rough go. She leaned against me. "Padre."

I chuckled. "Yes."

She kissed me on the cheek. "I'm a good kisser."

I laughed. "That's not all you're good at."

This time she laughed as well. "Yeah, I'm still real sorry I did that to your chapel. That's my bad."

Her honesty and ability to see herself clearly was a beautiful gift. Magnetic. I waited.

She kissed me again. Invading more of my personal space. "And my mom is a good dancer."

"Yes, she is." I tried to lighten the air. "Good kisser too."

Angel laughed. "Better than me?"

"She's pretty good."

Tears came easy. Her body was using them to flush out the toxins. "Don't take too long. Mom'll miss you. Me too."

"Deal."

She kissed me a final time and then spoke over her shoulder. "I'm saving you a dance." Before she walked through the door of the plane, she turned, closed her eyes, and raised her hands. Frozen. Soaking in the sun. Then she twirled and disappeared. A beautiful disappearing.

Clay was next. Dressed in his new suit and shoes, he tipped his hat, shook my hand, and stared at the G5. He shook his head. "My first airplane ride." Bones had paired him up with a specialist who was treating his particular strain of cancer. His chance of full recovery was good. Like all of us, Clay will die one day, but probably from old age.

"Catch a bit of a tailwind, and you'll bump up against the speed of sound."

"How fast is that?"

"Six seventy-five. Give or take. Depends on the air temperature."

"Miles an hour?"

I nodded.

"You don't say."

He was enjoying himself. Maybe more than at any time in his recent memory. He picked at his teeth with a toothpick. "'Mazing."

I patted him on the back. "Spring training starts soon."

His eyes widened. "Yes, it do."

"Got a favorite team?"

"The Yankees drafted me but traded me to the Dodgers 'fore I could get there."

"It's a short ride to LA. And they've got a pretty good team in Denver."

He eyed the plane. "We take this thing?"

"Whatever you like."

He shook his head. "I'll buy the hot dogs."

I shook his giant paw. His middle knuckle had taken seven stitches after he punched the flesh-trader in the face. He admired his handiwork. Before he climbed aboard, Clay turned and said, "Mr. Murphy."

I smiled. "Yes."

"Most of my life I been angry at men that look like you. With skin color like yours." A pause. "They took so much. Everything." He sucked through his teeth. "I lost count of the number of fights in prison." He glanced at his hand. "But then that man took Ellie and . . . I thought she was gone and I couldn't bear the thought of that little girl being . . . and then you stopped him, and he came running at me, and I reached back some sixty years and I took all the anger I ever knew and I sent my fist through his face." He straightened his jacket and his hat. "And now I'm not so angry anymore."

"That's good, 'cause they had to wire his jaw back together. He's drinking his meals through a straw."

Clay's face changed. "Prison won't be fun for him."

"Nope."

He shook my hand again. This time holding it. "Thank you."

From inside the plane, Ellie was laughing at Angel, who had just said, "You know, you never really get used to that new-plane smell."

I nodded. "Watch out for those two."

Summer was last. She stood beautiful against the evening sun, the wind tugging at her dress. Her legs tanned and firm. She lifted her sunglasses off her face, held my face in her hands, and kissed me. Once. Twice. Then a third time. Her lips were soft. Tender. Inviting. And gone was the tremble. She pushed my hair out of my eyes. "Dancing is better when two people do it."

"I'm not much of a dancer."

A sly smile. "I am."

I laughed.

She climbed a few steps, twirled once, then again, and disappeared into the plane. When she did, I felt a part of me go with her.

The pilot appeared from the cockpit. Bones. He stood in the doorway, broad chested, chiseled. Smiling like the Cheshire cat behind mirrored aviators. He loved this stuff. Now in his late fifties, he was fitter than most CrossFit fanatics. His face was tanned from too much skiing at Vail and Beaver Creek. He and I needed to have a conversation, but this was not the time nor the place. The look on his face acknowledged this. He gave me a thumbs-up, followed by rapid and practiced finger motions. When finished, they'd said, "91–11."

He shall give His angels charge over you, to keep you in all your ways.

The plane taxied, the jets roared, and within seconds they were little more than a speck.

I turned to Gunner, who was sitting next to me. Wagging his tail. "You ready, boy?"

He stood, ears trained on the disappearing plane, tail moving at six hundred rpm's.

We walked from the airport across the street to the water where *Gone Fiction* was tied up at a dock. Standing on the dock, wearing an enormous hat and sunglasses, stood a familiar face. She'd made her yearly trek to Key West. She was holding a drink in one hand and the printed pages of a manuscript in the other. I lifted Gunner, placed him on the beanbag, and wrapped him in a blanket. She stared down at me and gestured with the pages. "You sure?"

I shrugged. "One half of me says yes. The other half says no."

"Doesn't have to end this way."

I took a look inside. "My well is pretty dry. I don't know if I can . . ."

She nodded. "You want me to speak to you as your editor or your friend?"

My mind wandered to the six hundred miles ahead of me. "Think I need a friend right now."

"Write it out."

I stared out across the water, finally letting my eyes come to rest on the battered orange Pelican case strapped to the bow. The one that held Marie's ashes. My editor sipped from her drink and then pointed at the box. "I can hold the press." She weighed her head side to side. "Expensive but . . . you're worth it."

I cranked the engine. The water stretched out like glass before me. The breeze cooled my skin. Snook darted beneath the hull. Behind me, I heard Marie's echo, *Walk me home.* I nodded. "Maybe you should hold it."

She smiled, lifted her drink in a toast, and disappeared up the dock toward the next watering hole.

Gunner and I reversed out of the slip. I throttled into drive, and we idled up the south side of Key West, where the sun shone on that orange box. Six hundred miles stared us in the face.

And that was good.

CHAPTER 52

Bones released the videos of the men captured on the *Sea Tenderly* and *Fire and Rain*. Authorities began making arrests up and down the coast of Florida. Over fifty men. Famous people too. Most lawyered up and tried both to buy their way out and to silence the media circus, but it's tough to argue with video. Especially when little girls are involved.

Despite their attempts, the media couldn't sniff me out. All they could uncover was a mystery man who had rescued some twenty-six girls over the course of a week and driven a stake through the heart of a mafia-run sex-trafficking racket that spanned the East Coast. Several of the girls required medical attention, but each had been returned to their lives and their parents. A few were unable to be contacted as their numbers had been disconnected. Theory was they'd been relocated to parts unknown. Each was a bit wiser. The captain of the demon boat had been offered a deal if he talked. Reduced sentence. "Softer" prison. He was singing like a canary.

The ride home took a week. We idled much of the way. Nothing about me was in a hurry. Most nights I slept in my hammock, cradling the jar that held Marie.

The island had survived much as I'd left it. Over two hundred citrus trees fared well given that they're individually watered with automatic sprinklers. The weeds had returned with a vengeance, so I spent a few days beating them back—spraying or uprooting them. When I finally garnered the gumption to return to the chapel, my note still hung on the door. I thought about taking it down but couldn't bring myself to do it.

So I left it.

Gunner was hands down the peeing-est dog I'd ever seen. Marked every tree on the island. To speed his therapy, I got him out swimming. At first, I held him while he paddled gently in my arms, getting his strength back. Slowly, I let him go and he swam on his own. I knew when he started swimming against the current he'd be okay. A good sign.

I lifted *Gone Fiction* out of the water and spent several days giving her a deep cleaning. She'd earned it. I even pulled off the wrap, restoring her to her original color.

Sunset found me staring over a cup of coffee out across the shallow water where Marie and I had met as kids. Somewhere in the next few days, I grabbed my laptop and opened a white page. For the next month, I wrote the me I wanted us to be. I wrote the story I wanted to read rather than the story I'd lived. Proving once again that writing is an amazing transaction, and that the most powerful thing ever is a word.

When I'd finished, I read out loud to both Marie and Gunner as the sun dropped behind the palm trees. Then I read it again. Gunner wagged his tail and rolled over on his back. Maybe Marie liked it too. I knew my editor had bitten her nails to the quick, so I clicked Send and waited a few hours, and when my phone rang near midnight, she couldn't even talk. Usually a good sign. She managed two words. "Thank you." Followed by, "The wedding . . ." She paused. Blew her nose. "Most beautiful thing I've ever—" She couldn't finish. Proving that while she was my editor, she was a reader first.

I hung up, stared at a full moon, and felt the tug. I walked out to the bank, and Marie and I sat beneath a blanket and watched the sunrise.

Gunner sniffed me out at daylight and said hello by licking my face. "Okay, okay . . . I'm coming." He ran around me in circles, splashing, sinking his muzzle to his ears, chasing schools of mullet.

Standing on the beach where we'd searched for sharks' teeth as kids, I opened the box and lifted the jar. Then, holding her hand, I waded into the knee-deep water. Gunner paused, tilted his head, and stood wagging his tail. Below me, the outgoing tide tugged at my skin. Bait fish nibbled at my toes. I clutched the jar for some time. Remembering how the water glistened on her skin and the wind tugged at her hair. And how her hand found mine when we were snorkeling. A homing beacon. I closed my eyes and let the water wash over me.

Ellie told me the story her mom had told her after I'd rushed out to rescue Summer. The day of our wedding, she'd left ashamed. A betrayal unlike any other. While she knew I could forgive her, she could not forgive herself. So she ran. Medicating and drowning her pain in drink, drug, and people. Always one step ahead of me.

Seven years in, she tired of running and walked back into my life. We spent that night talking, and just before daylight, she'd given herself to me. The honeymoon we'd never had. Seven years to the day, and the only time I'd ever been with my wife. She left before dawn, then climbed into a rented boat and turned on the camera. Yet, sitting in that boat and tying herself to a concrete bucket, she had a problem. Her body felt different. Something was off. Or new. And like most girls, she knew what the "new" was.

So, wanting to complete the ruse for the camera, she followed the bucket. Twenty feet down, the knot came undone. Had she tied it loosely or was it something else? Hovering below the boat in what was to be her watery grave, she watched the bucket disappear. Darkness below. Light above. Something new inside. For reasons she had never been able to understand, she chose light.

Yet walking up to shore, how could she return to me? How could I ever trust her? After so great a betrayal. Twice. At least, this was her thinking. She returned north to the Hamptons and waited tables until the baby came. While there, she learned of an adoption agency that catered to the wealthy. Maybe they could give the girl a better life. So she gave birth to Ellie, signed the papers, and left the Hamptons on, of all things, a Greyhound bus.

During delivery, she'd had complications. They ran tests and determined she had several problems, the worst of which was an incurable virus that attacks the lining of the heart of otherwise healthy individuals, suffocating it. It comes in through needles and sex. Of which she'd known her share. They said she was lucky to be alive. Gave her a few months to live. Incidentally, the virus did not pass through the womb. Host only.

Having committed suicide twice, she couldn't bring herself to do it again. So she searched the yellow pages and found a convent in, of all places, Key West. She figured she could hide and die there. She inquired under a false name, they accepted her as a candidate, and she made the trip south. Burdened with guilt, she left bread crumbs along the way in the event her daughter ever wanted to know about her beginnings. About where she came from—without all the pain and betrayal. Marie arrived at Sisters of Mercy and was met by Sister June. Fast friends ever since.

She explained her life and situation to Sister June and asked permission to die in that cottage. Sister June obliged while telling her, "I have a feeling what's about to happen isn't going to happen the way you think it's going to happen."

So she walked the beaches. And waited. Feeling her ability to breathe and fill her lungs lessen with every day. But then a funny thing happened. One evening, nearly a year to the day she'd left me, she was walking the beach and found herself near the southernmost point. Breeze at her back. People-watching. Then this one guy caught her eye. Suntanned, sitting on a rock, scribbling in a notebook.

Handsomest man she'd ever seen. Day after day, she stood at a distance and peered through trees and disguises. Big hats and sunglasses. When he finished writing in his notebook, he'd walk to work, serve drinks, and keep writing—long into the night. Several nights she'd followed him home and waited 'til he turned out the light. Then she stood at his open window and listened to him breathe.

She knew his shifts, so one day, while he was at work, she let herself in his unlocked apartment and opened the oldest notebook. Over the next few days, she read each one from beginning to end. In dumbstruck amazement.

This man, this tortured creature, was writing a story he had not lived. A story he could only dream. Of love known. Shared. Of a woman unlike any other. He wrote of how she moved, how she smelled, how the wind dried the water on her skin, and how goose bumps rose around her hair follicles when she got cold. And he wrote of how when she slept, he'd place his hand on her stomach and feel its rise and fall.

Torn and tormented by her own life's decisions, her own selfishness, she photocopied the first notebook and sent it with a note to a woman she'd met in the Hamptons. An editor for a New York house. The note read, "There are sixty more of these. He tends bar at the 'End of the World.' Key West. You have one week to order a drink or I'm sending elsewhere." Five days later, she watched from the second-story window of a dilapidated bed-and-breakfast as the woman who would become my editor sidled up to the bar.

A year later, lying in the bed at her cottage, a bedside table full of steroids and medications, Marie and Sister June read the first release. Out loud. Five times.

When Sister June pressed her about telling me the truth, Marie shook her head and squeezed the hardcover to her chest. "I want his heart to heal."

Sister June had challenged her. "That all?"

Marie had shaken her head. "I want our love to live forever."

And she was right. It had. Until it didn't. Until thirteen years had passed and I could write no more. So I burned every book, loaded into my Whaler, and intended to return to my rock where I would walk out into the water and scatter our ashes and our memories and our hope and all my love into the waters where the Gulf kissed the Atlantic.

But love is a difficult thing to kill. Actually, it's the only thing in this universe or any other that you can't kill. No weapon that has ever been made can put a dent in it. You might punch it, stab it, whip it, and hang it out to dry—you can even drive a spear through it, pierce its very heart. But all you're going to get is blood and water, because love gives birth to love.

Marie settled into what she thought would be her last months. But with four book releases over a two-year period, the process slowed. There were days when she sat by the water's edge, her toes digging into the wet sand, my words in her hands, and felt as though she strengthened. As though the very words I'd written had reversed the virus. She watched in amazement as millions upon millions of copies circled the globe, movies were made, and yet this anonymous writer never came out of the shadows. Never stepped into the limelight. He simply wrote for love. She said there were days when her joy squeezed more tears out of her eyes than she thought humanly possible. But in the crying there was a washing. A cleansing.

Water does that.

Thirteen years passed, and she was still hanging on. Weakened, breathing extra oxygen, skin and bones, a shadow of her former self, paying the consequences of years of bad decisions—and yet there she was, just like the rest of the world, awaiting the next installment. An injection of words from his heart to hers that would give her a few more months.

But internet rumors suggested the author had come to his end. That he'd written his last love story. She and Sister June, oxygen tank in tow, boarded a train, rented a sleeping car, and didn't get off until the Hamptons. They rode into the city and took the elevator to floor seventy-something, and Marie introduced herself. At first, the editor was standoffish. Disbelieving. But only two people ever knew about the package of photocopies she'd received in the mail. Herself and the person who'd sent it. That person was sitting in front of her.

Marie confessed that she knew the identity of the writer and that she'd heard he'd written his last. The editor glanced at a printed manuscript sitting on her desk. Stained with tears. Marie asked to read it.

The editor responded, "And if I don't?"

Marie shook her head. "I'll go home. Brokenhearted. Same as you."

The editor agreed, and Marie spent the day wrapped in a blanket in her office staring down over a blanket of snow covering Central Park. When finished, she dried her eyes and sat shaking her head. The editor said she had begged me not to do this, but even she could hear it in my voice. I, the anonymous writer, was done. Well empty.

Marie ran her hand across the pages. "He's saying goodbye. He has come to the end of us. The end of me."

When Marie stood to leave, the editor asked, "What are you going to do?"

Marie had stared out the windows at the snow falling. "Give him a reason not to."

Then the waiting began. She did not know about Angel, Ellie, or Summer. She simply knew I was returning to Key West with a box and the ashes of our love. Fourteen years ago, love had brought me back to her. Now, some twenty-one years since our wedding day, maybe love would bring me back again.

When we'd appeared at Sisters of Mercy that afternoon, asking questions, she'd looked in the mirror and chickened out. Instructed Sister June to deny her existence. Turn us around. Then she saw us on the rock. Saw Ellie and found herself mesmerized. Knew her immediately. Saw me wade out into the water and spread the ashes. Saw the names tattooed across my back. Saw me trying to be strong for everyone else when she knew I was cracking.

When she saw Summer she knew I'd be okay.

When she finally made up her mind to summon us that evening, the virus struck with a vengeance. Given her weakened condition, it left her with hours rather than days. She spent her last hours with her daughter. Telling her who she was. Who I am.

I stood in the waters around my island, tears cascading off my face, clutching two jars. In one, I held Marie. My love. My heart. The middle of me. And in the second, the purple urn from the kitchen table, I held all the words I'd written about her over thirteen novels. It held everything I'd ever wanted to tell her.

The breeze washed across my skin. I stared across the water at my island. The upstairs of the barn I call an office. The window I look out of when I'm staring across the top of my laptop. There was so much left unsaid. Not knowing what else to say, I spoke out loud some of the words of Marie's obituary:

Some of us wear our limps on the inside. Some on the out. No matter where, we're all broken. All walk with a limp. I wish I had found you sooner. I'm sorry I did not. Although, I guess if you were standing here, you would tell me that I did. That every word I'd ever wished to tell you found you. And when I think about that, about how those words soothed your broken heart, that you slept with me tucked up against your chest and under your chin, I feel . . . better. I don't know if I'm okay, but maybe better.

I know you're wondering, so I'll tell you—I've decided to keep writing. Why? Because I have more to tell you. The story's not over. Least not yet. You are still loved. And nothing you have done or can do makes me love you any less. Our love will live on. All of us face the choice—how to get from slave to free. Run? Walk? Crawl? Is it worth it? Will it hurt? Will it kill me? Some take longer than others. Some never risk it. Some never make it. You did. And in the most beautiful gift you've ever given me, I got to walk you through the door.

In the years ahead, when I grow old and tired, and maybe when my well runs dry and the words fade and the scent of you grows faint, I'll walk back out into these waters, dive beneath the surface, and let you fill me up. Red sky at night.

Love is like water. No matter how you cut it, slice it, beat it, or blow it into ten trillion droplets, give it a few minutes and it will all come back together again. Like nothing ever happened. No scar. No shrapnel. Just one giant body of water. Clear. Clean. Cool. Love fills the empty places and flows from what was once the epicenter of the wound. And it's the flowing that washes out the residue of the pain and makes us whole again. That's the crazy miracle that is love. The more you pour out, the more you have to pour. I don't understand it, I just know it's true.

I turned the jar, and Marie's ashes scattered onto the water, spreading into a defined cloud around me. Clinging to my skin. Then I emptied the words I'd written. To keep her company. Keep her warm. Remind her when she forgot. If this water could talk, I wanted her to hear my voice. To hear me say with every ripple, current, and wave that there was not then and is not now anything she could do to lose my love. Nothing can separate us.

Love does that. It erases the pain. The darkness. The stuff that wants to hold our head under the water. Love reminds us who we are and who we were always meant to be. And there never has been nor ever will be anything that can kill it.

I shook the two urns and mixed the ashes until there was no distinction between them. We stood there, a slack tide. Marie, me, and the ink that etched the memories. Then the current swirled, tugged on my legs, its flow drawn by the moon, and carried her out to where the Atlantic kissed the sky.

In a few hours, she'd be swimming in the Gulf Stream. Free again.

CHAPTER 53

A few days later, I found myself sitting on the floor of the chapel. Angel's lipstick inscription just above my head. Tools scattered around me. A Dremel in my hand. I'd just finished carving five names into the wall of the chapel.

ANGEL

ELLIE

MARIE

SUMMER

CLAY

Then, for reasons I can't quite understand, I stood and inscribed a phrase above all the names:

THESE HAVE WALKED FROM BROKEN TO NOT.

FROM SLAVE TO FREE.

I sat back, leaning against the far wall. Staring at the names. The fresh cuts in the stones. I scratched my head. It was warm, so I'd stripped my shirt off and sat there sweating. Beads draining down. Cleansing me. As I stared at the wall, something bugged me. Gunner too. He lay on the cold stone floor, belly up, tail wagging, tongue dragging. He'd taken to island life just fine.

I circled the wall all afternoon, trying to place the missing piece. Wasn't until midnight, standing knee-deep in the incoming tide, that it dawned on me. I climbed out of the water, headed back into the chapel, and picked up the Dremel. Only took me a few minutes. When finished, I blew out the dust, wiped it with a wet rag, and stood back. Reading the two names. Over and over.

DAVID BISHOP

MURPHY SHEPHERD

Sometimes I can't wrap my head around where my life has taken me. The depth and the breadth. I nodded at the two names. They, too, had been cut loose from their tethers. A salty breeze washed through the chapel.

I wasn't quite sure who to be.

I packed a few things and closed up the island, and Gunner and I arrived at the tarmac midafternoon. The plane was waiting on us. We boarded, the G5 took off, and three hours later we touched down at a private airport ten minutes outside of Freetown. I unlocked my storage unit, backed out my Chevrolet diesel, locked it into four-wheel drive, watched the highway turn from asphalt to gravel, and began working my way to Freetown.

I never told them when I was coming. Not even Bones. Only the pilots knew and even that was just a few hours' notice. I drove back roads and parked at a trail that wound its way up to one of the Collegiate fourteen-footers but also allowed me backdoor access to the Eagle's Nest without being seen. I wanted some time to myself. In truth, I wanted to spy on Summer and Angel. Or rather, Summer.

I needed a few days to acclimate, so the climb was slow; I had yet to fully recover from my wounds. Actually, my climb was anemic. I had a ways to go yet. I made it to the Nest just before sundown. Although late summer, the temperature had dropped into the forties and the wind had picked up. Cold for a Florida boy. I built a fire, made coffee, and stared down from the porch at Freetown. I could recognize the body shapes and sizes. The cadence of each person's gait. I knew most by sight. And each sighting made me smile.

I would make my way down tomorrow. Tonight, I only wanted to see one person. Having some time and distance behind us, I needed to know if the sight, the sound, and the smell of her tugged on me. Or was my emotional connection to her just a function of the trauma we both had suffered in our ordeal? I stood staring down on the town, needing to know if I could give my heart to another. Was it healthy enough, and did I have control over it such that I could give it away? Was it even givable? I didn't know, which explained my staring through binoculars at the chateau where Summer, Angel, and Ellie had lived the last month or so.

Angel and Ellie were cooking dinner. Singing. Twirling over a pot of boiling water. Angel held pasta in her hand like a conductor's wand while Ellie sang into a microphone that looked like a wooden spoon. Angel looked healthy and happy; she'd even put on a few pounds, which she needed. Her hair had returned to its normal color—an auburn brunette. Ellie looked lighter and carefree. As if her new life was agreeing with her.

The radio had been turned up loud, and the two of them were currently blaring the Supremes. "Stop in the Name of Love." Every time Angel sang the chorus, she'd scream, "Stop!" at the top of her lungs and hold out a stop-sign hand, followed by more conducting with the pasta in the other. Quite comical. It also showed how far she'd come in her own healing and the loss of inhibitions. She had become comfortable in her own skin. Ellie continued singing into the spoon, her voice slightly louder than the projection from the speakers. I studied the house, the windows, and all the doors. The kitchen table had been set for four, but there was no sign of Summer.

The sun fell and the air grew cooler so I pulled on a Melanzana hoodie, stoked the fire, and wrapped my hands around a warm mug. I was about to retire to the couch when the sound of footsteps echoed from the shadows. They were light and quick.

Like a dancer.

Two hands wrapped around my waist, and I felt a woman's warm bosom press against me. I didn't need to turn.

She whispered, "Missed you."

I was struck by how healthy she looked. I was also struck by how incredibly glad I was to see her. Something in me actually fluttered.

She smiled. "You owe me a dance."

"I have a question for you."

"You're doing that thing again."

"Which thing is that?"

"The thing where you ignore the hard question by saying something out of left field."

I tilted my head. "Maybe."

She smirked, hands extended. "I'm waiting."

I struggled to find the words. I lifted her right hand off my neck and pressed it flat across my chest. "A long time ago, I gave my heart away. And I spent something like twenty years without one. I mean I had the organ, but part of it was missing. Then, here recently, it came back to me. And I have it again. The problem is that it doesn't fit in me anymore. While it was gone, it grew. The place in me where it used to go is too small to hold it. So it needs a home. And I was wondering if . . . you'd hold on to it. Maybe take care of it. I'm wondering if you'd be the keeper of my heart."

Summer leaned against me and pressed her face to my chest.

We stood swaying. I whispered, "For a long time, I felt my life was over. Measured in faces returned to those they love—most of whom never knew me. It can be an occupational hazard to get close to the girls and women I find. So I quit thinking about love a long time ago. Figured that was beyond me. Passed me by. Maybe I'd had my chance.

"Then I'm motoring south down the ditch, minding my own business, when I see you steal a boat and venture off into deep water when you couldn't even swim. And I thought, *What kind of woman does that?* Then you told me about Angel and you were so honest and self-effacing and just spilled your heart across my eggs and coffee. And you have that little twirl thing you do unconsciously when you're thinking or you're hurting.

"By the time we returned to the boat, I was swimming in the thought and smell and presence of you. I couldn't get you out of my mind, and something in the center of my chest started hurting. Some part of me that had been dead, or dormant, was waking up and coming back to life. And the pain I felt wasn't something dying but a muscle being flexed. And I thought, *Can't be. I've forgotten how. It's been too long. Who would think twice about me?*

"Yet ever since I stood on the tarmac and watched you all disappear into the clouds, you've been on my mind. Often. Most days I can't get you off my mind. I find myself rehearsing what I'd tell you if you were there, and then I say it out loud and it sounds stupid so I back up and say it again and sometimes again. 'Til I get it right. Then I'll walk up from the water and catch myself in the mirror and I see all these scars and I think, *There's no way. If she knows what's good for her, she'll walk away. Knowing that every time I answer this phone and run toward trouble, I might not walk back . . .*

"I don't know what to think. All I know is that I thought about hiring someone to teach me dance lessons so the next time I saw you and you asked me to dance, I wouldn't stumble around like such an idiot. I just know that I'm really tired of walking alone, and I'd—"

She pressed her finger to my lips. "Shhh."

"I'm trying to talk to you. I've been rehearsing this for—"

She dried her face and smiled. "I know. It's cute."

"But—"

She spun around me, tracing the lines of my shoulders with her finger. Never losing touch with her partner. Sizing me up. "If you want to do that thing you do where I ask a direct question and you change the subject, you can. Anytime is fine."

I tried to recover. "I don't know what life looks like from here, but I think it looks like . . ."

She raised her eyebrows and nodded knowingly. "Turn around."

"What?"

She spoke slowly. "Turn . . . around."

"But—"

"Turn."

"Why?"

"You live your life bouncing between variables. Constantly prepared for the what-ifs. It's one of the things I love about you. It's why there's a town in Colorado populated by girls and their mommas who dream and laugh and . . . these girls are safe. I know. I live among them. But not you. You choose to live alone in a slave chapel where you are reminded daily that evil is real. Not letting your guard down."

She traced her finger again along the lines of my shoulders. Stopping at each scar. Her fingertips barely touching each. "I—" She paused. Stared at my back. Slowly traced the letters. Finally placing one palm flat across the back of my heart. The other around my waist. She pressed her cheek to my shoulder. We swayed. She whispered, "I want to read you."

I turned. "I added four names."

She lifted my hoodie and studied my back. "Where?"

"You can't see them?"

"No."

"It's this new kind of tattoo. Permanent ink but tough to see with the naked eye."

Her confusion changed to playfulness. "Oh yeah?"

I placed her hand flat across my heart, which was pounding like a drum. "I wrote them here."

She pressed her face flat against my chest.

"Nothing can erase the ones written on the heart. Ever."

We swayed, my first dance lesson. She listened to me breathe. I marveled at the scent of her. Her tenderness. How every movement was a shared interaction. She even let me lead. Not wanting me to be embarrassed, she wrapped her arms around me and whispered, "You have good structure."

I wasn't sure how to take that. "Is that a compliment?"

She laughed. Then with little notice, she pulled me to her and kissed me. A long kiss. One she'd been holding. When finished, she stood back, stared at me, and kissed me again—only this time she placed her hands inside my hoodie, flat against my skin. Her hands were warm, and her fingertips traced the lines of the scars on my back.

Laughing, she pushed away from me and tried to hide the fact that her face was flushed. She grinned. "Air sure is thin up here."

"Yep."

She let go of me, walked to the door, and said, "Dinner is served in fifteen. Angel's cooking her favorite. Basil pesto pasta. Fried chicken. Sautéed spinach. You don't want to let it get cold."

It struck me again that the table had been set for four. "How'd you know?"

She smirked. "I'm a woman, not an idiot. I have my ways."

"Evidently."

Summer kissed me again and said, "Tell me."

"Tell you what?"

"That you're glad to see me."

"I'm glad to see you."

"Not like that. Like you mean it."

I held out my left hand, shoulder high, and she placed hers inside mine. I wrapped my right hand around her waist, and she followed my steps while I led her counterclockwise around the room. Dancing under a blanket of firelight. I raised my hand, and she twirled and came back to me. I raised it again, she twirled and twirled, and we ended up wrapped around each other. Intertwined.

She smiled, closed her eyes, and pressed her forehead to mine. "That works."

She walked to the chairlift, saying, "Fifteen minutes," then caught the first chair down. I walked back out on the porch and watched her ride solo down the mountain. If I had come here wondering what my feelings were for Summer, I had my answer. I didn't want to let her out of my sight.

CHAPTER 54

I had intended to shower and maybe even change my clothes, but when I turned and headed back into my small cabin, I found Bones. Standing in front of the fire. Warming himself.

In the month and a half since Marie's death, we had not talked about what he knew, when he knew it, and why he'd not told me. And while part of me was happy to see him, part of me wanted to put my fist through his face.

I figured we'd skip the niceties. "You owe me an explanation."

"I do."

"Well?"

"Won't do any good."

"'Course it will."

He shook his head. "Right this moment, you have something more important to deal with."

"Like what?"

He held up his phone. The picture of what looked like a ten- or twelve-year-old girl shone on his screen. I turned away. "I'm off duty."

"That's just it. You don't get to decide when you're on and when you're off when you choose this line of work." He pointed at Summer and Angel, dancing around each other in the kitchen. "And right now you've got to choose between"—he flashed his phone again—"eleven-year-old Macy and"—he gestured with his phone—"basil pesto pasta."

I glanced at the phone. "What happened?"

"Dance recital. They lifted her out the back door. Her father runs a tech company in Silicon Valley."

I swore beneath my breath. "That's not fair."

He stepped closer. Inches from my face. "You're right. It's not. Never has been. But until now, you've never been concerned with fairness. Only freedom."

I stared out over the expanse. My view stretched some seventy miles into the distance. "You should've told me about Marie."

"Maybe."

I turned quickly. More quickly than he could react to. My right hand caught him under the chin, and I lifted him, squeezing his esophagus as his heels came off the ground. I spoke through gritted teeth. "Love matters."

He held on to my one hand with both of his, nodded, and tried to speak. "More than you know."

I threw him down. "What do you know about love? If you knew anything about it, you wouldn't have kept her a secret. I died a little every day because of you."

"Clock is ticking. What's it going to be? Dinner and a warm fire"—he held up his phone—"or . . . ?"

"It never ends! There's always one more!"

He stepped closer. His voice no more than a whisper. "That's right. And in this moment, you've got to choose. The one or the ninety-nine."

"You should have told me."

"If you need to know why, then you can't handle the answer and you should stay home."

I pulled up my hood and grabbed the truck keys. I spoke as I was closing the door. He could tell from my tone of voice that I was serious. "Bones, there might come a day when you wake up to find my hands around your throat. And when you do, you'll know that I'm finished with you."

He nodded, but there was no anger in it. Only acceptance.

I descended the mountain on foot, stopping long enough outside Summer's door to smell the air and spy on her through an open window.

Angel and Ellie had moved on to dessert and were currently covering strawberries with two cans of whipped cream. Every few seconds each girl would tip the can upward, point the nozzle into her mouth, and shoot it full of whipped cream, all while trying not to laugh. Occasionally they managed.

Movement through the sliding-glass door caught my eye. Summer had just exited the shower and was wrapping a towel around her. She was humming. Her face aglow. Brushing her hair. Twirling every few seconds. The scent of her perfume wafted toward me. The cuts and deep gashes on her back from the oyster shoal had healed, leaving only thin scars. Gunner stood quietly at my feet. I inhaled and held it, imprinting the picture of her in my mind's eye.

Finally, I turned, cussed Bones beneath my breath, and headed for the truck while the sound of Angel and Ellie's singing accompanied my descent. The air had turned colder yet, and my breath had begun blowing smoke. Twenty minutes later, I rounded a corner and pulled open the cab door. When I did, I found Clay. Hands folded. Waiting on me. "You didn't think I was going to let you leave here without me, did you, Mr. Murphy?"

I shook my head and cranked the engine. "Apparently not."

"Where're we headed?"

"Vegas."

"Too bad I don't gamble."

I shifted into drive and pointed the nose of the truck downhill. "Neither do I."

I pressed on the brakes and pointed through the windshield. "Clay, I don't know what waits out there. If you want out, you'd better speak up. This is no place for an . . ."

He raised both eyelids. "What? Old man?"

"Yes."

Clay buckled his seat belt and said nothing.

I let my foot off the brake. "Don't tell me I didn't warn you."

"You did that." Then he turned, looked out the window, and picked at his teeth with a toothpick, speaking both to me and to the memory that had brought him to my front seat. "And don't tell me I didn't warn you."

Gunner stood with his hind legs in the back seat and his front propped on the console. He alternated between licking Clay's face and mine.

Finally, Clay spoke. "Mr. Murphy?"

"Yes, sir, Mr. Pettybone."

"After we find this girl, I was wondering if you could do me a favor."

Clay wouldn't ask if he didn't need me. "Is it important to you?"

He considered this, and I saw a tear form in the corner of his eye. "It's about the only thing that is."

The road turned from gravel to asphalt just as darkness settled over the valley. We had a couple hours' drive. "You might should get some sleep."

He crossed one leg over the other, leaned his head back, and closed his eyes. "Before I do, you'd better let me tell you a story."

DISCUSSION QUESTIONS

1. Who do you think the water keeper is? What are the ways water heals in the book?

2. The idea of leaving the ninety-nine to go after the one and that the needs of the one outweigh the needs of many is repeated throughout the story. What do you think about the choices Murphy makes to pursue the one? Have you ever had to make that choice? Have you ever had someone come after you?

3. When did you realize who David Bishop was? What were the clues?

4. Murphy says, "Love is an amazing thing. It takes the brokenness, the scars, the pain, the darkness, everything, and makes it new." How do you see this happen in the story? Is it also true for Murphy?

5. Before reading this book, how much did you know about sex trafficking? Were you surprised that it happens in the US, or did you think it was a problem more prevalent in other parts of the world?

6. Colorado told Murphy, "We don't love because people love us back. We love because we can. Because we were made to. Because it's all we have." How do each of the main characters struggle to give and accept love?

7. Do you agree with Marie's decision to fake her death? What about Colorado's decision to keep the truth from Murphy?

8. How do you feel about the ending? What do you think will happen to Murphy? He wrote his name on the wall in the chapel, but do you think he is truly free?

9. Colorado challenged Murphy to write down the names of all the people he loved. Who would be on your list? Whose list would you be on?

10. What do you think about the names Murphy has tattooed on his back? Do you think it's healthy for him to carry them on his body?

COMING JUNE 2021 . . .

Murphy Shepherd's journey continues.

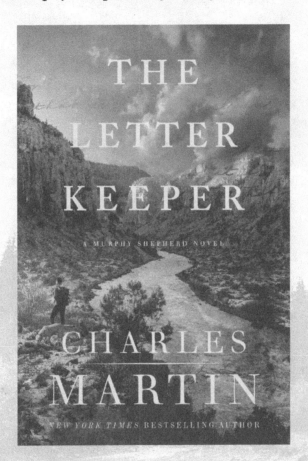

THE
LETTER
KEEPER

A MURPHY SHEPHERD NOVEL

CHARLES
MARTIN

NEW YORK TIMES BESTSELLING AUTHOR

"Martin excels at writing characters who exist in the margins of life.
Readers who enjoy flawed yet likable characters created by authors
such as John Grisham and Nicholas Sparks will want to start reading
Martin's fiction."

—*Library Journal*, starred review, for *The Water Keeper*

THOMAS NELSON
Since 1798

ABOUT THE AUTHOR

Photo by Kerry Lammi, www.soulwornimages.com

Charles Martin is the *New York Times* bestselling author of fourteen novels. He and his wife, Christy, live in Jacksonville, Florida. Learn more at charlesmartinbooks.com.

Instagram: @storiedcareer
Facebook: Author.Charles.Martin
Twitter: @storiedcareer